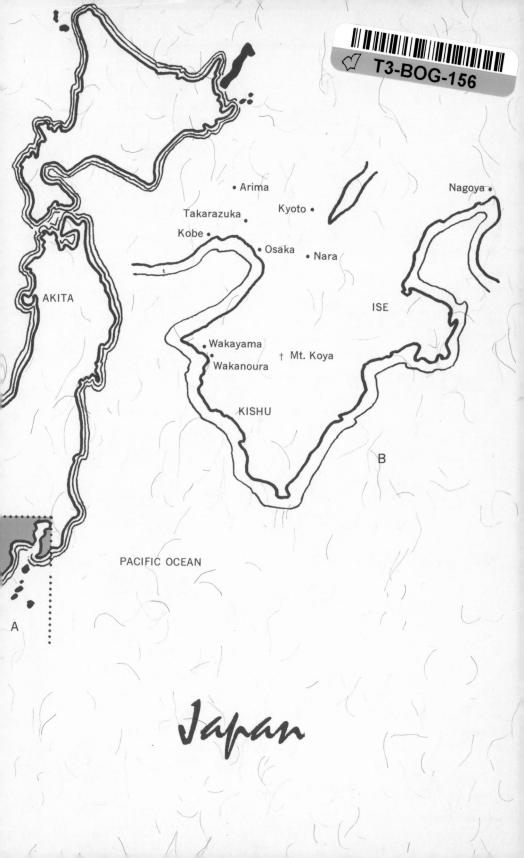

• Arima

Kyoto •

Takarazuka •

Kobe •

• Osaka   • Nara

Nagoya •

ISE

AKITA

• Wakayama   † Mt. Koya

Wakanoura

KISHU

B

A

PACIFIC OCEAN

Japan

The Wayfarer

NATSUME SŌSEKI (1912)

(Courtesy of Iwanami Shoten, Publishers)

The Wayfarer

KŌJIN

NATSUME SŌSEKI

TRANSLATED FROM THE JAPANESE
WITH AN INTRODUCTION BY BEONGCHEON YU

WAYNE STATE UNIVERSITY PRESS
DETROIT
1967

CONTENTS

The Wayfarer

INTRODUCTION

Since his death in 1916, Soseki has become a legendary figure in modern Japanese literature, even though few artists' lives have been so unromantic, unexciting and prosaic as his. Except for his last dozen years which were charged with a sudden, explosive creative energy, his life would command little attention. His was a life altogether devoid of colorful escapades; on the surface it was very monotonous indeed, showing no traces of flamboyant romantic rebellion. He was neither an *enfant terrible* nor a *poète maudit*. In short, Soseki was no citizen of Bohemia.

Instead, the Soseki legend is built mostly on anecdotes which serve to reveal his eccentricities and idiosyncrasies, such as his refusal to accept the first prize as the most popular novelist of 1909 and again his refusal to accept the government-created doctorate of letters. For Soseki, however, these gestures were something more than superficial. His refusal on both occasions had nothing to do with the artist's conscious pose. Indeed, they stemmed from his passionate desire to remain a private citizen, a free man in a society which was rapidly moving from a time-honored feudalism toward a new kind of bureaucracy. On both occasions his intent was to exercise his newly acquired freedom, the freedom of shaping his own destiny, the freedom of a non-aligned citizen, the sacred privilege of an artist bent on dedicating his whole being to his chosen vocation. His was in this sense an artist's declaration of independence. The Soseki legend thus is truly significant in that it signaled the birth of the professional artist in modern Japan. For this reason a discussion of modern Japanese literature which did not refer to Soseki would be incomplete. It is a legend about the birth of a new type of hero whose feats are accomplished not by the sword but by the pen, a legend of silent heroism.

Soseki's life, uneventful as it was, did have its drama, the drama of his own slow but deliberate choice. Natsume Kinnosuke—who is now better known by his pen name Soseki—was born of a once well-to-do family of Edo, present day Tokyo, in 1867, on the eve of the Meiji Restoration. As an unwelcome child, however, Soseki's early years were far from joyful; it was an unstable period which in later life Soseki remembered with some bitterness. More important to him, as to us now, is the very fact that his birth coincided with the most crucial juncture of modern Japanese history. That is, by his birth he was naturally an heir to the Edo culture which had in the past two centuries evolved something comparable in refinement and sophistication to that of Paris; by his early education he became a scholar of Chinese classics, which helped to foster his sense of tradition, a tradition far older than that of Edo culture; and then by personal choice he became a student of English literature, the field which seemed to promise to his generation a new world, a new order, and a new vision.

But a triple tradition, such as this, does not necessarily make an artist, as we all know. All indications are that, with such a background, Soseki might have become a refined dilettante or at most a gentleman scholar, rather than a novelist. (As a matter of fact he was both, an accomplished *haiku* poet and something of a painter.) Intelligent and perceptive as he was, Soseki's artistic ambition was rather vague in his early years and slow in forming. At one time he thought of distinguishing himself in Chinese, a dream feeble enough to be discarded without much regret at his elders' advice; at another he thought of becoming an architect so as to have a practical means of livelihood. Then as a student of English literature he also thought of accomplishing something significant in English, another dream which he eventually abandoned as he realized its near impossibility. This is all we know about his youthful ambition. Since he had to earn his own living, there was then only one path to follow: to specialize in English literature as his profession; in other words, to become a professor of English literature, which for the moment seemed the surest way for him. (He was graduated from the Imperial University of Tokyo in 1893, holding the country's second bachelor of arts in English.) And all his writings before graduation and after—articles on Whitman, English nature poets, Sterne, etc.—indicate his future career as a professor of English.

It was exactly with this understanding that the government chose to send Soseki to England, and Soseki himself agreed to go without the slightest idea of what the future had in store for him. His stay in England, of a little more than two years (1900–1902), proved to be a very trying experience which he would never repeat. For one who had reached the age of 34, who was already the father of one child, and who had to live alone on a meager government allowance, life in London was desolate enough, and difficult to adjust to. As an almost indigent stranger lost in that indifferent metropolis and engulfed in the vast ocean of books, Soseki longed for home; in fact a report was even sent to the home government that Soseki was on the verge of insanity. He was then suffering from his first attack of nervous strain which, along with his later chronic ulcers, was to afflict him for the rest of his life. But his was not the desperation of a sensitive soul under the crushing weight of reality. In reality, we can now say with confidence, Soseki was at the moment going through the first of his spiritual crises, and his agony was that of an honest soul reckoning with his own self, an experience which in itself brings forth the promise of rebirth. It was no longer the same Soseki; it was another Soseki, now resolved to commit himself to the pursuit of literature as the sole dictate of his own existence. By un-learning his fragmentary knowledge of literature, he launched on an enormously ambitious project which he called his ten-year plan. Instead of attending lectures at the University of London, he shut himself up in his room, reading everything possible and impossible, devouring books not only about literature, but also those concerned with the more fundamental branches of human knowledge, philosophy, psychology, sociology, ethics, and other sciences—with the determination to examine the raison d'être of literature in human society. "So I decided to lock myself up in my lodgings," Soseki wrote, recalling those days, in his preface to *On Literature*, "I stored all my books of belles lettres away in my trunk, for I came to realize that to study literature by reading these works would be as futile as to cleanse blood with blood. Instead, I was determined to enquire psychologically by what necessity literature came into being, and in what process it has evolved, and for what reason it has also decayed. Again, I was determined to investigate sociologically by what necessity literature came into existence, to what purposes it has contributed, and due to what causes it has also declined." In a word, the rise and decline of literature. And when his notebooks, filled with letters as tiny as flies' heads, reached the thickness of five or six inches, Soseki returned to Japan. It was the first month of 1903.

Soon after his return home Soseki found himself lecturing on literature at his alma mater as the first Japanese successor of Lafcadio Hearn. His lectures were all dryly objective and intensely analytical, a marked contrast to those of his famous predecessor whose poetic eloquence was still ringing in students' ears. Although unpopular among his students, Soseki might well have settled down as a respectable professor of English at the Imperial University of Tokyo. Yet destiny, it would seem, had been preparing Soseki for something far richer and more rewarding, if more difficult.

The chance came when the *Hototogisu*, a literary magazine, published Soseki's serial, "I Am a Cat" (1905–1906), a loosely connected but delightful satire of the contemporary scene as viewed by a non-human agent. Its success was instantaneous and sensational. Apparently encouraged by this sudden fame, Soseki let his pent-up creative energy take its own course. In the ensuing years innumerable pieces came from his pen, one after another, with phenomenal rapidity, *haiku* poems, critical comments, short stories, fantasies, translations, and adaptations. Judging from the fact that all these writings were widely various and experimental in nature, Soseki was then groping for some art form congenial to his genius. The more confident he grew of his worth the more acutely he became aware of the dilemma which tore him between an academic and a creative career. In 1907, when the *Asahi*, the largest daily newspaper of Japan, offered him a contract to write exclusively for them, Soseki knew that the moment of decision had at long last come. After much deliberation he accepted the offer. Rendering his resignation to the university authorities, Soseki was fully aware that he was forsaking a life of social prestige, traditional respect, and relative comfort to plunge into a future which was a large question mark. Yet he was evidently convinced that art was after all worth gambling a man's lifetime for, and that his kind of art demanded full-time devotion. And also he was the kind of person who knew no compromise in the matter of vocation. Only from the vantage point of time can we say that his was no doubt a fortunate although hard choice (for, as it happened, art alone could synthesize the two Sosekis—the dilettante and the scholar) and that in the following ten years he made the most of this choice.

Starting with *The Poppy* (1907) Soseki produced novels of medium length, averaging one work every year, with such intensity, rapidity, and maturation that one might suspect that Soseki somehow knew there were only ten years left for him to create his kind of fiction, and all the more determined to fulfill whatever promise destiny chose to dictate. His productivity during the period, his development as an artist, and his accomplishment in quantity as well as in quality were especially remarkable considering the fact that throughout this period Soseki also had to continue his mortal combat with a series of recurring nervous afflictions and ulcers of the stomach. ("It seems I was born to suffer from diseases," said Soseki in a moment of reflection.) So it is that the new standard Iwanami edition consists of 34 volumes of which 13 are novels, 4 short stories, 7 critical essays and reviews, 5 correspondence, and 5 miscellaneous writings.

2

Unlike *I Am a Cat, Botchan* (1906), an engaging melodrama, and *The Grass Pillow* (1906), a *haiku* novel of rare variety, *The Poppy* is a work of fiction in the most conventional sense. In this first contribution to the *Asahi* Soseki, understandably enough, was overly self-conscious. It is indeed his self-consciousness that damages the work: the elaborate style is quite out of place in fiction; his excessive fondness for symmetry becomes somewhat mechanical; and his way of resolving the dramatic situation still suffers from his sense of melodrama. With all these flaws it is respectable enough as a novelist's first attempt. And more importantly in it we find almost all the seeds of Soseki's central concerns, themes, characters, etc., which he was to develop in his later novels.

After *The Poppy*, Soseki learned his trade fast and well. None of the flaws evident in that novel of apprenticeship are found in any of the following works. Still he was a conscious experimentalist in matter of form, especially in narrative point of view, while he continued to explore, develop, and expand his major themes via basic human situations. Thus thematically and situationally, all of Soseki's novels following *The Poppy* seem to fall into three groups: the first trilogy, *Sanshiro* (1908), *And Then* (1909), and *The Gate* (1910); the second trilogy, *Until After the Spring Equinox* (1911–12), *Kojin* (1912–13), and *Kokoro* (1914); and the last group, *Loitering* (1915) and *Light and Darkness*, which was left incomplete at the time of his death.

Literally and metaphorically, Soseki was a child of Meiji Japan. In this most significant period of modern Japan, Soseki discovered the most exciting material for his art. To interested readers all of his novels provide a graphic chronicle of the era of dramatic transition from the old to the new Japan. It was an historic period when Japan, once aroused from her two-century-long feudal isolation, had to confront the rapidly changing complexity of the modern world in the second half of the 19th century. At this period of drastic re-orientation in all directions and on all levels, the most immediate problems for Japan to solve at any cost were modernization and westernization, although they were actually one and the same problem. In point of westernization Meiji Japan had to face much the same situation as 19th-century Russia; and in point of modernization it had to experience something very similar to what the West had already come through four centuries before with the disintegration of its medieval feudalism. It was thus this twofold re-orientation that made Meiji Japan so violent, so complex, so dramatic as a chaotic scene of human drama.

Against such a significant social, political and cultural background, Soseki set his own world, never ceasing to explore the moral dilemma of individuals caught in the historical vortex: those individual men and women liberated for the first time from the iron grip of their tradition and society. Many of Soseki's heroes and heroines are delighted in their discovery of their own individual selves, especially at moments of high passion. But their exhilaration is precariously short-lived, for at almost the same time they have to seek their souls' salvation, too. And astray somewhere between these two points, points of departure and destination, they can find no easy solution in dealing with their own newly discovered selves. That is, they are driven to experience life's birth and its death at once, with little interval for fulfillment.

Only in this light can we understand adequately what Soseki meant when he called himself an ethical writer or a moralist. It was his conviction that there was no genuine art without ethical or moral foundation. During the period of our literary history which lived by the gospel of art for art's sake, Soseki did not hesitate for a moment to point out the basic fallacy of its attempt to insulate art from life. He valued life too highly and took it too seriously to accept such a contrived rationalization. His spirit of artistic and moral independence as a non-aligned artist and citizen was nowhere more pronounced than in his attitude toward Romanticism and Naturalism, two major movements which were then almost simultaneously flooding Japan. No literary school, as he saw it, had enough to offer to warrant his relinquishing independence in its name.

Yet Soseki was far from aloof or arrogant. Despite his occasional misanthropic utterances and legendary eccentric behavior, he was far more warmhearted than appears on the surface. For instance, he never harbored professional rivalry or jealousy. While taking charge of the literary columns of the *Asahi* (November 1909–October 1911), he praised the merits of many an obscure writer, introduced new talent, and never spared his advice to beginning artists. As early as 1906, Soseki's friends, admirers, and disciples had begun to gather around his magnetic personality, meeting once a week for conversation, thus forming the so-called Thursday circle. Those admirers and disciples, an odd mixture of scholars and artists, came in due time to be called Neo-Idealists whose influence has been persistent in Japan till today, and whose contribution should never be underestimated in the intellectual history of modern Japan.

3

Kojin, the second novel of the author's second trilogy, is doubtless one of his most mature works. The first three parts of the novel, namely "Friend," "Brother," and "Return and After," appeared in serial form in the *Asahi* from December 6, 1912 till April 7, 1913, and the last part, "Anguish," from September 16 till November 15 after an interval of five months. (While working on the novel, Soseki, as was his wont, had to struggle with his ever-recurring nervous strain and, worse still, the third attack of ulcers.) And this interruption, interestingly enough, proved to be a boon rather than a deterrent in elevating the theme of the novel to another plane.

In Soseki's use of varying points of view, his deliberate unfolding of plot, and above all his intense psychological probing, *Kojin* has much in common with *Until After the Spring Equinox* and *Kokoro*, the other two works of the second trilogy. In all these three novels Soseki deals with situations which are potentially violent, yet he always has them well under artistic control. As a result they achieve both beauty of form and depth of theme. All this is noteworthy in view of the fact that Soseki rarely took the pains to revise his novels once they were off his pen—excepting only those simple mechanical matters which might obscure the general context.

Like many of his fellow artists, Soseki drew heavily on his own experiences. He had that enviable gift for weaving into the very texture of his literary fabric anything significant that was happening to him, to his mind, and even to those around him. For instance, it is known that some of the settings in *Kojin*, such as Osaka, Wakanoura, and Benigayatsu, were drawn from Soseki's recent experiences. Soseki was also a regular practitioner of his so-called art of artificial inspiration. When the time came around for him to discharge his contractual obligations toward the *Asahi*, it was his habit to pick up any novel near at hand and read some pages of it. And this, as he explained, often helped to induce in him a creative mood. Impossible as it may be to pin down which novel helped in this way to create *Kojin*, the work does certainly contain many literary allusions, some of the most obvious examples concerning Dante, Shakespeare, Meredith, Maeterlinck, Nietzsche. For all this, we know next to nothing about Soseki's own personal experience which might have provided the material for the central situation of *Kojin*. Although it has been suggested that the tension between Ichiro and Onao is somewhat similar to that between Soseki and his wife, Kyoko, this does not shed too much light on the Ichiro-Onao-Jiro, that is the Paolo-Francesca, situation. Nor does his diary entry help us too much, either. Far more important to us is the fact that Soseki is an impersonal artist through and through, not merely because, as with *Kojin*, he keeps mum about his source, but also because all his works, including *I Am a Cat*, take on an air of impersonality, a mark of a genuine art. Such impersonality is indeed rare in modern Japanese literature, which has often indulged in the confessional *watakushi shosetsu* ("I" novel).

Yet *Kojin* is by no means a perfect work; it has many flaws when judged by our standards. To those who are used to European fiction, especially contemporary fiction, *Kojin* may appear to be but a series of sharply-etched tableaux which lack the dynamic rhythm of action. However, in fairness to Soseki, it is well to point out that this static quality of *Kojin* is due in part to the very tradition of Oriental fiction and in part to the peculiar circumstances under which a novelist labors when writing his work serially for a daily newspaper. In fact, there is much evidence that Soseki was conscious of this problem and did his utmost to make virtue of necessity.

Aside from such an over-all objection, there are still more specific points to be weighed. For example, some, if not all, readers may complain of the apparent cleavage between the first three parts and the fourth and last part, although this apparent flaw can be easily justified as a thematic turning point. Others might wish that Soseki had been more specific about Ichiro's and Jiro's professions, and also about the previous relationship between Jiro and Onao; and that Soseki had not dropped Jiro's own problem unsolved. Also, some may express dissatisfaction with the denouement itself which is only suggested in H's letter in the last part. And so on. Some of these criticisms may well be sound; however, one must bear in mind that a *perfect* work is usually an artist's dream and a critic's hypothesis. It would be more profitable for us to probe into those qualities which make *Kojin* a significant piece of literature, whatever may be the defects that seem to draw attention away from its architectonic import.

In believing in fiction as art, Soseki was as firm as James, his western contemporary. And much like James Soseki experimented with its possibilities, selected what might be called a point-of-view technique, and shaped his structural pattern so that the theme might emerge out of his central situation. In *Kojin*, as in the other two works of his second trilogy, Soseki attempts a novel which consists of short stories or pieces. And in fact in tightening his work without damaging its organic wholeness Soseki here is more successful than in *Until After the Spring Equinox*. His narrative method in *Kojin* is unmistakably mod-

ern, akin to what we might call an oblique method. In the
present work Soseki employs it in two ways: First, to unfold the
whole story Soseki creates Jiro, who is sympathetic toward
Ichiro because they are brothers, and at the same time preju-
diced because he himself is intimately involved in the situation.
Until he receives H's missive, Jiro remains imperceptive. Then,
to complete Jiro's broken vision, Soseki introduces H and places
him in an inner circle—far closer to Ichiro than Jiro, and far
closer than any other character, for that matter, can ever be. It is
by way of H's detailed report concerning Ichiro that Soseki
heightens this basically domestic issue to the level of an intellectual, cultural, and even metaphysical issue. By the same means
Soseki is able to dispose of what he once regarded as an important but difficult matter in modern fiction, namely the treatment
of religion or a religious state. In *Kojin* Soseki deals with this
very state quite successfully. And his success is due largely to
this oblique method which enables him to offer just sufficient indications as to the direction of Ichiro's ultimate salvation.

Commensurate with Soseki's technical consciousness is his
sense of structure. On both points Soseki stands apart from
many of his Japanese contemporaries, as does his art from the
native tradition of fiction. Nurtured in one of the finest tradi-
tions of European fiction, Soseki knows how to make those
seemingly unrelated episodes and anecdotes function organi-
cally, centering on the principal situation. As one whose ambition once was to become an architect, Soseki knows how to
bring into play his sense of balance—contrast as well as parallel
—to make intricate the pattern of symmetry and thereby enrich
and carve rather than confuse or obscure the basic theme of the
novel. First, the impossible relationship between Ichiro and
Onao is made sharper by introducing Okada and Okane, and
Sano and Osada, two pairs, one established, and the other in
process, who should exemplify the norm of traditional matrimony. These two pairs, indeed, are made to serve as the very
norm set down by long feudal tradition they all accept matter-of-
factly. Presumably Ichiro and Onao married by arrangement, just
as did Okada and Okane, and just as Sano and Osada do, but

their marriage resulted only in deviation from the social norm, for Ichiro and Onao are a classic example of an incompatible couple forced to live together by tradition. Furthermore, they are, unlike their foils, new man and new woman dissociating their individual selves from society and seeking to value their hearts on their own individual terms. Yet the trouble is that they are and cannot be completely free or modern. In the world where everything is in transition, a very sudden and rapid one, their selves and hearts know only their conflict. What worsens their situation is that Ichiro, instead of quitting in compromise, tries to settle once and for all his personal problem on the absolute level, whereas Onao is not as forthrightly free a woman as, say, Ibsen's Nora.

Second, two other episodes, both pathetic and telling, that of Misawa's demented girl and that of the blind woman, also stand in contrast to Ichiro and Onao. Misawa's happiness is due to his remaining ever poetic or romantic, and his never trying to translate experience into absolute terms. As Ichiro is a philosopher, so is Misawa a poet. Misawa is content with his illusion, because as a man of poetic temperament he instinctively refuses to dissect the beauty which is the essence of that illusory image of the insane young divorcee. This contrast of attitude between Ichiro and Misawa becomes pronounced when Ichiro reacts to the blind woman's episode. When Ichiro denounces his father's practical solution, it is because to him his father's dealing is despicably cheap in comparison with the intensity of the blind woman's single-minded desire to grasp the heart of her lover who has deserted her some twenty years since.

4

Onao's tragedy lies precisely in the fact that, by virtue of her own egotism, she can never be insane like Misawa's young divorcee and thereby release her passion; at the same time she is just sufficiently freed from tradition to keep her heart in silence as does the blind woman. She is thus aligning herself with the long lineage of Soseki's heroines, who are all self-assertive in one way or another, and yet unlike their feudal counterparts, sufficiently awakened to their individual selves. Especially Onao, as Jiro describes her, is extremely elusive because she accepts the dictates of tradition, an acceptance which is in her case a silent defiance, and almost by instinct she keeps her heart to herself—as her only measure of self-protection.

Ichiro also is typical of the Soseki hero in that he suffers from his excessively cultivated intellect and introspective sensibility. He has his own share of passion toward Onao but, like her, he is also incapable of discarding his self. Neither Ichiro nor Onao knows an easy compromise; nor is divorce conceivable. Thus theirs is in a sense the battle of the sexes, a case similar to that of Strindberg's characters. What makes the situation worse still is that in their society the battle cannot be brought out into the open; it is a constant duel of two minds which allows for no finality.

It is true that the domestic impasse of Ichiro and Onao is the common tragedy of a new man and a new woman caught in the violent transition of Japan from feudal to modern society. Yet in *Kojin* this domestic tragedy is not the cause of Ichiro's plight; it is really a symptom of the general malady of an age Ichiro happens to represent. This point is vital for our correct reading of the novel. For this reason Soseki first depicts the personal situation by way of Jiro, and then by way of H's letter places it in a larger supra-personal perspective. Thanks to the latter device *Kojin* becomes something more significant, more profound than a mere domestic tragedy.

And that significance is first of all socio-cultural, in the sense that in Ichiro Soseki creates a modern Japanese intellect, a product of Meiji Japan, which is comparable not only to the Russia during the second half of the 19th century, but also to Renaissance Europe still trying to escape the shadow of the Medieval world. Only in these terms can we view the socio-cultural dilemma of Meiji Japan as an impossible hybrid of east-

ern and western civilization. In this sense Ichiro is more germane
to Hamlet than to Raskolnikov, for instance. Ichiro is a modern
Japanese Hamlet to whom the world is out of joint.

It would be a serious mistake to explain Ichiro's nervous tension as no more than Soseki's personal problem. In fact it was
Soseki himself who said as early as 1906 that the nervous breakdown is a malady peculiarly common to modern man, and then
added that the more faithful one tries to be to himself the more
acute the malady becomes. From this it becomes clear that in
terms of his own experience Soseki was actually diagnosing the
disease of his own Japan. In a speech he delivered in 1911 under
the title of "Enlightenment of Modern Japan," Soseki discusses
this very issue in more general terms: first, the paradox of modern Japan, says he, is that thanks to the current enlightenment
(which is in this case synonymous with westernization), Japan is
surely enjoying higher standards of living than at any period of
her past but, as Soseki sees it, from this it doesn't necessarily follow that the suffering or pain of existence has proportionately
been allayed. Her westernization is basically superficial because
the initial impetus came from outside, not from inside. All this is
perhaps historically inevitable, Soseki admits, but the point is
that this peculiar situation is the very cause of universal empti-
ness, malcontentment, and uncertainty. Meiji Japan, as Soseki
continues to point out, is trying to digest in a matter of decades
the western civilization that has through centuries evolved to the
present height. Thus, Japan is attempting something impossible
from the start, even though there is no alternative. Precisely
herein lies the real cause of nervous breakdown. What is worse,
there is no handy solution. It is a tragedy without any hope of
solution.

"Why, then, 'tis none to you; for there is nothing either good
or bad, but thinking makes it so: to me it is a prison." What
Hamlet here says about himself may also apply to Ichiro.
Ichiro's plight is the plight of the intellectual. He excels in the
abstract, but fails in the concrete. As when he recreates a night
scene of Osaka he is incapable of grasping the idea of people,
places, and events in their proper context. His memories of

these, graphic as they may be, still remain totally fragmentary. Take for instance those foreign names scattered all through the novel, an aspect which once more reminds us of those Russian novels by Turgenev, Dostoevski, and Tolstoi. Certainly we cannot justify their frequent appearance merely as the result of Soseki's known practice of creative reading or artificial inspiration, for that would be indicative of only pedantry. To do him full justice in this matter, at least two points must be noted. First, the allusions are completely functional in the context. (Besides, the novel teems with unspecified allusions to western masterpieces, especially some well-known situations. For instance, Ichiro's request that Jiro test Onao's honor echoes singularly that meaning-packed episode of the impertinent husband in *Don Quixote*. Both Ichiro and Anselmo are attempting something impossible. In a way *Kojin* contains the metaphysical theme of "El Curioso Impertinente" superimposed on the romantic situation of Paolo and Francesca.) Second, more significant is that in the novel all these foreign names, with a few exceptions, are supposedly an integral part of Ichiro's own thinking process. All his references, while highly functional in their respective context, take on an air of outlandishness. These names appear as alien to the novel itself as, according to Soseki's speech of 1911, western civilization in the culture of Japan. They are not completely blended; it is this failure in interfusion that indicates the root of Ichiro's tragedy.

Yet Ichiro's plight has a further signifiance, a universal one. His is also the plight of the modern intellect, and modern man in general. His plight is symbolic of the predicament of modern man in the hopeless isolation from his family, society, culture, and ultimately his own cosmos. This deeper implication becomes clearer when Ichiro interprets his personal case in the light of modern science which knows no moment of rest, only driving him on and on. In his talk with H, Ichiro states: "Man's insecurity stems from the advance of science. Never once has science, which never ceases to move forward, allowed us to pause. From walking to ricksha, from ricksha to carriage, from carriage to train, from train to automobile, from there on to the dirigible, further on to the airplane, and further on and on—no matter how far we may go, it won't let us take a breath. How far it will sweep us along, nobody knows for sure. It is really frightening." The theme, we know too well, has been one of the major themes of western literature since the later 19th century. The significance of Soseki's art here is, then, that while treating of the most concrete domestic situation, he can also expand its implication across many layers of human existence in the modern world, without losing its basic immediacy. And this is what he accomplishes in *Kojin*. Though Soseki's own favorite work was apparently *Kokoro* (in his announcement he urged those seeking their own hearts to read the work which did grasp the heart of man) it appears that *Kojin*, thematically and artistically, is more representative of Soseki the man and the artist.

In the above-mentioned speech Soseki designated the dilemma of modern Japan as a tragedy with no hope of solution. Soseki might have believed this to be still the case—at least on the collective level. On the individual level, however, it is certain that Soseki had by now come to see some possibility of it. This is suggested in *Kojin*. It is Ichiro himself who said in unequivocal terms: "To die, to go mad, or to enter religion—these are the only three courses left open for me." To Ichiro the absolutist of all or nothing, any practical expediency is out of the question from the outset. Yet no ordinary human solution is possible in his tragedy of self. It calls for some sort of transhuman measure which alone could deal with self to any satisfactory degree. And Soseki suggests that the only possible solution is the last of the three, namely religion as the only human way in which man can surpass himself—by surrendering his self to something larger than himself.

This would appear to contradict Ichiro who demanded in desperation that his friend H name any God as trustworthy as even a rickshaman. Just as in modern literature so many heroes in this dilemma have returned to their traditional religion, so does Ichiro seem to tend toward his own. The solution suggested in *Kojin*, unsatisfying and incomplete as it may appear to the western reader, is authentically Oriental. Soseki's hints as to this matter are given when H suggests that Ichiro resolve his plight by surrendering rather than asserting his small ego. The crab scene is a case in point. Soseki seems to agree with H in suggesting self-absorption as the only possible human solution—at least to Ichiro who knows no God he may turn to. This solution, however, is not the counterpart of Rousseau's return to nature; it simply points to the possibility of releasing the accursed self by way of aesthetic union, for in this basically mystic union there is no longer any difference between "Thou" and "I." True, this kind of solution might appear to the western reader no better than an escape from the issue itself or, worse still, the obliteration of self. But the traditional Orient has viewed the problem in a different light, always asserting this kind of self-absorption as a divine state for the reason that it simply means to expand, not obliterate, self as large as nature, the way which is the divine source of individual life. In other words, it is something comparable to what Christian mystics term one's total surrender to God. Nature is as much Ichiro's birthright as those foreign names are alien to him. Thus considered, Soseki's solution in terms of union with nature would be as valid as say Dostoevski's solution in terms of return to Christ.

It must be remembered that in *Kojin* Soseki is content with only offering this hint of solution. The solution here, vague as it may seem to some, is unmistakably in that direction. Indeed, Soseki has come a long way from the conclusion of his early novel, *The Gate*. In it Sosuke the hero, seeking a way out of the impasse, hopelessly knocks at the gate of a Zen temple. "He looked back. But he had no courage to retrace his way. Now he looked ahead. But there stood a solid gate obstructing his view forever. He was not meant to be the person to go through the gate; nor was he the person who could stand without going through the gate. In a word, he was an unfortunate being who stood motionless under the gate, only awaiting nightfall." Soseki's solution suggested in *Kojin* is therefore doubly meaningful: first, he is now able to take a positive forward step; second, his forward step is not in the direction of formalism which is often not free from its own theoretical or dogmatic basis, even though it be

Zen. Furthermore, Soseki's solution here definitely points to his much-discussed philosophy, *sokuten kyoshi* ("Conform to Heaven and forsake Self"). Whether Soseki personally attained this state is a matter of little consequence. It will suffice to say that in it Soseki finally saw the possibility of salvation for his hero, Ichiro. And here is the significance of *Kojin* in the long cycle of Soseki's novels.

A word must be said about the title of the novel. Ordinarily it would, if pronounced *kōjin*, mean a wayfarer or a messenger. If pronounced *gyōjin*, however, it would mean the living in contrast to *kijin*, the dead, in keeping with Lieh Tzu's usage. While following Soseki's own reading, I have adopted the more inclusive Wayfarer for the present translation.

The text I have used is the new Iwanami edition, *Sōseki Zenshū*. And for the notes, I, as do other readers of Soseki's novels, owe much to those of the editor, Professor T. Komiya.

In the process of translation I have in many ways been indebted to various friends, Richard Bedford, John Cutts, Bernard Levine, Frank Paulsen, Atsushi Takata, and Jack Wolkenfeld. And last, my gratitude is due to the Wayne State University Faculty Research Committee which granted a fellowship for this project.

B.Y.

PRINCIPAL CHARACTERS

THE NAGANO FAMILY

Father	A former government official now in retirement
Mother	Tsuna
Ichiro	Their first son; a university professor
Jiro	Their second son; the narrator, employed in an architectural firm
Shige	Their daughter
Nao	Ichiro's wife
Yoshie	Ichiro's daughter

OTHER CHARACTERS

Okada	Mother's distant relative; formerly lived with the Naganos as a *shosei*; now working in Osaka
Kane	His wife
Sano	Okada's office friend
Sada	Lives with the Naganos as a helper
Misawa	Jiro's friend
H	Ichiro's friend; a university professor

Throughout the novel, female characters are invariably addressed with either an honorific prefix *o* or an honorific suffix *san*, or often with both, depending on the relationship between addresser and addressee, as Okane, Osada, Oshige, and Onao, or Okane-san, Osada-san, Oshige-san, and Onao-san. The honorific suffix *san* is also used for male characters, as Okada-san, Misawa-san, Jiro-san, and Ichiro-san.

Friend

As soon as I got off the train at Umeda Station I hired a ricksha and hurried to Okada's as my mother had told me to do. Okada was remotely related to her, but exactly how, I had not the slightest idea. I remembered him vaguely as a distant kinsman.

I had my own reasons for calling on him right after my arrival in Osaka. A week before that, a friend of mine and I had agreed to meet in Osaka within ten days and climb Mt. Koya together and, if time permitted, go on to Nagoya by way of Ise. At the time we had made this plan neither of us could decide on a meeting place; then I had hit on the idea of giving him Okada's name and address.

"I should call this place as soon as I get to Osaka, then, to find out whether you are there?" my friend had tried to assure himself as we parted. But as I wasn't sure myself whether Okada had a telephone, I told him to telegraph or write me in case he didn't. His plan was to go first to Suwa by the Koshu line, and then come to Osaka by way of Kiso; mine was to take the Tokaido line as far as Kyoto, and after stopping there four or five days, partly on business, to proceed to Osaka.

I stayed in Kyoto as planned and then, anxious to contact my friend, I hurried to Okada's as soon as I got off at Umeda Station. So my haste was prompted mostly by my own convenience; it had nothing to do with my mother's errand. When my mother told me to call on Okada, and especially when she put a bulky can of goodies in my suitcase as a gift, it was, of course, largely from the old-fashioned sense of courtesy, but she also had in mind a more practical matter she was about to tackle.

I am the kind of fellow who doesn't even know how my mother and Okada branched from the family tree. I did not have anything particular to gain from my mother's errand or even any interest in it. Yet I was somewhat curious about Okada whom I was going to see after so long a time—a square-faced balding man of placid disposition, with hardly any of the moustache he was so eager to cultivate as a kind of compensation for his thinning hair. We had somehow missed each other on those several occasions when he had come to Tokyo on business. Consequently I missed the chance to see his square, alcoholic face. On the way to his house I counted off on my fingers the several years which had already gone by, though it seemed like just a few days, since I had last seen him. As I tried to visualize him, I reflected that perhaps the hair he had watched thinning with such great anxiety was by now completely gone.

In fact, Okada's hair was just as thin as I had imagined, but his house, on the other hand, was much neater looking and more newly finished than I had expected.

"You see," said Okada, "the house is really quite depressing with this high wall—in Kamigata style—where it isn't necessary. But it has a second floor. Go up and take a look." But more anxious to get in touch with my friend, I asked him if there had been any note from so-and-so. Okada gave me an odd look and said, "No."

2

Then I followed him upstairs. The view was fairly good, good enough for him to be proud of, but the sun glaring through the windows warmed the veranda-less room. I noted that a scroll-picture in the ornamental alcove had been warped by the heat.

"It's not the sun," he hastened to explain in earnest, "but the glue that does it, you know, because it is left hanging there all year round."

"Well, well, here is that nightingale and plum-blossoms," I felt like saying. It was the very scroll-picture my father had given Okada as a wedding gift, and which in glowing excitement he had come all the way to my room to show off to me. I remembered how angered Okada had been as I said jokingly, "Take my word for it, this Goshun is a fake. That's why the old man decided to let you have it."

Now looking at the scroll, both of us recalled those bygone days and simply laughed. Sitting on the window-sill, Okada seemed happy enough to chatter endlessly. Stripped down to my shirt and trousers, and lying on my back on the floor, I heard him telling me of the prospects of Tengajaya, of future expansion, about the convenience of trolley service, etc. As I half listened to all of this drivel I mused on my stupidity at having come all the way by ricksha when trolley service was available. Finally, we went downstairs.

And before long Okada's wife came back. Okane-san, as she was called, was not especially good-looking, but she was fair and smooth-skinned, and at a distance rather attractive. She was the daughter of a petty government official who worked for my father, and who had formerly come to the back door of our house bringing the piecework we occasionally requested. Okada was then our *shosei*, and slept, studied, napped and occasionally munched baked sweet potatoes in a room near the back door. Thus, apparently, they had come to know each other, though I could never understand how such an acquaintance had led to marriage. Although Okada was my mother's distant relative, he was treated as a *shosei*, and because of this our maids were inclined to be very frank with him about those things they dared not speak of either to me or my elder brother. Every now and then I would hear one of the maids say, "Okada-san, Okane-san said hello to you," but since Okada himself seemed so indifferent, I thought it all a joke. Then Okada graduated from a college of commerce and left for Osaka to work for some insurance company in which my father had secured him a job. About a year later Okada made a surprise visit from Osaka, and this time when he left he took Okane-san back to Osaka with him. They said that my parents had stepped in and arranged the matter. At the time I was on an excursion climbing Mt. Fuji and journeying along the Koshu Road. I was indeed a bit surprised when I found out about all this. As I alighted from the train at Gotemba, it just happened that Okada was at the same time on the way to Tokyo to claim his new bride.

Okane-san closed her parasol before the lattice, and carrying it in her arms together with a small bundle, passed through the front door toward the kitchen; she seemed a little awkward. Her face was damp and flushed after walking in the heat of the day. When Okada announced their visitor in an unrestrained loud voice, she said gently from the back of the house, "I'll be right there." Her voice instantly summoned up the memory of the girl who used to sew my cotton kimono and flannel underwear.

3

Okane-san's demeanor was plain and calm; there was about her none of the ineptness which might betray her as a member of the lower classes. The charming smile which crinkled around her eyes as she nodded, "We've been looking forward to your arrival for the last couple of days," made me recognize that she was not only more refined but also better-looking than my own sister. After just a few minutes of talk I was quite certain that it had been worth Okada's trouble to come all the way to Tokyo just for her sake.

Although I had known the voice and appearance of this young wife five or six years in her adolescence, we had never had occasion to exchange friendly words. Consequently, meeting her now as Okada's wife, I could not behave very familiarly. I spoke stiffly and awkwardly as one does with a strange woman of one's own social standing. Whether this was amusing or pleasing to Okada, he winked at me from time to time. What's more, he did the same to his wife every now and then. She pretended not to notice it. And when she had left the room, Okada dropped his voice noticeably and poking my knee teasingly, asked, "Why all the formality? You knew each other well."

"But what an accomplished lady she has become! I should have married her myself."

"Oh come on," Okada laughed still louder. Then a little more seriously he said, "But I heard you are the one who told your mother something about her."

"Did I really? What?"

"Well, you said: 'Poor Okada! He had to drag a girl like her back to Osaka. If he could have waited a little longer, I would have found a good one for him.'"

"That was a long time ago," I managed to say, feeling rather small and a bit confused. Now I understood why he had winked at his wife.

"I had a good scolding from my mother for that, you know. 'Well, what do you know, a greenhorn like you?' she said. 'As for Okada, your father and I arranged the whole thing for both parties. Mind your own business and don't meddle.' Yes, those were my mother's very words and a real scolding it was, too."

I described the situation in a somewhat exaggerated way as though my mother's scolding might justify my former blunder. But this made Okada laugh all the more, and he insisted on prolonging my awkward suffering even when his wife returned to the room.

"Jiro-san said very nice things about you, just now. Better thank him well."

"That's because you are saying such nasty things," she replied, while smiling at me.

Before dinner Okada and I, in *yukata*, strolled around the hill, and the sparsely scattered houses each encircled with its wall reminded me of the fringes of uptown Tokyo. Then all at once I uneasily recalled the appointment with my friend who had promised to meet me in Osaka.

"By the way do you have a telephone?" I asked, turning to Okada.

"A telephone—in a house like ours!" said Okada. On his face there was a look of cheerful amusement at my question.

4

It was a summer day and the evening lingered. There was still plenty of light on the hill where we were strolling. But as the distant woods blurred into the horizon, the color of the sky also changed rapidly. In the remaining daylight I looked at Okada's face.

"You are now far more cheerful than when you were in Tokyo. You really look very well . . . And I am delighted."

"Well, thank you," said Okada. His answer contained—though rather vaguely—a note of joy.

Then deciding that dinner must be ready we turned back. And on the way home I said to him abruptly, "You and your wife seem very fond of each other." Although I meant what I said, he must have taken it for a joke, for his only answer was a smile. But he didn't deny it either.

A while later, suddenly losing his cheerfulness, he lowered his voice and confided, while staring at the ground as if muttering to himself, "You know we've been married five or six years already and we still haven't had a child. That's what worries us . . ."

I said nothing. I had always believed that no one in the world would marry just to have a child. But whether children become desirable after a marriage was something I could not know.

"I suppose that once settled down people want to have a child," I ventured.

"Whether nothing is sweeter than a child, I still don't know. But after all, a wife should have a child, shouldn't she? Otherwise, she seems to me to have no right to be . . ."

In other words, I gathered, Okada wanted a child because that would make his wife fit the pattern. I wished I could tell him that, in the kind of harassing world we lived in, people wanting to get married often had to put it off a little longer merely because they couldn't afford to have children. Okada then added, "Besides, just two of us alone are so lonely."

"Just two of you—but that's why you are such a fond couple, isn't that so?"

"Would children lessen the affection between husband and wife?"

Okada and I thus talked knowingly about what was beyond our experience.

When we returned home the table was set and ready for us; it was neatly arranged with slices of raw fish, soup, and the like. Okane-san wore light make-up and as she served us beer she occasionally fanned me with a round fan. As each breath of air brushed the side of my face I could smell the faint fragrance of her powder. And to me it smelled good—far more enticing than the beer or horse-radish.

"Does he always drink like this at supper?" I asked her. "He is an insatiable tippler as you well see." So saying, she threw a glance at her husband. "She wouldn't let me drink that much, anyway," he said. He picked up a fan nearby and began fanning himself vigorously. At that unaccountably I once again thought of the friend I was supposed to meet here in Osaka.

"*Okusan*, didn't I get a letter or telegram from a Mr. Misawa while we were out for a walk?"

"Of course you didn't. Take it easy. My wife knows how to take care of that sort of thing. Don't you?" Okada added, turning to her. "Forget it. What difference does it make whether this Misawa comes or not? Be more comfortable, will you? After all, you must first settle that business, let me remind you."

With this, Okada let some beer gurgle into my glass. He was already tipsy.

5

So that night I stayed at Okada's after all. Given the six-mat room upstairs, I found the air inside the mosquito net unbearably muggy, and rolled open the shutters cautiously so as not to disturb the couple downstairs. As I lay with my head near the window I could see the sky through the net. I tucked up the red hem of the net and put just my head out. The stars were glittering in the sky. All the while I considered the past and present of the Okadas. I was somewhat envious of the happiness of a married couple who could be as fond of each other as they. At the same time I was uneasy about Misawa's silence, although it wouldn't be at all bad, I thought, to loll about for a few days as a guest in their cozy home until Misawa broke his silence. Certainly my least concern was the business Okada had spoken of.

The next morning I was awakened by Okada's voice calling from the small patch of garden below the window.

"Hey, Okane. That dappled one is opening up. Come and take a look at it."

Lying prone, I looked at my watch and held a match to a Shikishima, while expectantly awaiting her reply. But it did not come. Okada shouted again a couple of times, "Hey, Okane." Next I heard her say with annoyed distinctness, "You are really impatient. Can't you see I have no time for morning glories? I am busy enough right now here in the kitchen." I was aware that she had come out of the kitchen and apparently was standing on the living-room veranda.

"Pretty, aren't they, when opened up? How about the goldfish?"

"Well, they're swimming all right, but this one, I'm not sure . . ."

I smoked my cigarette, anticipating some sentimental words from her about the sad fate of the goldfish. I waited and waited, but she said nothing. Nor did Okada. I snubbed out the cigarette, arose and descended the fairly steep stairs, treading heavily on each step.

The three of us finished breakfast, and it was time for Okada to go to work. He apologized for the fact that he could not take time to show me around town. I told him I had not expected any such thing. Looking up at him I noticed that he had donned a white jacket buttoned to the throat.

"Okane," he said, as if hitting on a good idea, "you'd better show Jiro-san around, if you have the time."

But this time at least she rather oddly made no answer to either of us.

"Don't worry about that," I said, rising. "Let me go with you as far as your office. I'll just ramble around."

At the front door, handing me my umbrella, she said simply, "See you soon."

I was escorted on and off a couple of streetcars. Left to myself I walked around the stone office building where Okada was working. Two or three times I caught a glimpse of water, although I wasn't sure whether it was the same river. Meanwhile the heat of the day had become oppressive, so I returned to the Okadas' house.

I went upstairs—to the six-mat room which I had come to think of as my own since the night before. Then, sprawled out relaxing, I heard footsteps on the stairs. I was startled as Okane-san appeared, and covered myself hastily. She had changed her low pompadour of the day before to a round chignon, with a pink band visible through the strands of hair.

6

Before me Okane-san placed a black tray on which were a bottle of Hirano carbonated water and a glass.

"Would you care for some?" she asked. As I said "Thanks," and was going to pull the tray toward me, she picked up the bottle quickly, saying "Please let me do it." At that moment I was staring in silence at her white hand. There shone a ring which I hadn't noticed the night before.

As I raised the glass to drink, she pulled a postcard from her *obi* and, smiling half teasingly, said, "It came a little while after you left." I recognized the name of Misawa. "What you were so anxious about has finally arrived . . ."

Smiling, I turned over the card.

"I may be a day or two late." That was all he had written in bulky characters.

"It sounds just like a telegram, doesn't it?"

"Is that why you were smiling?"

"Not really because of that. But still it's too much . . ."

She stopped talking and somehow I wanted to catch that smile again.

"Too much of what?"

"A sheer waste, it seems."

She then related to me an amusing story about her own father, a very methodical person who usually did his business by postcard—even when writing to her—and chose letters, as tiny as flies' heads, precisely aligned in about fifteen rows. I forgot about Misawa altogether and chatted with Okane-san.

"*Okusan*, don't you want a child? It must be boring to keep house all alone like this."

"Not that bad, I tell you. Maybe because I have known enough hardships, coming from a family with too many children. There seems to be no greater torture to parents than their own children."

"But one or two wouldn't be bad, I suppose. Your husband tells me he misses having children very much."

She said nothing but gazed out of the window. Even after she turned toward me she did not look at me, but instead stared at the Hirano water bottle on the floor.

Not quite realizing what I was saying, I went on, "I wonder why you can't have a baby."

She flushed at this question, and I was immediately sorry that my friendly remark had created such an unhappy result. But it was too late to catch myself, and knowing I had embarrassed her I of course lost the chance to find out exactly why she had turned red.

Seeking some way to pass over her embarrassment, I decided to change the topic and turned to Okada's so-called business in which I had so far shown little interest. Okane-san immediately recovered her composure. But she said little, apparently in the hope of leaving such responsibilities mostly to her husband. Nor did I go on prying.

7

However, it was that very evening that Okada first chose to broach the matter of the business formally. I had taken my seat on the veranda where I might be closer to the freshness of the evening dew. Okada, who had been seated face to face with his wife in the room, rose and came out on the veranda as soon as the talk began.

"It's difficult to talk at such a distance," he said as he lowered himself on to a patterned cushion dropped before me. Only Okane-san did not leave her seat.

"Jiro-san, you saw the photograph, the one I sent some time ago?"

It was of a young man who was working with Okada in the same office. When the photograph came we had passed it around and—unknown to Okada, of course—had made various comments.

"Yes, just a look."

"What did they all say?"

"Someone said he is a bit beetle-browed."

This made Okane-san laugh. I myself was tickled, for I had really been the first to take notice of the beetle-brow.

"It must be Oshige-san who made a nasty remark like that. Really, no one can escape her sharp tongue."

He had been convinced of my sister's acerbity ever since she had said that his face looked just like a chessman.

"Well, let Oshige-san say whatever she pleases. But what about the party most concerned?"

When I left Tokyo I made sure that my mother had already informed Okada there would be no objection on the part of Sada. So I told him that was the way Osada-san herself felt. The Okadas then gave me many details about this candidate, Sano— about his personality, character, prospects, and that sort of thing. Finally they pointed out that Sano himself was very keen about the successful outcome of this attempted match-making.

I should point out, perhaps, that in her looks and education there was surely nothing special about Osada-san. In fact, all that could be said about her is that she had been a burden to our family.

"I'm somewhat uneasy about the fact that the other party is so anxious. When you get there, please try to find out which way the wind blows."

This had been my mother's request. With but slight interest in Osada-san's future, I could nevertheless see that her being so suspiciously desired might mean something risky as easily as something fortunate.

As I had all this time been listening quietly to the Okadas, I now blurted out, "But why has he taken such a fancy to her? He hasn't even met her yet."

"Mr. Sano is such a steady person that I'm sure he would prefer a hard-working wife," offered Okane-san, looking toward her husband as she speculated about Sano's point of view. "That's right," agreed Okada without hesitation and apparently with no other thought in mind.

Anyway Okada and I agreed to meet Sano the next day, and I returned to the six-mat room upstairs. Laying my head on the pillow, I wondered if my own marriage would be settled as simply as this. It was a little frightening.

8

The next day Okada quit his work at noon and came home. He slipped off his suit and took a quick bath in the back of the house. Then, as if prompting us, he asked, "Shall we go now?"

Okane-san had already opened a drawer of the chest and had taken out her husband's kimono. What he was going to wear was none of my concern; however, completely unaware, I had been watching as she helped him put on his kimono and pass his *obi* around his waist. I started when he asked, "Jiro-san, are you all set?"

"Today, you're coming with us, too," Okada said to his wife.

"But . . ." Okane-san, while holding a *haori* of silk gauze, looked up at her husband's face. "Please come with us, *Okusan*," I said from halfway up the stairs.

By the time I descended outfitted in my suit, she had already changed her kimono and *obi*.

"You're really quick."

"Yes, a fast change."

"You don't look especially smart, though," said Okada.

"This is good enough for that sort of place," replied Okane-san.

Then, braving the heat of the day, the three of us went down the hill to the station and caught a trolley right away. Every now and then I looked at Okada and his wife sitting together opposite me. At intervals I also recalled that whimsical postcard from Misawa, and wondered from where in the world it had been mailed. Thoughts of Sano, whom we were on our way to meet, also entered my mind occasionally. Every time they did, however, they were accompanied by the word odd.

All of a sudden Okada leaned forward and asked, "What do you think of this?" I replied simply, "Fine." Okada straightened himself and said something to his wife. On his face there was a proud look. Now it was her turn. "Wouldn't you also like to settle here?" she said, leaning toward me. "Thank you," I said quite unwittingly. Now I understood what Okada meant by his abrupt question.

The three of us got off at Hamadera. A stranger in this area, I admired its loveliness as we passed through tall pine trees and the sands. Here, however, Okada did not repeat his question, "What do you think of this?" And Okane-san, too, hurried along beneath her open parasol.

"Do you think he has already come?"

"Well, maybe he has and is waiting for us."

Listening to their conversation, I followed them along the

vestibule of an enormous restaurant. At first I was impressed by its vastness, but as we were shown in I was even more amazed at the distance we had yet to travel. We went down the steps and passed through a narrow hallway.

"We are now going through a tunnel."

When Okane-san told me this I thought we couldn't possibly be underground, and supposing that she was only joking I simply laughed and passed through.

In the room Sano was sitting alone at the door sill, with one knee raised. He was smoking and gazing out at sea, but when he heard our footsteps he turned toward us. I was the first to exchange glances with him when we entered the room, and noted immediately how his gold-rimmed glasses glared beneath his forehead.

9

Sano was far more beetle-browed than his photo had suggested. This impression was probably due to the fact that he had a broad forehead and it was also emphasized by his short, summer haircut. When we were introduced to each other he nodded his head politely and said, "How do you do? Glad to know you." Yet this routine greeting, while common enough, under the present circumstances sounded a bit peculiar to me. It made me feel all the more restraint in this matter for which I could feel no strong sense of responsibility.

The four of us talked around our table. Okane-san seemed quite familiar with Sano, and even made fun of him across the table from time to time.

"Sano-san, I hear your picture is much talked about there in Tokyo."

"Much, in which way? Probably in my favor, I hope."

"That's certain. But if you don't trust me, why not ask him yourself?"

Sano laughed and glanced at me quickly. I felt that I had to say something. "Well, I must say they make better pictures here than in Tokyo," I said with a straight face.

"O come now, you are not talking about a *jōruri*," bantered Okada.

My mother's distant relative as he was, Okada had the habit of speaking to me and to my brother in a manner notably deferential, perhaps because he had been our dependent so long. I had especially noticed this in the last two days after our long separation. But now before Sano he suddenly began to speak to me as to an equal, probably for appearance' sake. At times I felt he even became overbearing.

From our room we could look up at the second floor of another wing of the same house. There in the hall cleared of sliding doors we saw a large group of young shop boys, one of them dancing with a towel thrown over his shoulder. We had decided it was something like a shop clerks' get-together when a boy of sixteen or so came over to the railing and vomited profusely on the overhang. Then another boy of about the same age emerged puffing a cigarette and in a pure Osaka accent said, "Oh, cheer up, man. Nothing to be afraid of. Here I am with you." Or some such nonsense. Although we had been frowning at the spectacle, at this we burst into roars of laughter.

"Look. Both are drunk . . . just shop boys, too," said Okada.

"Just like you, if I may say so," was Okane-san's comment.

"Which of them, may I ask?" asked Sano.

"Both of them, of course—throwing up and babbling away," said Okane-san.

Okada looked rather jolly. I was quiet. Only Sano continued to roar with laughter.

At about four o'clock, while it was still light, we left the restaurant and started for home. When we parted on the way Sano took off his hat and bid us good-bye. The three of us left the platform.

"Well, what do you say, Jiro-san?" Okada looked at me at once.

"He seems to be all right."

I could not answer otherwise. Yet even as I said this I felt that I was being too cavalier. At the same time I thought that matchmakers must often of necessity experience this oddly irresponsible feeling.

10

I stayed at Okada's for two or three more days, expecting momentarily to hear from Misawa. As a matter of fact the Okadas wouldn't let me stay elsewhere. During this time I saw as much of Osaka as I could. The crowds here, due probably to the narrowness of the streets, seemed to me noticeably more lively than in Tokyo. Equally attractive were the houses, situated in more regular rows than those in Tokyo, and the innumerable waterways, which crisscrossed the city, with their currents quiet and abundant. Each day I ran into some new fascination.

As for Sano, I saw him again the evening following the day we had dined together at Hamadera. This time he came attired in a *yukata* to see Okada. I talked with them for a couple of hours, but I could form no new impressions since it was no more than a repetition on a small scale of the previous meeting. All I did find out about him convinced me that he was just an average person. But I began to recognize that as a matter of obligation to my mother and Okada I couldn't possibly remain indifferent. During these two or three days, therefore, I finally wrote a report to my mother in Tokyo about my meetings with Sano.

For want of anything better to say, I stated that Sano looked much like his picture, that although he was a drinker he did not get red, and that he said he was taking lessons in *gidayū*, just as my father was in *utai*. And finally I described what a fond couple the Okadas were and assured my mother that she could rely on their recommendation. In my conclusion I said, "In short, in no way does Sano seem to differ from many married men. Since Osada-san is best qualified to become an average housewife, you might as well give your consent."

When I sealed this letter I felt I had finally done my duty. Yet when I thought that this letter was to decide the future of Osada-san forever I was somewhat ashamed of my own frivolity. So I just put the letter in an envelope and took it to Okada. Okada glanced over it and said, "Fine." His wife wouldn't touch the rolled letter at all. I sat down before them and looked from one to the other.

"Does it sound all right? Once this thing is sent off, you know, the matter will be closed as far as we are concerned. Consequently Mr. Sano will find himself committed."

"That will be fine. That's what we are most hoping for," said Okada with a grave face. Okane-san echoed this in a feminine way. Their matter-of-fact reaction made me feel uncertain rather than relieved.

"Why are you worrying now?" asked Okada with a smile, puffing on his cigarette. "As I recall, you have been most indifferent throughout this entire affair."

"No doubt I have been, but the whole business is so simple that I feel a bit sorry for both parties."

"Far from it. You've written a nice long letter that will satisfy your mother. After all we were agreed on this from the start. So what could be finer than this? Don't you think so?"

And with that Okane-san turned to Okada, who looked as much as to say, "Of course." I did not want to argue. So in their presence I put a three-*sen* stamp on the letter.

I I

I wanted to leave Osaka as soon as I sent off my letter. Okada agreed that I need not await my mother's reply, nevertheless he repeated, "Why, please take your time."

Although I appreciated their good intentions I could well imagine their inconvenience. Inconsiderate guest though I was, I was not altogether at ease either. I felt like cursing Misawa who had not written since that postcard as cryptic as a telegram. Finally, therefore, I made up my mind to go ahead and climb Mt. Koya if I didn't hear from him in a day or so.

"Well then, let's go to Takarazuka with Sano, tomorrow," said Okada. I wasn't at all happy at the prospect of Okada's taking time off from his job to entertain me. To be more cynical, I felt it would certainly be an affront to his wife if we went to such a spa for the pleasure of carousing. At first glance she looked glamorous, but this was due rather to her fair complexion and demeanor. Actually she was far more practical than one would expect—for a person from Tokyo. And I had an inkling that she was thrifty indeed even in handling her husband's pocket-money.

"Your life must be better because of it," Okane-san declared enviously when she was told that I was no drinker. My guess though was that what she really disliked was not her husband's getting drunk but the expense that was involved. I noticed that when Okada, his face all red with sake, said, "Jiro-san, it's been so long. Let's have a wrestling bout," she looked very happy, in spite of her mock frown.

I declined the kind offer to take me to Takarazuka therefore and promised myself that the next morning I'd go alone by trolley and look around after Okada had gone to work.

"Well," said Okada regretfully, "the Bunraku might be a good place to go, but it is closed during the summer."

The next morning I started out with Okada. Suddenly on the trolley he brought up the problem of Osada-san's marriage— which I confess for me was already half-forgotten.

"I am far from regarding myself as your relative. Rather I have always considered myself the beneficiary of the generosity of your father and mother. I owe both my present position and my wife to your parents. I have always thought of paying back my debt somehow. That's why I am so interested in settling the matter of Osada-san's marriage. I have no other intentions."

Since his point was to help marry off Osada-san, a burden to my family, as soon as possible, I was placed in the position of family representative thankful for his goodwill.

"Isn't it everyone's wish to dispose of her quickly?" asked Okada.

Indeed that was the wish of both my parents. However, at the moment I envisioned Osada-san and Sano, total strangers, together as well as separately.

"Would they make a good match?"

"Of course they would. Just look at me and my wife. Since we got married we haven't had a single quarrel to speak of."

"You may be an exceptional pair, though . . ."

"All married couples, no matter who, are much the same, I tell you."

With this Okada and I dropped the matter.

12

Just as I feared there was no news from Misawa even by the next afternoon. I had no patience and it was maddening to have to wait for such a negligent fellow. This time I made up my mind to leave alone.

"Can't you stay and wait another day or so?" asked Okane-san out of politeness. All eager to have me stay, she tried to detain me as I was about to go upstairs to pack my things in the suitcase. Then, not yet satisfied to let me go, she appeared at the top of the stairs when I was through packing, and said, "O my, you are already through with the packing. Let me make some tea. You still have plenty of time." And she went downstairs.

I sat at ease cross-legged and studied the train schedule. As I discovered that it wouldn't work out well, I lay on my back resting for a while. Soon Misawa's figure came to my mind. For some reason I recalled that he had slipped and fallen, breaking a big jar of Kimmei-water hung from his waist as we had climbed down Mt. Fuji toward Subashiriguchi. I remembered how he had tied the broken jar to his belt and walked on. Then, roused by the footsteps of Okane-san ascending, I sat up quickly.

"O just in time," said she, standing before me, evidently relieved. She then sat down and handed me Misawa's letter which she indicated had just arrived. I tore it open impatiently.

"So he has finally arrived."

For a moment I couldn't quite muster an answer. As a matter of fact, Misawa had arrived in Osaka three days earlier, stayed in bed for a couple of days, and then had been taken to the hospital. Pronouncing the name of the hospital I asked Okane-san

47

where it was. She knew it all right but beyond that could tell me nothing about it. Anyway, I now decided to leave Okada's house, taking the suitcase with me.

"That is too bad," Okane-san repeatedly expressed her sympathy at my friend's plight. And over my protest she had a maid carry my suitcase to the station. On the way I tried to send the girl back but she wouldn't listen. I could figure out what she said, of course, but no stranger like me could possibly reproduce that odd Osaka dialect. When we parted I gave her one *yen* for her past kindness, and she said, "Good-bye . . . I wish you luck."

Getting off the streecar I hired a ricksha, and this vehicle crossed the railroad track and sped straight down a narrow street. Careening along wildly as we were, several times we almost bumped into oncoming bicycles and rickshas. I was somewhat shaken when I got off in front of the hospital.

Carrying my suitcase, I went up to the third floor and had to look into various rooms before I could locate Misawa. With an ice bag on his stomach he was lying in an eight-mat room at the end of the hallway.

"What's the matter with you?" I asked, entering the room. Misawa merely grinned. "I bet you overate again," I said chidingly. I sat cross-legged beside his bed and threw off my jacket.

Misawa turned up his eyes and indicated a cushion in the corner. Gazing at his eyes and cheeks I wondered how serious his illness was.

"Have you got a nurse?"

"Yeah. She just went out somewhere."

13

Misawa had always suffered from poor digestion. He had a tendency to vomit and to experience bouts of diarrhea. Friends agreed that it was because he did not take proper care of his health, although Misawa explained it away as something he had inherited constitutionally from his mother. He often browsed through books about digestive diseases and used terms like atony, ptosis, and tonus. Occasionally, when I ventured advice he looked at me as if to say, "What do you know, a layman like you?"

"Now look. Can you tell which absorbs alcohol, the stomach or the intestines?" he would ask. Yet whenever he became ill he sent for me. I felt like saying "I told you so," and yet I always visited him without fail. He usually recovered in two or three days although occasionally he was disabled for a week or more. He took his own disease lightly, though somewhat more seriously than an outsider such as I would have taken it.

This time, however, I was first surprised by his hospitalization; and my surprise doubled when I saw an ice bag on his stomach. I had thought that an ice bag could be applied only to the head or chest. Somehow it made me uneasy to stare at the pulsating ice bag, and the longer I sat by his bedside the less capable I felt of offering cheering words.

Misawa had his nurse send for ice cream. And while I was still finishing my first dish he began insisting on having the second. Afraid that it might be harmful for him, I tried to stop him from consuming anything other than his medicine and diet, but this only angered him.

"Do you know how strong a stomach one must have to digest a mere dish of ice cream?" he started arguing in earnest. As a matter of fact I didn't have the slightest idea. The nurse thought it was all right, and after going all the way to the office to make sure, she came back with permission that he could have a small amount of ice cream.

On my way to the washroom, I called the nurse aside without Misawa's knowledge, and inquired about his case. Something was probably wrong with his stomach, she replied. When I asked for further details, she said indifferently that she knew nothing more, having been assigned by the nurses' agency that very morning. So I had to go downstairs and ask a man in a white gown about it. He didn't even know Misawa's name, but after leafing through the files, he could tell me that his was a case of slight inflammation of the stomach.

I returned to Misawa's bedside. The ice bag still lay on his stomach. He told me to look out the window. There were two windows at the front and another at the side, all western-style, and higher than the familiar ones. When the patient was lying on a Japanese pallet, all that he could see was the intense color of the sky slashed diagonally by a portion of the telegraph lines.

But I put my hands on the window-sill and looked down. And the first thing that came into sight was a cloud of smoke rising from a tall chimney in the distance. While I watched, the smoke was creeping over a large building and looked as if it were about to engulf the whole city.

"You can see the river, can't you?" said Misawa.

Indeed a big river was partly visible to my left.

"The mountain, too," said Misawa, again.

I had already noticed the mountain directly ahead.

That was the Kuragari Pass, explained Misawa. Once it had apparently been covered with huge trees, but now it had been transformed to a clear pass. And soon Nara-bound electric trains were going to run through the tunnel under the mountain— Misawa related cheerfully all these things that he must have just heard from someone. Relieved therefore that his illness could hardly be any cause for alarm, I left the hospital.

14

Having no special destination in mind, I got the name of Misawa's hotel and rode a ricksha up to it. The hotel, which the nurse said was close by, was actually quite a distance, or so it seemed to me.

The hotel didn't have much of a vestibule; nor did any maid greet me when I walked in. However, I was shown into the up-stairs room which belonged to Misawa. A wide river flowing just beyond the railing looked very cool when viewed from the room, yet the wind direction was away from the hotel and no breeze entered the room. Thus, although the glitter of the night lights across the river added some charm, there was certainly no freshness.

Although Misawa believed that he had lain sick here for two

days and was hospitalized on the third day, I learned from a maid that he had checked in one afternoon earlier and, leaving his suitcase, had gone out and had not come back until after ten o'clock that night. When he checked in, said the maid, he had with him several companions, but when he returned he was alone. Although I speculated as to who had accompanied him I got nowhere.

"Was he drunk?" I asked the maid. She did not know for sure, but she suspected he must have been, for she had noted that he had thrown up a little later.

That night I had a mosquito-net hung around my bed and turned in early. But soon a couple of mosquitoes came in through a hole in the net. Just as I had fought them off with a fan and was about to fall asleep, I heard voices in the adjoining room. Apparently a guest waited on by a maid was drinking sake. I was told that he was a police sergeant or something of the sort. Somewhat curious, I had just about decided to listen in on his talk when my maid came up to my room and said I had a telephone call from the hospital. I sprang up in surprise.

Misawa's nurse was on the other end of the line. Half fearful that her patient might have taken a sudden turn for the worse, I asked her what all this was about. It proved to be nothing but a message from her patient urging me to come as early as possible the next morning, because he was bored to death. From this I decided that his was after all not so serious a case.

"Is that all? Don't bother me any more by relaying such ridiculous messages," I said roughly. Then I felt sorry for the nurse and said, "Well, I'll be there, anyway, if that's what you want me to do." I returned to my room.

The maid must have noticed the hole in my mosquito-net and was mending it with a needle and thread. But the mosquitoes were now trapped inside the net, and occasionally buzzed around my forehead and the tip of my nose as soon as I lay down. Yet I had once again fallen into a doze, from which I was awakened by voices coming from the next room on my right. They were the voices of a man and a woman. A little surprised, for I somehow took it for granted that no guest was staying on that side, I decided from the way the woman repeated two or three times, "Now, will you let me go?" that he had probably been escorted back by her from a tea-house, and I again dozed off.

Once more, when I was finally roused from sleep by the noise of the shutters the maid was rolling up, a white thin mist was hovering over the surface of the river. Altogether I slept only a few hours.

15

Misawa's ice bag was still on his stomach that day.

"Still icing it?" I asked, in surprised disbelief—probably disappointing him.

"This is not a cold in the head," he said.

I turned to the nurse and said simply, "Thanks for your call last night." She had a pallid and swollen face. Probably because of her looks which so much resembled that of a blind man drawn in a picture, her white uniform was not at all becoming. Without waiting to be asked, she told me that she was from Okayama and that as a child she had had her right eye damaged by blood poisoning. Indeed, one of her eyes was covered with a white film.

"Nurse, if you are too nice to a patient like him, you can never tell what he will demand next. You'd better not take such good care of him."

The nurse grinned at my deliberately suggestive joke. Then suddenly, Misawa said, "Hey, more ice," and lifted the ice bag.

I heard the cracking of ice out in the hallway as Misawa again demanded my attention.

"You may not know it, but this disease, if I strain myself, is bound to develop into an ulcer. That's why I am lying like this wearing an ice bag. I came in here neither on a doctor's advice nor at the recommendation of my hotel. I came here voluntarily because I realized something needed to be done, and I'm certainly not here for fun."

While I had no great confidence in Misawa's medical knowledge, I had no courage to bandy with him now that he had become so serious. Besides, I had not the faintest notion about his so-called ulcer.

I rose, went over to the window, stealing a view of the distant Kuragari Pass, whose parched soil was reflecting the blinding light of the day. I was seized with the sudden desire to visit Nara.

"From the way you look, I guess you can't keep your promise."

"I am trying to improve my health to do just that."

Misawa was a very stubborn fellow. If I should put up with his stubbornness I would have to be cooped up in this stuffy town until his health allowed him to take a trip.

"Seems you can't get rid of your ice bag so easily."

"Because I want to get well fast—that's all."

In exchanging this sort of talk with him I could very well see not only his stubbornness but also his willfulness. At the same time I could also recognize my own selfishness in wanting to get away from Misawa as soon as possible.

"I hear you had some companions when you arrived in Osaka."

"Well, I shouldn't have drunk with those fellows."

I knew some of the names he now mentioned. It seemed that, bound as far as Bakan, Moji, and Fukuoka, they had all taken the same train at Nagoya, and, having decided to celebrate their reunion after a long separation, they had gotten off at Osaka to have a party.

Anyway I decided that it would be best for me to wait for two or three more days to see how the patient was getting along. Then I could act accordingly.

16

In the meantime, I spent most of my afternoons and evenings at the hospital, as though I had been Misawa's attendant. Indeed, he was lonely and eagerly awaited my daily visit. In spite of all I did, he never thanked me when we were together. Even when I troubled to take him flowers he was often sulky. I read books by his bedside, chatted with the nurse, and badgered the patient to take his medicine regularly. As the bright morning sun shone into his room I was even asked to help the nurse move his bed into the shade.

In due time I came to know the director of the hospital who made his rounds every morning. He wore a black dress coat, and was accompanied by his intern and nurse. Dark-complexioned and very handsome, he had a manner of speech and bearing as dignified as his looks. When he appeared Misawa asked the same questions as a layman would who has no medical knowledge: "Will it still be difficult for me to travel around?" "Would it be dangerous if this developed into an ulcer?" "Was it after all a good thing that I made up my mind to come in here for treatment?" Whenever he asked these questions the director answered simply, "Why, yes." It was amusing that Misawa, despite his usual snobbish display of difficult medical terms, became so timid with the director.

His illness, seemingly light and yet somehow serious, was an odd one in any case, and Misawa absolutely refused to have his people informed of it. Even as the director informed us that there would be little to worry about so long as the patient had no nausea, he nevertheless seemed puzzled at the fact that Misawa did not have as much appetite as he should. I myself was at a loss what to do next.

The first time I saw his tray brought in there were only raw bean curds, seaweed, and a bowl of dried bonito soup. He was not allowed to have any more than that. He must have a long way to go, I thought; it was pitiful to see him sipping a bowl of thin soup. Every time I left the room to go to a western-style restaurant nearby and came back, he invariably asked, "Was it good?" His expression made me feel all the more guilty.

"The ice-cream we quarrelled about the other day came from that place," said Misawa, laughing. I wished I could stay on with him until he showed improvement.

Once back at the hotel, however, I struggled inside the sultry

54

mosquito-net, and often thought of going off to the cool country. The guest whose chattering with a woman had disturbed my sleep before was still staying in the adjoining room. He always came in, drunk, at just about the time I was ready for bed. Once he drank sake in his room and roared for a geisha. The maid tried to put him off with various excuses and finally advised him to forget about the girl. She would say nice things when she was with him, said the maid, but would call him names behind his back. I heard the man shout back that he would be perfectly happy with her flattery even if it lasted just while she was with him, and that he wouldn't give a damn what she might say later since he wouldn't have to hear it, anyway. At another time the geisha started a serious discussion and he had a hard time putting her off. The geisha got mad at that and cried, "You are spoiling my story."

This was the kind of thing that, much to my annoyance, disturbed my sleep.

17

One morning, groggy from lack of sleep, I stumbled across the bridge toward the hospital, having made up my mind to quit nursing the patient once and for all. I found Misawa still fast asleep.

From the third floor window I could see the narrow street leading neatly away from the hospital. Across from me stood a fine, high wall. As I watched someone, probably the owner of the house, came out of one of its side entrances and diligently dampened the street with a watering-pot. Within the wall the dense dark green foliage of what might have been a Chinese citron spread out over the tiled roof.

Within the hospital a janitor was mopping the hallway with a rag tied to the end of a T-shaped stick. Since it was not rinsed, the rag only left white soap marks on the mopped area. Those patients who were not in serious condition bustled back and forth to the lavatory where they splashed and gasped the morning ritual. I heard the nurse bustling about dusting here and there. Borrowing a pillow, I decided to try to catch up on the sleep I'd missed the night before and entered a vacant room adjoining Misawa's.

It happened that the room was in the direct morning sun, so I had to settle for a catnap, during which my face became damp and unpleasantly greasy. My rest was interrupted by a telephone call. It was the third time Okada had called me up at the hospital. Routinely he would ask: "How is the patient doing?" or "I'll come and see you within a couple of days," or "Please let me know if there is anything I can do for you." He would always wind up by adding some words about his wife: "Hello from Okane," or "She too wants you to come and see us," or "Her household chores keep her so busy that . . ."

That day for several minutes Okada went on in his usual manner. At the end, however, he dropped a strange hint. "Within a week—well, though I can't be too definite—anyway fairly soon, I may have a suprise for you." Not knowing what to make of it, I kept asking him what he was up to. All he said was "Just wait, you'll find out soon enough." Still puzzling over what he meant, I returned to Misawa's room.

"From the same fellow again?" asked Misawa.

With Okada's telephone call still on my mind, I was reluctant to talk about leaving Osaka. Unexpectedly it was Misawa who brought it up. "By now you must certainly be tired of Osaka. Don't stay on just because of me. Go ahead if you have to go somewhere." After all, he told me, even when he left the hospital he would have to keep away from mountain-climbing for the time being.

"Well, I'll think about it."

Saying this, I remained silent for a while.

The nurse left the room without saying a word. Waiting until the flapping of her straw sandals had died away, I dropped my voice and asked Misawa if he had enough money with him. Since he had not yet let his people know of his illness, I feared that if I, his only available friend, should desert him, it might be even harder on him financially than emotionally.

"Can you raise some?" Misawa asked.

"There's no one in particular I can depend on," I said.
"How about that fellow?" said Misawa.
"You mean Okada . . . ?"
Misawa laughed at that. "Oh, I can manage if necessary. You won't have to get any money. I have some with me anyway."

18

No more was said about money. I hated the thought of going to Okada to borrow money, and I really hadn't the slightest desire to do so even for the sake of my sick friend. Thus I frittered away my time, unable to make up my mind whether I should leave the city or stay on.

That phone conversation with Okada aroused my curiosity so much that I even thought of calling on him to get at the truth. But overnight my curiosity waned and I forgot the matter.

Still I continued my daily visits to the hospital. At about nine o'clock in the morning when I stepped into the vestibule it often happened that the hallway and lobby were crowded with out-patients. At this sight I was always greatly impressed by the number of sick our modern society could afford to take care of, and I glanced at them reflectively as I began climbing the stairs. It was indeed on one of these occasions that I happened to notice the woman. I call her the woman, that being also the way Misawa was to refer to her.

Curled up in the dim corner of a bench in the hallway, the woman showed only her profile. By her stood a tall, matronly woman with her freshly washed hair wrapped around a comb. When first I caught sight of this matronly back, I thought she was screening my view of someone. Then the matron stepped aside, and the screened figure appeared. The woman was sitting still, curled up, an image of endurance. There was scarcely any trace of anguish either in her complexion or her expression, so much so that when I first saw her profile I could not believe it was that of a sick person. She was doubled up so terribly that her chest was nearly touching her stomach. I felt a wave of re-vulsion sweep over me; and while mounting the stairs I envisioned the perseverance and suffering concealed behind this woman's beautiful face.

Misawa was listening to the nurse's gossip about a certain hospital assistant. He was a young man who played the bamboo flute in the evenings when he was free. Being a bachelor, he lived at the hospital—in a room on the same floor as Misawa, at the end of the hallway. Although he was a familiar enough sight padding about in his flapping slippers, he hadn't been around for the last couple of days. In fact, Misawa and I wondered what had become of him.

The nurse used to laugh at the odd sight he presented as he limped to the latrine. She frequently commented on seeing a hospital nurse enter his room from time to time with antiseptic gauze and a metal basin. With a sullen look apparently meant to show his lack of interest in such gossip, Misawa said simply, "Well" or "Yes."

Again he asked me how long I was going to stay in Osaka. Now he frequently asked this same question when he saw me, particularly after he had given up the idea of traveling. The question was annoying, for it sounded as though he wanted me to stay yet urged me to leave.

"Of course I can leave any time I please."

"That's what I want you to do."

I stood by the window and looked right down. I kept watching but the woman did not come out of the gate.

"What are you trying to do, stand in the sun?" asked Misawa.

"Just watching," I said.

"Watching what?"

19

Ignoring him, I continued to stand at the window. Across the way on the drying-stand crowded with a half dozen pots of dwarf pine trees, pomegranate-trees, etc., a young woman with a *shimada* coiffure was busily hanging things on a clothes-line. I glanced that way for a second, and then looked down toward the gate again. I kept waiting, but there was no sign that the woman would come out. Finally, unable to stand the heat of the sun any longer, I returned to Misawa's bedside and sat down.

"What a stubborn fellow," he scolded, peering at my face. "The more you are reminded, the more you insist on exposing your face to the sun. Now look how red your face is."

Thinking that no one could be more stubborn than Misawa, I answered with exaggeration, "Mine is quite different from your kind of stubbornness. I was sticking my head out for a good reason." But this made it even more difficult for me to mention the woman.

Shortly after Misawa asked again, smiling, "Were you really watching something?" By now I was ready to talk about the woman although I felt sure that Misawa would dismiss the story as ridiculous or nonsensical and scoff at me. Not that I was bothered by that, for I could then merely hint that for some reason I had come to take a special interest in the woman. I rather enjoyed the idea that by telling that much I might keep Misawa in suspense.

However, Misawa's reaction wasn't anything like I had expected. Apparently much impressed, he listened to every word I said. And in my zeal I strung out the story to three times its real length, when actually I could have finished in a couple of minutes. At last when I paused for a moment, Misawa asked, "Of course, she isn't a professional, is she?" I became aware that with all the details I had given him about the woman, I somehow had never used the word geisha.

"If she is a geisha, then she may be the one I know."

Now it was my turn to be startled, although I still imagined that he must be merely joking. Even when his eyes suggested the contrary, a vague smile played about his mouth. Misawa kept asking me about her features, but I could supply none of these details since all I had seen while mounting the stairs was her profile. The only thing that was vivid in my memory was her peculiarly pitiful pose, of being doubled over, almost crumpled up.

"It must be the same one. I'm going to have the nurse find out her name," said Misawa with a faint smile. There was no indication that he was playing a trick on me. And already somewhat taken in, I was eager to hear what he might know about the woman.

"You shall have it—as soon as I make sure she's the one."

A nurse announcing the doctor's visit cut short our conversation. Whenever that time came, to avoid the confusion that would follow the visit, I usually slipped out of the room and hung around in the hallway or went up where the water tank was. That day, however, I picked up my hat and went all the way downstairs to the first floor. With a vague feeling that the woman might still be there somewhere, I paused at the entrance and looked around. But I saw no patients either in the hallway or in the lobby.

20

That evening when the wind quieted in the hush of sunset, I hurriedly climbed the winding stairs to Misawa's room. He must have just finished his supper, and now sat cross-legged on the mattress, seemingly pretty much contented with himself.

"I can now go to the latrine all by myself. And I can have fish, too," he said, beaming proudly.

All three windows of his room were wide open. Because there was nothing to obstruct the view from his third-floor room, the sky appeared very near; and the glittering of stars grew brighter every moment. "Must be some bats flying?" said Misawa, fanning himself. I caught the whiteness of the nurse's uniform as she moved toward the window and leaned out. I was more interested in the woman than in bats.

"Say, have you found out anything?" I asked.

"Yes, she's the one—just as I thought."

Misawa replied with a meaningful wink. "So—it is she," I said. My high-pitched voice must have revealed my excitement, for Misawa suddenly flapped his fan in my face. Then he pointed with its handle to a room diagonally opposite.

"She went into that room after you left."

Misawa's room was at the end of the hallway, looking over the street; whereas hers, at the corner of the same hallway, let in the light from the courtyard. As the weather was warm, the entrances of both rooms were left open and the sliding doors removed, so that from my seat I could see about a quarter of the entrance of the room Misawa indicated with his fan handle. But all I could see inside was the corner of her pallet which seemed like a triangular design on the floor.

For a while I stared at this corner of the mattress, without saying a word. "She has a severe ulcer that makes her spit blood," Misawa whispered. And I was reminded that Misawa had told me he had come to the hospital to avoid developing an ulcer. The term ulcer hadn't impressed me at all then but now it sounded singularly ominous. It sounded as if death lurked menacingly behind it.

A little later, faint gagging sounds came from her room.

"There—now she is vomiting," said Misawa, frowning. Then a nurse carrying a little metal basin appeared at the entrance. Slipping into her sandals, she darted away, giving us a quick glance.

"Is there any hope of her recovering?"

I again saw the profile of the young woman as I had caught it just that morning, sitting still on a bench, with her chin pressed onto her chest.

"I am not so sure—from the way she vomits," said Misawa. His expression was not one of mere pity; rather it was shadowed with concern.

"Do you really know her?" I asked Misawa.

"Yes, of course I do," he answered earnestly.

"But isn't this your first visit to Osaka?" I pressed him.

"Yes, it is, and I had never seen her before," explained Misawa. "As a matter of fact it was from her I heard about this hospital. When I registered here I had an inkling that she might also come, but I didn't really think this would be likely to happen until I heard from you this morning. Since I hold myself responsible for her illness . . ."

21

It seems that on arriving in Osaka Misawa and his friends had gone to drink at a certain tea-house, and there he had met her.

Apparently even then Misawa had had some stomach trouble due to the warm weather. Celebrating the occasion of their re-union, Misawa's companions got him drunk as though they were throwing a party just for him. Not wanting to spoil their fun, Misawa had drained the cups one after another as they came round. Yet all the time he had been growing more uncomfort-able, with the sickness mounting inside him. At times he had had to gulp fast, making a face. Sitting beside him, she had talked to him in her Osaka accent. She had offered him medicine, some Gem pills, and he accepted, throwing five or six of them into his mouth. When he returned the pill case he noticed that she did the same thing, taking several of the tiny pills in her white palm and swallowing them down.

For some time Misawa had noticed how languid she was and had asked if she felt well. With a sad smile she complained of her poor appetite, due probably to the warm weather. In the past week she had become averse to rice even and in fact was taking nothing but ice. She told him that as soon as she swallowed the ice she experienced an uncontrollable craving for more of it.

Misawa suggested that it was probably indigestion, and urged her to see a specialist. She told him others had said the same thing, and confessed that in fact she had thought of seeing a good doctor. "But my trade being what it is—" She was re-luctant to go on. It was then that he had learned of this hospital and the director's name.

"Well, I myself might go to a place like that. Something seems to be a little funny with me, too."

Misawa said this partly in jest, partly in earnest, but she knit her brows disapprovingly as if to say "Good Heavens!"

"But let's put it off until we have drunk our fill," Misawa had said, drinking off the cup. She had gently filled the cup he held out.

"Why don't you drink, too? You may not feel like eating rice, but you can certainly drink sake at least."

He drew her near and kept pressing the cup on her. To this, she submitted. Finally, however, she begged him to excuse her from drinking. And she continued to sit calmly and did not leave her seat.

"Come on—drink and drive out those worms, then you will want rice. But first you've got to drink."

Hopelessly drunk, Misawa by then was speaking roughly and forcing her to drink even though his own stomach was swelling with violent pains.

Misawa's story made me shudder. Why in the world should he treat his own body so cruelly? Worse and more of it, his self-torture was foolish enough, but why insist on torturing that poor girl?

"God only knows why. She really knew nothing about my condition; nor did I suspect her suffering. And as for those around us, they of course couldn't know. But that isn't all. In fact neither of us really knew our own condition. Besides, I was furious with my own stomach and I tried to coerce it with alcohol. Maybe she felt the same way."

22

She was lying in such a position that her face could not be seen from the hallway. Our nurse suggested that if I came closer to the door post I could look in, but I didn't have the nerve to do it.

Perhaps because it was so warm, the nurse who attended her spent most of the time leaning against the post and looking outside. Moreover, she was exceptionally good-looking for a nurse —in fact, so much so that Misawa often got sulky and complained as if that was somehow insulting. His own nurse too, for very different reasons, did not speak well of the pretty nurse.

She told us all sorts of things she had found out about the nurse: that she was completely inattentive to her patients; that she was unkind; that she wasted time mooning over love letters from a lover she had in Kyoto; and so on. As an example of her negligence our nurse also described how the other girl had once dropped off to sleep, forgetting to remove a bedpan from under her patient.

Indeed, it was plain even to us that the nurse, good looking as she was, did not take her duties very seriously. And Misawa often said with a sour face, "That nurse ought to be replaced; she is no good for her patient." Yet when the nurse leaned against the door post dozing, Misawa used to stare at her from his own room.

Our nurse brought us frequent reports on the patient's condition, too. It seemed that her disordered stomach would not tolerate milk, soup, or any other liquid no matter how light; she couldn't even take her medicine—would throw it up almost as soon as she swallowed it.

"Does she vomit blood?"

Misawa grilled the nurse, and every time I heard this question I felt sick.

Although she had visitors all the time, no sound of gay voices came from her room as it did from the other rooms. Lolling in Misawa's room, I watched many women visitors with *shimada* or butterfly coiffures going in and out. There was one who exclaimed at the entrance, "O dear, dear—" but that happened only once. And as soon as she had put her parasol down on one side of the hallway, she vanished into the room, and everything was quiet again.

"Have you visited her?" I asked Misawa.

"No," he said. "But I am doing more than just visiting."

"Then she may not know yet, I mean, that you are here."

"She wouldn't know unless the nurse has told her. When she came in I was startled at the sight of her. But she didn't see me and probably she doesn't know."

Misawa told me that one of her regular patrons who happened to be a patient on the second floor, had not only written her a ditty: "You for the stomach; I for the bowels, and we both suffer for sake," but also taken the trouble to visit her, in full dress, when he was about to leave the hospital. Misawa grimaced as though to say "What an ass!"

"They should leave her quiet and avoid exciting her nerves. They should go in and out of her room on tiptoe."

"Seems very quiet, though?" I said.

"That's because the patient is reluctant to talk," and he added, "That's a bad sign."

23

It turned out that Misawa knew a great deal more about her than I had expected. Each time I visited the hospital he brought her up as a matter of his primary concern. Apparently during my absence he gathered information about her private life, which he later divulged to me as though it had been a confidential story about his own lady friend. He even seemed to take pride in doing this.

As Misawa told the story, she was a popular geisha, treated well as the owner's prized daughter. Fragile as she was, she took great satisfaction in her role and devoted herself to her trade. Even when she didn't feel well she never shirked her duties. Even when once in a while she was forced to take to her bed she was impatient to get back to work . . .

"The woman in there now is a long-time maid of the geisha house. Of course she is really a maid in name only. Being an old-timer, she has considerable power, so naturally she doesn't behave like a maid. In fact she acts more like an aunt or somebody like that. Apparently she is the only one who can persuade the patient to take the medicine or who can curb her, because she listens only to this maid."

Misawa ascribed all this inside information to his nurse, and related everything as if learned at second hand. However, I began to have some doubts about this. While he was gone to the lavatory I took the opportunity to ask his nurse, "Well, that's what he says, but doesn't he sneak in for a chat with her when I am not here?" "Heavens, no," replied the nurse curtly. She then explained that the woman couldn't possibly tell her story to anybody like Misawa. But she also revealed the depressing fact that the patient was gradually taking a turn for the worse.

With her nausea still persisting, the normal way of taking nourishment was no longer possible. The day before they finally had tried a nutrient enema on her. But this was a failure, for her exceedingly weakened bowels seemed unable to retain even the simple milk-and-egg mixture.

The nurse seemed to imply that nobody could enjoy chattering about the life story of a patient in such serious condition. She was right about this, I thought. Oblivious to Misawa for the moment, in my mind I contrasted the picture of a popular geisha girl in her gala dress and the young woman in the other room suffering from a virulent disease.

Thanks to her personal beauty and her valued talents, she had been treated well as the prized daughter of the house. But now that they were no longer saleable, I wondered if she would still enjoy such fine treatment. Should that lessen in proportion to her illness, life would be hopeless indeed for her now struggling with this foul disease. Her parents, who had sent her to the geisha house, were undoubtedly lowly people, and certainly could not be expected to do anything since they could not afford to keep her.

All these things went through my mind. And when Misawa returned from the lavatory I asked him whether her parents were still around, and if they were aware of her condition.

24

Misawa said he had seen her mother only once.

"Even then, just from behind," he qualified.

Her mother, just as I had guessed, was obviously not well off. In fact, she could barely manage to make herself presentable for the hospital visit. When she made her periodic visit she always crept in timidly and then hurried down the stairs and slipped away unnoticed.

"Any parent in her situation would be as shy, I suppose," said Misawa.

All of the visitors were female, and most of them quite young. Moreover, they were all beautiful since, unlike ordinary women, they depended on their charms for their livelihood. In the midst of these beautiful women this mother of hers must have looked more than merely plain and shabby. I imagined to myself the rear view of this poor, aged mother, and felt sorry for her.

"As a parent she must be very anxious to sit with her own daughter, when she is in such a serious condition. It can't be pleasant to see an outsider such as that maid giving orders while she as a parent is treated almost as a stranger."

"But parent or not, she can do nothing about that, for not only has she no time to sit with the patient, but even if she had, she has no money to pay the bills."

I felt miserable and brooded on the fact that a woman of such a gay profession, and glamorous as her life might normally seem, should have to suffer all the more once she had fallen ill.

"She must have her own patron, though?"

Misawa had evidently not thought about that, for when I mentioned it he made no answer. The nurse, who was the source of all his information, could shed no light on this matter either.

The geisha's fragile body was holding out somehow, despite the heat. Misawa and I talked about this as though it had been a miracle. For fear of being thought too forward, we dared not steal a look at her even from behind the door post, and we could only imagine how she must be worn down by now. Even as we heard of the futile result of her nutrient enema treatment, Misawa could not think of her except as a beautifully dressed geisha girl. All I could imagine, on the other hand, was the sallow face I had caught a glimpse of as she was being admitted to the hospital. Actually even as we spoke of hers as a hopeless case, neither of us really believed that she would die.

In the meantime, patients of all varieties entered and were discharged from the hospital. One evening a woman of the same age, who had been on the second floor, was carried away on a stretcher. This patient, who might die any day, was taken back to the country by her mother who had been attending her in the hospital, but once complained to Misawa's nurse that the ice cost so much—some twenty *yen*—and that they had no other choice but to leave the hospital.

From the third-floor window I looked down at the stretcher heading for the country. Although I could not see the stretcher in the dark, the lanterns moved off. As my window was high up and the street narrow, it seemed as though the lights were moving silently along the bottom of a ravine. When they had vanished around the farther street corner, Misawa turned and said to me, "I hope she will hold out until she gets home."

25

While one patient was forced to leave the hospital in such misery, there was another, seemingly of ample leisure, who, carrying a child on his back, prowled around the hallway and the lookout post, and even invaded others' rooms.

"He must imagine the hospital is some kind of recreation center."

"Which one is the patient, anyway?"

It was amusing and puzzling, too. From the nurse we learned that the carrier was an uncle, and the child his nephew. The child had been nothing but skin and bones when he had been brought to the hospital, but now was chubby, thanks to his uncle's devoted care. He was said to be a hose maker; in any case he plainly had no worry about money.

There was another strange patient in a room a couple of doors from Misawa. Carrying his suitcase he went around as freely as any healthy person. Occasionally he even stayed away overnight. When he came back he stripped himself stark naked and enjoyed his hospital meal. Nonchalantly he would reveal that he had just been to Kobe the previous day.

There was also a couple from Gifu who had been staying in the hospital ever since they had been admitted while visiting Kyoto to worship at the Hongwanji Temple. In their alcove hung a scroll-picture of the haloed Amitabha. They were often seen relaxing over a game of *go*. Yet when asked the wife solemnly said that she had brought her husband to the hospital because the previous spring while having rice-cake he had vomited one-and-a-half sake-cupfuls of blood.

As I was saying, though, the geisha's nurse had the habit of leaning against the door post, cradling her knees with her arms. Our nurse criticized her to us, saying that the hussy was so proud of her own good looks that she was sitting there only to be seen. "Certainly not," I tried to defend her. But it was obvious that from the outset the woman and her pretty nurse remained indifferent to each other. Theirs, I explained, was a case of two good-looking women who in jealousy had come to hate each other instinctively. Misawa denied this and asserted that their mutual indifference was due to the fact that in Osaka nurses were so haughty as to look down upon geishas and wouldn't have any dealings with them. Yet, despite all this, he didn't seem to dislike the nurse. Nor did I. And when Misawa's ugly nurse declared, "Well, well, a pretty face has everything to gain and nothing to lose," her phrasing sounded so funny that we both laughed.

In the midst of these surroundings Misawa was regaining his health, and his interest in the woman grew proportionately every day. Here I use the word interest, for Misawa's attitude being neither that of love nor of unalloyed kindness, I cannot think of any other words more fitting than that.

When I had first seen her in the lobby I was just as attracted to her as Misawa apparently had been. But the moment he had revealed his acquaintance with her, that settled the matter of priority, and from then on whenever we talked about her Misawa invariably assumed the superior role. I must admit that for a while I had been carried away and imagined that my initial interest was growing keener. Yet once he had made me aware of my secondary position my interest in her waned.

26

When my interest waxed, his waxed hotter. While my interest ebbed somewhat, his grew all the more keen. Blunt as he was, Misawa was at heart a man of uncommonly tender feelings. He was capable of displaying an immediate and intense passion for whatever interested him.

I wondered why he wouldn't visit her room now that he had recovered enough to wander about the hospital. Unlike me, he was by no means shy. Certainly it would be in character if he visited this sick geisha—whom he had met but once—to cheer her up with a few words of sympathy. I even went so far as to suggest, "If you're so much concerned about her, why not go see her yourself and brighten her up?" "Yes—yes, I would be happy to go but . . ." and he was hesitant. With him, this was an unusual enough reaction, I thought, and I puzzled over it. Yet though I could not figure it all out I confess I really hoped that he would prefer not to pay her a visit.

One day I borrowed a fortune-book from her nurse— somehow the geisha's nurse and I had occasionally struck up a conversation, though our acquaintance didn't go beyond casual exchanges about the weather, when sitting against the door post, she glanced up at me as I passed by. At any rate, from this pretty nurse I borrowed an amateur fortune-book called Horoscope Chart or something like that, and amused myself with it in Misawa's room.

All I had to do was to take disks shaped like go stones, painted either red or black on both sides, and arrange them on a mat, while keeping my eyes closed. Then having counted the number of the reds and the blacks, I located those two numbers on the chart, lined horizontally for red and vertically for black. Where the two columns intersected was a symbol which, when looked up in the book, yielded the type of oracular proverb that can be found on divining papers.

With my eyes closed I arranged the stones one by one on the mat, and the nurse, after counting the reds and the blacks, looked up my fortune—which turned out to be: "If this love were to be realized you would be bound to disgrace yourself." Even while reading, the nurse burst out laughing. Misawa also chuckled.

"Say, you'd better watch out," said Misawa. For some time he had been alluding in jest to something fishy about my bowings to the woman's nurse.

"I say you are the one to watch out," I countered. He immediately became serious and demanded, "Why?" I kept silent, for at this point to say anything more to this stubborn fellow might only get me in more hot water.

I continued to wonder that he showed no inclination to visit her room. On the other hand I was afraid, considering his excitable nature, that whatever had happened in the past he might undergo some unanticipated change at an unpredictable moment in the future. This seemed quite likely since he had already gained enough strength to descend the stairs alone to the lavatory every morning.

"Say, isn't it time now to get out of the hospital?" I ventured. I had decided that if his hesitation was due to his financial distress I would approach Okada for a loan to spare Misawa the time and trouble of having money sent over from home. But Misawa did not rise to my suggestion, instead asking when I was going to leave Osaka.

27

As a matter of fact, only two days before, Okane-san unexpectedly had come to see me from Tengajaya, and as a consequence I at last learned what Okada had previously been hinting over the phone. Already, that is, I had been bound by his prediction that within a week he might have a surprise for me. Misawa's illness, the nurse's pretty face, the young geisha whose voice and figure I could neither hear nor see, and the temporary lull in the agony of her bed-ridden life —all of these were by no means the only matters that had kept me lingering in Osaka. Lapsing for a moment into poetic phraseology, I might say that I had stayed on at that stuffy hotel, ever expecting a certain prophecy to fulfill itself.

"All in all it seems wisest that I stay a little longer," I told Misawa gently, but this made him somewhat unhappy.

"That means we can't go together to the seaside for a rest."

There it was, and Misawa was certainly an odd fellow. As long as I had tried to be kind to him he had repulsed me; and now as I retreated, he seemed to grab me by the sleeve and hold fast. Our friendship was indeed a continuous repetition of such oscillations.

"Have you really been thinking of going to the seaside with me?" I tried to clarify the point.

"I wouldn't say I haven't," he replied, as though he might be envisioning the distant sea. Just for that moment I had the impression that in his vision both the woman and her nurse had been supplanted by the image of me, his friend.

Thus, although I left him agreeably that day, I recalled while returning to my hotel the unpleasantness that had preceded our agreeable parting. When I urged him to leave the hospital, he had in turn asked how long I would be staying in Osaka. Superficially that was all there had been in our exchange of words. And yet both Misawa and I had tasted its strange and bitter meaning.

Although my interest in the woman had waned, I did not wish to leave just as Misawa and the woman seemed likely to grow more intimate. Moreover, although Misawa had given no evidence of having designs on the pretty nurse I had observed that he had not remained calm about my getting close to her. Perhaps, it was a secret struggle we were neither conscious of; a conflict compounded of that selfishness and jealousy inherent in all of us; a clash of centerless interests never capable of developing into either harmony or discord. In short, it was a battle of sex, although neither of us would like to admit it frankly.

I felt ashamed of my own baseness as I walked along, and at the same time I hated Misawa's, too. But I was well aware that, wretched creatures that we were, it would be virtually impossible to eradicate this baseness, however long our friendship might last. I felt very forlorn and sad indeed.

The next day, upon arriving at the hospital, I immediately declared, "I won't urge you to leave the hospital any more." I said this, feeling almost penitent. Misawa also said, "I can't go on lolling like this, either. Following your advice I have finally decided to leave." It turned out that that morning he had obtained the director's permission to leave, and he was proceeding straight to Tokyo for fear that much activity might do him harm. I was stunned by the abruptness of his decision.

28

"But what induced you to leave the hospital so suddenly?" I couldn't help asking. And before replying, Misawa stared me full in the face. I felt that through my face he was reading my inmost thoughts.

"Nothing in particular. I just decided it's time to leave . . ."

That was all he said. I had no choice but to keep silent, and we sat face to face more pensive than usual. As the nurse had already gone, the room seemed exceptionally desolate. Misawa, who had been sitting cross-legged, suddenly threw himself down on his back and, turning up his eyes, gazed out of the window —at the blue sky, intensely tinted as usual, but now flooded with the heat of the glaring sun.

"Say," he then said, "that fellow you often speak of. Does he have money?"

Of course I knew nothing about Okada's financial situation, and when I thought of his frugal wife I became nervous at any mention of the word money. Already the day before, however, I had made up my mind to go through at least that much trouble if by doing so it would get Misawa out of the hospital.

"Being thrifty, he may have some, I guess."

"Get me a loan then, will you? I don't need much."

I thought that he was pressed for the money to settle his hospital bill, so I asked him how much he was short. But the fact was quite contrary to what I had expected.

"I have some here, just enough to pay the hospital and my train fare back to Tokyo. If that's all I needed, I wouldn't bother you."

Misawa was by no means a lucky fellow born in the lap of luxury. As the only son, however, he had considerably more freedom in such matters than some of the rest of us did. Furthermore, he had in fact some money with him, which he had planned to use in Kyoto to do some shopping for his mother and relatives but which had been left untouched since he had come directly to Osaka with his companions.

"Then, you mean to take some with you just in case?"

"No," he said curtly.

"What are you going to do with it, then?" I pressed him for an answer.

"Look, whatever I do with it is my business. All I want you to do is get me a loan."

There it was again and I felt my temper rising. He was treating me like a stranger, and I was so offended that I kept an angry silence.

"Please don't get mad at me," said Misawa. "I am not trying to conceal anything. You have nothing to do with this. I didn't want you to think I was advertising it. So I thought it would be best to keep it to myself."

I was still silent. And Misawa, still lying on his back, looked up at me.

"In that case I'll let you have it," he snapped and added, "I haven't gone to see her yet. And she is, I am sure, not expecting that either. Nor am I under any obligation to visit her. Yet I can't but feel guilty for the fact that her illness has reached this critical point. All this time I have been thinking that I would try to see her again—just once, whichever of us would be first to leave the hospital. Not just to visit, but to apologize. It will do if I simply say how sorry I am for the trouble I have caused her. And as I can't just go, empty-handed, I asked for your help. But if that is inconvenient to you, never mind. I'll manage it somehow. I may wire my family."

29

So circumstances forced me to approach Okada. I told Misawa to hold off sending the telegram,

74

and slipped out of the hospital gate. Okada's office, situated in the opposite direction from Misawa's room, could not be seen from his windows, but it was only a short distance. However, it was so warm that as I hurried along I felt sweat soaking my back.

When he saw me Okada exclaimed as though we hadn't seen each other for a long time, "Hello. How have you been?" And then he released the greetings he used to repeat over the phone so many times.

Only lately were Okada and I being so formal with each other; in by-gone days we had never stood on ceremony. I remember having done him the favor of lending him a sum of money. So to screw up my courage I began by reminding him of our old days. Not guessing what I was up to, Okada rose, saying spiritedly: "Well, what do you think of my prediction? That surprise seems to be coming within a week, doesn't it?"

But I quickly got down to my immediate business. At first he seemed surprised at my request, but after he had heard me out he consented readily, "Why, certainly. That much, I can take care of."

Naturally he did not have that much money with him. He asked, "Is tomorrow all right with you?" Once more I had to press forward, "I'd like to have it today—if possible." He looked a little at a loss.

"Well, I can't see any other way. Let me write a note which you can take to my house and show to Okane. You don't mind, do you?"

As much as I hated to deal directly with her about this matter, it seemed unavoidable. With Okada's note in my pocket, I was off to Tengajaya. When she heard my voice Okane-san rushed out to the front door and said in surprise, "O my—and in this warm weather. Won't you please come in." She repeated this, but standing there I answered that I was in a hurry, and merely handed her Okada's note. Still on her knees before the door, she opened it.

"I am sorry you've had to come all the way. I'll be ready to come with you right away." She quickly disappeared into the house. I heard the drawer handle of the dresser rattle.

Okane-san and I went as far as the terminal of the trolley line, and parted. Opening her parasol, she said, "I'll be seeing you later." I hurried back to the hospital by ricksha, washed my face, sponged off my body, and chatted with Misawa for a while. As expected, I was soon called down to the door, where Okane-san pulled a bankbook out of her *obi*, drew out the money inserted between the pages, and put it in my hand.

"Will you check the amount, please."

I counted it perfunctorily and thanked her. "This is fine. Many thanks for all the trouble, and especially in this heat." Indeed, she must have rushed; both sides of her Fuji-shaped forehead were wet with tiny beads of sweat.

"Won't you come up and cool yourself for a while?"

"No thank you. I'm in a hurry today. I must be going. Please give my regards to your patient. I am so glad he can leave the hospital soon. My husband has been much concerned and has often phoned the hospital about his condition, I understand."

With these expressions of solicitude, Okane-san opened her cream-colored parasol and left.

30

I was also in a hurry, and with the money in my hand I almost ran up the stairs to the third floor. Misawa was less composed than usual. He immediately threw the cigarette he had just lit into an ash tray and took the money from my hand, with no word of thanks. I reminded him of the sum of the money and asked if that would do. Yet all he said was simply "Yes."

He stared at her room. At this time of the day there wasn't even one pair of visitor's straw sandals on the other side of the hallway. Her room, which had always been too quiet, now seemed doubly desolate. The pretty nurse, as usual, leaned against the door post, studying a book on obstetrics or something.

"I wonder if she is asleep."

Misawa seemed rather afraid to disturb her sleep now that a favorable chance to visit her offered itself.

"Maybe she is," I thought.

A little later Misawa said in a low voice, "Perhaps I should have that nurse find out if it would be convenient." Since, however, he had never spoken to her, I had to take care of that part. The nurse looked at me in puzzled amusement, but noticing my seriousness without a word she turned and went into the room. Not more than a minute or two had gone by when she reappeared smiling. She said that the patient could see him since she was feeling better. Misawa rose without saying a word.

He looked neither at me nor at the nurse; he rose in silence and vanished into the woman's room. From my seat I blankly watched his disappearing back. Even after he was gone I kept on staring at the empty space where he had been. The nurse remained aloof. With a somewhat derisive smile on her lips she glanced at me; then once more she leaned against the post and resumed her reading.

The room, even after Misawa entered, was as quiet as before. Of course no voices could be heard. Occasionally the nurse suddenly raised her eyes and looked in. But without making me a sign she again dropped her eyes to the pages of her book.

In the early evening hours I had enjoyed, from this third floor, the refreshing chirpings of summer insects, but not once in the daytime had I heard the noisy shrill chirrup of cicadas. Now the room where I was sitting was quieter than at midnight. And this dead silence got on my nerves as I anxiously waited for Misawa to come out of her room.

Finally Misawa strode out of the room. Crossing the doorsill, he smiled and said to the nurse, "Pardon me. Working hard, aren't you?" That was all I heard him say.

He returned to his room, stamping his slippers somewhat determinedly, and said, "Now I am through." "How did it go?" I asked.

"I am through, finally. Now I can leave."

Misawa simply repeated this. He said nothing else. I could get nothing more out of him. At any rate I thought that it would be best to expedite the discharge procedure, and began putting away the things scattered around. Nor did Misawa, needless to say, sit still.

3 1

Both of us hired rickshas and
left the hospital. Misawa's rickshaman, who started off first, was
quite a dasher; in fact he ran so spiritedly that I was almost
obliged to call after him to stop. Misawa looked back and waved
his hand. As he seemed to be saying, "I'm all right, I'm all right,"
I let the man alone and paid him no more attention. When I got
to the hotel, Misawa, his hands resting on the riverside railing,
was gazing at the broad current flowing below.

"What's the matter? Do you feel all right?" I asked him from
behind. Without turning around he said simply, "Yes," and then
added, "I had completely forgotten this room until I came back
and saw this river."

He remained facing the river. I left him there as he was, and
sat on the cushion. Still impatient, I pulled my pack of Shikishima out of my sleeve and began smoking. I had finished a
third of the cigarette when Misawa at last left the railing and
took his seat before me.

"It seems only yesterday and today that I've been in hospital.
But come to think of it, it's been quite a long time," said Misawa,
counting off the number of days on his fingers.

"You won't forget that third-floor hospital room for some
time," I declared, looking at his face.

"That was an experience I had never expected. Maybe it was
fated," Misawa said, now looking at me.

He clapped his hands and had the maid who appeared make a
reservation for a berth on the night express. He then pulled out
his watch and noted how much time would be left after supper.
Unused to standing on ceremony, we threw ourselves down to
relax.

"You think she will recover?"

"Well, she may if she is lucky, but . . ."

Our talk about her was interrupted right there, however,
when a maid came up the stairs, carrying the bowlful of fruit I
had ordered. I ate the fruit sprawled out as I was while Misawa

quietly watched my mouth moving. Then he said in the tone of a sick person, "Well, I wish I could have some, too." I had for some time noted his glum face, and now urged, "What matter! You may as well eat. Why don't you take some?" Luckily Misawa had forgotten the day when I wouldn't permit him ice cream. But he merely grinned and turned sideways.

"No thanks. Don't force them on me, much as I like them. I know they won't do me any good. I certainly don't want to suffer like her."

All along Misawa, apparently, had been thinking of her; and he persisted in thinking about her.

"Did she remember you?"

"Sure she did. After all, she had met me just recently—and I forced her to drink."

"She must have resented it."

Misawa, who had been talking with his face averted, now suddenly turned round and looked at me hard. Noticing this change in him, I also quickly took on a serious air. But I could not discover what kind of talk they had had after he walked into her room.

"She may die. If she does we shall never see each other again. And if she is lucky enough to recover, even then we shall never see each other again. This meeting and parting in human life is so strange, though I suppose that may sound exaggerated. But at least that's the way I feel. When she heard of my plan to return to Tokyo tonight she smiled and said good-bye. And I am afraid I may dream about her forlorn smile on that train tonight."

32

That was all Misawa said. He was probably envisioning her forlorn smile, even before he had the dream. Although I was familiar with his tendency to sentimentalize, it was puzzling how he could have become so fascinated by this woman on such slight acquaintance. Still anxious to hear the details of their farewell talk, I tried futilely to pump him a little. I was therefore left all the more mystified, for

Misawa was behaving like one who wouldn't let anybody else have even half-a-loaf simply because he was afraid that would mean the loss of his own half.

"Shall we get going? The night express usually gets crowded," I finally urged him.

"It's still too early," said Misawa, showing me his watch. It was, indeed, for we still had a couple of hours before the train was scheduled to leave. I decided not to mention the woman any more and, trying to avoid referring to the hospital even, I began chatting with him as we lay there. He responded just like any other person, but somehow he remained out of sorts and looked cheerless. Yet he didn't leave his seat. And finally, as conversation lapsed into silence, he sat merely gazing at the river.

"You're still brooding," I ventured. Misawa, taken by surprise, gave me a scornful look which I had learned meant, "What a vulgar fellow!" This time, however, that did not seem to be his intention.

"Yes, I am," he said almost casually. "I've been debating with myself whether I should tell you this or not."

It was indeed a strange story that he then told me. Even more surprising, it had no direct bearing on the woman.

It seemed that, five or six years before, Misawa's father had helped the daughter of one of his friends marry into another friend's family. As ill luck would have it, she had to leave her husband in a year or so under difficult circumstances. Moreover, she could not return to her own people again, due to some other complicating factors. As the one who made the match, Misawa's father had to take care of her, at least for the time being. And this young divorcee Misawa had grown accustomed to calling *musumesan*.

"Probably she was too worried; in any event she was not quite in her right mind. Whether it had started before she had come to stay with us or after, I do not know. However, it was not until some time after she came that we took notice of it. Undoubtedly she tended that way from the start, yet at first glance no one could have told that. She simply kept quiet and was depressed. But this *musumesan* . . ."

At this point Misawa became a little hesitant.

"Now this may sound funny, but—she would follow me to the door every time I went out. In fact, she never failed to follow me to the door no matter how quietly I tried to slip out. And always she said, 'Please come back early, will you?' and nodded if I said, 'Yes, I'll come back early. You be good and wait until then.' If I said nothing, she would keep saying, 'Please come back early, will you?' Of course nothing could be more embarrassing to me in front of my family. Yet for all that, since I felt sorry for her, I always tried to come back early when I was out. I even got into the habit of going to her upon my return and standing there, saying simply, 'You see I am home now.'"

Misawa paused there and checked the time.

"We have still got some time, haven't we?" he asked.

33

I feared that Misawa might have to cut short his story about the *musumesan*, but luckily there was still enough time, and Misawa, without being pressed, went on with his story.

"It was all right once we knew for sure that she was out of her mind. But before that I myself, as I have just now said, was much annoyed by her boldness. My father and mother frowned, and our maids giggled among themselves. I felt I couldn't stand all this any longer. Once when she followed me to the door I was going to upbraid her harshly, and glared back at her two or three times. But the moment our eyes met I just couldn't get mad; nor could I even say cruel things to such a pitiful creature. She was a pale complexioned girl, her face beautiful with her black brows and her large dark pupils—always moistened with a rapt, faraway look, in which there was a faint hint of sorrow. As I looked back to scold her, there she was, on her knees there at the door, turning up those dark eyes toward me, as if to express an extreme loneliness. Each time this happened I felt that she was clinging to my sleeve and imploring, 'Please help me out of my unbearable aloneness in this lonely world.' I mean her eyes. Her large dark pupils so appealed to me."

"Wasn't she in love with you?" I was tempted to ask.

"As for that, she was sick, so no one could tell whether it was love or mere sickness," Misawa replied.

"What they call nymphomania, isn't it something of that sort?" I asked him again.

Misawa was apparently disgusted.

"A nymphomaniac snuggles up to any man, doesn't she? She wasn't at all like that. All she did was to follow me to the door and say, 'Please come back early, will you?'"

"I see."

I had tried to make my answer seem as noncommittal as could be.

"Whether it was because of her sickness or something else, I'd like to think only that she loved me. That's the way at least I would like to see it," said Misawa, staring at me. His face had grown more tense. "But the truth seems quite otherwise. As I heard the story, her husband, whether a rake or a sociable man, soon after their marriage fell into the habit of staying out or coming home late, and apparently this tortured her unmercifully. Yet she somehow had endured this treatment, not uttering a word of complaint to him. With this experience still haunting her, even after the divorce, and the onset of her sickness, she was only saying to me what she had wished to say to her husband . . . But I don't want to believe it. In fact I insist on believing that it is not true."

"Did she please you that much?" I asked him again.

"Yes, she came to . . . the more serious her sickness became."

"And—what has become of her?"

"She died. After she was sent to the hospital."

I dropped into silence.

"When you urged me to leave the hospital I realized that it would soon be the third anniversary of her death. That thought was enough to induce me to go back home." Misawa thus explained what had prompted his decision to leave the hospital. I still kept silent.

"O yes, I've forgotten to tell you the main point," Misawa then exclaimed.

"What is it?" I asked automatically.

"The face of the woman in the hospital bears a remarkable resemblance to hers, to tell you the truth."

I caught a sort of smile working at his lips as if to say, "Now you can understand."

Presently we hired rickshas and hurried to Umeda Station, which was jammed with passengers awaiting the express. Together we crossed the bridge to the other side, where we waited for the Tokyo-bound train. And within ten minutes, clattering and shaking the ground, the train came in.

"Well—see you again."

I gave Misawa a firm grip in memory of both women. Then in an instant he had vanished into the darkness, with the roaring of the train's departure.

Brother

The day after I saw Misawa off
I had to return to the same railroad station to meet my mother,
my brother, and my sister-in-law.

It was of course Okada who had from the start contrived this
visit, which seemed almost inconceivable to me, and eventually
worked it out successfully. He was always fond of manipulating
such a trick and bragging about his success. Indeed it was he
who had called me up just to predict that something might soon
take me by surprise. Later, when Okane-san called on me at the
hotel and explained it, I was really startled.

"What are they coming for?" I asked.

Before I left Tokyo I had happened to learn that the front
portion of my mother's suburban lot was to be condemned to
make room for a new trolley line. "With the money you'll get,
you may as well take others along and do a little traveling this
summer," I suggested to her and got laughed at. She said only,
"Jiro-san is at his old game again." But, as it turned out, when
that money came into her hands, my mother was able to realize
her long-treasured wish to visit Kyoto and Osaka. And the invitation from Okada was to round out her grandiose plan. Yet I
wasn't sure about what made Okada extend such an invitation.

"There isn't anything special about it, I'm sure. He just wants to show them around and repay all their past kindnesses. Besides, he has that matter to discuss."

By that matter Okane-san meant Osada-san's marriage. Yet I still couldn't quite understand why my mother would come all the way to Osaka in behalf of Osada-san, her favorite though she was.

I was by then already running out of money; furthermore, I had borrowed some from Okada. Other matters aside, their coming seemed to offer a good opportunity for me to improve the state of my sad resources. It even seemed likely that Okada's willingness to lend me the money had been influenced by his knowledge of all of this.

In any event, I went to the station with the Okadas. While we were waiting for the train, Okada asked, "What do you say, Jiro-san? Surprising isn't it?" Having already heard this sort of thing many times, I made no answer. But Okane-san said to him, "You've been so puffed up with yourself all along. I'll bet Jiro-san is tired of listening to that kind of talk." As she spoke, she turned to me and added apologizingly, "Aren't you?" In her winsomeness there was a hint of sophisticated coquetry that suddenly upset my verbal response. Pretending not to notice it, she continued to talk with Okada.

"*Okusama* must have changed much. It's been a long time since I last saw her."

"Just the same old aunt as when I saw her last time."

Okada called my mother aunt and Okane-san, *okusama*. This difference sounded somewhat odd to me. But I said laughingly, "When you are with her all the time, you can hardly tell whether she is really growing old."

The train arrived on time. Okada mentioned the hotel reservation he had made especially for the three, and directed the rickshas toward the south. Clinging to the flying ricksha I marvelled at the way Okada could take others by surprise. Come to think of it, when he had shown up in Tokyo unexpectedly, snatched up his bride, and carried her away with him, it had certainly seemed to me one of his most dazzling feats.

85

2

My mother's hotel was not big, but its style was far more refined than any mine offered. Her room was furnished with an electric fan, a Chinese writing desk fitted with a lamp, and other comforts. My brother at once filled out one of the telegram forms informing those in Tokyo of their safe arrival and handed it to a maid. Okada took out of his sleeve several picture postcards he had thought to provide and, after addressing each specifically to my father, Oshige, and Osada-san, passed them around, saying, "Please a line on each."

On the one addressed to Osada-san I wrote "Congratulations." My mother in her turn added, "Take care of your illness," to my surprise.

"Is she ill?"

"Actually I thought it would be a good idea for her to come with us, but when all was set, she suddenly complained of a stomachache. It was too bad."

"But not so serious. She can now have gruel," my sister-in-law interrupted. She was pausing over the card addressed to my father. When Okada suggested, "For a person of taste like uncle a poem might be better," she answered, "You want me to write a poem? Impossible." On the one to my sister, however, Okada wrote respectfully in tiny characters, "Missing your sharp tongue." "So you still seem mad about that chessman," my brother remarked teasingly.

The cards done with, we chatted briefly. Then the Okadas took leave of us, over the protests of my mother and brother. They promised to return soon.

"Okane-san has become really wifely, hasn't she?"

"I can hardly recognize her; she has changed so much from those days when she used to bring back the piecework."

These comments my mother and brother made about Okane-san seemed to imply the faint melancholy realization that they themselves had aged that much.

"Mother, Osada-san also will be like that very soon," I interjected.

86

"Why certainly," said my mother, probably thinking of Oshige, for whom no suitable man had appeared yet. My brother looked around and said, "I hear you couldn't go any place because of Misawa's illness." "No," I replied, "I was stuck in a nice mess and couldn't leave." My brother and I used to speak to each other in this rather reserved way, possibly because of some age difference, but also because our old-fashioned father had disciplined his elder son to accept the role of supreme authority. Indeed, when my mother occasionally attached the respectful "san" to Jiro, in calling me, I decided it was probably a carry over of her habit of referring to my brother as Ichiro-san.

We were all so much engrossed in our chat that we forgot to change to *yukata*. My brother rose and, slipping into a heavily starched one, urged me, "How about you?" Handing mine over to me, my sister-in-law asked, "Where is your room?" My mother, who had gone over to the railing and been dully looking at the high, plastered wall directly beneath her, volunteered the remark, "This room is nice but a bit gloomy. Is yours also like this, Jiro?" I went over to her and looked down at the courtyard oblong like a cloth-stretcher, sparse with slender bamboo. There was also a rusted iron lantern on a rock. The rock and the sparse bamboo were wet all over with sprinkled water.

"Small but fancy, isn't it? But you don't have the river view my room offers, Mother."

"Oh where is the river?" said my mother. Following her, my brother and sister-in-law also insisted that their room be changed for another with a view of the river. I gave them some idea about the location of my hotel. Then I said that I would go back to the hotel, pack my things, and join them here. With this promise I left the hotel.

3

That evening I checked out of my hotel and went over to theirs. Supper must have been a little late. The table had not been cleared yet, and they were using toothpicks. I suggested a walk, but my mother begged off, saying she was too tired, and my brother seemed to think it was too much trouble. My sister-in-law alone seemed interested, but my mother discouraged her, saying: "You'd better not go out tonight."

My brother then lay down and started a conversation. From the way he talked one might think that he was very familiar with Osaka. On further questioning, however, it was obvious that he knew only place names, such as the Tennoji Temple, Nakanoshima, and Sennichimae. As for his sense of geography, it was as vague as any dream could be.

Yet apparently he did remember fragmentary scenes, judging from the way he described those enormous rocks of the stone wall of Osaka Castle, a dizzy view from the tower of the Tennoji Temple, and the like. The one that sounded the most interesting of all to me was a night scene at a hotel where he had once stayed.

"It stood at the corner of a narrow street. From the railing I could see a willow tree. With its close packed houses it was a quiet area; from the window I enjoyed a picturesque view of a long bridge. Even those vehicles crossing the bridge sounded very pleasant, though my hotel itself was embarrassingly inhospitable and shabby . . ."

"What part of Osaka was it?" asked my sister-in-law, but he had no notion whatsoever. He couldn't even recall the direction. And this was typical of my brother for, while retaining a remarkably vivid memory of the phases of a certain incident, he tended to forget completely the names of places and the dates, although this peculiarity apparently never bothered him.

"What good is it if you can't tell us where it is?" said my sister-in-law. Over this kind of point my brother and sister-in-law often collided with each other. It was all right when he was in a good humor, but it sometimes created friction.

"I really don't care where it was as long as that isn't the end of the story. Now go on and tell us the rest of your story," interrupted my mother, who had the knack of dealing with touchy situations like this.

"I don't think this would interest you mother or Onao," he first declared, and then spoke to me, "Jiro, what interested me when I stayed on the second floor of that hotel was . . ." Now I assumed the role of a listener to his story.

"Yes, what happened?"

"That night, as I woke up from a nap, a bright moon was out, shining on the green willow tree. I lay still looking at it, when suddenly I heard a shouted yo-ho! down below. The sound seemed particularly sharp since the area was exceptionally quiet. I rose instantly and, going out to the railing, looked down. Under the willow tree three fellows all stark naked were taking turns lifting a huge *takuan* stone, apparently in a contest of strength. And the cry of yo-ho! echoed each time one of them, straining mightily, lifted the stone high above his head. All three were much absorbed in it, so much so that no one spoke a word. It made me feel very strange to watch their shadowy nakedness moving in the bright moonlight. Soon another began turning round and round something long like a pole . . ."

"Now that sounds like *Suikoden,* doesn't it?"

"Even then it did not seem quite real. As I look back now, it seems just like a dream."

My brother was fond of recalling moments like this. And their charm was something that neither my mother nor sister-in-law could understand, something that only we menfolk appreciated.

"That was the only thing I found interesting in Osaka at that time, although I certainly can't associate that with Osaka any more."

I recalled the neat and narrow street which could be seen from the third floor of the hospital where Misawa had stayed. And I wondered if the pole-player and strong men my brother had then seen were young people from such a neighborhood.

The Okadas, true to their word, called on us again that night.

4

Okada brought with him a very elaborate sightseeing plan which he had prepared at home, and showed it to my mother and brother. The minuteness of the plan seemed to dazzle my mother and brother who could only comment, "Oh my!"

"Roughly how many days can you stay? We can adjust our plan accordingly. Unlike Tokyo, we have a lot of places to see here, once we get out of the city."

Okada's statement echoed some dissatisfaction, while at the same time betraying a touch of triumph.

"You seem to be bragging about Osaka, if I may say so."

Okane-san laughingly chided her too serious husband.

"Not at all, this is not bragging. This is not bragging, but . . ."

Now intimidated, Okada grew even more serious, and seemed so comical that everyone present burst out laughing.

"Okada-san, you've taken to Kamigata style completely in the last five or six years, haven't you?" my mother teased him.

"Well, he has retained his Tokyo accent at least," my brother said, poking fun at him.

"So, another rough customer to deal with, after so long. Tokyo people are all sharp-tongued," replied Okada, gazing back at my brother.

"Ah but remember, Okada-san, he is Oshige's brother," I broke in now.

"Come help me out, Okane," Okada said at last. He picked up the plan in front of my mother, and put it back in his sleeve. "What nonsense! A ribbing for all my trouble!" He now pretended anger.

The momentary bantering was concluded when my mother, as I had expected, brought up the Sano matter. In completely changed and carefully precise terms, she warmly expressed her gratitude to Okada. Okada, on his part, in stilted fashion, replied, "By all means." I thought they were both exaggerating a bit. Then, Okada urged her to take this opportunity to meet the young man involved, and began making arrangements. My brother must have decided that it was now fitting to join in the conversation, and did so, puffing his cigarette. I wished the sick Osada-san might witness this scene and tell me whether she felt grateful to them, or annoyed. At that very moment I found myself recalling the unhappy marriage of that beautiful demented girl whose touching story I had heard from Misawa before his departure.

My sister-in-law and Okane-san knew each other only slightly but, both being young women, they chatted for a while, although with the characteristic reserve of unfamiliarity. Since by nature my sister-in-law was taciturn, and Okane-san was lively, one could speak ten words, the other could manage only one, and whenever they ran out of a topic it was always Okane-san who supplied the next. At last they got around to talking about a child, and now all of a sudden my sister-in-law occupied the stage. With marked animation she spoke of her only daughter's everyday life. Although Okane-san pretended to listen admiringly to her tedious account, it seemed to me that she was altogether indifferent. In fact, only once did she appear genuinely interested as she said, "She can stay home all by herself? How remarkable!" "Oh only because she is so much attached to Oshige-san," replied my sister-in-law.

5

To my surprise, my mother, brother and sister-in-law were going to stay only a few days. Apparently they had come intending to return to Tokyo within a week, after spending several days in and out of Osaka.

"You might as well stay a little longer, since you have come all the way. It won't be so easy to arrange another trip; it takes too much effort."

Okada urged this though he couldn't possibly afford to take every day off to show my mother around if she stayed. She was also concerned about those left at home in Tokyo. My mother, brother and sister-in-law seemed to me odd traveling companions, in the first place. Ordinarily my father and mother would have come together, and my brother and sister-in-law would have gone to a summer resort by themselves. And if Osada-san's marriage problems were the main purpose, then either my mother or father certainly could have come with her to settle the matter quickly after she got well. In any event, they surely had some other more natural course of action. From the start I had not understood how things had come about in just this peculiar way. It would seem that my mother was keeping all that to herself, although I guessed that my brother and his wife were very likely as aware of that point as was my mother.

Their meeting with Sano came off without a hitch. Yet, although my mother and brother thanked Okada, even after Sano had left neither of them commented about him. It seemed as though the whole matter had been concluded and there was nothing more left to be discussed. They agreed that the ceremony would be held toward the end of the year when Sano could come up to Tokyo.

"It seems so odd," I said to my brother. "The whole thing is going swimmingly, and yet the person most concerned has no idea of what's going on."

"Of course she knows," my brother said.

"She couldn't be happier," my mother assured me.

I didn't say a word. But a little later I said, "Well, I suppose no Japanese woman could conclude this matter all by herself." My brother kept silent. My sister-in-law gave me a queer look.

"Not just women. Even a man shouldn't be allowed to carry it off. I wouldn't want that either," my mother reminded me.

"Well, that might be better," said my brother. Perhaps it was his rather cool tone that made my mother frown and caused my sister-in-law to make an odd face; however, neither spoke.

After a while my mother finally said, "Anyhow, having Sada settled will take a load off my mind. Then there will be only Oshige left."

"This, too, thanks to our father," replied my brother. But my mother did not detect the faint touch of irony in his words.

"That's right. All thanks to your father. The same with Okada, who is now doing fine." Poor Mother appeared so very satisfied. Apparently she took it for granted that our father retained his former social influence. On the other hand, my brother, to his credit, was quite aware that our father, now virtually retired, could hardly enjoy even half of it.

Although I happened to be at one with my brother in this, I couldn't but feel that my whole family were conspiring to cheat Sano. But to look at it in another way, I somehow had a feeling that Sano would get his just deserts.

Anyway, the meeting was over to everyone's satisfaction. My brother insisted on leaving Osaka soon, complaining that the muggy weather was a strain on his nerves. Naturally, I agreed with him.

6

Osaka was then enduring a hot spell, and our hotel was especially steamy. The small courtyard with its high wall wouldn't let in either much sun or enough breeze. At times it was like sitting in a damp tea-parlor, surrounded by a roasting fire. Once, when I kept a fan on throughout the night I was scolded by my mother, who said, "Don't be foolish. You may catch cold."

When I agreed with my brother that we should get out of Osaka it occurred to me that a cool place like Arima might do his nerves good. Although I was not familiar with this famous spa, I related a story I had once heard: A ricksha man was climbing a steeply sloping road with the aid of a dog tied to the shafts. Every time the dog, now overheated and thirsty, tried to drink from a mountain stream the ricksha man thrashed it with his bamboo stick, forcing it whining and panting to continue pulling the vehicle.

"Oh, I wouldn't care to ride that kind of ricksha . . . The poor thing," said my mother, knitting her brows.

"Why doesn't he let his dog drink? Is it because the ricksha will be delayed?" asked my brother.

"They say once a dog drinks on the way it becomes tired out and then is no good for anything," I replied.

"Indeed. But why?" asked my sister-in-law now, puzzled, and I did not know what to say in reply.

Thus the Arima plan fell through—though probably not because of concern for this dog. Then my brother surprisingly proposed a visit to Wakanoura instead. It was a beauty spot I had always wanted to see, and our mother also agreed readily, the name having been familiar to her since childhood. My sister-in-law was the only one who seemed to find nothing to choose between the two places.

Now my brother was a scholar, and a man of principle, but he was also a likable fellow with the purity of a poet. However, as the elder son, he was inclined to be wilful, and I daresay he was far more spoiled even than is normally the fate of the eldest son. When in good humor he was extremely pleasant not just to me but also to Mother and his wife; but in a perverse mood he would make a sour face and not speak a word. Yet, when he was with outsiders, he became a completely changed person, an altogether desirable companion who would seldom lose his gentlemanly manner. As a consequence, all of his friends took him to be a gentle, affable soul. My parents never ceased to be amazed whenever they heard of his reputation, although they were also pleased, for he was their son after all. When I for one heard some such evaluation while we were at odds with each other I really smouldered and yearned to set everybody straight.

Thus, it seemed to me that when my mother readily agreed to visit Wakanoura she was merely revealing her thorough understanding of his temperament. As a result of her continuous solicitude to foster her son's ego, she now found it her fate to kneel down before that very ego on all occasions.

On the way to the lavatory I saw my sister-in-law standing absent-mindedly beside the wash-basin. "How are things? Is Brother cheerful or moody?" I asked. "As usual," was all she said. Yet I noted that there was now a forlorn dimple in the middle of her lusterless cheek.

7

Before leaving I wanted to clear up my debt to Okada. Of course he would not have minded if I had told him that I'd return the money upon my return to Tokyo, but I thought I would feel better if I returned it as soon as possible. So when no one else was around I enlisted my mother's help.

My mother, as I have indicated, loved my brother as heartily as she indulged him. Yet she was somewhat reserved with him, perhaps because he was her first-born or simply because he was a difficult person. She was very reluctant to give him advice for fear of offending him. On the other hand, she tended to treat me like a mere child, and would scold me unsparingly, "Jiro, don't be so unreasonable." But for that reason also she pampered me more than my brother. I remember on several occasions asking her for pocket money without his knowledge. Nor was it rare for her to retailor my father's kimono to fit me, without my knowledge. Such indulgence on her part did not please my brother at all. He became easily peevish at trifles, and as a consequence would cast his own gloom over our otherwise sunny home. Quite often my mother, knitting her brows, would whisper to me, "Ichiro is venting his spleen again." At such times, when my mother took me into her confidence, I was elated and said nonchalantly, "Well, that is his habit. Let him alone." But as I came to realize that his behavior was due not merely to his difficult temperament but to his sense of justice which made him detest whatever intrigues he might sense behind his back, I felt too ashamed to venture further thoughtless remarks. But since there were so many matters which just couldn't be satisfactorily attended to if I tried to obtain his consent openly, I was invariably tempted to seize the chance to monopolize my mother's confidence.

On this occasion she was amazed when I explained how I had borrowed the money from Okada for Misawa.

"I fail to understand why Misawa-san had to spend money on that kind of woman. It's so absurd," she said.

"But that was something he thought he was obliged to do," I explained.

"Your kind of obligation is beyond me. Well, if he was truly sorry he could as easily have gone to see her empty-handed. But if that made him still feel awkward he could have taken along a box of sweets. Wouldn't that have been enough?"

95

I kept silent for a while.

"Even if he thought it was his obligation to do it, I still can't see why you were obliged to borrow money from someone like Okada."

"Oh well, forget all about it then," I replied. I rose and was about to go downstairs. My brother was taking a bath, and my sister-in-law was having her hair done in a small room downstairs. My mother was alone in the room.

"Wait a moment," she called me back. "I never said I wouldn't help you out, did I?"

In her words there was a touch of helplessness, as if to say, "Since your brother alone is more than enough, why must you too torture your old mother?" I sat down again, as I was told. I felt so sorry for her that I could not bear to raise my face. And, awkward as a child, I received the needed sum from my mother. When in her usual lowered voice she murmured, "Don't mention this to your brother," I was suddenly overwhelmed with inexplicable discomfort.

8

We were to leave for Wakayama the next morning. Since we would have to return to Osaka once anyway, I thought I might perhaps delay repaying until then. However, being impatient, I just did not want to keep the money in my pocket that long. I made up my mind to slip it to Okada when he showed up at the hotel that evening.

My brother came out of the bath. Throwing on a *yukata*, without tying the *obi*, he walked over to the railing and hung up his wet towel.

"Sorry to have kept you waiting."

"How about you next, Mother?"

"You go ahead first," my mother said. And glancing at my brother's neck and chest, she complimented, "You look very well. What's more, you seem to have put on some weight." My brother was naturally scrawny. Although everyone in the family agreed that it was due to his nerves, and suggested that he try to put on a little more weight, it was my mother of course who worried the most. As for my brother, he loathed his own leanness as if it had been some sort of punishment, and yet could not gain an ounce.

When I heard my mother's words I was somehow sorry that she felt it necessary to console her own son with such a forced compliment. I raised my body, which in its sturdiness contrasted sharply with my brother's, and said to my mother, "Then, if you'll excuse me I'll go ahead," and went downstairs. Peeping into the little room next to the bath, I noted that my sister-in-law had just completed her chignon and was using two mirrors to retouch the side-locks and the back-hair.

"Are you through, already?"

"Yes. Where are you going?"

"To take a bath, that is if I may go first."

"Why certainly."

Stepping into the bathtub, I wondered what made her decide on the extravagance of the chignon. I called out to her. "Yes, what is it?" she replied from the hallway.

"Sorry you've had to go to so much trouble in such warm weather," I said.

"With what?"

"What? Your extravagant hairdo—is that Brother's wish?"

"Oh please."

I heard the sound of her sandals echo sharply through the hallway and up the stairs.

In the courtyard facing the hallway I saw a stump of Japanese fatsia as I looked out while an attendant was washing off my back. Then other footsteps approached from the exit along the hallway, and soon Okada passed by dressed in a white suit with a closed collar. "Say," I blurted out.

"Ah so, taking a bath. It's so dark in here I didn't even notice you," Okada replied, turning around and gazing into the bath.

"I have something to tell you," I said suddenly.

"Something to tell me? What is it?"

"Step in, will you?"

Okada looked as if to say, "No kidding?"

"Hasn't my wife come?"

When I replied "No," he asked, "How is everyone?" When I answered, "They are all here," he seemed puzzled and asked, "Didn't you go anywhere today?"

"Yes, we did. And we've already come back."

"I am on my way home from the office. Awfully warm, isn't it? Say, I guess I better go up and greet them, first. Excuse me."

And having cast this remark over his shoulder, Okada vanished toward the stairs without finding out my business. Soon afterwards I came out of the bath.

9

That evening Okada drank a great deal. He repeated his regret to my mother and brother that his colleague's absence due to illness made it impossible for him to carry out his original plan to accompany us to Wakanoura.

"So this is going to be our last evening. Well, I suppose you'd better get drunk a little," my mother suggested.

Unfortunately none of us was a good enough drinker to keep up with him. So we excused ourselves and went ahead with our supper. Okada seemed rather glad to be left alone at table and went on draining his cup.

By nature a spirited man, he habitually became even gayer as he drank sake. And regardless of whether anyone was listening or not, he rattled on as he pleased, now and then interrupting himself to roar with laughter.

He seemed immensely satisfied with his statistics illustrating such matters as how much Osaka's wealth had multiplied in the last twenty years, and how many scores of times it would multiply in the next ten years.

"Forget about Osaka's; how about your own wealth?" said my brother with just a shred of irony.

Okada laughed, and resting his hand on his baldish head, said: "But whatever I am today—and I may sound big—the fact that I can get along somehow—all this I owe to Uncle and Aunt. This at least I never forget, even though I may get drunk and talk nonsense."

Thus, Okada expressed his gratitude to my mother—seated right beside him—as well as to my father in far-off Tokyo. As he got drunker he became repetitious, stressing his appreciation several times—although he slightly modified it each time. Finally he insisted on treating my father to an order of the pomfret for which the Nadaman Restaurant was famous.

This reminded me of a certain New Year's eve when Okada, then still staying with us, had gotten drunk at another's expense and, lurching home, had prostrated himself before my father and offered the three-inch-long leg of a red crab, saying that he was respectfully presenting my father with a delicacy from the North Sea. My father, angered at this, had shouted, "What is this thing like a vermilion-lacquered paper weight? I have no use for it. Take it right away."

But now Okada was continuing to drink and would not leave. His talk, which at first had amused us, was gradually becoming boring. My sister-in-law yawned behind her fan. Finally I had to take him out and walk him for several blocks in the fresh air. Then I took the money out of my bosom and handed it to him. As he received it his mind seemed remarkably clear despite everything. "It doesn't have to be now, you know—although I'm sure Okane will be delighted. Thanks," he said and put it into an inside pocket.

The street was quiet. Quite unconsciously I looked up at the sky. Up there the stars looked dim with a peculiar dullness which seemed an ominous weather forecast. All of a sudden Okada said, "Ichiro-san used to be a difficult person." And this called an old scene to mind: Once when my brother and I were playing chess he had lost his temper at something I had said and suddenly threw a chessman at my forehead.

"Even then he was so headstrong. But now he looks cheerful

99

enough, doesn't he?" Okada remarked. I made a vague, non-committal answer.

"Why, it is quite some time since he married. The kind of person he is must be a great strain on his wife."

Still I made no answer. And as we parted at a street corner, I said simply, "Give my regards to Okane-san," and turned back.

10

On the following morning we left by train and had lunch in its cramped dining car. "The interesting part is the waitresses. Some are quite charming in their white aprons. So don't forget to have your lunch on the train," Okada had urged me. Although I kept my eyes on the waitresses who were carrying plates and serving soft drinks I thought none of them particularly attractive.

My mother and sister-in-law were looking out of the window curiously, both apparently enjoying the rustic scenery. The view through the window was indeed a change for us after Osaka. Especially as the train ran near to the seashore the green pine trees and the indigo sea reflected their bluish freshness to our smoke-wearied eyes. Even the tiled roofs glimpsed through the trees was something we couldn't see in the Tokyo area.

"Peculiar, isn't it? It looks like a temple, but it isn't. Jiro, I wonder—can it really be just a farm-house," said my mother pointing at a relatively large roof.

I was sitting next to my brother, and seeing that he was pondering something I wondered if his usual trouble was starting, and hesitated to decide whether I should humor him or ignore him in silence. Since he had the habit of assuming such an air, I really couldn't tell whether he was irritated or merely musing over some difficult, scholarly matter.

But finally I decided to break the spell, especially since I caught my mother stealing a glance at him from the opposite seat now and then while she chatted with my sister-in-law.

"By the way, I heard an interesting story," I said, turning toward him.

"What is it?" he asked, as curtly as I had expected. But having been prepared for it, I continued.

"Just recently I heard this story from Misawa . . ."

I then related the tale of how when the demented girl, that poor divorcee who had come to live at Misawa's, had seen him off she always told him to come back early. As I paused at this point, my brother suddenly appeared interested and said, "That story, I heard, too. And when she died Misawa kissed her cold forehead, as I remember it."

I was dumbfounded.

"Did he? But Misawa didn't mention any kissing. Did he, then, kiss her while others were around?"

"That, I don't know—I mean whether he did that when others were around or when he was all alone."

"Still it doesn't seem likely that Misawa was left alone with her body. But if he kissed her when no one was around?"

"That's why I say I don't know."

Lost in thought, I wondered.

"And how did you happen to know that story?"

"I heard it from H."

H was my brother's colleague, and had once been Misawa's teacher. Furthermore, as Misawa had used him as a reference, their relationship seemed intimate enough. But how H had gotten hold of such a delicate story and related it to my brother, I couldn't find out from him.

"Then why didn't you tell me that story before?" I asked. With a sour face my brother said, "Because there was no need to." And while I was wondering if I could possibly press him further, the train reached its destination.

I I

Coming out of the station and finding a trolley waiting, my brother and I, suitcases still in hand, helped the women on and jumped aboard.

But as the four of us were the only passengers who got on, the streetcar did not start for some time.

"What a leisurely thing this is!" I declared somewhat condescendingly.

"Perhaps we could have brought our luggage with us," said my mother, looking back at the station.

But soon a couple of other passengers got on—one carrying books like a student, the other, a merchant, flapping a fan, and as they took seats the driver started spinning the tiller.

We rode along a narrow, deserted street beside the mud wall which apparently marked the outer limits of the town; after two or three stops we saw a moat encircling the base of a high stone wall. The moat was covered with the floating green leaves of lotuses, whose scattered crimson flowers caught our eyes.

"My—and this is the ancient castle," said my impressed mother, whose aunt had formerly served at the inner quarters of the House of Kishu. And suddenly I recalled that feudal title, Lord Kishu, which I had often heard as a child.

Passing through the city of Wakayama, our trolley ran along a country road for a while, and in time arrived at Wakanour. The always efficient Okada had arranged to have rooms reserved at a first-class hotel of the locality. But as it turned out the rooms with a good view had already been taken by a crowd of summer visitors. So we quickly took rickshas and, following the shore line, managed to locate another tall three-storied hotel fronting the sea, and were shown into a room on the top floor.

Our room was large and faced south and west. The building itself was no better than respectable boarding-houses in Tokyo and, as far as taste was concerned, it couldn't match the hotels in Osaka. The second floor consisted of one single, undivided enormous hall which might be used for a large group. Its empty vastness and the wavy surface of cheap mats presented a dreary sight.

My brother was apparently attracted by a fine painting of the peculiarly shaped leaves of a bamboo done on a six-panel screen which was serving as a temporary divider of this large hall. He had an eye for such things, thanks to our father's instruction. My brother, turning around suddenly, said, "Say, Jiro."

We were on our way down to the bath, and carrying our

towels. I was standing about four yards behind him as he paused to gaze at the bamboo. I was certain he would make some comment about this painting.

"Yes?" I said.

"That story of Misawa's we talked about on the train . . . what do you think of it?"

His question really was something unexpected, especially as only a while back on the train when I had asked why he'd never told me the story, he had said irritably that there was no need to.

"Do you mean that story about his kissing the dead woman?" I asked again.

"Not that. I mean the part about her always following him to the door and telling him to come home early."

"To me, both parts are interesting—but that about his kissing seems somewhat more pure, more beautiful."

We were halfway down the stairs from the second floor. Right there my brother stopped short.

"Yes, poetically speaking. Certainly both parts would be equally interesting, poetically viewed. But that is not what I'm concerned with. I am talking about it in a more practical sense."

12

Since I could not quite see what my brother was driving at, I merely continued quietly down the stairs, and he had no choice but to follow me.

Stopping at the bath entrance I turned and asked, "What exactly do you mean by a more practical sense? It's not too clear to me."

Impatiently, he explained, "In a word, whether that woman really cared for Misawa as he seems to have thought she did, or whether in her insanity she had merely begun voicing all that she had tried in vain to convey to her husband—which do you think was the case?"

This was the question I had also given a little thought to when I heard the story. But realizing that it was the kind of question which could find no clear-cut answer, I had dropped it. Now, therefore, I could offer no particular opinion in answer to his question.

"It's beyond me."

"Really?"

My brother stood still, making no attempt to get ready for the bath. I also refrained from taking off my clothes. I first looked into the dark bath, which was smaller and more old-fashioned than I had expected, and then turned back to my brother.

"Do you have any idea, then?"

"I can only believe she took a fancy to Misawa."

"Why?"

"Whatever the reason, that is just the way I look at it."

The two of us got into the bathtub without settling the point. As we came out to let the women take their turn, the afternoon sun flooded the room and the surface of the sea was blazing hot like molten iron. To keep away from the sun we moved into the next room, but no sooner were we seated together face to face than my brother once more brought up the subject.

"I cannot think of it any other way . . ."

"I see." I was listening deferentially.

"There are a lot of things people ordinarily just can't speak their mind about—for the sake of decency or obligation, much as they may like to."

"I am sure there are."

"But once they become insane—I guess a doctor would laugh at my lumping all sorts of mental diseases together—anyway, once they become insane, they forget their inhibitions, don't you think?"

"Maybe. I suppose there are some patients of that sort."

"Now, let's suppose that the woman is a victim of this type of insanity. Then all that ordinary sense of propriety would completely vanish. And if so she could then speak her mind freely, regardless of the consequences. Looked at this way what she said to Misawa ought to be far more sincere and genuine than the usual empty amenities."

Terribly impressed by his reasoning, I said, "Very interesting, indeed," and clapped my hands, in spite of myself. This seemed somehow to displease him, however.

"Interesting or not, it is no frivolous matter. Jiro, do you really think I've got it figured out?"

"Well—" and somehow I was hesitant.

"Ah, then can we never find out what a woman really is like, unless we make her insane?" sighed my brother painfully.

13

Below the hotel was a rather big canal. I had no idea how it was connected with the sea, but towards evening a couple of fishing boats glided out of nowhere on the canal and passed by slowly.

We walked a couple of hundred yards along the canal to the right and, turning to the left, crossed a lane running through some rice fields. Farther on, the fields merged into a gently sloping hill topped by a bank on either side of which stood a long stretch of pine groves. We heard the roar of heavy waves dashing against rocks, broken waves, hurling their white foam up into the air, which we had seen from the third floor of the hotel.

By and by we came out on the bank. Most of the waves smashed to myriad pieces against a thickly built dyke, but every once in a while a heavy one broke over the dyke, pouring down inside.

For a while we stood fascinated by this awesome sight, and then resumed our walk—in the midst of the roar of waves. While we were walking, my mother and I guessed idly that those were doubtless the famous so-called surging waves. My brother and sister-in-law, both dressed in *yukata*, my brother carrying a cane and my sister-in-law wearing a narrow hempen *obi* of golden pattern, walked nearly forty yards ahead of us, side by side, but about a yard apart. From time to time my mother half-concernedly cast a glance at them, a look so nervous I decided that for some reason she must be concerned about the couple. Trying to avoid a serious talk, however, I pretended not to notice anything unusual and deliberately walked rather slowly. And trying to project a sense of relaxation I said funny things which might make my mother laugh.

"Jiro," she finally said, as usual, "if everyone could go along like you, I imagine there would be no worry in this world."

But a little later, unable to stand it any longer, she spoke up, "Jiro, just take a look at that."

"What are you talking about?"

"I really don't know what to do," my mother said, gazing at the backs of the two walking ahead.

Feeling that the least I could do now was to appear to catch her meaning, I asked, "Has something happened again that might irritate him?"

"He is such an odd one, I can't be sure. But between husband and wife—it's after all up to her—no matter how difficult. It seems to me it's up to Nao to try to humor him at least. Look at them. They are like two strangers who happen to be heading in the same direction. Even Ichiro, I am certain, wouldn't tell his own wife not to get closer to him."

Of the couple walking apart in silence ahead of us, it was my sister-in-law that she wanted to blame. I must admit I felt pretty much the same way. I think it was a reaction natural to anybody observing their marital relationship.

"He must be brooding about something again. That's why she's restrained and keeping quiet."

I hoped to ease my mother's mind by this feeble reasoning.

14

"Even if he is thinking about something—so long as Nao is indifferent like that, how can he talk to her? Why, it almost seems as though she is walking apart on purpose."

To my mother, who sympathized with my brother, my sister-in-law's back must have appeared really heartless. But I made no answer and simply walked along, trying to think more objectively about my sister-in-law's personality. Not that my mother's criticism was altogether wrong, but at the same time I also suspected her bias as an over-indulgent mother led her to criticize unduly.

As I see it my sister-in-law was by no means a warm-hearted woman, but she was the kind who, once warmed, could project warmth. While she did not possess any inborn charm she was also the kind of woman from whom one can with tact elicit much charm. I had noticed more often than not an offensive coldness in her after her marriage, and yet I could not believe that she was hopelessly unfeeling or cruel.

Unfortunately, my brother also had much of the temperament I have just ascribed to his wife. From this it would follow that the couple couldn't hit it off together for, being of the same nature, they each expected from the other exactly what both needed and neither could supply.

Her cheerfulness when my brother was in a good humor clearly seemed due to the efficacy of the warmth which my excitable brother could elicit from her. Thus, just as my mother criticized my sister-in-law for her apathy, so might my sister-in-law criticize my brother.

While walking along with my mother, I thought of the couple ahead of us in this manner, though I of course could not attempt to trouble her with such complicated reasoning.

"Strange, though," said my mother. "Nao is certainly no born charmer, but she is always cordial with your father and me. Isn't she that way with you, too, Jiro?"

My mother was entirely right about this. Although I am by nature quick-tempered, loud-mouthed, and blatant, I realized that not only had I experienced no unpleasantness with my sister-in-law but also at times had even been able to talk with her more openly than with my own brother.

"Yes, she has always been that way with me, too. Come to think of it, it is a bit strange."

"That's why I cannot help thinking Nao is deliberately spiteful only to Ichiro."

"Oh, that can't be."

To tell the truth, I obviously had not given as much thought to this matter as my mother apparently had and therefore I had no grounds for such suspicion, and wouldn't have been sure about its cause, in any event.

"But he certainly should be the most important, I mean, to her."

"That's why I say I simply can't understand."

Now I was suddenly aware of how ridiculous it was to ramble on about my sister-in-law behind her back, especially when such fine scenery lay spread out for our enjoyment.

"One of these days I'll sound her out about this matter. You really have little to worry about, I'm sure," I declared and dashed up the dyke from the tea stall overhanging the break-water, where I shouted at the top of my voice, "Hello! Hello!" Startled, my brother and sister-in-law turned around and at that moment the waves smashing against the stone breakwater inundated my feet and sent up spray, soaking me to the skin.

Dripping water and chided by my mother, I accompanied the three back to the hotel. All the way the roar of the waves beat against my eardrum.

15

That night my mother and I slept beneath a white mosquito-net, made of something far thinner than ordinary hemp, and looking very cool as the breeze played with its pretty lacing.

"A nice net isn't it? Let's get one like this," I suggested to my mother.

"This thing may look pretty, but it isn't really so expensive. Our white hempen net at home is of a better grade. This one is made light and all in one piece; that makes it look delicate."

My mother, being old-fashioned, prized our hempen net which had been made somewhere around Iwakuni.

"For one thing, ours is better because it keeps you from catching cold while sleeping," she said.

But a maid had come to shut the doors and the net had ceased rustling.

"It's gotten stuffy all of a sudden, hasn't it?" I sighed.

"It certainly has," she said calmly, obviously undisturbed by the heat. But I could hear the faint sound of her fan.

As my mother stopped talking I closed my eyes. In the next room, just on the other side of the partition, my brother and his wife were sleeping. They had been quiet for some time. Somehow their room seemed even quieter now that ours had quieted down suddenly, leaving me with no one to talk to.

I kept my eyes closed, but was unable to get to sleep for a long while as the stuffiness, perhaps emphasized by the silence, became acute. Finally I sat up on the mattress cautiously, careful not to disturb my mother, and tucked up the hem of the net. Intending to go out on the veranda I was about to slide open the door gently, when my mother, who I thought had fallen asleep, suddenly challenged me, "Jiro, where are you going?"

"It's so stuffy I am going out on the veranda to cool myself."

"You are?"

Her voice was so clear and calm that I could tell she had been wide awake all this time.

"Haven't you gone to sleep yet either?"

"No. It's rather uncomfortable. Maybe because I'm not used to this bed."

I just passed the *obi* around my *yukata,* slipped a pack of Shikishima and a box of matches in the top folds and went out on the veranda, where I found a couple of chairs draped in white slipcovers. I pulled a chair up and sat down.

"Don't make noise and disturb your brother," my mother warned.

I smoked and contemplated the dreamy scene before me. It was indeed a blur as the moonless night made the shapes of things all the more dark and creepy. Only the rows of pine trees which I had noticed on the bank during the day stood out in black starkness, stretching out at length right and left. And also visible in relative sharpness below was the nocturnally white foam of the ceaseless movement of those breaking waves.

"Don't you think you'd better come in now? You may catch cold," my mother cautioned from inside.

I leaned forward in the chair and urged her to join me in enjoying the night scenery, but as she ignored my invitation I meekly crept back under the net, and laid my head on the pillow.

During all this time my brother's room remained quiet as ever, and even after I had returned to bed it remained wrapped in the same silence. Only those waves smashing against the breakwater kept roaring all night long.

16

The following morning, when I sat down to the table, it was obvious that all four of us had had a bad night. The want of sleep affected all of us around the table and our conversation naturally was rather gloomy.

Ill at ease, I said, "That steamed redsnapper we had yesterday evening didn't seem to agree with me," and making a face, I left my seat. I went over to the railing and gazed at a near-by signboard advertising "The Orient's No. 1 Elevator." Unlike an ordinary indoor elevator, this one was so devised as to lift curious sightseers from the ground to the rocky hilltop. Obviously out of place, it could only spoil the view, and still unknown then even at Asakusa its novelty had attracted my attention the previous day.

Sure enough, early risers had already begun boarding it, in twos and threes. My brother, already finished with his meal, had moved over behind me unnoticed, and was picking his teeth as he joined me in watching the steel box ascending and descending.

"Say, Jiro. Let's try that cable car this morning," he said suddenly and so much like a child that I glanced back.

"Wouldn't that be a lot of fun?" he continued, betraying a childishness unworthy of him. But I didn't mind taking a ride, although I wasn't sure whether it would take us any place interesting.

"I wonder where it will take us."

"What's the difference? Let's go now."

Assuming that my mother and sister-in-law would come

along, I had called out, "Would you like . . ." but my brother stopped me at once.

"Let's go alone—just the two of us," he said.

Just then my mother and sister-in-law showed up and asked where we were going.

"Jiro and I are going to try that cable car. It's too risky for women. Mother, you and Nao had better not come. Let us try it first and find out how it rides."

My mother looked at the steel box rising in empty space and took on an uneasy look.

"Nao, what are you going to do?"

At this my sister-in-law smiled her typically lonely, dimpled smile, and said, "As you please," in a way which might sound obedient, indifferent or even sullen, depending on how it was taken. I somehow felt sorry for my brother and at the time thought this sort of attitude would only put her at a disadvantage.

We left the hotel in *yukata* and got on the car right away. It was a box of two yards square. As soon as five or six passengers got on, the door was closed and it started off. Unable to stick our faces out between the iron bars, we had to be content to peer out through them. It was quite depressing.

"It's just like a jail," my brother whispered.

"Yes, it certainly is," I responded.

"And so is life."

My brother had a habit of philosophizing like this. "Yes, indeed," I said simply, although I could understand only the vague outline of his remark.

The terminal of this jail-like box was at the top of the small rocky mountain. The sparse green tints of dwarf pines clinging to the hillside broke its monotony and greeted our eyes with summer freshness. On the tiny level spot of ground stood a tea stall, where they kept a monkey which we fed potatoes and played with for ten minutes or so.

"Is there any place where just the two of us could have a talk?" My brother said, looking around, apparently intent on locating some quiet place where we could talk undisturbed.

17

Thanks to the height we had an extensive view all around. In particular, the famous Kimii Temple could be seen set far off in a densely wooded grove, and at the foot of the hill the water of an inlet glistening calmly suggested a lakeshore of an intricate color pattern, rather than a seashore. A man next to me pointed out the drooping pine tree celebrated in a *jōruri*. True to its name, the tree trailed its branches over a cliff.

My brother asked a woman at the refreshment stand if there was a good place nearby for a quiet talk, but perhaps because she didn't properly understand his question he could not learn anything from her. She ended every sentence with a peculiar localism.

"Well, then shall we go to the Gongen Shrine?" he finally asked.

"That's also a scenic spot. That will be fine."

The two of us descended at once. Without ricksha or umbrella, wearing only straw hats, we trudged along a hot sandy road. That day, for some reason, I felt uneasy about riding the lift and visiting the Shrine—alone with my brother. Ordinarily I found it rather awkward to be face to face with him, and I was more restless than usual that day. This peculiar feeling had begun the moment he had said, "Say, Jiro. Let's go, just the two of us."

Our foreheads were slick with sweat. I really had been somewhat affected by the steamed redsnapper we had had the previous evening. Moreover, the gradually rising sun beat down so ruthlessly on my swimming head that I could only walk along in dazed silence, more or less conscious of the grating sound of our shabby hotel clogs in the sand.

"Jiro, what's the matter with you?"

My brother's voice had taken me completely by surprise.

"I feel a little funny."

And again in silence we walked on.

Finally we reached the foot of the Shrine. Peering up at the narrow, steep stone steps, I was simply appalled at their height and felt I hardly had the courage to climb them. My brother slipped on a pair of the straw sandals arranged at the foot of the steps and climbed alone ten steps or so. Then noticing that I wasn't following, he called sharply, "Hey, aren't you coming up?" Helpless, I paid the old woman a fee for a pair of the sandals and barely managed to climb the steps. From about halfway up I had to support my weight by resting both hands on my thighs. And as I glanced up I saw my brother impatiently standing at the corner of the shrine gate at the summit.

"Look at the way you're floundering up those steps. Weaving just like a drunk."

Indifferent now to whatever I might be called, I threw my straw hat on the ground and stripped myself to the waist. Having brought no fan, I wiped off my chest with my handkerchief, nervously half expecting to hear a derisive "Hey, Jiro" behind me, but ignoring everything I kept dabbing at myself with the wet handkerchief, muttering over and over, "Gosh! What heat!"

Soon my brother came down to me and sat on a nearby stone. Behind the stone grew young bamboo which extended all the way down to the edge of the stone wall, their ranks broken only by the brownish white trunks of camellia trees which stood out conspicuously here and there.

"Well, this is a quiet place. Here I think we'll be able to have a long talk," said my brother, looking around.

18

"Jiro, I have something to talk over with you," said my brother.

"Well, what is it?"

For a while he hesitated. Since I didn't care to pursue it I did not urge him further.

"This is a cool place, isn't it?" I said.

"Yes, a cool place all right," my brother echoed.

As a matter of fact, it was a shady height, cooled by passing breezes. After mopping myself with the handkerchief for a few minutes, I quickly slipped my *yukata* on. Behind the gate there stood an aged sanctuary; the building was no doubt very old, for the head of a carved lion under its eaves was half-discolored.

Passing through the gate, I headed towards the sanctuary.

"It's cooler over here. Won't you come on over?"

Failing to gain any response, I idly strolled to and fro before the façade of the sanctuary, glancing at the soaring evergreens which obstructed the rays of the scorching sun. Just then my brother, with a determined look, came up to me.

"Hey, didn't I say I have something to talk over with you?"

I had no choice but to sit on the steps leading to the sanctuary. He joined me.

"Well, what is it—if you don't mind my asking?"

"To be frank with you, this is about Nao," my brother finally stated, apparently very conscious of the delicacy of the subject. The sound of the name Nao made me shudder. Of course I was more or less aware of the state of affairs between my brother and his wife, particularly since my mother had already complained about it to me. I had even promised her I'd seize the opportunity to sound out my sister-in-law fully, and then approach my brother more positively. I had secretly nursed the fear, however, that I might be forestalled by my brother. In fact, my uneasiness that morning when he had said, "Jiro, let's go, just the two of us," was prompted by the suspicion that he might bring up this very matter.

"What about her?" I asked him, again reluctantly.

"Isn't Nao in love with *you?*"

My brother's question was very abrupt, and moreover, totally unworthy of him.

"Why do you say that?"

"I am lost if you ask why, and worse still if you resent my bluntness. Certainly I am talking without any material evidence, no love letters or embraces witnessed. To tell you the truth, as husband I couldn't possibly ask anyone else such a question, but as it happens to be you I have been able to bury my own self-respect and dare ask you such a delicate question. And I want you to give me a straight answer."

"But she is my relative—a married woman—and especially she is my own brother's wife," I replied, not knowing what else to say.

"Yes, of course that's how anybody would answer merely for the sake of formality. And it may be natural for you to speak in such an ordinary fashion. That sort of reaction is enough to put me to shame. But Jiro, I know you have inherited our father's honesty. Besides, you have lately professed that frankness is your highest principle. That's why I am putting this question to you. I know your formal answer without asking. All I ask is to know your most sincere and truest feeling. I want you to tell me what your innermost feeling is."

19

"Does it seem possible that I could have any such feeling?" I replied, staring at the roof of the temple gate rather than at my brother. For a moment I did not hear him say anything, but then his voice rang in my ears, high-pitched and strained.

"Listen, Jiro, how can you be so frivolous? Aren't you and I brothers?"

Confounded, I looked at his face, somewhat pale perhaps because an evergreen shaded it.

"Of course. Just as I am your brother. I meant what I said. What I have just now said is not empty at all. I have said so because that's the true fact."

I was as excitable and quick-tempered as he was sensitive. Ordinarily, I could have made no such answer. He fired one simple question.

"Are you sure?"

"Certainly I am."

"Why, then, are you blushing?"

Maybe I did blush as he pointed out. While his face seemed particularly pale, I felt my cheeks flush, in spite of myself. Furthermore, I simply did not know what answer to make.

For some obscure reason he rose abruptly from the steps. With his arms folded, he began pacing to and fro before me as I sat, uneasily watching. His eyes remained fixed on the ground, and not once did he look at me as he passed before me a couple of times. Then as he passed the third time he turned to me and stopped short.

"Jiro?"

"Yes."

"I am still your brother, and I am awfully sorry I have talked childish nonsense."

His eyes were filled with tears.

"What do you mean?"

"After all, I am supposed to be more learned than you. Until today, in fact, I have regarded myself as a man of greater knowledge than the average. And yet I find myself blurting out such silly remarks. I am really ashamed of myself. Please try not to despise me."

I repeated the simple question. "Why—what do you mean?"

"Don't ask why so seriously. What a fool I am!"

And with this he held out his hand, which I grasped at once —noting as I did that it was as cold as mine.

"Simply because you blushed I doubted your word! How insulting that was. Please forgive me, won't you?"

I was well aware of my brother's temperament, like a woman's, as changeable as the weather. A characteristic of his high-mindedness, this made him seem at times like an artless, innocent child, and at other times like a poet of flawless purity. Although I respected him, I nevertheless found him somewhat too pliant.

"Brother, something must be wrong with you today. Enough of this foolishness for now. Let's go," I said, retaining my grip on his hand.

20

But suddenly my brother dropped my hand and stood stock-still staring down at me silently.

"Can anyone read another's mind?" he asked abruptly.

Now it was my turn to stare back at him.

"Do you mean to say you don't know my mind?" I said after a while. The tone of my answer contained rather more firmness than did my brother's question.

"Oh your mind I know well enough," he said without hesitation.

"Then isn't that enough?" I replied.

"I don't mean yours. I am talking about a woman's mind."

In the last phrase of his remark there was a fiery sharpness, a sharpness which sounded to me very strange, indeed.

But as I was saying "Whether a woman's mind or a man's—" he cut me short.

"You are a lucky fellow. Perhaps you haven't had to study a thing like that."

"That's because I am no scholar like you . . ."

"Don't talk nonsense." He blew up and shouted. "I'm not talking about any remote academic subject. I am asking if you have ever known what it's like to be ceaselessly driven to study the mind of another person, somebody right beside you, one who ought to be dearest to you."

In a flash I understood what he meant by one who ought to be dearest.

"Aren't you perhaps thinking too much, as a result of your learning? It seems to me you might be better off if you were more of a fool."

"It is the other party who deliberately forces me to think like this. By taking advantage of my over-wrought brain, she never lets me be the fool."

At this point I was hard pressed to think of a word of consolation. I felt terribly sorry for my brother, many times smarter than I, and yet racking his brains over such a bizarre matter. Both of us were well aware that he was now far more excitable than I, but since he had never before behaved so hysterically I was badly thrown off balance.

"Do you know a man named Meredith?" asked my brother.

"Yes, by name only."

"Have you read his correspondence?"

"Have I read—! I haven't even seen it."

"No—no I suppose you haven't."

With that he sat down beside me again. Then somehow I happened to remember the pack of Shikishima and the box of matches. I lit a cigarette and handed it to my brother, who took it but smoked mechanically.

"He says in one of his letters—I envy those who are satisfied with a woman's appearance. I also envy those who are satisfied with her flesh. I for one can never be satisfied until I can grasp her soul or heart, what we call her spirit. That's why I can have no love affairs."

"Was he then a bachelor all his life?"

"That I don't know. It wouldn't matter anyway. But Jiro, one thing is certain, I am married to a woman whose soul, heart, and whatever it is we call spirit I haven't grasped."

2 1

Acute anguish was visible on my brother's face. And as much as I respected him in many ways, at that moment I felt in my heart a certain uneasiness bordering on fear.

"Brother," I said with forced calmness.

"What?"

At his reply I rose, and paced back and forth two or three times right in front of him, just as he had done a little earlier, although for an entirely different reason. But he seemed altogether indifferent to me, with the fingers of both hands stuck like a comb deep in his rather overgrown hair, and his eyes cast downward. He had very glossy hair; every time I passed before him, my eyes were attracted by the fine joints of his fingers stuck in the raven blackness of it. His fingers had always appeared to me delicate though angular, symbolic of his nervous temperament.

When I called again he finally raised his head heavily.

"It may be impudent of me to say this kind of thing to you. But I don't think we can ever fully tell another's mind, no matter how much we may read and study. Since you are more learned than I, I suppose you must already realize this: we may feel that there is a tacit understanding between parents and children, between brothers, but as a matter of fact they are always separated from one another, no matter how intimate—just as much in heart as in mind. And there is nothing we can do about it."

"We can study another person's mind from outside, but can never quite become one with him. That much at least, I think I know."

My brother spoke scornfully and languidly. At once I followed this up.

"Isn't it religion that can transcend this? Well, I am not very bright about such things but since you are a thinking type . . ."

"By thinking alone no one can get at faith. Religion is not something to reason out; it is something to believe in," he declared in profound disgust. Then he went on. "Much as I try, I can't believe; no, I cannot believe. I can only think, think, and think; that's all. Jiro, please help me to believe."

Although he spoke like a well-educated man, he acted like a boy of eighteen or nineteen. To observe him in such a state made me sad; indeed at that moment he seemed almost like a mudfish hopelessly thrashing in the sand.

This was the first time that my brother—in every way so much my superior—had even taken such an attitude toward me. Saddened as I was, I also feared that if he kept on he might lose his senses sooner or later.

"Well, in fact, I myself have already given some thought to this matter . . ."

"I am not interested in what you think. The reason I have

brought you here today is I have a favor to ask. Will you do me a favor?"

"What is it?"

The matter was getting more complicated. However, he wouldn't come directly to the point. And meanwhile three or four men and women, obviously sightseers, appeared at the foot of the stone stairs, each changed from clogs to sandals and began to ascend the steep steps. No sooner had my brother noticed them than he rose quickly. "Jiro, let's go back," he said and started descending the steps. I followed him immediately.

22

We retraced our steps. Although I had been sick in the stomach and nursing a headache when we had set out, on the way back I felt even worse, due probably to the growing heat of the day. Unfortunately since we had both left our watches in the hotel, we couldn't be sure about the time.

"I wonder what time it is," my brother asked.

"Well," and I looked up at the glittering sun, "I don't think it is noon yet."

We thought we were retracing our way, but by some mistake we came out on the very briny seashore near a shabby cluster of fishermen's huts, some grocery stores, and a steamship company's waiting-house topped with a weather-beaten flag.

"We seem to have taken the wrong way."

My brother still walked with his eyes downcast and apparently wrapped in thought. Shells were scattered all over the ground, and our footsteps grinding them to bits added a peculiar rustic note to our monotonous walk.

My brother paused for a second, looked around and asked, "Didn't we come this way?"

"No, we didn't, I'm afraid."

"Really?"

And we resumed our walk. He was still looking downward. I became worried that, now seemingly far off our course, we might get back to the hotel rather late.

"This is a small place anyway. No matter where or how we get lost we can make it back all right."

Saying this, my brother marched on briskly. And looking at his back reminded me of that old expression: as one's legs carry one. In this instance there was no greater relief to me than to walk a dozen yards behind him.

Inwardly I prepared to hear his so-called request at any moment as we looked for the way back. However, as he chose to confine his speech to monosyllables and merely hurried on, I felt oddly uneasy as well as very relieved.

At the hotel we found my mother and sister-in-law sitting face to face, still in *yukata*, while over the railing hung their outdoor kimonos, of either striped silk gauze or Akashi silk crepe. When my mother saw us she exclaimed in surprise, "Oh my, how far did you go?"

"Didn't you go anywhere?" When I asked, glancing at the clothing drying over the railing, my sister-in-law said, "Certainly we did."

"Where?"

"Guess where."

Such a familiar tone taken by my sister-in-law in my brother's presence made me feel somewhat guilty. Moreover, he might choose to interpret this as a deliberate display of her friendliness to me. I secretly shared his pain.

But she remained completely unconcerned; I couldn't tell whether through coldness, indifference, or defiance of common sense.

As it turned out, they had been out to visit the Kimii Temple. My mother explained to my brother that by passing before the Tamatsushima Shrine one could go out to the street and catch a trolley which stopped exactly in front of the temple.

"The stone steps were so steep. Just to look up at them was enough to make me dizzy, I tell you. I thought I couldn't possibly make it, and I didn't know what to do. But I had Nao help me up and somehow managed to visit the temple at least. Thanks to that, though, my kimono was soaked with sweat . . ."

"Oh, really?" interjected my brother half-heartedly from time to time.

23

That day went by without event. The four of us spent the evening playing cards. In the game we played each player in turn must pass four cards, face down, to the next, who tries to form matching pairs which he lays down on the floor. By gradual elimination the one left with the ace of spades is the loser. It was a very simple game popular in such resort places.

Both my mother and I, whenever the spade came around, looked so funny that we were readily suspected. My brother also occasionally smiled a grim smile. The most composed was my sister-in-law, who feigned indifference whether holding the spade or not. I think her nature rather than any pretense gave her an advantage. In any event I was quietly amazed at the way my brother had his wrought-up nerves under such firm control —after our earlier conversation.

That night I couldn't sleep, and it was in fact worse than the night before. In the intervals between the rumbles of roaring waves I listened intently to the adjoining room where my brother and his wife were sleeping, but all was as quiet as the night before. And that night I could not dare to go out on the veranda for fear of being questioned by my mother.

The following morning I took my mother and sister-in-law to the Orient's No. 1 Elevator, and we fed potato to the monkey on the hilltop as I had done the day before. However, this time we were accompanied by a hotel maid who was better acquainted with the monkey, and we had a far livelier time holding it and making it gibber. My mother sat on a stool in the tea stall and, pointing out a bald, brownish hill called Shin-Wakanoura, inquired about it. My sister-in-law kept excitedly demanding a telescope.

"This is not the Atago Shrine of Shiba, you know," I reminded her.

"But they should at least have a telescope, surely," she complained.

That evening I was finally dragged out to the Kimii Temple by my brother. On the pretense that the women had already visited the place on the previous day, the two of us decided to go alone, but of course the fact was that I was being invited to hear my brother's request.

Plunging straight up the steep stone steps which had frightened my mother at a glance, we found ourselves on a kind of landing halfway up the hill and sat down on a bench which commanded a good view. The main temple, flanked by a five-storied pagoda, had a more antique look than ordinary Buddhist temples. The white rope hanging from the middle of the overhang somehow looked very serene indeed.

We sat silently on the bench before an uninterrupted scene. "Now this is a fine view," I said.

Right below the wide sea glittered like a sardine's belly, entirely suffused by a dazzling afterglow whose glare flushed our cheeks. A little nearer than the sea a meadow pond of an irregular shape also spread its surface flat as a mirror.

My brother was silent, his chin rested on his cane, but soon he turned toward me resolutely.

"Jiro, I have a favor to ask of you."

"Yes, of course—I've come all the way up here to hear it. But there's no hurry. I'll do whatever I can."

"Jiro, this is really a delicate matter to broach."

"You can tell it to me even if it is."

"Then, I am going to speak up—since I trust you. But don't be shocked."

So warned, I was shaken even before he began, for I was fearful as to just what he could possibly request. My brother's mood, as I had said before, was changeable, but I knew that once he spoke out he would persist in having his own way.

24

"Jiro, don't be shocked," he repeated and looked at me scornfully as I sat already chilled in shock. As he was now, my brother struck me as an altogether different person from what he had been at the Gongen. It was plain that he was now determined to confront me.

"Jiro, I trust you. What you say already proves your innocence, and there should be no mistake about that, should there?"

"Of course not."

"To be frank with you, I want you to test Nao's honor."

When I heard him say, "test Nao's honor," I was thunderstruck. His repeated warning, "Don't be shocked," had no effect whatsoever. Indeed, I was thoroughly dumbfounded.

"Why, do you look like that now?"

It was miserable imagining how my appearance might have seemed to my brother. Our positions now were clearly the reverse of what they had been during our last talk. But I somehow pulled myself together.

"Testing my sister-in-law's honor! You'd better drop that sort of idea."

"Why?"

"Because it's ridiculous."

"What's ridiculous?"

"Well, perhaps it isn't—but there is no need for such a thing."

"Oh yes, there is, and that's why I am asking you."

I kept silent for a while. As there were no other visitors in the vicinity, it was exceptionally quiet. And as I glanced around only to find the two of us alone in a corner a vague uneasiness again crept over me.

"You ask me to test her, but how am I supposed to go about it?"

"All you have to do is go with Nao to Wakayama and stay there overnight."

"Nonsense," I rejected the idea point-blank. Now we both fell into silence. Over the sea the afterglow was thinning out as the dying rays, still pale-red, lingered on the horizon.

"You don't like it, do you?" my brother asked.

"I might have considered something else. But this—you must excuse me," I declared.

"Then, I won't ask. But this may make me suspect you all my life."

"I hope not."

"Well, if you hope not, then please do as I ask you to."

I dropped my head. Ordinarily he would have already struck the first blow. With my face down I waited for him in a fit of rage either to pound my hat in with his fist or slap my cheeks. By taking advantage of the reaction which would often follow the fit, I still hoped to calm him down. More acutely than anyone else, I was aware of my brother's temperament which was susceptible of this reaction.

But my patient wait for his clenched fist came to nothing. He remained deadly silent, so much so that I finally had to steal a look at him. He was pallid, and gave no evidence of making an impulsive move.

25

Moments later, however, my brother said excitedly, "Jiro, I do trust you. But I suspect Nao. And the suspect's partner happens to be you, unfortunately. It is unfortunate for you, I mean, but may turn out to be fortunate for me. That's because, as I have just now tried to make clear, I can believe whatever you may say and can speak my mind to you freely. That's why I am asking you to do me this favor. Don't you see the sense in what I am saying?"

It was then that I felt the first glimmer of suspicion that there might be some deep meaning implied by his words. Now suspicious that there was some sexual intimacy between his wife and me, wasn't he being unreasonable in his insistence?

"Brother," I said, meaning to speak forcefully, no matter how I might sound to him. "Brother. But this raises a very, very serious ethical problem . . ."

"Indeed it does."

He replied very coolly and in a way which both surprised and aroused my suspicion even further.

"I would rather not do a cruel thing like that—even for my own brother."

"But it is she who is cruel to me."

I didn't even want to know what he meant by this reference to her cruelty to him.

"Let me hear about it another time. I must decline this request of yours in any case. After all, I have my own integrity to think of. Certainly you do not expect that even for your sake I could possibly abandon my own integrity."

"Integrity?"

"Of course it is a question of integrity. I don't like, among other things, to test a person at someone's request. Much less that kind of . . . I am no detective."

"Jiro, I am not asking you to act vulgarly toward her. All I am asking you to do is go with her somewhere, as brother and sister-in-law, and stay together at a hotel. It has nothing to do with your integrity."

"Brother, you suspect me, don't you? That's why you are making such an unreasonable demand of me."

"No. I am asking you because I trust you."

"You say you trust me, but it seems clear that at heart you suspect me."

"Don't talk nonsense."

Talk such as this was repeated many times between us and with each repetition both of us became heated, and then one right word calmed us down as suddenly as if a fever had abated.

While we were heated there was a moment when I seriously wondered whether his was not a genuine mental case. But once the fit left him, as swiftly as a passing gust, he also seemed to be very normal.

Finally I said, "As a matter of fact I have for some time thought over this problem, and on the first chance wanted to sound out her mind thoroughly. If that is all, I will certainly see to it. Soon we'll be going back to Tokyo."

"Then, I want you to do it tomorrow. Tomorrow noon you and she will go to Wakayama together and return before dark, if you don't mind."

For some reason I remained reluctant. Personally I preferred to take my time and wait for a suitable occasion after our return to Tokyo. But since I had turned down the first request, I could hardly decline the second. So at last I agreed to take her to Wakayama.

26

The next morning when we woke up the sky was dotted with clouds. Moreover, the wind was blowing so high that we could hear the thunderous roar of waves dashing against the breakwater. From the railing we could see quantities of white foam rolling all along the shore. And none of us cared to go down to the beach.

Past noon the sky looked a little calmer, and now and then the sun shone through the cloud folds. Nonetheless, four or five fishing-boats came rowing their way into the canal before the hotel earlier than usual.

"It is threatening. We may be going to have a storm," my mother said, scanning the ominous sky and then returning to the room. My brother rose promptly and went over to the railing.

"It's all right. I doubt if there is going to be anything serious. Mother, I can guarantee it. Let's get started. Rickshas have already been called."

My mother looked at me without saying a word, and then remarked, "I wouldn't mind going of course. But since we are all going anyway, why not go together?"

To me that was far preferable. I very much wished to accompany my mother and forget about the trip to Wakayama.

"In that case, we might also go together to the cut in the mountain," said I, rising from the seat. In an instant my brother threw me an angry look. And on second thought I saw that I had no choice but to carry out the promise.

"But I remember I have made a promise to Sister-in-law."

To my brother I had to feign innocence. And it was my mother who next gave me a wry look.

"Forget about Wakayama, will you."

I looked from my mother to my brother, wondering what to

do. While caught between them I was baffled how to act. My sister-in-law remained indifferent as ever and said scarcely anything.

When my brother said, "Nao, isn't Jiro supposed to take you to Wakayama?" she said simply, "Yes." Nor did she protest when my mother urged, "Oh not today." As I turned round and asked, "What do you say?" she said, "Well, whatever you will."

When I went downstairs for something, my mother followed me, looking somewhat nervous.

"Do you really mean to go to Wakayama with Nao?"

"Why yes, I do—and Brother knows about it, too."

"Yes, apparently. But I certainly don't like it. Please don't go."

Somewhere in her face there was a hint of uneasiness. But whether she was uneasy about my brother or about my sister-in-law and me, it was rather difficult to determine.

"Why shouldn't I?" I asked.

"Why? Because I don't think it looks right for you and Nao to go off together."

"Do you mean it's bad for him?" I asked bluntly.

"Not just for your brother but . . ."

"Then, bad for her and me?"

This last question was even more blunt, and my mother merely stood there speechless. In her expression, however, I was surprised to detect what I thought was a shadow of suspicion.

27

As I had been certain of my mother's trust and love, her expression made me suddenly timid.

"Then I will give up. In the first place it wasn't my idea to take her out, believe me. The reason we are going is simply that he insists on it. I am certainly ready to give up the idea if you don't like it. But won't you please go talk with him so that we don't have to go? I gave him my word, you see."

And having spoken, I stood awkwardly in front of my mother

since I didn't have the courage to leave her. At first she seemed a bit puzzled, then she replied as if she had made up her mind, "Well, let me speak direct to your brother, and you wait here meanwhile. If you come up to the third floor with me there may be more trouble, I am afraid."

Watching her retreating figure I thought that with the matter so tangled up I certainly wouldn't feel like taking my sister-in-law to Wakayama, and that nothing could be settled by it even if I did. I hoped that the whole matter would take the turn my mother desired. I nervously paced up and down the large room.

Soon my brother came down from the third floor, and the instant I glanced at his face I knew there was no choice for me but to go.

"Jiro, you can't possibly break your word now. Be a man, my boy."

On those occasions when he called me "boy," I was always alarmed and alerted for possible trouble to come.

"Sure, I am going—though Mother tells me not to."

At this moment she came down from the third floor, still anxious, and walked straight up to me, saying, "Jiro, forget what I said a while ago. Ichiro says something about the promise you made at the Kimii Temple. Well, I guess it can't be helped. You'd better do as you promised, after all."

"Yes, I will."

With this reply I decided not to say any more.

Soon my mother and brother got into the rickshas which had been awaiting at the door and disappeared rattling away from the hotel to the right.

"Shall we get started too?" I asked, not feeling very well but looking around at my sister-in-law. "Or don't you have the nerve to set out?"

"And you?" she countered.

"Of course I do."

"Well, if you do, I do too."

So I rose and began to change my clothes, my sister-in-law helping me slip into my jacket. Half in jest she said, "Somehow you don't seem to have much nerve today." She was right. My nerve had drained away.

We walked together as far as the trolley line, but unfortunately we made a poor choice in taking the short cut, and her thin clogs and white *tabi* sank in the sand with every step.

"Difficult to walk, isn't it?"

"Yes it is," she replied. Still holding her parasol in her hand, she glanced back at my heels. While my ox-blood shoes were embedding themselves in the sand I was trying to consider where and how it would be best to carry out my task. As I was having trouble walking and thinking our conversation remained stiffly sparse.

"Do you know you are unusually quiet today?" my sister-in-law finally reminded me.

28

In the trolley car I sat side by side with her, but conscious of the important task which lay ahead, I could not speak easily.

"Why are you so quiet?" she asked for the second time since we had left the hotel. I thought perhaps she was hinting that the two of us might enjoy a chat.

"Have you ever said such a thing to Brother?"

But my look must have been rather grim, for she quickly turned to look out of the window. Then, she said, "What fine scenery!" Although the scenery through which we were then passing was not bad by any means, it was too obvious that she was looking out deliberately. Insistently I repeated my previous question.

"Why do you ask such a silly question?" she answered as if it were unworthy of consideration.

The car continued on its run, and before it got to the next stop I again asked the same question.

"You are silly," she flared back at last. "Why do you ask such a thing? After all, we are a married couple. I might have said things like that to him. But why do you make so much of it?"

"No reason. All I ask is that you always make some effort to say such friendly things to him."

Her pale cheeks flushed slightly and, perhaps because it was so very slight, it seemed as if her cheeks were warmed by the flickering of distant interior candles. Yet I didn't give much thought to how that blush might be interpreted.

At Wakayama as we got off I realized for the first time that this was my first visit to the city. Since I had brought my sister-in-law here ostensibly to show her around the place, we had to visit some of the well-known sights, even perfunctorily.

"My—although you haven't been here before yourself, you bring me here to show me around. You really are an easy-going person, I must say."

As she looked around rather helplessly, I was a bit embarrassed.

"Shall we let the ricksha men choose our route or shall we stroll toward the castle?"

"Well."

She glanced at the distant sky, paying no attention to me. Here too, as at the shore, the sky was overcast. Overhead hung masses of mottled clouds which made it seem muggier than the direct sun would have. Besides, a portion of the sky had already darkened and it threatened to shower any moment. And the blackened circle of the sky, shading off, glimmered menacingly over Wakanoura from which we had just come. It was apparently this ominous spot that she was looking at with knit brows.

"Do you suppose it will rain?"

Quite certain it would, I decided it would probably be best to hire rickshas and see as many sights as possible. I told the ricksha men to take us as quickly as possible to whatever points of interest there were. Thus, given free rein, whether they understood or not, the pullers ran along a narrow street, then around the moat laden with blooming lotuses, and into another street; but there wasn't any special place to speak of. And then I realized that seated separately in our flying rickshas we couldn't possibly discuss the impending issue. So I instructed the men to take us some place where we might sit comfortably and have a talk.

29

The ricksha men exchanged knowing looks and dashed on. While I was still marveling at their spirited reaction we turned down a narrow side street and suddenly passed through a big gate. Before I could stop them, the shafts had already been laid down along the vestibule and there was nothing more we could do; besides, now a young maid, all dressed up, had come out to welcome us. We had no other choice than to go in.

"I didn't expect to come to a place like this," I blurted out apologetically.

"Why not? This is a nice tea-house. I like it," replied my sister-in-law. From the way she responded it seemed to me that she had all along been expecting to come to such a place.

As a matter of fact the room was very clean and solidly made as she was quick to point out.

"This does look even better than those cheap restaurants in Tokyo," I agreed, appraising the timber of posts and a scroll-painting hanging in the alcove. She went over to the railing and gazed out at the courtyard. There at the bottom of an old plum-tree stump was a pale-dark cluster of orchids, and clinging onto the trunk of the plum tree were elongated mossy patches.

A maid arrived, bringing *yukata*, to show us to the bath. I didn't want to waste time on a bath, particularly as it seemed to be getting dark already. I had hoped to be able to get the whole thing over with as soon as possible and, as I had promised, to return to the hotel while it was light.

"What do you say to taking a bath?" I asked.

My sister-in-law had her reply all prepared, having received instructions from my brother to return before dark. And now she drew a watch from her *obi*.

"It's still early, Jiro-san. We have enough time to take a bath."

She attributed the seeming darkness to the weather, and indeed, beneath the lowering turbid clouds, everything had taken on a somberness inappropriate for the hour her watch showed. I was also concerned at the possibility that rain might fall any minute, and decided that it would be better to return as soon as the expected shower ended.

"Then shall we go and bathe?"

And we did. When we came out of the bath dinner was brought in, though it was really too early for that. I had made up my mind to keep away from sake since I was by no means a good drinker, and I simply ate the soup and picked at the sliced raw fish. As the maid seemed in the way, I dismissed her saying I would call her if needed.

I then weighed whether I should formally broach the matter to my sister-in-law or in the course of conversation lead her casually to the point. However, the further I continued these deliberations the more both courses seemed good—and bad, as well. Finally then, with my hand cupped around the soup-bowl, I stared vacantly at the courtyard.

"What are you thinking about?" she asked.

"Well, I've been thinking it may rain," I replied noncommittally.

"I see. And does the weather really frighten you? How unbecoming."

"No, of course I'm not frightened. But it would be awkward if we had a cloudburst."

While I was saying this, rain began falling. In the upstairs hall of the opposite wing I could see two or three figures in crested *haori*. Perhaps it was an early party, I decided, as from that direction I heard the sound of a geisha tuning her *samisen*.

I had already felt nervous when we left the hotel at Wakanoura, and by now I was positively jittery. Fearfully I half recognized that I could not summon up the nerve to start a quiet talk. I berated myself for having agreed to undertake such an extraordinary errand on this particular day.

30

But all of this was something my sister-in-law could not possibly sense and, somewhat puzzled, she nevertheless continued to rebuke me for worrying about the rain.

"Why in the world are you worrying so much about a shower? Afterwards it will be nice and cool."

"The trouble is we can't be sure when it will stop."

"What trouble? Certainly you can't be blamed for breaking a promise in such weather."

"But I have a responsibility to Brother."

"All right, then let's be off this minute."

And she rose at once, a determined look on her face. In the room opposite us the invited guests must all have finally arrived, for the *samisen* had begun to twang resonantly through the sound of falling rain. I noticed that the lights had already been turned on. And half-spurred by my sister-in-law's resoluteness, I was also about to rise when I realized that I hadn't yet raised the important question. I would have no excuse to offer my mother and brother—or myself for our late return—if I failed to broach the matter now to her.

"Wait," I said to her, "it doesn't look as if this rain will let up soon. Besides I have brought you here to speak about a certain matter."

I glanced obliquely at the sky and then turned to my sister-in-law. Neither she nor I started getting ready for departure, although she was already standing. She seemed armed at all points, all alertness to make her move, depending on my reaction. Stalling now, I again leaned out toward the edge of the eaves and peered up. The view of the sky from our room was rather limited as we were hemmed in by the large, two-storied structure with a hall across the courtyard. It was not too easy to see what course the storm was taking. One thing was certain, however, that the garden-trees were shaking violently, more menacingly than earlier. I was far more appalled by the gathering fury of this wind than by the rain or the sky.

"You are really odd. A minute ago you insisted we had to go back, yet now that I am ready, you refuse to budge."

"Don't say you are all ready. You are just standing."

As I said this, she broke into a smile, and examined her sleeves and skirt as if she had realized the very fact for the first time. Then she dropped down once more in front of me as I watched her with a matching smile.

"What is this important matter you keep hinting at? I don't think I can ever understand anything as difficult as you imply. In fact, I rather prefer to listen to the *samisen* in the room across the way."

The rain seemed not only to patter on the eaves; rather it seemed to be seized by the wind and driven against now one part of the house, now another, at random. At intervals, the notes of the *samisen* were wafted past our ears capriciously.

"But if you have some business, why don't you come out with it?" she urged.

"Don't press me please. It isn't that simple."

In fact as she drove me, I lost all notion how to start. She grinned.

"How old are you?"

"Please don't be so mocking. This is a really serious matter, I tell you."

"Well, then, come out with it quick."

More and more I disliked the idea of trying to assume a solemn air while pretending to give advice. And now inescapably in her presence I could not get rid of the feeling that she was more than ever enjoying my discomfort. And yet I could not but feel a certain intimacy in her manner.

31

"How old are *you?*" I asked abruptly.

"Old as I may look, I am still young. Much younger than you."

From the start I had had no intention of comparing ages.

"How long have you been married to my brother?"

"Well, let me see," she said nonchalantly, "I have no memory

135

for that sort of thing. I sometimes even forget my own age, to begin with."

This feigned ignorance was very characteristic of her. And this unnaturalness, which seemed to me rather coquettish, was very likely to displease my serious brother immensely, I thought.

"I see that you are indifferent even to your own age," I commented ironically. Yet realizing how frivolous I sounded as I said it I felt suddenly uncomfortable at having done my brother injustice.

"Well, you may be as indifferent to your age as you please. But at least you might be a little more kind and considerate to my brother."

"Do I really seem so unkind to him? You know, despite appearances I think I'm doing as much as I can for him—not just for him but even for you, am I not, Jiro-san?"

I was about to say that I wouldn't mind her being less kind to me so long as she should try to be a little more kind to him, but as I looked into her eyes it came over me once again suddenly what a sentimental fool I was. I even understood that, once face to face with her, I was unable to do anything genuine and sincere for my brother. I did not lack words, and in fact I could have spoken fluently in his behalf, if I had wanted. No matter what I said, however, it was likely that I would be aiding my own cause rather than that of my brother. I was not a man worthy of such a trusted mission, after all, and now I regretted the whole venture.

"But now you've stopped talking all of a sudden," she said as though she wanted to hit me in a sore spot.

"All this time I've been pleading with you for my brother's sake. Yet you don't take me seriously. That's why."

I said this deliberately to help erase the consciousness of my shame. She only smiled a singularly lonely smile.

"But that's unreasonable, Jiro-san. I am so dull that often things slip my notice, and perhaps I give the impression of indifference. And yet I really believe I am doing as much as I can for him . . . I am really a fool. Somehow nowadays particularly I sometimes feel as if I'm an empty shell."

"But must you be so depressed? Can't you try to be a little more positive?"

"Be more positive? Tell me, please, how. Should I say nice things? I very much dislike flattery, and so does your brother."

"I guess no one can be satisfied by flattery. But if you try just a little perhaps, that will make him happy—and things will be easier for you too . . ."

"That's fine. Yes—that will do for now," she said, and no sooner had she finished than large teardrops streamed down.

"I am sure an empty shell like me doesn't please your brother. But I am happy as I am. That must be enough for me. So far I haven't complained to anyone about him. At least that much you must have known . . ."

Sobs interrupted her speech—and fragments of it burned into me with fierce intensity.

32

An experienced elder of mine once told me that a woman's tears are seldom genuine diamonds; they are mostly imitations. I then noted the justice of this remark with admiration. However, it was nothing but a piece of abstract knowledge. Thus witnessing my sister-in-law's tearful eyes I, an inexperienced greenhorn, had a vague feeling of pity for her. Under different circumstances I might have taken her hand and wept with her.

"Everybody certainly knows my brother is a difficult person. It surely must be no easy thing for you to put up with him. But for all that he is upright, perhaps too much so, and honest, too honest perhaps. And—he is a high-minded fellow. Why, he is a respectable man, believe me . . ."

"Oh, without your telling me all that, I think I understand his character. After all, I am his wife."

And at this she once again broke into sobs. I felt all the more sorry for her, particularly as I happened to notice that a small handkerchief with which she had been wiping her eyes was soiled with tears. Although I felt an irresistible urge to pat her face, to dry her eyes and cheeks with my own dry handkerchief, something within me seemed to stay my hand.

"Frankly, do you really care for him or not?"

And only then did I realize that these words were a natural, verbal substitute, indeed, for my desire to wipe away her tears. From behind the handkerchief and through her tears, she peered into my face.

"Jiro-san."

My simple "yes" slipped out without the least resistance and consciousness on my part, like an iron filing inevitably attracted to a magnet.

"Why in the world do you ask such a question—whether or not I care for your brother? Do you think I may love someone else?"

"No. That's not what I meant, but . . ."

"Haven't I been telling you all this time that look of indifference is merely due to my stupidity?"

"You might at least stop flaunting what you call your stupidity. No one in the family, believe me, speaks ill of you."

"No one need tell me I am stupid, for I know very well, myself. Yet stupid as I am, I remember occasional praise for my kindness and so it doesn't seem I'm really as bad as I am made out."

Once when she had embroidered in various colors figures of dragon-flies and flowers on my large cushion, I had said, "You are very kind."

"Oh—do you still have that? It is so pretty, isn't it?" she said.

"Yes, it is; and I'm taking good care of it," I said, acknowledging that fact as well as the fact that she had been kind to me.

Suddenly I became aware that the sounds of the *samisen* had vanished although an occasional drunken voice of some remaining guests echoed now and then. Fearing that it must be quite late, I reached for my pocket watch, when a maid hurried over the stepping-stones and came around the veranda.

From her we learned that Wakanoura had been caught in a storm, that the telephone lines were cut off, and that the trolley traffic was tied up by the blown down roadside pines.

33

My mother and brother came to
my mind suddenly, and I felt a terrible urgency. I had visions of
their hotel at the mercy of raging winds and whirling waves.

"We are in trouble now," I said turning to my sister-in-law.
But she didn't seem much alarmed. It might have been mere
fancy that her pale cheeks looked far paler than usual. Yet she
apparently did not want the maid to detect the signs of crying
which lingered on her pale cheeks and around her eyes for, turning her face away from the revealing light, she was taking pains
to look away from the entrance as she asked, "You don't think
we can return to Wakanoura then, somehow?"

Whether this question was directed toward me or the maid
was rather difficult to tell, but sharing the burden I faced the
maid.

"We can't go even by ricksha, can we?"

The maid repeatedly pointed out how risky that would be,
and although she didn't use the word hopeless, she advised us to
stay in Wakayama at least for the night. Her serious look certainly mirrored her genuine concern for our safety, and even as I
began to accept the inevitability she implied the more anxious I
grew about my mother.

There was a distance of about a third of a mile separating the
breakwater and my mother's hotel. I thought that even if the sea
rose up over the dyke, it was not likely that it could reach a
third-floor room. But perhaps a tidal wave sweeping over all at
once . . . that was another matter.

I blurted out anxiously, "Say, has a tidal wave ever swept all
the hotels in that area?"

The maid reassured me that nothing like that had ever happened, although she added that a couple of times the sea had
poured over the dyke to flood the interior just like a lake.

"In any event it must have been rather hard on those houses
under water," I remarked.

At worst, the maid said, the houses might be turned round and round but they wouldn't be carried out to the sea. And in spite of my anxiety I could not but laugh at her nonchalant answer.

"As if spinning round and round wouldn't be bad enough, but now suppose they were carried out to the sea, as well. What a disaster!"

The maid merely giggled and said nothing. But seeing that my sister-in-law was now composed enough to face the glare of the electric light, I asked her.

"What do you propose?"

"What do I propose? Why, as a woman I can't tell you what to do. If you say you're going back I must of course go with you, no matter how risky."

"I am certainly willing to go—but what a mess! Do you think we should stay here tonight?"

"If you're going to stay here I have no choice but to stay. A woman just can't go alone all the way to Wakanoura, dark as it is now."

The maid looked from one of us to the other, and her look indicated that she had just realized she had guessed wrong.

"But are you very sure we can't get a call through?" I asked her just to make sure.

Her "Yes sir" didn't encourage me to go to the telephone and try myself.

"We can't help it then. I'm afraid we had better stay," I said, turning toward my sister-in-law.

"Yes—"

Her answer was simple and calm as ever.

"We can get rickshas here in town, can't we?" I asked, again turning to the maid.

34

Preparing to go to the hotel recommended by the restaurant, we got ready and stepped down from the vestibule. The glaring lights and the ricksha men's lanterns, in sharp contrast with the beating rain and shrieking wind, looked like spotlights on the raging Furies. My sister-in-law promptly concealed her bright colored figure behind the black hood of her ricksha, and I quickly followed, settling myself behind the uncomfortable oil cloth of my vehicle.

Once behind the hood I had little chance to look around the gruesome streets; my mind was constantly tossed by the tidal wave which I had never experienced. Worse still, I mused gloomily over the fates that had decreed such perverse weather —weather that was forcing me to carry out my brother's request after I had once flatly rejected it. My mind could not relax, whirling wildly in a fiery chaos.

Soon the rickshas drew up to the door of a hotel-like structure. I remembered vaguely that we passed through the entrance sign-curtain and on to the earth-floor beyond. The vestibule was rather deep for its width, and there was no office or attendant. With only one maid to show us in, it was an uncommonly desolate scene for early evening.

We stood there quietly. Somehow or other I didn't feel like speaking and my sister-in-law also kept silent, resting the point of her slanted silk parasol on the floor.

The room to which the maid led us was time-worn and was fronted by a veranda and a bamboo-blind hung from the eaves. The posts shone black with age, and the ceiling was also soot-colored all over. My sister-in-law hung her parasol on the clothes-rack in the adjoining room and said: "In this place, thanks to the tall building over there and the plastered wall over here, you can't hear the wind blow much. But in the ricksha the wind shrieked terribly, and you could feel how hard it was pressing down on the hood. I thought the ricksha might be blown over any minute."

Although I had been a trifle too excited for such observations, I did not have the courage to admit it and merely mumbled, instead, "Yes, it was a horrifying wind."

"If it is this bad here, it must be really terrible in Wakanoura," she said.

And at this first mention of Wakanoura my heart began leaping once again.

"Say, is your telephone line also cut off?" I asked the maid.

But without awaiting her answer, I went over to the telephone near the bath. Fumbling through the directory, I kept trying to call the hotel in Wakanoura where my mother and brother were staying. Strangely enough, I thought at one point that I heard a few words on the other end of the line. But when I inquired about the storm over there, I was cut off immediately and completely. As my repeated "Hello" and ringing served no purpose whatsoever, at last I gave up and returned to our room.

My sister-in-law, whom I found seated on a cushion sipping tea, turned on hearing my footsteps and inquired, "How was the telephone? Could you make any contact?" But upon hearing the details of my futile attempt she said, "That's more or less what I thought. It's no use trying to call tonight. The wind has probably blown down the lines. You can tell from that noise."

And just at that moment gusts of wind snarling out of opposite directions suddenly passed each other with a weirdly blended moan, and again rose high up into the air.

35

As we listened intently to the passing gusts, the maid came to show us to the bath and asked if we would like to have supper. I was in no mood for supper, but asked my sister-in-law.

"What do you say?"

"Well, it makes no difference to me," she replied. "But since we're going to stay perhaps we might as well."

As the maid disappeared the lights all over the place suddenly went out. The room, already gloomy with its black posts and sooty ceiling, now was thrown into total blackness. And I felt as if my sister-in-law might be sitting right under my nose.

"Aren't you scared?"

"Yes, I am," she answered from a likely part of the darkness. But there was nothing in her voice that would suggest her fright; nor was there anything of the feigning of a young hussy.

Both of us sat, without stirring and without a word, in the dark silence. With everything gone black, the storm outside seemed to blast our ears even more harshly. While the rain, scattered by the wind, did not sound very menacing, the shrieking wind swept frantically over the roofs, walls, and utility poles. Our room, much like a cellar above the ground, was surrounded on all sides by solid buildings and thick plastered walls, and even the little courtyard in front of the veranda seemed relatively safe. But a certain fierce sound rose in all directions from that inscrutable, threatening darkness which no men can well withstand.

"It will soon be over. Have patience. I'm sure the maid will fetch a light now."

Saying this, I inwardly hoped to hear my sister-in-law's voice from her direction. But she made no answer. I felt a bit uneasy at the thought that the total darkness could be so overpowering as to damp even a woman's gentle voice. Indeed, I grew uncertain even of the reality of my sister-in-law who I supposed was seated beside me, and I called to her.

Yet still she kept silent, and even as I conjured up in my imagination her figure as she had been sitting there in front of me just before the light went out, I called her once more.

"Yes," she finally answered seemingly annoyed.

"Are you there?"

"Of course I am. Do you forget I am a human being? If you don't believe it, come over here and touch me with your own hand."

I had an impulse to grope for her in the darkness, but lacked the nerve. And soon I heard the rustling of a woman's *obi* from the direction where she was sitting.

"Is—is something going on there?" I asked.

"Well—yes."

"What are you doing?" I asked again.

"I am taking off my *obi*. I thought I might as well change to that *yukata* the maid brought in a while ago," she replied.

As I was listening to the rustling of the *obi* in the dark, the maid came along the veranda bearing an old-fashioned lighted candlestick. She put it on the desk by the alcove, and with its flames dancing to and fro, the area animated by the flickering light, not to mention the black posts and sooted ceiling, seemed to careen wildly, to my forlorn anxiety, in the wavering glow. The scroll-picture hung in the alcove and the flowers arranged in a vase before it seemed to stand out especially ominously in the candle light. I seized a towel and went to the bath, which was lit by a weird-looking metal hand-lamp.

36

Searching around in the mournful light I somehow found a pail and slashed some water over my back. As I came out I tried the phone again, but there was no likelihood that it would go through and I finally gave up.

My sister-in-law bathed in turn and, returning presently to our room, commented: "So dark and eery. Besides, the pail and tub were so shabby I didn't feel like lingering long in that bath."

At that moment, with the maid sitting respectfully before me, I was in the process of signing the hotel register.

"What shall I put down in the book?" I asked my sister-in-law.

But "As you please," was all she said, taking out of a pouch a fancy-figured folding paper-case containing combs and such things. Turning her back to me she began doing something at the dressing-table now bathed in candle light. Resignedly I wrote down our Tokyo home address and her name—specifically adding wife of Ichiro—and my own, followed by brother of Ichiro.

Before dinner was served the electric lights which had been out for some time suddenly came on all at once, and a joyful cry of excitement rose from the kitchen. I noted that despite the maid's apology for the lack of fish due to the stormy weather, there was some now on the lighted table.

"Now we can breathe again," my sister-in-law said.

But the next moment the lights blinked off again and, surprised, for a moment I held my chop-sticks suspended in mid-air.

"O my!"

The maid shouted to one of the other maids to supply us again with candle light. During the brief interval when we had electric light, I happened to have noticed, to my fascination, that my sister-in-law had already applied her make-up. Now that the lights were gone again her face still seemed to hover in the darkness.

"But when did you do your make-up?"

"O please, don't say that when everything is gone black. When did you notice?"

The maid chuckled in the darkness as she admired my acuity.

"So you've even brought powder with you at a time like this. You really are meticulous," I said to my sister-in-law.

"No. I didn't bring any powder, just cream."

Somehow I felt an extraordinary sense of pleasure at being able to joke there in the dark, especially in the presence of a maid.

In time another maid brought in a couple of lighted candles. In the naked candle light the room tilted and swayed. As with knitted brows my sister-in-law and I stared at the flickering tongues of the flame, we both felt something which could only be defined as a kind of uneasy sadness.

Soon afterwards, we prepared for bed. Gazing up at the sky through the window while on my way to the toilet, I saw that the storm which seemingly had calmed till then was now gathering force anew as the night advanced. The inky sky seemed to heave and turn unceasingly, as if enormous black bolts crashed against each other and volleyed their ebony darts, making a monstrous roar in the darkness. I was awe-struck at the thought.

When the maid came to spread the bedding she placed a paper-shaded night lamp outside the mosquito-net. But it gave off such an antique and dismal light that one might even prefer the unlighted darkness to its ghastly glow. Amid the gloom I struck a match and smoked.

37

I wasn't able to sleep at all for some time. While in the toilet, I kept smoking and thought about many things. But as these came all at once incoherent and jumbled, I somehow couldn't quite discover what the main issue was. More often than not I was unaware as I struck another match and lit my cigarette again. Suddenly becoming aware of my own forgetfulness, I placed the cigarette-holder in my mouth once more; and then, for some reason it tasted especially bitter.

Now the black unfathomable sky I had just seen was moving with rhythmic violence within my head. The three-storied hotel where my mother and brother were staying was also whirling there nearly submerged beneath manifold waves. Hardly had these visions receded when I began to brood about my sister-in-law who was sleeping in this very room. I wondered how possibly to justify our being together here, though it had been necessitated by a natural calamity and, perhaps even after finding some justification, how then to restore my brother's humor. Yet at the same time out of nowhere welled up a thrill of joy at the rare adventure I happened to be sharing with my sister-in-law. And when that joyous sensation came over me I forgot everything—wind, rain, tidal wave, and mother and brother. Then suddenly the joy would change to a kind of horror—a premonition of horror which seemed a symptom of that anxiety which lurked somewhere. At such a moment I seemed to detect a prophecy that the raving storm outside would not only uproot trees, tear down walls, rip off roof-tiles, but would also smash to pieces that person smoking a tasteless cigarette in the faint lamplight.

While I was chasing these thoughts, my sister-in-law, who had till then been very quiet, turned over suddenly beneath the mosquito-net, and gave a long, audible yawn.

"Aren't you asleep yet?" I asked through the cigarette smoke.

"No. I just can't sleep in this downpour even if I wanted to."

"Neither can I, with the sound of that wind roaring in my ears. They say the lights went out because a couple of utility poles near by were blown down."

"Yes, the maid said something about that a while ago."

"I wonder how things are with Mother and Brother."

"That's the only thing I've been thinking about all this time. But I doubt if the sea will come up that far. Even if it does, all it could carry away might possibly be one of those poor straw-thatched huts near the pine trees on the bank. If a real tidal wave should come in and sweep away everything in the area, that's something I wouldn't want to miss."

"Why is that?"

"Because I would like to see such a terrific scene."

"What a joke!" I said cutting her off. But soon she continued in earnest.

"Yes, I am serious, Jiro-san. If I had to die, I would certainly not want to have to do it by hanging myself or by slashing my own throat; I despise something so petty. I would rather die violently and at a single stroke—either carried away by a flood or struck down by a lightning bolt."

It was the first time that I had ever heard such a romantic utterance from my sister-in-law who had certainly never seemed a great lover of fiction. And as I thought of it I concluded that it must by symptomatic of her excited nerves.

"That sounds like the way they die in some kinds of books."

"Whether in books or on the stage, this is what I really think. If you think I'm bluffing, let's leave right now for Wakanoura. And I'll show you that I'd really jump into the sea or gladly be swept up by a tidal wave."

"You're nervous tonight," I said trying to pacify her.

"You know I'm many times calmer than you. Most men are cowards in a difficult situation," she replied.

38

For the first time it came over me how little I know about women. Indeed, my sister-in-law was the kind of woman who is unmanageable no matter where and how you might approach her. That is, faced up to positively, she would yield only too easily. And then when you backed off she would suddenly show great strengths where they were not in the least expected. Some of them, indeed, were formidable enough to frighten you off. Or if you were to decide to contest her, others would vanish at once even while you hesitated. Although throughout our talk I had the feeling that I was at her mercy, I derived immense pleasure from this supposedly unpleasant feeling of being tossed around.

But at last she had mentioned her tremendous determination. Swept away by a tidal wave, struck down by a lightning bolt or whatever, in any case she preferred to die an uncommon, sublime death. Always, and especially since we had come to Wakayama together, I had felt somehow uneasy about her, despite my overwhelming physical superiority. Yet this sense of uneasiness was, singularly, accompanied by another sense of intimacy.

Inasmuch as my sister-in-law was more or less a stranger to poetry and fiction, I was all the more eager to find out what had so excited her as to bring out that declaration regarding death by a tidal wave.

"I think tonight is the first time I've ever heard you mention death."

"Perhaps—it may be the first time I've spoken out, but not even one day has death, this question of death, been out of my mind. That's why I have told you if you think I'm bluffing to take me to Wakanoura. You will see how readily I will plunge into the sea and kill myself."

It was harrowing to hear these words spoken by a dim night lamp, and while the storm roared outside. Normally she was a quiet woman: she would scarcely show anything hysterical; she would rarely speak and her cheeks were always pale; and yet for some reason or other her eyes would suggest an intense, inexplicable meaning.

"You are really strange tonight. Is there something making you unusually nervous?"

I could not see any tears; nor could I hear any sobbing. However, suspecting that she was perhaps at that point, I peeped into the mosquito-net by the dim lamplight. There she was lying on the doubled over red mattress, neatly covered to the shoulder with a hemmed white hempen quilt. As I looked at the figure in

the dim light, she shifted the pillow and stared back at me.
"You keep commenting on my nervousness, but I'm much
calmer than you. Because I am always ready."

I could offer no reply. Instead I silently lit another Shikishima
by the dim lamplight, simply gazing at the clouds of smoke
which streamed from my nose and mouth. Occasionally turning
my uneasy eyes to look through the net, I found her figure lying
as still as ever. But just as I had decided that she had fallen asleep,
the upturned face called "Jiro-san."

"Yes," I said.

"What are you doing there?"

"Smoking. I can't sleep."

"You'd better turn in soon. It's not good to miss your sleep."

"Yes, I will."

And raising the hem of the mosquito-net I slid into my bed.

39

The following morning a beau-
tiful sky greeted us, a complete change from the previous day.

"It's fine weather now," I said.

"Yes, indeed," my sister-in-law agreed.

But because of the poor night we both had had, we didn't feel
at all as if we were awakening from a happy dream. In fact the
sky was now so tinted with blue that on rising we still felt somewhat as if we had emerged from a nightmare.

At breakfast when I saw the sunbeams streaming under the
overhang I was suddenly aware of a change of mood. The
woman I was now facing seemed to me altogether different from
what she had been the night before. Now her eyes cast no romantic shadow. Only her eyelids, heavy from lack of sleep, betrayed a certain languor, too languid to resist even the freshness
of the sunlight. Nor were her pale cheeks now any different.

We finished our breakfast as hurriedly as possible and left the
hotel. Warned that no trolley service had been restored yet, we
hired rickshas. When we stepped out of the earth-floor the

ricksha men, at a glance, took us for a married couple. As soon as we entered the rickshas the man lifted my shafts, first. Intent on stopping him, I repeated "After hers." And understanding, he signaled, "Hey, his lady first." As my sister-in-law's ricksha passed by, she said "Before you," showing her familiar dimple. Although I replied "Go ahead, please," I was much disturbed by my man's "his lady," but my sister-in-law, apparently unconcerned, raised her amber-colored, embroidered parasol as soon as she passed by me. From the rear she looked very fresh indeed. It seemed that she was calmly riding along, utterly indifferent as to what she had been called.

Looking ahead at her back, I considered her character once more. Ordinarily I was confident that I could understand something of her nature; but since I had earnestly determined to learn the truth from her directly, I had felt as though entering even deeper into a veritable labyrinth.

Could it be that all women, from the male point of view, ultimately turn out to be as mysterious as she? I wondered, lacking in experience. But at the same time I was convinced that this mysteriousness was something unique with my sister-in-law, something that one could hardly expect to find in other women. In any event, long before I was able to fathom her real personality, the sky had cleared up. Feeling like an idiot, I still stared at her back.

Then suddenly I realized that on returning to the hotel I would be obliged to report to my brother on her, and I really didn't know what to report. As much as there might be to tell, I didn't have the courage to itemize all of it for him. And even if I could, it would boil down to one final, simple point: that she was a mystery. Wasn't this also the point which my brother, just like me, had reached after his frustrated attempt to understand her true character? If I became a plaything of fate as my brother had, it might indeed rack my nerves worse than it had racked his. At this thought I felt the first chill of fear.

But when our rickshas arrived at the hotel there was no sign of either my mother or my brother on the third-floor veranda.

40

In a shaded room on the third floor my brother was lying on his back, his glossy black hair resting on a pillow. He was not asleep, and was in fact very tense. His bloodshot eyes were wide open as he lay staring at the ceiling. No sooner had he heard our footsteps than he fixed those bloodshot eyes full upon us. I knew him well enough to anticipate this, yet I was a little shocked when, standing with her at the door, I saw the fierce red eyes which were clear evidence of the restless night he had spent. As usual I looked for my mother to act as moderator in a situation such as this. However, nowhere, neither in the room nor on the veranda, was she to be seen.

While I was thus occupied in looking for my mother, my sister-in-law sat down beside my brother and said simply, "I am home."

He made no answer. My sister-in-law sat there and did not move. Obviously, I thought, I had to break the ice.

"I heard that you had a terrible storm here last night."

"Yes, we had a very heavy wind."

"Did the sea come over the stone bank and down from that row of pine trees?"

That was the question she asked. My brother looked her in the face for a moment, and then replied slowly.

"No, it wasn't that bad. There wasn't any damage to the house."

"Then we could have come back if we had tried hard."

So saying, she looked back at me. I turned to my brother, instead of to her.

"No, we couldn't possibly have made it. In the first place, there were no trolleys."

"I guess not. Yesterday evening the sea was running very high."

"Did this place shake during the night?" she asked.

And this time he promptly replied, "Yes, it did. In fact it shook so much that Mother got nervous and went downstairs."

I was not relieved, however, until I was finally certain that, in spite of his severe look, there was nothing ferocious about his manner. He was indeed more hot-tempered than I was impatient, yet he had always shown a sort of inborn ability to master his temper when the occasion demanded.

Soon my mother returned from her visit to the Tamatsushima Shrine, and was genuinely relieved to see me back.

"O, I'm so glad you could come back early. O my but I was frightened last night, Jiro. It was more than I can tell you. Why —every time this post creaked the room swayed to and fro. On top of it, that roar of the waves—even now it makes me shudder . . . to remember it!"

Apparently she had been really frightened by the storm, especially the roar of the waves smashing against the dyke.

"I want no more of Wakanoura, no more of the sea. No more of anything. I only want to go home at once."

My mother frowned as she spoke. My brother screwed up his hollow cheeks, grinning.

"Where did you both stay last night?" he asked.

I named the hotel in Wakayama.

"Was it a nice hotel?"

"Somehow or other, no—it was just dark and gloomy, wasn't it?"

At that moment my brother turned his flashing eyes on his wife.

Looking at me, she said, "It was just like a haunted house."

Toward the evening I met her at the foot of the stairs and inquired, "How is Brother? Is he mad?" "Oh, I can't tell what's in his mind," she replied, going upstairs with a forlorn smile.

41

As my mother had urged our early departure, we all agreed to seize the occasion to cut our visit short and leave as quickly as possible.

"However beautiful a place may be for a couple of days, it certainly becomes boring if you stay any longer, doesn't it?" said my brother, agreeing with her.

My mother asked me in secret, "Jiro, what are you going to do?" First, I wondered if perhaps during my absence my brother might have confided everything to her. But judging from his usual way, it seemed quite unlikely that he would have been that frank.

"Did he seem angry because we failed to return last night?" At this she was silent for a moment.

"Last night, because of the rough sea and the wind, you know, there really wasn't much time to talk about it, but . . ." That apparently was as far as she was willing to go.

"Mother, you seem to be suspicious that there is something between Sister-in-law and me, though . . ." My mother, who had been staring at me, interrupted me promptly at that point by waving her hand.

"Nothing of the sort. Least of all your mother."

This seemed unequivocal indeed as she stared at me sharply. Yet it was impossible to read her mind. I had long ago learned that more often than not my own parents and I, their own son, were capable of telling lies to each other with a completely straight face. In fact I had become resigned to the conclusion that no one in the world could tell the truth all the time.

"I am supposed to talk to him about all of this, since that's the way we arranged it. So there is nothing for you to worry about. Please make yourself easy about it."

"Well then, Jiro, perhaps you'd better do it as soon as you can."

It had been decided that we were returning to Tokyo by an evening express the following day. There were still many sights around Osaka which might have occupied us, but my mother was no longer willing to go sightseeing, nor was my brother interested. Neither of them was inclined to lose time in transferring at Osaka, and both insisted that we continue straight to Tokyo by sleeper.

It was therefore necessary that we leave Wakayama for Osaka

by a morning train the following day. My mother asked me to send a telegram to the Okadas.

"We don't have to send another to Sano, do we?" said I, looking from my mother to my brother.

"I think not," answered my brother.

"Just one to Okada will do. You may forget about Sano. I'm quite sure he will come and see us off, anyway."

With the telegram form in my hand, I recalled the beetle-brows and gold-rimmed eyeglasses of Sano who had insisted on taking Osada-san for his wife.

"All right. Let's forget about Mr. Beetle-brows, then."

My remark made everyone laugh. I had, from the start, been particularly impressed with those overhanging brows, and so the others seemed to have taken special notice of that very same peculiarity.

"Certainly more prominent than his picture suggests," remarked my sister-in-law, looking very serious.

Thus taking refuge in a joke, I wondered how to seize the occasion to make my report to my brother on his wife. Unnoticed I stole a glance at him every now and then; however, he seemed wholly indifferent, quite contrary to my expectations.

42

It was shortly after this, nevertheless, that he called me to another room. He seemed to be his usual self—which, according to his wife, was sheer pretense—as he said quietly, "Jiro, I would like to have a word with you. Will you come to the other room." "Yes, certainly," I replied obediently and rose. While rising, I chanced to glance at my sister-in-law's face. It was a casual gesture of which I was then wholly unconscious, but which, I have since realized, might have been arrogant. The moment we glanced at each other, my sister-in-law, as was her wont, smiled with her dimple. To others, our eyes might have appeared to shine with triumph. Looking back at my mother who was in the next room folding *yukata*, I was instantly petrified, in spite of myself. Her eyes seemed to suggest that she had covertly been observing us. Feeling that her suspicion had cut me to the heart, I entered the room where my brother was waiting.

It was about the time of the Feast of Lanterns by the old calendar, a time when the sea was normally rough. Probably for that reason not so many tourists, to say nothing of regular guests, were to be seen around. In the spacious three-storied hotel more rooms were vacant than were occupied; so we could always make free use of a vacant room for a while at least.

My brother must have already arranged for it with the maid; there I found a couple of hempen cushions facing each other, with a fancy cigarette tray between them, and even fans had been provided. I took my seat in front of him but, uncertain as to how to begin, I kept silent. He too was reluctant to speak. Recognizing that in such a case it was in his nature to come out positively, I purposely kept smoking.

Analyzing my state of mind at the moment, I must now confess that I was, indeed, goading my brother if not making sport of him. Although I can't quite understand what could have made me so bold toward him, perhaps I had unconsciously taken on some of his wife's attitude. Now I feel deep repentance for my attitude—which is, nevertheless, irrevocable and irreparable.

In silence, then, I kept puffing a cigarette until, as expected, my brother finally began.

"Jiro, now do you know Nao's true nature?"

"No, I am afraid I do not."

His question had been so severe that without thinking I snapped out a curt answer. Afterward, when I realized regretfully how perfunctory it was, it was too late.

In any case, he neither asked another question nor made any answer. The silence grew very painful for me, and it must have been even more so for him. I can see that now.

"Jiro, as your brother I never expected to get so indifferent an answer from you as simply, 'No, I am afraid I do not.'"

His voice was low and trembling. Clearly out of consideration for my mother, for the hotel, for me, and also for the problem itself, he was apparently fighting desperately to keep his voice under control, to keep from shouting.

"Do you think you can get away with such an indifferent answer? Don't be childish."

"No, I never intended that," was all I could manage to say. And when I said this I was indeed a gentle and respectful brother.

43

"If that's not what you meant, then let me hear you further," my brother continued with a wry face, and staring at a picture on his fan. Relieved of his withering stare, I observed him furtively. Although it may sound, much to my regret, as if I despised him, I must admit that his expression at that moment, or rather his attitude, betrayed a childishness quite unworthy of a grown man. Now I think I have gained the insight necessary to respect his utter simplicity; I was too immature then. Even in dealing with such problems, that is, I was guided by a spirit of calculation, assuming it a wise policy to take whatever advantage offered itself.

Thus for a while I kept watching him. And it occurred to me how easy it would be to grapple with him. He was out of temper; he was impatient; and he was consciously trying to control himself. He was all tense. Yet I felt that his was the bouyant tension of a balloon, for in a moment it would be bound to either explode or fly away somewhere.

It was then at last that I came to realize that herein lay the very reason why my brother was no match for his wife. I also thought that hers might be after all the most ingenious strategy to insure her own existence. Until then I had noticed only my brother's front; hence my timidity, uneasiness, and at times even awe toward him. But as a result of the previous day's experience with my sister-in-law I was quite unexpectedly able to view him

from the other side and thereby take him somewhat more lightly. At no time had I got a cue from her as to how to regard him,
yet at no time had I felt more courageous in his presence. Now
therefore with relative coolness I could stare at the forehead of
my brother who in turn stared at his fan.

Then suddenly he raised his head.

"Jiro, do say something." His intense tone struck my eardrums, and at the sound of his voice I came to myself with a
start.

"I was about to. But the matter is so complicated that I am at a
loss how to begin. Brother, this is no ordinary matter. I shall
have to ask for your patience and forbearance. Please don't be
all grim and stern—like a judge. After all that can only make the
words stick in my throat."

My brother was sensible enough to see my point at once.
"You are right. I'm sorry. You are quick-tempered, and I am
easily angered. So here we are beside ourselves. Well, Jiro, when
do you think you can talk freely? So far as I am concerned, I am
ready right now."

"Will you please wait until we get back to Tokyo. Surely that
will be soon enough. We will be going back on the express tomorrow night. Then I shall have more time to consider and let
you know what I think."

"That will do," he said calmly, as if his confidence in me had
cooled his hot temper.

"Then let us leave it that way." So saying, I rose. My brother
nodded assent. However, he called me back as I was crossing the
doorsill.

"Jiro, you will give me the details when we are back in
Tokyo. But I wonder for the moment—can you tell me your
opinion in a word?"

"About her, you mean?"

"Of course."

"About her integrity there is nothing you can doubt."

At this he changed color but said nothing. And with that I left
the room.

44

Actually at the moment I was afraid that he might hit me a hard blow with his fist or heap curses on me from behind. Having angered him and, in leaving my seat, deserted him I must have taken him lightly indeed, certainly far more lightly than usual. Furthermore, I was ready to defend my sister-in-law even by force if necessary. That is, I felt added sympathy for her, though not because she was an innocent party. In a word, I had begun to despise my brother. And as I left my seat I even felt a certain amount of belligerence toward him.

When I went back to the room my mother, having finished folding the *yukata*, was busy packing a small wicker suitcase. However, her mind was apparently on other matters, for at the sound of my footsteps she turned around quickly.

"And your brother?"

"He will be here soon."

"Have you already finished your talk?"

"Finished or not—it's not so serious a talk, to begin with," I said purposely, with an annoyed look to put her mind at ease.

My mother continued to stuff and rearrange sundry things in the suitcase. In her presence I was abashed, and did not dare look at my sister-in-law who happened to be behind her lending a hand. And yet almost imperceptibly a cold smile passed over her youthful, lonely lips.

"Are you already packing? Isn't it a bit too early?" I chided my aged mother teasingly.

"Well, once we are to leave, the sooner we get ready the better."

"Yes, that's right," my sister-in-law responded as if to forestall whatever I might say.

"Then, let me do the roping at least. You know that's a man's job."

Unlike my brother, I was very skillful at this kind of rough work reserved for ricksha men and workmen. In fact, tying up the suitcase was my specialty. As I started looping the rope around it, my sister-in-law rose quickly and went to the room where my brother was. Abstractedly I followed her with my eyes until she disappeared.

"Jiro, how was your brother?" my mother asked me, pointedly lowering her voice.

"About as usual. There is nothing you need worry about, I can assure you," I said rather sharply, while bearing down on the creaking suitcase lid with my right foot.

"As a matter of fact, I have something to tell you too. But we can wait until we get back to Tokyo."

"Certainly we can."

I answered in an off-hand manner, at the same time speculating vaguely as to what the discussion with her would be like.

A little while later, my brother and sister-in-law came out of the other room. All the time I was nonchalantly chatting with my mother I had been nonetheless concerned about their talk and its outcome. My mother seemed relieved to see them at last emerge together. And I too felt somewhat relieved.

Struggling to rope the suitcase I sweated profusely all over, and baring my arms I used the sleeves of my *yukata* to wipe off the sweat.

"Look at how hot he is. You'd better fan him a little," my brother said, turning to his wife. She rose quietly and fanned me.

"That's all right. I'll soon be finished," I declared. And indeed soon we had finished packing for our departure the next day.

Return and After

I had returned from Wakayama wondering how the relationship between my brother and sister-in-law would develop. It turned out just as I had expected. When I left my brother, I noticed obvious signs of a sort of mental turmoil in the wake of the natural storm. But these peculiar symptoms were to subside considerably—within ten or fifteen minutes after she talked with him.

I was astonished at this change, and once again I could only admire her ability to placate my brother whose nerves were as sharp as a needle. I was particularly happy to note my mother's relieved cheerfulness.

My brother was still in a good humor when we left Wakanoura, and was to remain so throughout our train ride to Osaka. He even joked with the Okadas who came to see us off.

"Say, Okada. Any message to Oshige?"

Still unable to catch his point, Okada asked again, "You mean just to Oshige-san?"

"That's right, to Oshige, your old foe."

Only then did Okada take the hint and laugh as did Okane-san, now the riddle was solved. Sano, who, as my mother had predicted, came to see us off, also took occasion to laugh unreservedly—much to our suprise.

Until then I had not asked my sister-in-law how she had managed to humor my brother; nor did I subsequently have the opportunity to ask her. But I thought that she certainly must have been blessed with a marvelous art, to cope with him so well. I also suspected that she was employing or not employing her art, depending on the occasion and place as well as on her own whims and caprices.

The train was crowded as usual. Somehow or other we got hold of four berths which, conveniently enough, formed one compartment. My brother and I, as the physically stronger members of our party, took the upper berths, giving up the lower ones to the ladies. My sister-in-law was lying below me.

Amid the rattle of the train speeding in the dark, I somehow couldn't forget her lying there. I found it both pleasant and at the same time unpleasant to think of her. I had the sensation of being entwined by a pliant striped snake.

Across the abyss my brother was sleeping in a literal sense—not so much physically as mentally. And the striped snake appeared to coil tightly around his dormant mind, crisscrossing it from top to bottom. The ductile creature, in my imagination, grew hot at one time and cold at another, as it loosened and tightened its coils. And my brother seemed to change color according to these variations in its temperature and flexion.

Lying in my berth, half in imagination and half in dream, I found myself associating this striped snake with my sister-in-law. I was suddenly roused from this fantasy by a station porter crying out "Nagoya, Nagoya." The instant the train halted I heard the sound of a shower. The soles of my feet felt damp and I sat up. Reaching beneath the silk gauze dust curtain, I hastened to close the window at my feet, and asked the others how their windows were. Only my sister-in-law said that the rain seemed to be coming in, and I had to jump down and close her window.

2

"Looks like it's raining, doesn't it?" my sister-in-law asked.

"Yes, it is."

161

The thick curtains had been half blown together by the wind, and as I drew these damp curtains to one side, my mother turned over and asked, "Jiro, where are we now?"

"In Nagoya."

Through the wind-swept gauzed window I looked out at the nearly deserted station in the rain. The cry "Nagoya, Nagoya" could still be heard far away, and then the plodding footsteps echoed as if alive of themselves.

"Jiro, will you please close the one at my feet, too, while you're at it?"

"Oh, isn't yours closed either? I called you a minute ago but you seemed sound asleep, so . . ."

As soon as I was through with my sister-in-law's window I moved on to my mother's. Drawing up the thick curtains, I fumbled for the window. Surprisingly, the window was closed tight.

"Mother, it certainly can't rain in this way. It's perfectly secure. See . . ." I said, tapping the window at her feet.

"O you say it can't?"

"Of course not."

My mother smiled.

"I don't have the slightest idea when it started raining," she said amiably and apologetically. "Thanks, Jiro. Go back to sleep. It must be awfully late."

My watch showed it was past midnight. Gently I climbed up into my berth. The compartment became as quiet as before. My sister-in-law had stopped talking as soon as my mother spoke. My mother also was silent after I was back up in my berth. My brother was the only one who had kept his silence all this while; in fact, he appeared to be sleeping as peacefully as a saint. I cannot yet account for his seemingly contented sleep.

My brother, as he often professed, was more or less neurotic, and frequently he suffered from insomnia. He complained of it quite openly to everyone in the family, yet he had never mentioned his sleepy spells.

Even with Mt. Fuji coming into sight, and everyone else up to admire the view of the rain-wet clouds as they seemed to head flying toward the train, my brother continued to sleep comfortably, mindless of what was going on around him.

The diner was open and many passengers had finished breakfast. As I rose hungrily, escorting my mother along the narrow aisle to the rear section, she told my sister-in-law, "Wake him up soon and come along. We'll be waiting there." "Yes, we'll join you in a minute," my sister-in-law replied, flashing her familiar lonely smile.

Leaving the porter to clean our compartment, we entered the diner still crowded with people bustling in and out along the narrow aisle. At about the time I was helping my mother with black tea and fruit, my brother and sister-in-law at last appeared at the entrance. As there wasn't a vacant table near us, they sat down near the entrance, and laughing and chatting, like any other married couple, looked out of the window. While sipping tea with me, my mother from time to time glanced at them contentedly.

3

At home In Tokyo things seemed to be going as usual, with little change to speak of. Osada-san, with sleeves hitched up behind her, went about her daily chores matter-of-factly. On the morning of the day after our return, gazing after Osada-san, busy washing, her hair covered with a towel, I remembered that she used to be far more serene.

Yoshie was the only child born to my brother and his wife. During our absence Oshige had taken care of her. Usually attached to both my mother and sister-in-law, Yoshie was a docile child whom Oshige could handle easily all by herself. I thought that perhaps this was either because the child inherited her mother's disposition or because Oshige had winning ways.

"Oshige," my father had once declared with feigned surprise, "I'm really amazed at the fine care you have taken of Yoshie! Why, apparently you are a woman, after all." She became sulky at this and complained to my mother, "What a father!"

I had learned of this on the train.

163

A couple of days after our return, I teased her, saying, "Oshige, I hear you got mad when Father said, 'You are indeed a woman, after all.'" "I certainly did," she replied simply and, changing the water in a vase in my father's study, wiped up some water with a dry cloth.

"Are you still mad?"

"Still mad? I've already forgotten that . . . Pretty flowers, aren't they? What do you suppose they are called?"

"But Oshige, you were being praised, for it meant that you have a kind heart worthy of a woman. So you shouldn't be angered at that."

"Oh, I don't care, however it was meant."

With this, swinging her *obi*-hidden hips right and left, Oshige carried a vase toward my father's parlor, as though using her hips to express her annoyance.

Yoshie was handed from Oshige back to my mother and sister-in-law as soon as we returned home. Although they vied with each other in picking up the child, for me it was always a puzzle to witness how the innocent Yoshie could be so deeply attached to my seemingly cold sister-in-law. This child, who was dark-pupiled, glossy-haired, and—like her own mother—uncommonly pale-cheeked, followed her aloof mother around. And my sister-in-law in turn showed this off to every one in the family as something like the greatest glory of Japan. It could be taken as not just a demonstration to her husband of her pride, but perhaps even as a kind of spiting of him. A scholarly person, always immersed in books and thoughts, my brother was rewarded with little intimacy, no matter how dearly he might love the child. Naturally he, who happened to be a man of sentiment, was irritated by this, and showed it every once in a while even at table. Oshige, more than anyone else, found this situation intolerable.

"Yoshie-san, you are a mamma's baby; why don't you go to papa?" she asked pointedly.

"Because . . ." Yoshie said.

"Because what?" Oshige asked.

"Because I'm afraid," Yoshie replied deliberately in a low voice. But to Oshige this could only sound more provoking.

"What did you say? Afraid? Of whom?"

Such an exchange of questions and answers was often repeated, and at times lasted as long as several minutes. At such times with her characteristic smile, my sister-in-law remained unperturbed. Finally my father and mother, to pacify both parties, would try to induce Yoshie to take fruit or cakes from my brother and, to smooth over the matter, would say, "That will do. Now get something good from your papa." Oshige still revealed her annoyance to every one present. My brother, as was his wont, would retreat into his study, silent and alone.

4

That year for the first time my father learned from someone how to cultivate morning glories, and constantly tended a variety of the plant. However, as they were but the ordinary species which curled up and became hardly distinguishable, no one in the family took kind notice of them. We were all impressed by my father's zeal, by his early rising, by his array of pots, by the fine sand, and last of all by the strikingly writhing shapes of the flowers and leaves.

My father arranged them in a row on the veranda and talked of them eagerly to whomever he could capture.

"Yes, very interesting indeed," even my overly candid brother was forced to say admiringly.

My father always occupied the two inner rooms far apart from ours. And pots of morning glories were usually arranged on the veranda of his rooms where the bamboo-blinds were hanging. It was, therefore, to this place that he usually called us children. I withdrew after offering more flattering compliments than my brother, and as soon as I was out of hearing confessed, "It's really awful to have to admire morning glories like those. But enough of his whims."

Indeed, my father loved to make speeches and as a man of ample leisure was in the habit of summoning someone to hold forth on various things. More often than not, Oshige, when she was called, begged me to go in her place, for invariably he talked about things which were well above her head.

When we returned from Osaka, however, I noted that my father took no more interest in the morning glories although they were still blooming.

And I was prompted to ask, "What is the matter with your pet variety?"

"Frankly, morning glories are not promising. No more after this year," he replied with a wry smile. I concluded that the odd-looking flowers and leaves he had proudly shown off to us must have been judged failures by a connoisseur on the subject and, saying so, I laughed aloud in the living room. The loyal Oshige and Osada-san came immediately to my father's defense.

"That's not true. With so much to be done, even he has given out. Why every one said nobody else could possibly have accomplished even that much."

My mother and sister-in-law then looked at me and laughed as if to ridicule my ignorance. Even little Yoshie, who happened to be with them, laughed meaningfully, just like her own mother.

Indeed, while busying ourselves with such trifles, we became less and less mindful of the relationship between my brother and his wife. And in spite of my earlier promise, I began to think that it was no longer necessary to give my brother the report about his wife. Nor did I readily expect to hear from my mother about that serious talk which she had said she wanted to have on our return to Tokyo. Last of all, my brother himself, once so anxious to learn about his wife, had gradually calmed down. In fact he spoke less to me or to my parents. Even when it was warm, he busied himself in his closed-up study.

"Is he working?" I asked my sister-in-law.

"Yes, I think he is preparing the next term's lectures," she said. Indeed, that must be it, I thought, and wished he would so divert all of his attention as to keep himself busy for a long time. My sister-in-law, on the other hand, moved around as usual somehow resembling a forlorn autumn flower. Every now and then she smiled wanly with her single dimple.

5

In the meantime summer waned gradually. The evening stars shone more and more intensely every night. The rustling leaves of Phoenix trees in the morning and evening breezes evoked a touch of shivering chill. As fall set in I often thrilled to a sensation of rebirth. I recalled that my brother, who was more poetically-minded than I, looking up at the transparent autumnal sky, had once said that surely it was a sky worth living for, and continued to gaze contentedly at the deep blue.

"Brother, we are now in the season worth living for," I said as I stood on his study veranda.

Reclining in a wicker chair, he replied, "We haven't quite caught the real autumn mood yet. Have to wait a little more." And he picked up a thick book laid face down on his lap. It was just before supper time. With this, I was about to leave his study to go downstairs, when then suddenly, my brother called.

"Is Yoshie downstairs?"

"She is, I think. She was in the backyard a little while ago."

I opened the northside window and looked down. Below stood a swing which the gardener had made especially for her, but Yoshie was no longer to be seen. And as I wondered where she had disappeared to, I heard her shrill laughter coming from the bath.

"Oh, there she is. She's taking a bath."

"Is she with Nao? Or is she with Mother?"

Listening I heard my sister-in-law's surprisingly deep voice intermingled with Yoshie's laughter.

"She is with her mother," I said.

"They do sound cheery, don't they?"

Involuntarily I glanced at him when he said this. But as his head was hidden behind the bulky book he was holding in his hands I was unable to see his expression at that moment. From his tone, however, I could tell very clearly what he meant.

After some hesitation, I said, "You just don't know how to handle a child."

My brother's face was still behind the book, but putting it away quickly, he said, "It is not just a child I cannot manipulate." In silence I fixed my eyes on his face. "Not only am I unable to handle my own child; apparently I do not possess the technique of handling my own parents. And worse yet, I have no idea how to handle my own wife. I have spent my years just studying, and thanks to that I haven't gotten around to picking up such useful arts. Indeed, Jiro, a certain technique of that kind seems absolutely necessary for a happy life."

"But if you can produce good school lectures, isn't that enough to make up for all that?"

I was ready to beat a retreat, depending on how the wind was blowing. My brother showed no signs of discontinuing the conversation.

"I wasn't born merely to prepare school lectures. I find that on account of writing lectures and reading books I have been unable to experience the most important thing: the enjoyment of human feeling in a human manner. Or it might well be the other party who hasn't any longer been able to let me do so."

Behind his words I spotted a rankling bitterness toward those around him. I had to say something in reply, and yet I was at a loss exactly what to say. I was frightened at the looming crisis, as this course seemed likely to stir up once more the case of his wife. Unfair though it may have been, I struggled to prevent our talk from drifting in that particular direction.

"You're thinking too much, and that makes you talk that way. Let's make better use of such fine weather and take a long walk, say next Sunday. Shall we?"

"H'm," he murmured his consent languidly.

6

A shadow of loneliness flitted over my brother's face, from the broad forehead to the hollow cheeks.

"Jiro, I've always been a lover of nature. Perhaps that's because I'm out of tune with other humans, with no alternative but to turn to nature."

I felt sorry for him at this and tried to reject such a notion flatly. But seeing that this could not satisfy him, I shifted quickly and declared, "I tell you it runs in the whole family. You know well enough how it is with me, not to mention Father. Besides, even our Oshige is fond of flowers and trees, odd as it seems. Why, quite often recently I've found her gazing at landscape paintings with genuine admiration."

As I was doing my best to console him, Osada-san came upstairs to tell us dinner was ready.

"You must be happy these days. Look, you're all smiles," I said to her.

As soon as I returned from Osaka, she had withdrawn into the stuffy maid-servants' quarters and rarely appeared. We had all had a good laugh as we discovered that her shy behavior had been prompted by the "congratulations!" I had put down on our joint postcard sent from Osaka. For this reason she had deliberately avoided me—a fact which tempted me to tease her all the more on those rare occasions when we ran into each other.

"Osada-san, what are you so happy about?" I now pressed her further, yet only half in jest. And continuing to press her hands to the floor she blushed to the tips of her ears.

From the chair my brother spoke to her, "It's a woman's best time when she blushes at marriage talk. But when you're married you will find out it is nothing you're so happy or bashful about. Why, it isn't worth your blush. On the contrary, with your partner in marriage your character is more likely to be destroyed than if you'd stayed single. You have to pay dearly. You mind that."

It was plain that Osada-san could not follow my brother at all. Confused, she did not know what to say, but tears were falling from her eyes.

Noticing this, my brother said, "Osada-san, I'm sorry for having offered such unnecessary opinions. It was only a joke. I should have said such things to a wild fellow like Jiro, and surely not to a gentle girl like you. It was my mistake, and I hope you will forgive me. Well, is there something good for dinner? Let's go and have our meal, Jiro."

Hardly had my brother stirred from the chair when she rose and hurried down the stairs, ahead of us. As we were about to leave the room together, he turned and said, "Jiro, we haven't gotten around to that matter of the other day yet. Although very anxious to hear what you have to say, I have been too busy reading and writing to do anything about it. Sorry. But soon I mean to make time for it and want very much to hear your story." I thought of feigning ignorance by asking "What do you mean by that matter of the other day?" but as I could not bring myself to that, I merely replied lightly.

"After so long, this thing is almost like stale beer; it is less easy for me to talk about. Of course I don't mind if you insist on holding me to my promise. But wouldn't it be better to forget all about that rubbish and instead take a nice long walk, now that we are in what you have called an autumn worth living for?"

"H'm. A long walk may be fine, too. But . . ."

Exchanging these words, we entered the room where a dinner table was set. There we found my sister-in-law seated with Yoshie at her side.

7

At table my parents also happened to touch on Osada-san's wedding. My mother said that she was going to dye the crest on some white crepe she had earlier bought from a draper. At this the embarrassed Osada-san, who had been waiting on us, abruptly rose from her seat and went out, leaving a black-lacquered tray on the rice server.

Gazing after her as she went away, I couldn't help laughing. My brother, on the other hand, made a wry face.

"Jiro, don't make fun of her so thoughtlessly. You ought to use more delicate language to an innocent girl like her."

"Jiro is just a busybody," said my father in an amused and yet reproving tone. Only my mother looked mystified, as my brother explained.

"Why, Jiro is making her bashful every time he sees her by saying congratulations, good wishes for her happiness, and what not. Just a little while ago upstairs he did just that and made her run away. You see she is by nature altogether different from Onao; she ought to be handled more gently, I should think . . ."

My mother seemed to have caught the meaning of this and grinned. My sister-in-law, who had already finished her meal, gave me what seemed a sort of wink. As my father remarked, I was something of a busybody, but at that moment I had not the slightest desire to return her wink before both my parents.

Then, without saying a word, she rose and turned at the door for a moment to beckon to Yoshie, who also scrambled up instantly.

"Well, are you leaving without even having dessert?" Oshige asked. Yoshie stood there, apparently confused as to what to do. "Well, aren't you coming, Yoshie-san?" my sister-in-law said very gently as she stepped into the hallway. No sooner had she disappeared than Yoshie, who had so far been hesitant, must have made up her mind, for she scampered after her mother.

Visibly disapproving, Oshige followed her with her eyes. Both my father and mother, with stiff faces, were staring at their own plates. Oshige looked askance to my brother. But he seemed faraway, the way his eyes were staring out from beneath his arched eyebrows.

"Please let me have that pudding if you don't mind," Oshige said to my brother, and then jabbed at it mutely with her spoon. It seemed as if she was eating something she really didn't care for to suppress the rage that was boiling inside her.

A short while later my brother rose from his seat and returned to his study. With strained ears I listened to the soft flap of his slippers going up the stairs. The study door banged upstairs and after that everything was quiet.

Since my return to Tokyo I had frequently witnessed such scenes. My father too seemed to have noticed them. But it was my mother who worried the most. Her moods, looks, and behavior all betrayed her desire to marry off the spiteful Oshige as quickly as possible—to keep her out of any possible conflict— and then to find me a wife as soon as she could to remove the source of contention between my brother and his wife. But in this entangled human world, things wouldn't turn out as conveniently as she wished. I was whiling away my time as usual, while Oshige grew ever more hostile toward my sister-in-law. Strange as it was, Oshige was fond of Yoshie—so long as my sister-in-law was not present—and Yoshie also clung to Oshige when her mother wasn't around. As for my brother, deeper and deeper lines channelled his scholarly forehead. More and more he immersed himself in books and thoughts.

8

Thus it was altogether contrary to my mother's expectations that Osada-san's marriage, to which she had paid least attention, was the first to materialize. But as both my parents deemed it their duty to marry her off sooner or later, they were indeed grateful for Okada's goodwill, and certainly regretted nothing. It was also for this reason that her marriage had become a sort of family matter. Oshige wouldn't leave Osada-san alone, and Osada-san, for her part, discarding her usual embarrassment, apparently consulted Oshige about various matters, not excluding her future.

One day I returned home and had just come out of the bath when Oshige asked with characteristic bluntness, "Brother, what kind of person is this Sano-san, anyway?" It was the second or third time she had put the question to me since my return from Osaka.

"What is this all of a sudden? It seems to me you're too indiscreet."

Oshige, who was apt to be peevish, stared back at me mutely. Sitting cross-legged writing a postcard to Misawa, I stopped writing for a second.

"Now Oshige, don't get mad again. Sano-san, as I've already said, is beetle-browed with a pair of gold-rimmed eyeglasses. Isn't that enough? The same old story no matter how many times you may ask."

"That he is beetle-browed and wearing eyeglasses, I can see from his photograph without your telling me. After all I do have eyes."

Her tone was still far from conciliatory and, quietly putting aside the postcard and brush, I asked, "What do you want to know, anyway?"

"What exactly did you find out about him?"

By force of habit, familiarity, impetuosity, or childishness, she always tended to treat me as her equal once she got into an argument.

"About him?" I asked.

"Yes, about his character."

I never took her seriously, but once confronted with a serious question of this kind I really didn't have anything solid in reserve to fend her off with. Coolly I began smoking a cigarette, however, much to her humiliation.

"How can you be so nasty, considering how important this is to Osada-san?"

"Well, isn't Okada's assurance enough?"

"But how much do you trust Okada? You know he is only a chessman."

"Whether he looks like a chessman or not . . ."

"I'm not talking about how he looks. I mean he is basically frivolous."

I became annoyed and impatient; I no longer wanted to argue with her.

"Now don't you worry about Osada-san. A smarter thing for you to do would be to try to get married yourself soon. You ought to realize what a relief it would be to Father and Mother if you were to get married, rather than Osada-san. So forget about her; get married yourself and settle down. Then you'll make them happy as a dutiful daughter."

Oshige started crying as I anticipated, for whenever we quarreled and she did not cry I was disappointed at her passivity, felt something was amiss. I kept puffing indifferently.

"Then perhaps you too had better find a wife and become independent. That would make them much happier than my get-

ting married. You're always taking sides with Sister-in-law
. . ."

"And you are too ready to antagonize her."

"Of course. I am Big Brother's sister."

9

Fresh from a bath I had intend-
ed finishing the postcard to Misawa, first, and then applying the
razor to my cheeks. Annoyed by her grumbling I asked, "Oshige,
would you mind going to the bath and fetching a bowl of hot
water?" But apparently a bowl of water was the last thing in the
world she could bother about. She sat frowning as though
pondering life's problems ten times more serious. I ignored her,
therefore, and summoned a maid to fetch the needed hot water.
Then I set a portable mirror on the desk, placed the ivory-
handled razor beside it, and in a deliberately comical manner I
puffed out my cheeks now wet with hot water.

With an elaborate flourish I wielded the shaving brush,
spreading white lather all over my face, when my sister, who had
been sitting beside me and watching for some time, burst into
tears with a pathetic cry. I knew it was her nature to come to this
point sooner or later, and had anticipated a shriek such as this.
Therefore, I blew up my cheeks all the more and cheerfully
started scraping off the white lather with the razor. This was perhaps humiliating to her, and she raised a yet more clamorous
howl. Although I had been intentionally slighting her, I admit I
was a trifle startled at the sharpness of her voice as she said,
"Brother."

"What do you want?"

"Why do you take me so lightly? After all, I am your own
sister. And even if she is your favorite, Sister-in-law is a stranger,
isn't she?"

I laid down the razor and turned my lathered face toward her.

"Oshige, you're really upset. You don't have to tell me that
you are my own sister and she is a stranger married into our family. I know all of that."

"I'm just reminding you. It's none of your business to tell me to get married quick. Why don't you marry somebody like your favorite sister-in-law?"

I felt like slapping her face but didn't dare for fear of the fuss she might make around the house.

"Well then you too ought to find a scholar like Brother for yourself."

Hearing these words, she became furious, and seemed on the point of flying at me. But her rage soon dissolved in tears as she declared that everyone scorned her because she couldn't get married ahead of Osada-san, and at last branded me as a barbarian who knew nothing of brotherly sympathy. Certainly, if I had wanted, I could have been as abusive as she, but straining my patience I chose silence instead. Even then, she would not let me alone; she rattled on offering not only facts, but all of the sheerest fantasy she was capable of. Her favorite subjects were the link between our sister-in-law and me which she took every opportunity to allude to with the most malicious innuendoes. I found that most vicious of all and even wished at that moment that I could seize the lead from Oshige and marry any girl, however plain-looking, and leave this woman all to herself, to chatter ridiculously about the marital relationship, of love between man and woman, and what not. I also seriously considered the plan favored by my mother, as a solution to the problem of my brother and his wife.

I still remember my sister's sulky face, tearful as if rain pelted, and Oshige, I am told, can never forget my face, grotesquely lathered as though I had just emerged from a wash-basin.

10

Because of intense sympathy for our scholarly and lonely brother Oshige clearly disliked our sister-in-law.

"What will he do when Mother is gone? I am really sorry for him," she said, unable to conceal anything. It was, of course, long before I, with my lathered face, took up the quarrel with her. Deciding to give her the cold shoulder, I simply admonished, "A sensible person like Brother won't need your kind of meddling in family affairs. That won't happen. You'd better keep quiet. Besides, there are Father and Mother."

Already then, I saw quite clearly that with personalities as different as fire and water it would be almost impossible for Oshige and my sister-in-law to live together in peace.

"Mother, we'll have to marry off Oshige quickly," I even ventured to advise. Although my mother then did not ask why, she seemed to understand my point. "You need not remind me of that. Your father and I are worried to death. It's not just Oshige, though. You can't realize how much we're troubling others about a girl for you, too. But all of this depends on fate, as you know . . ." she said, looking very hard at me. Not understanding what my mother was driving at, I said simply, "I suppose so," and withdrew like a mere child.

Oshige became serious rather easily about everything. Moreover, my father loved her more than my mother did for her single-mindedness and frankness, and my brother loved her too of course.

Even when Osada-san was proposed to, my father said, "It would be more proper to marry off Oshige, first," and he was supported in this view by my brother. My mother pointed out, however, that for Osada-san, who had been asked for specifically by name, it would mean loss on both sides to let such a rare opportunity pass. A sensible person, my brother readily concurred with her view which was more reasonable from a practical standpoint. And there was then little trouble in persuading my father, who was always somewhat conciliatory toward my brother's opinion.

To Oshige herself, who had remained quiet, this must have been very unpleasant, however. But from the eager way she talked with Osada-san about the latter's marriage, it was plain that my sister harbored no ill feeling toward her, even though Osada-san had gotten ahead of her.

It appeared that Oshige couldn't stand being near my sister-in-law. Although she was living in her own parents' house and like a child was allowed to have everything her own way, she could hardly bear my sister-in-law's cool and contemptuous look.

It was while she was in such a fretful mood that she chanced to enter my sister-in-law's room to pick up a woman's magazine or something of the sort. And there she noticed the wedding garments which my sister-in-law was sewing for Osada-san.

"Oshige-san, this is for Osada-san. Isn't it nice? You too ought to get married to someone like Sano-san soon," my sister-in-law said, turning the garments right side out so that Oshige might see them better. This, to Oshige, apparently was an all too obvious innuendo. It could be taken to mean, "Be quick to find someone to marry and do your own sewing." Or perhaps there was the sarcastic hint, "Well, how long are you as a sister-in-law going to spend your time annoying me?" Lastly, perhaps most jarring was the implication that she should get married to someone like Sano.

In tears Oshige went to my father's room to complain. But he must have found it too troublesome. On the following day, without seeking a word of explanation from my sister-in-law, he took Oshige to the Mitsukoshi for shopping.

11

Two or three days later my father had a couple of guests. He was by nature sociable, and professional necessity put him in touch with people from a large number of circles. Even after he had left government service, there was a ceaseless traffic of acquaintances, either by force of habit or inertia. And yet among those who came all the time there were no great celebrities or greatly influential people. One of the guests that day was a member of the House of Peers, and the other a comptroller of a company.

These two guests were apparently, like my father, devotees of Noh drama: every time they came they all enjoyed reciting from a Noh drama. At my father's request Oshige, having for some time taken lessons in drumming, was often called upon to furnish the proper musical accompaniment for them. I still remember her conceited face on such occasions.

"Oshige," I once made a special point to rail at her, "your drumming is fine, but your face is just awful. Take my advice and don't beat the drum for a while after you get married. No matter what an *utai*-maniac your hubby may be, he will be thoroughly disgusted with you if you put on such airs."

Osada-san, who happened to have heard my abuse, said with a shocked look, "What a thing to say! Why, that is simply terrible." And I realized then that I had gone too far. However, Oshige, ordinarily fiery, seemed completely undisturbed by what I had said.

"Dear Brother, for all that, my face is still better; my drumming is really awful. There is no time in the world that I hate more than when we have Father's *utai*-friends," she stated very frankly. Perhaps I had paid so much attention to her look that I hadn't realized her drumming was so bad.

That day too the reciting began as planned, about an hour and a half after the guests arrived. Certain that Oshige would be called before the company, I went to the sitting-room where she was absorbed in dusting several small dinner tables, intending to have a little fun with her.

"No demand for your drum beating today?" I asked teasingly. But with an oddly vacant look she glanced up at me as I was standing there.

"Right now I've got to prepare the dinner tables. I excused myself by saying I'm too busy."

Knowing that my mother would certainly scold me if I carried this bantering too far while the kitchen and living room were in such confusion, I returned to my room.

Later, when I came back from an after-dinner walk, my mother stopped me as I was entering my room.

"Jiro, I'm so glad you've come back just in time. Will you go in and listen to your father reciting?"

Having grown accustomed to his *utai*, I really didn't mind listening to one piece.

178

"What are they reciting?" I asked my mother. But unlike me, she wasn't at all interested in *utai* and answered, "I'm sure I don't know. Go right in. They're waiting for you."

Having sized up the situation, I was about to pass on into the inner section of the house, when I happened to notice Oshige standing out on the dark veranda.

"Hey . . ." I involuntarily cried even as she motioned me to keep my mouth shut. "Why in the world are you standing there in that dark spot?"

"Never mind," she replied. But still unsatisfied, I stood waiting, and she said, "You see they've sent repeated requests for me and I've had to ask Mother to say I don't feel well."

"But why so shy today?"

"Because I'm tired of beating the drum: it seems so silly. Besides, what's coming next is so difficult I don't think I can handle it."

"Well, well, even a girl like you can acquire some idea of modesty. That's great," I declared and went in.

1 2

In the inner room both of our guests were seated in front of the alcove. Both were refined-looking; and their thinly bald heads harmonized well with Tanyu's trio of scroll-pictures hung in the alcove behind them.

Both the guests were in *hakama*, but had slipped off their *haori*. My father alone was without *hakama*, but had retained his *haori* at least.

As we were well acquainted with one another, I nodded to the guests and said by way of greeting, "Would you permit me to enjoy your . . . ?" "You are certainly welcome," they said touching their hands to their heads as if slightly embarrassed at the implied compliment. In reply to my father's inquiry about Oshige, I said, "She seems to have a slight headache right now— she was very sorry she couldn't come to offer her greetings."

Looking toward the guests, my father said, "Oshige's not feeling well—that's as incredible as the Devil afflicted with cholera."

Then he asked me again, "A little while ago your mother said something about Oshige's stomachache. Now is it a stomachache or is it a headache?"

"What a blunder!" I thought and said, "Probably both, I guess, since they often go together. In any case it's not serious enough to worry about. I'm sure she will be all right soon." The guests, having injected their elaborate expressions of sympathy, finally said, "Too bad indeed, but shall we get started?"

My brother and his wife comprised the audience; and were already seated sideways, politely together. With a solemn face I took my seat next to my sister-in-law. Sitting down, I asked, "What's on?" and she, who had no knowledge of nor taste for this art, replied, "They say it's *Kagekiyo*." She did not offer any more.

One of the guests, who was ruddy-faced and portly, was to play the leading part; the other, the member of the House of Peers, sat next to him and was to support him; my father as host was to play the double role of the girl and the attendant, both minor parts. Having a fairly good ear for *utai*, I was, from the start, anxious as to what kind of *Kagekiyo* we were going to get. My brother, on the other hand, seemed somewhat pensive with his absent look, listening dreamily to the voices of the now decaying era. But on my sister-in-law's ears I'm afraid even that vital "*shomon*" passage fell with the unpleasantness not so much of human voices as of the roars of beasts. For some time I had taken interest in this Noh, *Kagekiyo*. Once or twice I had even been moved to tears by a certain heroic and pathetic mood rising from the intensity of that speech by the blind Kagekiyo and also by the devotion of his daughter who, in search of her father, travels all the way down to Hyuga.

But that was when accomplished singers were each playing their own parts competently and raptly. I wasn't in the least inspired by the kind of *Kagekiyo* we were now subjected to, this *Kagekiyo* faltering along the *utai* notes.

As soon as they were through Kagekiyo's heroic tale and had come duly to the finale, I became a trifle uneasy, not knowing what to say of the performance.

My sister-in-law, person of few words that she was, said, "It's certainly brave."

And I also said, "It certainly is."

But my brother, who was hardly expected to say anything, turned to the ruddy-faced guest and commented, "There was a passage: 'As, indeed, a true warrior of Heike, I shall recite a tale of . . .' I have particularly enjoyed that phrase, 'As, indeed, a true warrior of Heike.'"

Since my brother was honest by nature and regarded it part of his intellectual integrity to be wholly candid, there was no reason to doubt his remark. But unfortunately his remark, being concerned not so much with their *utai* performance itself as with the quality of the poetic style, made no impression on the guest.

Always tactful in such a case, my father first praised the guest's singing, saying, "Yes, indeed, that part, I've thoroughly enjoyed," and then he said, "Now this reminds me of a very interesting incident. It is something like that passage adapted to a popular drama, so to speak, and Kagekiyo transformed into a woman—a situation far more fascinating than that of the *utai*. Furthermore, it really happened, you know."

13

Good mixer that he was, my father carried many such quaint stories in his head, and he felt free to make good use of them while exchanging sake cups with guests. Although we lived together, it was the first time that I had heard of this anecdote about a female Kagekiyo. I was all ears as I watched my father's face.

"Now this happened just recently and it really happened—that's why I'm going to tell you about it. It started long ago—well, not as far back as the Gempei Era, to be sure, but some twenty-five years ago. I shall say at the time when I was a humble public servant . . ."

After this introduction which made everyone chuckle, he got to the main subject. It seemed that one of his friends, or rather a man many years his junior, had become involved in a kind of love affair. Naturally my father refrained from revealing the man's name. Although quite familiar with the names and faces of those who came in and out of our house, much as I tried, I couldn't place any of them in this particular anecdote. I decided, in fact, that my father must no longer be openly associated with the man.

In any event the whole thing started when the man was twenty or so, just after he had entered a college or perhaps when he was in his second year at most—about this my father's account was quite vague and in either case it was none of our concern.

"He was a nice fellow—yes, there are various types of nice fellows; anyway, he was a nice fellow, let me just put it that way. And since even now he is so, you can well imagine that at about twenty he must certainly have been a charming fellow."

Having thus described the man roughly, my father went on to tell of the unfortunate circumstances in which the man had an affair with a maid-servant in his house.

"Having been overly protected, so to speak, the fellow had until then been completely innocent of such an experience as a love affair. It was impossible for him even to imagine himself loved by a woman. But then the miracle suddenly dropped out of the clouds, much to his surprise."

The guests, thus addressed, responded with gravity, "Yes, indeed," whereas I thought it very funny. I noted also that a somewhat lonely smile played over even my brother's cheeks.

"What was stranger still was that the fellow was passive while the woman was so active. When I asked him how he had sensed her fancy, he quite seriously said all sorts of things. But something I still remember, maybe because I thought it most amusing of all, was that, once as he was eating crackers or something of the sort, she had come and asked him to let her have one too, but then had quickly grabbed at his half-eaten cracker and had thrown it into her mouth."

Thus presented, the humorous side of the story was emphasized more than the underlying seriousness. So after the three of us had joined our guests in a hearty laugh, there seemed nothing

else to it. Moreover, the guests laughed as though they had practiced the art of laughing somewhere. But of all the company it
was only my brother who was relatively serious, and finally he
asked in a tone hardly fit for joking.

"Anyway, what was the result of it? Did they marry hap-
pily?"

"No, that's what I am going to tell you about. As I said a moment ago, that's where the story begins to take on the quality of
Kagekiyo. What I have offered so far is merely an introduction," explained my father triumphantly.

14

As my father continued, then,
the affair between the man and the woman was as short-lived as
a summer night's dream. Yet when they sealed a pledge of love
his friend seemed to have declared his intention to take her for
his future wife. Moreover, as my father took pains to explain, it
was by no means the term she had demanded; rather in the heat
of passion the man had made a spontaneous declaration, an emo-
tional outburst which was sincere, to be sure, but which would
prove difficult to carry out.

"That is, you see both were of the same age. One was a student still depending on his parents for support, with a long way
to go, while the other was a poor maid expecting to live her life
as a domestic. And the promise, however firm, would take a
good many years to be realized, during which time all sorts of
events might occur. So the woman, I understand, asked, 'You'll
be twenty-five or six when you finish school; I will then be
about as old. Do you think you will find that satisfactory?' "

Having come to this point, my father abruptly interrupted his
story to fill the tiny silver-tipped pipe which was near his knees.
As he blew the first pale-blue smoke from his nostrils, I was so
impatient that I asked, "What was his answer?"

Tapping the pipe against his hand to knock the ashes out, my
father said, "I was certain that you would ask something.
Doesn't it sound interesting, Jiro?" Then, looking at me, "Let

me tell you there're all sorts of people in this world." I said simply, "Well, yes."

"As a matter of fact, I myself asked the fellow what kind of answer he had given her. But what an innocent babe he was! For this was what he told me: 'I knew of course my own age, and also hers, but how old she would be when I graduated never occurred to me; still less had I been aware of the remote future. That is, I hadn't considered that she would also be fifty when I was fifty.'"

"What innocence!" said my brother rather admiringly. And the guests, who had so far remained silent, quickly nodded in agreement with my brother, saying, "Yes, sheer innocence, indeed," and also "Yes, young people can really be that blind!"

"Hardly within a week the fellow began having regrets; well, the woman was calm as ever, but the fellow grew even more appalled at the enormity of the situation. He was as chicken-hearted as he was innocent. But being honest, he finally proposed in earnest that they cancel their marriage pledge, and I understand that, in addition, he awkwardly apologized by saying 'Beg your pardon' or something of that sort. Whereas the other party, though of the same age, was indeed a woman. To hear his childish apologies, she must have thought him rather cute, but perhaps silly too."

My father had a big laugh. The guests echoed him. My brother alone, whether it was funny or disgusting, had an odd face. To his mind all such matters seemed grave problems of life. In fact, from his point of view, the way my father was relating the story must have sounded frivolous.

Soon after the woman, according to my father, left her job for good. The young man brooded for the next few months, and wouldn't bestir himself, as though his mind had been transfixed on one spot. Once when she dropped in during a return visit to the neighborhood, he hardly spoke a word whether or not there were other people present. And as it happened to be lunch time she waited on him as before, but he remained silent as with a stranger.

Never since had the woman crossed the threshold of his

house. But in the meantime he had grown oblivious to her existence, left school, established a family, and so on, and had no contact with her for twenty-some years until just recently.

15

"Now all this might alone make more or less an anecdote. But fate is something dreadful . . ." My father continued to tell his story.

I was so interested in what he was going to say that I could hardly keep my eyes off his face. And to sum up my father's story, it was roughly as follows:

Twenty-some years after she had gone completely out of his mind, they were once again brought together quite unexpectedly by the guiding hand of fate. It was in the heart of Tokyo that they met; more specifically, it was at the Yurakuza, one chilly evening, at a concert sponsored by the Meijinkai or the Bionkai.

It was hardly five minutes after the fellow, with his wife and daughter, had taken their reserved seats somewhere toward the rear of the auditorium, that the woman came in, led by the hand by a young woman. Apparently they had also reserved their seats by phone, for the two women were shown to the seats tagged "Engaged" right next to his, and sat down quietly. Thus, strangely enough, the man and the woman by chance were sitting side by side. And stranger still was something utterly beyond all his imagination: the woman, now sightless, expressionless, and completely unaware of her neighbor, gave her rapt attention to the sound of music flowing from the stage.

When he first noticed the face of the woman sitting beside him he was startled as if his memory of the past twenty years had been turned upside down. And then he was struck with a sense of helplessness as he gradually realized that she no longer looked anything like the old image—the fixed stare of her dark eyes—he had held of her.

Until past ten o'clock, scarcely stirring and totally deaf to what was happening on stage, he was literally petrified in his seat. He spent his time exploring various ways of unsnarling the dark threads which fate had knotted ever since their separation. The woman, on the other hand, neither looked at, nor was even aware of the proximity of, her old lover. Only a pensive crease between her dark eyebrows revealed that in this music of the past, now fading inevitably, she was barely able to remember her lost youth.

Their reunion was as sudden as their parting, and even after their parting he was often haunted by thoughts of her. Especially disturbed at her loss of sight, he was determined to discover her whereabouts.

"Being as persistent as he was simple and honest, the fellow finally was successful in his search. Although I once knew how he accomplished this, it was such a complicated story that I have completely forgotten. It seems to me that the next time he went to the Yurakuza, he was able to make a profitable contact with the usher. Anyway, I recall he had to go to a great deal of trouble."

"Where did she live?" I asked, anxious for any facts which would confirm my suspicion.

"Ah, but that must remain confidential. Her name, her address —it was our understanding that I would not reveal such information. But, in any event, this fellow begged me to go and see the blind woman at her home. What his motive was, I do not know; he seemed to feel the necessity of something like a friendly visit. Educated man that he was, he stretched his specious reasoning infinitely. In a word, he hoped to join the past and the present together so that his mind might find peace. Secondarily, he seemed much concerned with how she had lost her sight. Yet he himself didn't dare go and see her. For one thing, he had no desire to stir their old flame afresh and, for another, he had his wife and children to consider. Moreover, all of this was really of less concern than the fact that as they had separated many years before he had said, 'Since I intend to continue my education a little longer, I won't be able to marry you until I am thirty-five or six. So I want you to agree to cancel our previous pledge.'"

"And the fellow had married almost as soon as he left school.

That, I fancy, had made his conscience more than a little uneasy. So it was settled that I go and see her."

"O my, how silly!" said my sister-in-law.

"Yes, but silly as it was, I did go at last," replied my father. Both the guests and I, much amused, could not restrain our laughter.

16

There was something oddly waggish about my father; in fact, some called him an upright man while others called him a jolly fellow.

"That's the whole secret of how the old man has worked his way up. And that seems to be the way the world really is. Those going through formal education, shaping ideas in earnest, are never appreciated by society. They are only looked down upon."

My brother had once confided that to me without quite revealing whether his remarks were to be taken for either complaint or sarcasm, innuendo or fact. Temperamentally, I think I was rather closer to my father than to my brother. Besides, I was then too young to understand what he was saying as clearly as I can now.

As I see it, it was probably his inborn curiosity that led my father willingly to undertake the mission.

In due time my father agreed to call at the blind woman's house. As my father was setting out, the man handed him a large box of cake, together with a ribboned wrapper containing a one-hundred *yen* bill, and had a ricksha rush my father to her house.

Although cramped, the house was neat and cozy enough. In a corner of the veranda was a round wash basin of carved granite, and over the towel-rack new Mitsukoshi towels flapped in the breeze. With its few occupants the house was as silent as a tomb.

When he met the blind woman for the first time in this sunny but tastefully aged room, my father had apparently been at a loss what to say.

"It might sound ridiculous that a talkative fellow like me could be hard up for words. But the truth was I really didn't know what to say, for you see she couldn't see at all."

With this disarming confession my father amused the company.

At last it seemed he revealed the name of the man he represented. As he placed the gift before her, the woman's hands fumbled over the package and she said courteously, "It's really kind of you . . ." But as she happened to touch the envelope attached to the package she picked it up at once, and asked puzzled, "And this?" as if to make sure of it. Being of such a jolly temperament, my father had burst into a roar of laughter, saying, "That, too, is part of the gift. Kindly accept it." But the woman, still holding the knot of the ribbons, then asked again, "Could this possibly be money?"

"Well, yes. Just a small present from Mr. ——. Won't you please accept it?"

At this the woman dropped the envelope to the floor, and directed her closed eyes straight at my father. "Widow as I now am, I was until recently the wife of a respectable man. My children are yet well and strong. No matter what there was between us in the past, if I accept money, I would show myself unworthy of my deceased husband, thanks to whom I am now living in comfort. Please be so good as to return this." And with this she began to weep.

"Perhaps you can imagine how really dumbfounded I was by all this," said my father, glancing around at us. But somehow apparently no one felt like laughing at this. I could not help thinking that the situation must have been hard on even such a seasoned tactician as my father.

"Yet dumbfounded as I was I thought at that moment that Kagekiyo, if a woman, might certainly be something like her. I was really impressed, you know. Why in the world I thought of Kagekiyo was—not just because both are blind—that woman's attitude was . . ."

My father paused, musing. "Yes, I think it is because they both seemed so resolute," said the ruddy-faced guest, who sat

188

diagonally opposite him, as if deciphering a very difficult puzzle.
"Yes of course, in their resoluteness," my father agreed readily. With this his story was over, I thought, and offered as if in
comment on the whole story, "Certainly, it is an interesting
story." Then, my father added, "Ah but not yet. There's still
something to follow. And that is just as interesting. Especially to
a young fellow like Jiro."

17

Thus shattered by the woman's
unexpected display of dignity, he felt obliged to leave. For the
first time, however, she turned on him a sweetly feminine expression and entreated him to stay. She asked exactly when and
where Mr. —— had seen her, and my father had frankly told
the blind woman what had happened at the Yurakuza.

"As I understand it, he was seated right beside you. Although
you may not have noticed, he seemed to have recognized you
from the very start, but since he apparently found it impossible
to address you in the presence of his wife and daughter, he had
to leave without clarifying matters."

And then—for it was the first time my father had ever seen
tears streaming from blind eyes—he inquired, "I hope you will
excuse me for asking, but have you had trouble with your eyes
very long?"

"Six years or so have passed since I lost the use of my eyes.
Yes, it was hardly one year after my husband passed away. And
unlike those born blind, I did have a very hard time of it in the
beginning."

He didn't know what words of comfort to offer. She then revealed that her husband had been a contractor or something of
the sort, and although a big spender in his life-time he nevertheless had left her an adequate bequest. Thus, my father explained,
thanks to that she had been able to live well in independence
even after her loss of sight.

She had a son and daughter, of both of whom she could be
proud. Her son, though obviously without any higher educa-

tion, held a position with a certain firm on the Ginza, and had an income good enough to make him independent. Her daughter, on the other hand, following old urban custom, occupied herself with singing practice and the study of the *samisen*. Thus, everything considered, there seemed nothing to connect her and her old lover, except for one speck of memory glazed on the remote past.

When my father told of the Yurakuza incident the woman said with tear-stained eyes, "Really, there is nothing more wretched than our loss of sight. Don't you think so?" And this seemed to have gone right to my father's heart.

"Well, what—what is Mr. —— doing now?" she asked my father as if seeking to create an image of something in empty space. He had then told her of Mr. ——'s career following his graduation, adding, "He is now quite a personage—not superannuated as I am, for instance."

"Surely, he must have married a fine lady, didn't he?" she inquired gently, apparently oblivious to my father's comment.

"Yes. And he already has four children."

"Ah—but how old is the oldest?"

"Well, let me see. Now perhaps twelve or thirteen, I think—a pretty girl, too."

In silence the woman began a curious counting on her fingers. My father was suddenly frightened at this sight, for he realized what an irreparable blunder he had been guilty of.

But shortly after, the woman said merely, "How nice!" smiling a little pathetically. It was her way of smiling, in fact, that struck my father more sharply than tears or rage would have.

Finally my father gave her his friend's address, saying, "Please go with your daughter to see him. It will be a pleasant experience. It's a pretty nice house. As a matter of fact he has asked me to say that he usually can see you in the evenings."

"It wouldn't be proper for people of our kind to visit so fine a residence," she replied in a moment, frowning. Then for a second she seemed to pause in thought, but spoke out resolutely in a serious tone, "No, I shall not. I would have to decline his invitation. But there is just one thing I want to hear from you. Since we won't see each other again. kindly tell me this one thing, and then we shall part friends, I hope."

18

When the woman had said this, my father, who was rather timid for his age, had apparently been intimidated not a little by the threat which she might be considering.

"Her sightlessness worked in my favor, for she didn't see what sort of confusion I was in," my father added expressly. And this is what she then said:

"As you can doubtless understand, since I lost my sight everything has gone black. Even the sun, the brightest of all things in this world, I can no longer enjoy. When I would like to go out for a little while, I can't do so without troubling my daughter. It makes me feel miserable to think by what fate I am afflicted with such an incurable disease while a great many elderly people can get about without any inconvenience. These sightless eyes do not give me much pain; what is most painful is to know that with both eyes wide-open it's still impossible to fathom another person's intentions."

"Why yes, of course," replied my father, and he added, "Certainly," even though her meaning wasn't at all clear to him. He admitted, in fact, that he had never encountered such a difficult situation. When she heard his vague, noncommittal reply, she seemed to urge agreement as she said emphatically, "Don't you think so?"

"Well yes, there are, I guess, some such cases," said my father.

"If that is all you can say, what's the use of your having come all the way over here at his request?" said the woman. And so my father described how he had been backed to the wall.

At that moment I glanced at my brother's face by chance. And the contrast between his nervously intent eyes and my sister-in-law's lips, around which seemed to play a faint sneer, reminded me suddenly of the strange tension that had for some time been brewing between them. I was also conscious of the odiousness of my own involvement in this tension. Gradually a feeling of uneasiness crept over me as I wondered what reason had prompted my father to choose this particular story, even if he intended mainly to amuse our guests. But it was already too late. My father, quite indifferently, went ahead with his story.

"Still I was in the dark, so I asked her frankly, 'Since I've come all the way over here at his request, if I return without having gotten to the main point, that would be regrettable for him, not to mention you. So please speak your mind freely. Otherwise, it will be very difficult for me to report satisfactorily to him when I return.'"

Then at last she said with a determined look, "Well, then I shall. Since I take it that you are very close to Mr. —— considering the pains you have taken on his behalf." And with this preliminary remark, she unburdened her heart to my father.

It seems that scarcely a week after his marriage promise Mr. —— had decided to break it. Did this decision stem from some turn of events or had he suddenly discovered, after having made the promise, something about her that displeased him? More than anything else, she wanted to find out precisely what had been the truth of this matter.

The woman was devoured by curiosity, and welcomed a chance to uncover this secret which had been buried at the bottom of her old lover's heart for more than twenty years. In fact, to her it was far more painful to suspect that she might have failed to gain the heart of her plighted lover than to have lost her precious eyesight and to have to endure being treated as disabled.

At that point my brother suddenly interrupted to ask, "What kind of answer did you give?" His face appeared to express uncommon compassion rather than ordinary curiosity about the story.

"Well, I had no choice but to say, 'Depend upon it, I can

assure you there was nothing frivolous about him,' " my father rather proudly directed his contrived answer to my brother.

19

"And was she satisfied with that kind of thing?" my brother asked in a way which seemed charged with sheer intensity. Indeed, his tenacious insistence sounded almost obsessive.

"At first she didn't seem satisfied; you see what I've just said was very shaky from the start. To tell the truth, I couldn't give any straight answer since the fellow, as I said a little while ago, was downright naive and all mixed-up. It seems, however, that one fact at least is certain, that once having become involved with her he had become overwhelmed by what he had done."

Apparently disgusted, my brother looked at my father. My father for his part oddly passed both palms over his long cheeks a couple of times.

"Although I'm a bit hesitant to mention such things in your presence . . ." my brother began. And wondering what kind of argument he was going to venture, I listened, ready to try to turn some of its force, if necessary, and so divert it that it would not be an embarrassment to the company. He continued:

"But it seems to me, sir, that a man loves more passionately than does a woman until his desires are gratified. Once he gets what he wants, his love gradually dwindles. On the other hand a woman, once involved, becomes increasingly affectionate toward a man. In view of evolutionist theories and also of actual happenings in life this, I think, is the case. Thus, couldn't we say, following this principle, that the man merely lost interest in the woman and consequently broke off with her?"

"What a strange idea! This is the first time I've even heard such a thing—though that kind of reasoning is too difficult for me as a mere woman. Yes, very interesting."

At this reaction from my sister-in-law I noted a certain unpleasant expression spread over my brother's face. Feeling it better that the guests not become aware of this, I was hurriedly about to say something as a cover-up. However, my father had gotten in ahead of me.

"Well, theoretically you can explain it in various ways. Yes, it may be that he really came to dislike her, but as I see it the fellow was first of all confounded. Besides, as he was cowardly, impulsive and naive he might well have decided to cancel it even if he hadn't come to dislike her."

While giving this reply my father remained unperturbed.

One of the guests, who had his *utai*-libretto on the alcove, then turned to my father, saying:

"Anyway women, I daresay, can be that tenacious. Imagine, harboring a thing like that in her bosom for twenty-some years! Well, I must say you certainly did a charitable deed. If by saying that you could ease her mind, it must have made her very happy."

"Now that's the tact of all human dealings. If everything could be done that way, I am sure it would be most convenient to all parties concerned."

As the other guest took his turn to say this, my father said, "Well, thanks," nervously scratching his head. "To tell the truth, at first, just as I said, it wasn't enough to remove her doubts, to my dismay. But by giving coloring to my story and making up all sorts of wild things, I had somehow convinced her. Anyway it was a tough job." My father seemed a bit elated.

By and by the guests wrapped up their *utai*-librettoes and departed through the dew-laden gate. While the rest of us were chatting my brother, looking glum, went alone into his study. I listened to every step of his slippers which somehow gave off a characteristic chill with their heavy sound. His door closed with a bang.

20

Two or three weeks went by after that and autumn was advancing. The deep-colored amaranths caught my eyes every time I looked out at the garden.

My brother went off to school by ricksha, and when home from school he busied himself in the study. Even we as family members had little chance to see him. When some business turned up it was our wont to go upstairs and knock on his door. We usually found him poring over ponderous-looking tomes or else writing something in his typically minute characters. Sometimes, however, we were surprised to find him hunched over his desk staring vacantly, his cheeks in his hands.

Apparently he was brooding about something. Being a scholar, he naturally enough often engaged in deep contemplation. Yet those who, on opening the door, saw him in this state could hardly wait to get out once the immediate business was over, for they all said they somehow felt a chill. Even my mother, who was closer to him than anyone else, was obviously not at all eager to go to his study.

"Jiro, are all scholars as eccentric as that?"

When I heard this question I felt oddly happy that I was no scholar. But I chuckled and tried to pass it off by saying simply, "O well." My mother then put on a serious look and said, "Jiro, without you this house, I'm afraid, would seem really deserted. But I suppose you had better try to find a nice girl fast and establish your own home." Her implication seemed plain to me —that if only I got out and started a family my brother might possibly be a little more cheerful. I wondered also if he was still entertaining such a queer idea. But as I was already old enough to be independent, and moreover had a position offering an income adequate for the management of a separate house, this idea had in fact occurred more than once to me, nonchalant as I was.

"Of course," I said to my mother, "to leave the house is no problem at all. I might if you say so be gone tomorrow. But as for the question of a wife, it is certainly not my way to find just anyone, no matter who, as if she were a puppy." Since I knew my mother was going to agree, saying, "Of course not . . ." I purposely interrupted her.

"Mother, if you'll excuse me, I would like to talk a little about the state of affairs between Brother and Sister-in-law. Various complicated circumstances aside, the fact that initially I knew her slightly seems to have caused you unnecessary worry; I am sorry for all this. But to come to the root of the matter, it was after all his own fault; acting as if he thought he was better than the rest, he left everything else to others. However precious his time for study, and however important his school lectures, he ought to have thought of his wife, with whom he must live for the rest of his life. For his part, I'm sure, he must have some personal reasons peculiar to his scholarly profession. But in any case his attitude is something we non-scholars can hardly afford to emulate."

While I was rattling away so recklessly, my mother's eyes were beginning to brim with sparkling tears. Shocked upon suddenly noticing this, I stopped.

Perhaps I was too thick-skinned or forward, but whichever the case, it was I rather than any of the others who knocked on his door, the door which they would shun in deference to him. And although the feeling I had on stepping inside his study was a bit unpleasant even for me, in a matter of ten minutes or so, he became as cheerful as anybody else. In fact, I very much prized my own technique for changing my brother's mood, so much so that at times I may have visited his study largely to gratify my vanity. To confess, it was at such a moment of triumph that he caught me, trapped in the jaws of death, so to speak.

21

Now I do not remember distinctly what I was talking about. Perhaps, having been subjected to my brother's knowledge of the history of billiards, I was being shown a Louis XIV copper-plate print of the billiard-board.

I had learned that once in my brother's room it was safest for me to listen obediently to his newly acquired knowledge on such subjects as this. Chatterbox that I was, I myself often, in other fields than his, made a display of my learning by using such terms as Renaissance and Gothic, with a knowing look. For the most part it was my practice to experience just such talk on such

erudite matters and then leave his study. On this occasion, as it
happened, my brother's pet theories on heredity and evolution
had come up following his remarks on the copper-print plate.
Since I probably had nothing to say, I was listening in silence,
when unexpectedly my brother said, "Jiro, you're Father's boy."
"Yes, I am," I said, rather tartly.

"Speaking just between ourselves, don't you think there's
something peculiarly shallow about him?"

That my father, in my brother's opinion, was no more or no
less than that I had long been aware. In this instance, however, I
felt uneasy about how to reply to him.

"Perhaps, but I guess it has nothing to do with what you call
heredity or disposition. It seems to me he is inevitably so, due to
the pressures of present-day Japanese society, which won't let us
be otherwise. The world is full of those far more shallow than
Father. You are perhaps unaware of it, however, since you are
always so preoccupied, spending your time as you do in your
study and at school."

"That I know, too. Exactly as you say. Present-day Japanese
society, and perhaps the same might be said of western society,
works in such a way that only superficial, clever fellows can
live."

Having said this, my brother was silent for a while. Then he
raised his languid eyes.

"However, Jiro, Father's is an inborn disposition, I'm sorry to
say. Not matter in what society, it would be awfully difficult
for him to live in any other way."

Such was the attitude of my brother who, too lofty and yet
too ignorant thanks to his education, was not only treated by the
whole family as an odd fish, but day by day alienated himself
from his own parents. Confronted with this sad fact, in spite of
myself I dropped my head and stared at my knee-caps.

"Jiro, your way is the same as Father's. I can't see any trace of
sincerity in you."

I had the same savage tendency as my brother to become
angered, yet in this instance as I heard his words, somehow I felt
no resentment.

197

"You can lump me with the common frivolous, but when you try to do so with Father, you are really going too far. You're too much alone and shut up in your study, and consequently can make nothing but such biased observations."

"Then shall I give you an example?"

My brother's eyes flashed all of a sudden and involuntarily I held my tongue.

"You remember his story about that blind woman the other day when his *utai*-friends came, don't you? As his friend's emissary, he simply dodged the question that had troubled the woman for twenty-some years. At that time I couldn't help feeling a deep sympathy. But more than that, for I really couldn't feel sympathy for a woman whom I didn't know, I really felt like crying at Father's frivolity. I pitied him . . ."

"If you approach life as a woman does, everything, I'm sure, must seem frivolous."

"Your saying that only proves that you have inherited his bad side—I asked you about Nao, and ever since I've been waiting for your report. But you're pretending ignorance on one pretext or another."

22

"Now I think that's a bit too harsh, don't you, to say I'm pretending ignorance? After all, I've had no chance to speak—nor have I had any need to."

"You have had a chance every day. And you may have no need, but I certainly do. That's why I asked that special favor of you."

There I was stuck. As a matter of fact, since that incident I had tried to avoid the painful meeting with him to talk seriously about his wife. So I tried to sidetrack the conversation.

"No longer do you trust Father; you don't seem to trust me, either, because I am his son. And doesn't that seem to you to contradict what you said in Wakanoura?"

"What?" cross-questioned my brother, sounding a little annoyed.

"You ask what, but surely you must recall that at the time you said, 'I can trust you because you've inherited Father's integrity. That's why I've confided in you and am asking such a favor of you.' "

As I said this I could see that I had checkmated him. Seizing this opportunity, therefore, I declared with special emphasis:

"Since I made the promise, I wouldn't mind in the least telling you all the details about her, right here and now. From the start I thought it so silly I had no intention of speaking about it unless there was such an occasion. Moreover, I knew that even if I did speak the entire matter could be summed up in very few words. As long as you seemed unconcerned I couldn't feel any urgency. That's the sole reason I have kept silent about it till today. But if you still insist on having some sort of report from me as though from a government clerk sent on an official errand, well, what else can I do? At this very moment I am going to tell you exactly what I found. But let me warn you in advance. In my report there will be no such odd fantasy as you are expecting. Because that is only in your head; it exists nowhere else, objectively."

As he heard these words, strangely enough, his face betrayed but the slightest twitch. He remained still, his elbows resting on the desk, and as his eyes were cast down I couldn't quite discern his facial expression. He was a man of reason, to be sure, and at the same time he had a weakness of being easily beaten by the very same reason. Noticing his complexion now turned somewhat pale, I assumed that he had obviously been vanquished by my strong language.

From a cigarette case I took a cigarette and held a match to it. For a moment my attention alternated between the pale-blue smoke creeping from my nostrils and the appearance of my brother's face.

"Jiro," said my brother at last, revealing neither strength nor tension.

"Yes?" I answered—perhaps somewhat haughtily.

"From now on I am not going to ask you anything about Nao."

"I see. Yes—I think that will be better for you, for her, and also for Father. Be a good husband; then, she will be a good wife too," I said, partly trying to balance the defense of my sister-in-law and the admonishment of my brother.

"You fool!" he shouted suddenly. The shout, which must have been audible even downstairs, took me completely by surprise.

"Father's son that you are, you may know how to get on in the world, but you are not cut out for gentlemanly intercourse. Why should I listen to you concerning Nao? You frivolous creature."

At that I suddenly rose from my chair almost unconsciously and walked toward the door.

"How could I trust your report after hearing such a false confession as Father's?"

Feeling this volley of fiery words directed at my back, I closed the door and emerged on the dark landing of the stairs.

23

For a week or so after this I did not meet my brother except at supper. Inasmuch as everyone used to deem it almost my duty to keep the dinner table lively, my sudden silence made for a peculiar bleakness. To those around the table even the friendly chirping of crickets somewhere sounded cold.

In the midst of such a desolate family scene Osada-san continued waiting on us with tray on lap, as if there was nothing in this world to think of but her approaching wedding day. My father, whose gaiety was never dampened regardless of what was going on, kept telling his usual stories as he pleased. But there was no longer any easy reaction. Nor did my father on his part seem to expect any, as far as I could tell.

So only Yoshie could at times induce us to burst into laughter. Every time the conversation paused in a lull of uncertainty, my mother would address Yoshie as a pretext to turn our attention and set us going again. Her unnaturalness then got on my brother's nerves.

Whenever I left the dinner table and came back to my own room I took a long pull on my cigarette, drawing in a long breath.

"Miserable. It's worse than a bunch of strangers dining together. I wonder if other families are as unpleasant as this."

Time after time I made up my mind to leave home at once. When the atmosphere about the table grew too unpleasant Oshige eagerly followed me to my room. At times she began to sob there, without saying a word. Or else she might glare at me bitterly as if to demand why I did not at once apologize to my brother.

Living at home grew more and more intolerable. As indecisive as I was quick-tempered, I nevertheless finally decided to make a break for the time being by renting a room elsewhere. I went to seen Misawa about this. Yet when I told him, "All this has happened because you were sick in bed so long in Osaka," he replied, "On the contrary, it's because you have been hanging around Onao-san too long."

As often as I had met him since returning from Osaka I had never said a word about my sister-in-law. Nor had he mentioned her before either.

In fact, on this occasion—the first time I had ever heard him mention her name—his words seemed to hint at some relation between her and me which could be taken as quite serious or as if poking fun. I fixed my surprised and suspicious eyes on Misawa and, apparently finding indignation there, he said, "Now don't get mad at me." Then he added pacifyingly, "My own peculiar fantasy—to be loved by a demented girl, and even that a dead one—might be safer." As I remained silent, he tugged at my shoulder playfully saying, "What do you say?" Whether he was serious or joking, I could not clearly tell. In either case I did not feel like explaining or justifying anything to him.

However, I did get some information from Misawa about a

couple of suitable rooms, and on the way home I stopped by to inspect a room I was going to take. Upon my return home, I called in my sister before anyone else, and announced, "Taking your advice, I have finally decided to move out of the house." She stared at me quizzically and her expression seemed to indicate that the news was half-expected and half-unexpected.

24

As brother and sister, we were not very intimate. I informed her first of my intention to leave the house out of spite rather than out of affection.

In an instant her eyes were filled with tears, and she replied, "Please do leave the house quickly. In the meantime I'm going to marry whomever I can as quickly as possible."

I kept silent as she continued.

"Once you leave, you won't come back; you're going to marry and establish your own home, aren't you?"

Being put on the spot in this way, I replied, "Of course," and the pent-up tears fell from her eyes onto her lap.

"Why in heaven's name are you crying like that?" I asked, suddenly making my voice gentle, for I was surprised at these wholly unexpected tears.

"Because I'll be left behind all alone . . ."

And this was all I could hear distinctly; the rest was garbled and muffled in her shuddering and continuous sobs.

I lit a cigarette and calmly waited for her to stop crying. Soon she wiped her tears away with her sleeves and rose to leave. Looking at her retreating figure, I suddenly felt sorry for her.

"Oshige, we've been quarrelling with each other constantly. From now on there will be little chance for bickering. Why not shake hands and be friends? Come on now."

And I held my hand out. Rather embarrassed, she hesitated.

I thought it was time to inform both my parents of my intention to leave the house and obtain their consent. Last of all I had to go to my brother and reveal the same news and this was the only painful duty.

It was on the following day, I think, that I disclosed my intention to my mother, who seemed surprised at my sudden decision. "If you left at all, I thought it would be after you had taken a wife—O well, it can't be helped." Then she looked at me pensively. From there I turned to go directly to my father's parlor when she called me back.

"Jiro, even after you leave the house . . ." At that my mother's voice faltered, and as I asked, "What did you say?" she fired a seemingly irrelevant question, "Have you already told your brother about this?"

"No, not yet," I replied.

"I think you'd better tell him yourself. He may be offended if your father or I give him the news."

"Yes, I suppose you're right. I'm going to try to clear things up before I leave."

Then I proceeded to my father's room and found him writing a long letter. He explained:

"The other day another inquiry came from Okada in Osaka about Osada's wedding. Much as I wanted to write an immediate answer, I somehow hadn't gotten around to doing it. So today I finally decided to discharge this overdue task. And I'm doing it now. By the way, let me tell you your character *kei* of the salutation *haikei* is wrong. If you want to simplify it, you ought to write it like this."

One end of the long letter happened to be sticking out toward where I was sitting, and although I looked at the character *kei* sideways I couldn't tell where I had been wrong. While he continued filling the sheet I made mental note of the yellow chrysanthemums arranged in a vase in the alcove, and the scroll-picture hung behind them.

25

Finally, folding the long letter, my father said, "What can I do for you? Money again? If you need money I just don't have it." Then he addressed the letter.

After disclosing my intention very briefly, I wound up with

some such formal courtesy phrase as "For a long time I've been a burden to you, but . . ." My father, however, said simply, "H'm, I see." Then he fixed a stamp at one corner of the envelope and said, "Ring the bell for the maid, will you?" "It's quite all right; I'll have it mailed," I said and took the letter. "Leave your address with your mother," he reminded me. Then he made various comments about the scroll hanging in the alcove.

Thus with only this, I left my father's room. Now I had only to bid goodbye to my brother and sister-in-law. With my brother, I had exchanged few friendly words since the last incident. I had lacked the courage to stand up to him. I was aware that if I had had it, I would have blown up at the time I had fled his abuse. I wasn't the type of fellow who could be easily scared out by fear of something like a plaster bust thrown at his back. But at the moment at least my resentment seemed to have dissipated itself. I had beaten my retreat as silently and effortlessly as a ghost. Thereafter, I just had not been able to bring myself to go and knock at his study door, to apologize candidly to him. So only at the dinner table did I see my brother and his ever-sullen face.

Lately I had hardly talked with my sister-in-law, either. In fact, it might be more proper to say since our return from Osaka than to say lately. For her own use she had a small room furnished with her dresser. But during the day there wasn't much time when she could play with Yoshie alone in that room, for most of the time she was helping my mother in sewing and sundry other housekeeping tasks.

On the morning following the day I had informed both my parents of my future plans, however, I ran into my sister-in-law on the veranda which connected the toilet and the bath.

"Jiro-san, I hear you're going to move to a boarding house. Don't you like your own home?" she asked abruptly. Her manner of speaking indicated that my declaration had already been conveyed to her via my mother.

"Yes, but I've decided to get out for a while," I replied casually.

"That seems wise. Perhaps that will save trouble," she said, staring me in the face, apparently expecting me to offer something additional, but I said nothing.

"And then, you should marry someone soon," it was again she who led. Still I kept silent.

"And the sooner the better," she added. "Shall I find you one?"

"By all means," I spoke out for the first time.

With both corners of her thin lips she smiled a faint, half-scornful half-teasing smile. And deliberately noisy she headed toward the living room.

In silence I gazed at a copper wash basin leaning in the corner of the cement floor between the bath and the toilet. This wash basin, more than two feet in diameter, was so ponderous and huge that I could scarcely lift it. Since my childhood I had always amused myself with the thought that it was used for grown-ups' bathing, and I was quite fascinated by that idea. Now the basin was neglected and grown dusty. Beyond the low sash-door the begonias, another childhood memory, with their annual colors, seemed somehow pathetic. Standing between them I recollected those bygone early autumn days when my brother and I beat down the Chinese date tree which stood in front of the vestibule and ate the dates. Now realizing that, young as I was, behind me stretched a long continuous past of just such innocent memories, I was overwhelmed with the vast changes that had occurred. The contrast was all the more sharp now that, having exchanged unpleasant words with my brother, who had once been such a bully, I was about to leave home.

26

That day, returning home from the office, I asked Oshige if my brother was home. "Not home yet," she answered.

"Is this the day he usually spends running his various errands?" I asked again.

"I'm not sure. Do you want me to go to his study and look up the schedule on his wall?" asked Oshige.

I asked her merely to let me know when he was back, and went to my room without seeing anyone else. I did not bother to change my clothes but lay down as I was. Without willing it, I fell fast asleep and dreamed fitfully. My dream was so fast-changing, so involved that I could hardly have explained to others what it was all about. I was only roused from it by Oshige.

"Big Brother is home now."

On hearing this I rose at once, although my mind was still hazy, still continuing to pursue the dream. From behind me, she suggested, "Perhaps you'd better wash your face before you go." Muddled as my mind was, I couldn't even imagine why that would be necessary.

And I entered his study as I was. My brother was still in his suit. Hearing the door creak, he instantly turned his eyes toward the entrance. Their glitter indicated some anticipation on his part. It was customary for his wife, accompanied by Yoshie, to bring up his everyday kimono when he returned home. I had overheard my mother on occasion advise her, "Do it this way, will you?" Absent-minded as I was at that moment, I could tell from my brother's look that he had been anticipating the appearance of his wife and Yoshie, not just his everyday kimono.

Only because I was really half asleep could I open his door so casually and unannounced, but upon seeing me standing at his threshold my brother didn't show the slightest sign of anger. Quietly he stared at my suited figure; nor did he give any indication that he was about to speak.

"May I have a word with you?" I broke the ice at last.

"Won't you come in," he said calmly. And he sounded as though he harbored no hard feelings about our last meeting. He even took the trouble to put a chair in front of me and motion me to sit down.

I avoided sitting down, however; instead, merely resting my hands on the back of the chair, I stated something more or less identical to what I had already said to both my parents. Like a respectable scholar he listened calmly. As I finished my statement, he said, "Well, sit down, anyway, won't you"—as though neither delighted nor saddened, he might be receiving a familiar guest.

He was dressed in a black dress coat, puffing at a cigar which did not have a very good aroma.

"Certainly, you may leave if you feel you must. You're old enough now to be doing for yourself," he said and kept smoking away for a while. He then said, "But I wouldn't want anyone to think that I pushed you out of the house."

"Not at all, since I am leaving at my own convenience," I replied.

My head, fogged with sleep, became gradually clearer, and now anxious to withdraw from my brother's presence as soon as possible, I glanced back at the entrance. He continued.

"Right now Nao and Yoshie are in the bath, I gather. So there is no chance of interruption. Don't be restless. Turn on the light. Take your time and speak."

I rose and flipped the light switch. Then, picking up a cigar, the same brand as my brother's, I lit it.

"Eight *sen* apiece. Very poor stuff, isn't it?" he said.

27

"But when do you plan to leave?" my brother asked.

"About next Saturday, I think," I answered.

"Just yourself, I suppose?" he asked again.

And at this odd question I was stupefied for a moment, only staring at his face. I couldn't quite decide whether this was deliberate, spiteful sarcasm or was prompted by some sort of disorder in his brain. So long as I was undecided, I could not make up my mind which tack to take.

His speech was always loaded with much irony. But I felt very strongly also that his attitude was but the product of his intelligence which was a great deal more sensitive than ours; otherwise, though, there was no intentional malice. Yet his words, striking my eardrums now, continued to echo hotly there.

Staring at my face, he chuckled and even in that laugh I perceived a flash of hysteria.

"Just yourself, no doubt. You have no need to take anyone with you."

"Of course not. All I want is to be alone and get some fresh air."

"Fresh air, that's what I would like to get too. But in the breadth of Tokyo there isn't any place where I can get fresh air."

In a way I pitied my brother for his self-imposed isolation. And I also felt some sympathy for his over-wrought nerves.

"How about travel? That may freshen you up a little bit."

As I said this, he pulled a watch out of his vest pocket.

"We still have some time before dinner, don't we?" Then he sat down once again and said, still studying my face, "From now on there will be little chance to talk with each other. Let's have a chat here until dinner is ready."

Although I said, "Surely," I was by no means enthusiastic about the prospect. What's more, I could think of no topic we might chat about. Then suddenly my brother asked, "You know the love affair of Paolo and Francesca, don't you?" It sounded vaguely familiar and yet I couldn't for the moment place it, so that I made no immediate answer.

My brother went on to explain that it was a tragic story about two lovers, Francesca and her brother-in-law Paolo, who carried on their clandestine love affair behind the husband's back only to be discovered finally and murdered by him. This story, I was further told, appears in Dante's *Divine Comedy*, but rather than focusing sympathetically on the plot of this sad story I immediately was suspicious about my brother's probable implication. I could scarcely control a feeling of disgust therefore as I met his stare wreathed in clouds of foul smoke as he related this Italian story of the thirteenth or fourteenth century. Finishing the story, however, he fired a question at me which caught me completely off guard.

"Jiro, why does the world forget the name of the wronged

husband, and remember only those two names, Paolo and Francesca? I wonder if you can tell me why."

"Just as in the case of Sankatsu and Hanshichi, I guess," I said reluctantly. Apparently he was a bit puzzled by my unexpected answer. However, at last he spoke up.

"Perhaps, but this is the way I explain it. The natural love of those lovers is, after all, more sacred than the man-made relationship of husband and wife. Consequently, as time passes we are left only with a ringing voice, that voice which admires the law of vast nature transcending the rigid moral code set up by a narrow-minded society, aren't we? At the moment, then, all of us side with morality and accuse the lovers of adultery, to be sure. However, it is so because our sense of morality is meant only to regulate the moment when that affair becomes known; it is, as it were, a passing shower; and what is left behind is only the blue sky and the bright sun, that is, Paolo and Francesca. Now don't you think so?"

28

At my age and being as I was, I would normally have seconded my brother's theory with all my heart. But in this particular instance I could not see his point; I could not fathom his reason for discussing the love of Paolo and Francesca; I could not understand why he was elaborating on the immortal fame of the two lovers, so that my natural curiosity was altogether dulled by a feeling of unpleasantness and frustration. Hearing him voice such provocative innuendo I felt like demanding, "So what, just what are you implying?"

"Jiro, that's why those who side with morality may surely be temporary victors, but they are losers for all eternity while those who follow nature may be temporary losers, but they will be eternal victors."

I said nothing.

"And I for one can't even be a temporary victor. For all eternity I am a loser of course."

Still I made no answer.

"Whatever tricks you may learn, you must be a poor wrestler when you don't have any strength. In fact, you don't even have to worry about mere form. If only you have strength you will win, that's certain. Yes, you are bound to win. All that is mysterious in the art of wrestling is but petty human tricks, whereas physical strength is nature's gift . . ."

In this manner my brother went on to discuss his futile philosophy, futile because he was only tilting with a windmill. And I felt myself imprisoned in his eery fog as I sat before him. Indeed, it was far more punishing to attempt to brush aside this dense fog than it would have been to bite through a thick hawser.

"Jiro," said he at last, "You are going to remain a victor, in the present, in the future, and throughout all eternity, aren't you?"

Quick-tempered as I was, I was not so reckless as my brother. In particular I then had to consider, first of all, whether he was altogether sane or whether, as a result of over-excitement, he was possibly in a sort of momentary abnormal mental condition. Furthermore, I was made all the more acutely conscious of the fact that in any case I was being held responsible for producing this mental agitation in him.

Without venturing a reply, I simply listened. I even wondered if it wouldn't be a real relief to him to divorce his wife, of whom he harbored such serious doubts.

But just then my sister-in-law came up the stairs, carrying his everyday kimono and leading Yoshie by the hand.

As she appeared in the doorway her normally pallid cheeks, probably fresh out of the bath, were flushed pleasantly pinkish, her fine skin seemed alluringly smooth.

She glanced at my face and said nothing to me, but she greeted my brother.

"I'm awfully sorry for being so late—you must really be uncomfortable. As we were in the bath I couldn't bring your kimono right away."

Then she directed Yoshie, who stood beside her, "Say to

Daddy 'Welcome home.'" Yoshie, as her mother instructed, dropped her head and mumbled "Welcome home."

For a long time I had not seen my sister-in-law reveal such wifely charms to my brother; nor had I before seen his eyes shine as his mood was softened by this winsomeness. I knew that in the presence of others he seemed a man of extremely strong self-respect. But since I had grown up with him from childhood, it was easy enough for me to guess what was passing through his mind.

Concealing my relief at such an unexpected rescue, I left his room. As I was leaving my sister-in-law nodded slightly to me as though greeting an inferior stranger; rarely indeed had she treated me as coolly as that.

29

Two or three days later I at last left the house, an old history-filled house wherein lived both my parents, my brother and sister. Yet upon leaving I felt almost no sentiment to speak of, and I rather resented the cheerless appearance of my mother and sister sorrowing over our parting, for I somehow felt they were trying to restrict my freedom of action.

Only my sister-in-law showed me her lonely smile as she said, "Are you all set to leave? Well—goodbye, then. But do drop in occasionally."

This single word of courtesy cheered me up somewhat, especially after seeing the glum faces of my mother and sister.

After moving to my lodgings I went to the office at Yurakucho every day as usual. Misawa had found me a place there. The office was run by an uncle of H (my brother's colleague), who was Misawa's former reference. The man was an expert in his field, had been a longtime resident abroad, and also was an old hand at home. He had the odd habit of plunging his fingers into his gray-streaked hair and vigorously rubbing dandruff off his head; and sometimes when sitting face to face around a brazier, the rest of us were annoyed by the odd odor which then came from the fire.

"What is your brother working on nowadays?" he often asked me. And I would give a very general answer, "Well, he is shut up alone in his study doing something."

One morning when the Phoenix trees had shed all their leaves, he caught me unexpectedly and again asked, "How has your brother been lately?" Yet much as I was accustomed to such questions from him, it came as a surprise attack that I simply didn't know how to meet.

"How is his health?" he asked again.

"It doesn't seem very good," I replied.

"He ought to take a little more care. Overwork won't do him any good, you know," he said.

I stared him in the face, and his expression conveyed a certain seriousness.

Only once had I visited the house since I had moved out. On that occasion I had called my mother aside and asked her about my brother.

"Lately he looks somewhat better," she said. "Sometimes he even goes out in the backyard and pushes Yoshie on the swing . . ." This eased my mind somewhat, and from that time till this moment I had not tried to contact anyone at home.

During the lunch hour, as I was eating part of the *à la carte* meal which I had had delivered, Mr. B, the boss, again asked, "Is it true that you have taken a room somewhere?" I replied simply, "Yes."

"Why? Wouldn't your spacious house be more convenient? Or is there some trouble?"

I was hesitant and gave a very evasive answer. The piece of bread which I had just swallowed felt suddenly dry and hard in my throat.

"It may be more carefree to live alone though, than to huddle together . . . By the way you are still single, aren't you? Well, how do you feel about getting married and settling down?"

Even to this remark I couldn't reply as readily as usual.

"You seem to have the blues today," and having said this, Mr. B changed the topic and began a silly and totally irrelevant chat with the others. As for me, only half listening to the laughter around me, I sat in silence and stared at the tea leaves floating erect in my cup, as though they might foreshadow something, and wondered if perhaps I was the one who had grown jumpy lately. That is, I considered the possibility that something might have gone wrong with my head because of my solitary life at my lodgings. I made up my mind that when I returned home that evening I would call on Misawa for the first time in a long while and have a chat.

30

When I was shown up to Misawa's room that evening I felt envious to see him comfortably sitting cross-legged in his room with its bright lamp and warm brazier, altogether insulating him from the early winter chill outside. Although from his complexion and physique I had already observed that his chronic condition had gradually been improving as the autumn wind had increased, that he should be so relaxed, in such contrast to my uneasiness, was something I had not expected. Recalling those bygone days when at the hospital in Osaka he spent hours looking up restlessly at the high warm sky, I had the feeling that we had almost changed places with each other.

Having lost his father recently, he had now established himself as master of the household. Even when Mr. B had offered him a position through Mr. H, Misawa had passed this kind offer over to me, perhaps out of unselfish goodwill or perhaps out of mere fastidious choosiness.

I looked around his brightly lighted room and chatted for a while about the elegant etchings and water-color paintings which covered all the walls. But in hardly ten minutes such discussion of art had exhausted itself.

Then suddenly Misawa spoke out, "By the way, your brother." At the mention of my brother I couldn't but be startled. "Again!" I thought.

"What about him?"

"Oh, nothing special, but . . ."

Saying this much, Misawa looked at me, and I couldn't help linking mentally his words and Mr. B's of that morning.

"Don't stop halfway like that. Out with it if you're going to talk at all. What do you have to say about my brother? Just this morning Mr. B asked me the same kind of question and I'm rather puzzled."

Misawa stared intently at my impatient face, and then said, "All right, I'll let you have it. Mr. B's story, like mine, I guess, has come from the same Mr. H. And Mr. H's story, I hear, in turn came from the students. As I get it, your brother's lectures are normally lucid, fresh and very popular with his students; but frequently there pop up in those lucid lectures one or two points which are not quite consistent with the context. And when students ask him about these your brother, by nature an honest man, tries over and over again to explain them but still can't make himself understood. Finally he presses his hand to his forehead, saying, 'Of late something seems to be wrong with me, my head . . .' And then he stands still for a long time looking vacantly out the window. So the students withdraw, promising that they will save their questions for the next time. And it seems this has happened a few times. Mr. H said to me, 'Next time you see Jiro Nagano you'd better tell him about this. His brother's may turn out to be a case of serious nervous breakdown.' But I had forgotten it completely until this minute when I saw you."

"When was this noticed?" I asked restlessly.

"At about the time when you moved to your lodgings, but I don't remember exactly when."

"Is he still that way?"

Looking at my tense face, Misawa said consolingly, "O no. It seemed to be merely a temporary thing. Nowadays he isn't any different from his usual self—or so Mr. H told me a couple of days ago. So you may be easy about it. But . . ."

My mind flashed back to that hardly forgettable interview with my brother at the time when I left home. I felt helpless and

frightened as I wondered if my suspicion at that moment had
not been confirmed by this trouble at school.

31

I deliberately put thoughts of
my brother out of my mind, and in doing so I remembered the
demented girl about whom Misawa had spoken at the hotel in
Osaka.

"Were you in time for that girl's memorial service?" I asked.

"Yes, I was in time all right. Yet her parents were really rude
and disgusting," he said as harshly as if lashing out with his fist.
I was startled at this and asked for some further explanation.

It seemed that, representing his family, Misawa had visited
her family cemetery in the precinct of the Honganji Temple in
Tsukiji that day. After a long prayer had been read in the
somber inner temple, Misawa, among other guests, offered a
wreath of incense before her white mortuary tablet. According
to him, it was doubtful that any other person bowed before the
soul of this beautiful, young woman with as sincere a feeling as
he had.

"Her parents and relatives were so indifferent that they
seemed to be merely observing a quiet festival. I, a stranger, was
the only one who shed genuine tears."

Actually, Misawa's fuming about this seemed a bit comical to
me, yet I nodded sympathetically. Misawa continued, "I couldn't
possibly be angry if that was all there was to it. But what
followed made me mad."

After the memorial service, as was customary on such an occasion, he was invited to a certain restaurant near the temple.
During the meal her parents, while talking to him, began to
make certain sly insinuations. At first, since Misawa bore no ill
feeling, he failed to catch the innuendo, but in the course of the
conversation he at last came to see what they were getting at.

"What could be more ridiculous? Frankly it was that I had
been the cause of the girl's misfortune, and also her dementia.

Moreover, they were inclined to believe that the husband who had divorced her was not at all responsible."

"What could have made them think so? It seems ridiculous. Perhaps you misunderstood," I suggested.

"Misunderstood?" he said loudly, and I became aware that I had better hold my tongue. Yet Misawa wouldn't stop enumerating her parents' stupidities; nor would he stop denouncing her former husband's frivolity.

"Why then hadn't they let me marry her in the first place?" At last he said: "Merely for the sake of money and social status they . . ."

"Did you ever propose?" I interrupted.

"No," he replied. "Because it was after her mind had snapped I began to—that a vision of her large moist eyes began to recur to my mind. Yes, it was after she had started her habit of bidding me come home early."

As he said this he still seemed to be envisioning her large, beautiful eyes. Indeed, his tightly closed mouth bespoke his firm determination, a determination to surmount any difficulties, should she be still alive, to wrest her forever from her stupid parents and her frivolous husband, and to clasp her fast in his own arms.

But now my imagination switched from the beautiful-eyed woman back to my own brother whom I was trying to forget. And the more the mad fury which had shattered her mind burst on my ears in the telling, the more I became worried about my brother. On the train to Wakayama he had declared that the girl really loved Misawa, and even ventured as his reason for it that her mental disorder had now freed her from any normal scruples. I began to see that it was possible that my brother might wish his wife to suffer from such insanity so that she might also lay bare her inmost thoughts which perplexed him. But to outsiders, he himself might rather seem to be becoming insane. Indeed, with his mind deranged as a result of his nervous breakdown, he might go wild and rave through the house shouting all kinds of terrifying things.

So involved in my own thought, I had no time to spend in looking at Misawa.

32

Earlier I had promised, at my mother's request, to go to Misawa, at the first opportunity, to sound him out about whether he would be interested in marrying Oshige or not. That evening, however, I could not bring myself to do so. Unaware of my own feelings, he urged me to think about marriage. Since my head was neither calm nor clear, I was unable to make any warm response. I fumbled through a noncommittal reply and left his house. Outside, winds clashed and high up in the sky stars twinkled, seeming to gather their powder-tiny strength as resistance against the wind. With hands folded over my lonely heart, I returned to my lodgings where I at once slipped into my frigid bed.

Two or three days went by. I was still uneasy about my brother and I was constantly assailed by conflicting thoughts. At last I went over to Bancho, but reluctant to face him I did not go upstairs. I chatted as casually as a friendly visitor would with my mother and the others. The pleasure of my family circle without my brother made me feel more relaxed and warmer.

Before taking my leave I called my mother to the adjoining room for a moment and inquired about my brother. She was glad to tell me that his nerves had now calmed down considerably. Although her words did ease my mind, I was rather concerned about the possibility of some abnormality somewhere which might have escaped her notice. Even so, I could not summon up the nerve to go and test him. Nor could I tell her Misawa's story that his lectures had shown temporary though strange lapses.

Although I had nothing more to say, I still stood absently and bleakly in the dark behind the sliding panels. Nor did my mother, still facing me, depart but she seemed to realize the need to say something.

"The other day, though, when he had a slight cold he said something in his delirium," she offered.

"What did he say?" I asked.

But she dismissed my question by saying, "It was just because of his fever—nothing to worry about."

"Did he have that high a fever?" I shifted.

"His temperature was running no higher than 38° or 38.5° but I thought it couldn't be and asked the doctor. Well, he said that when anyone suffers from nervous breakdown even a slight fever can affect his brain."

Although I had not even a rudimentary knowledge of medicine this new information was enough to make me knit my brows, in spite of myself. In the dark my mother couldn't see my face.

"But when we cooled his head with ice the fever left him immediately—much to our relief . . ."

Yet still anxious to find out what he had said in his delirium before the fever had left him, I remained standing there hopefully behind the chilly panels.

The adjoining room was lighted brightly, and every time my father made fun of Yoshie everyone had a merry laugh. Through the laughing voices, however, my father suddenly called me, "Hey, Jiro."

"Hey, Jiro," he repeated aloud, "You are asking your mother for pocket money again, aren't you? Otsuna, don't be so easily taken in by his tales."

"Nothing of the kind, I tell you," I said equally aloud.

"Then, what is it you're whispering about with your mother there in the darkness like that? Stick your face out here where it's light."

At this everyone in the bright room burst into gales of laughter. At my father's insistence I said, "Yes, I certainly will," and had to appear before the rest, without having found out from my mother what I wanted to know.

33

For some time thereafter, when I saw Mr. B or called on Misawa, nothing about my brother came up in conversation. Feeling a bit easier, I tried to forget about my family as best I could. But overwhelmed by the dullness and solitariness of my room I spent a great deal of time at Misawa's or else dragged him out in search of amusement.

Misawa never tired of talking about the demented girl. And every time I listened to his account of his weird affair with her I was annoyed to find myself thinking of my brother and sister-in-law. By look and words—something like "what again!"—I often showed my annoyance. But Misawa on his part remained unyielding as ever.

"Out with your story. Then we'll be even," he jeered at me. We sometimes came near quarrelling in the street.

Such was the way this demented girl haunted Misawa—like a shadow—that there was little chance for me to speak of my sister, as I had promised my mother. Oshige's looks were probably well above average, I thought, even though I was no great admirer of her. But unfortunately her looks were altogether different from those of the girl who clearly had meant so much to him.

Showing none of my reserve, Misawa freely recommended a candidate to me. "Wouldn't you like to just take a look at her somewhere, one of these days?" he once suggested. And noncommittal as I was in the beginning, I finally came around to thinking seriously of meeting her. But Misawa began postponing the date of our interview further and further under the pretext of its not being opportune, until at last I got tired of the whole business and her vision itself faded away.

On the other hand, the plans for Osada-san's marriage were materializing. Old as she was, she was surely the naivest of all at home. She had no outstanding qualities to speak of, but easily blushed at whatever we might say—in a charming way peculiarly her own.

Late at night when I came back with Misawa along the cold street and slipped into my icy bed, I often remembered Osada-san. Pulling her equally icy covers over her head, warmed by her dream of the future, she might, at that very moment, be burying her dreamily smiling face half in the velvet band of the quilt.

Two or three days before the wedding, Okada and Sano alighted at Shimbashi Station, shivering from the ice-dripping train. I had been sent there to meet them; Okada, spotting me, shouted, "Hullo," and then, "Jiro-san, you are jolly as ever." Okada never seemed aware of his own jollity.

On the following day when I went over to Bancho the whole house was noisy and lively, thanks to Okada. My brother, probably making an exception on this occasion, kept quiet and seemed to have abandoned his usual wry mask as he also was drawn into the maelstrom.

"Jiro-san, it's really silly to have rented a room away from home. That only makes the house seem lonely, doesn't it, Onao-san?" he urged my sister-in-law's support. But at the moment she remained mute, with an odd expression on her face. I didn't know what to say either, although my brother seemed to take notice of nothing. Okada, already tipsy, rattled on freely.

"I don't think, though, that Ichiro-san is right either. Look, there isn't any sense in locking yourself up in your room and studying all the time. Anyone with your educational background is in no danger of coming off as a loser, believe me. Also Onao-san and Aunt, not to mention Jiro-san, are not quite right. Though Ichiro-san says he doesn't care for anything but his study, here he has gladly come downstairs as soon as I decided to drag him down, and we have had an interesting talk. Isn't that so, Ichiro-san?"

Saying this, Okada looked at my brother who remained silent, grinning feebly.

"Well, Aunt?"

My mother also remained silent.

"Well, Oshige-san?"

Apparently he was going to ask around one by one until he could get a favorable response.

"Okada-san," Oshige said finally, "you don't seem to be cured of your chattering sickness, no matter how old you get. What a noise you're making!" And this made everyone laugh, somewhat to my relief.

34

"Uncle, will you come in for a second?" From the adjoining room Yoshie motioned me with her tiny hand. As I rose saying, "What is it?" and went over, she dragged a large cloth carry-all from somewhere and said, proudly looking at me, "This is Osada-san's. Would you like to see what's in it?"

She then drew a velvet-covered square box from the cloth pouch. I picked up a pearl ring from the box and looked at it curiously. "This one, too," Yoshie said, producing a maroon box this time; in it was a plain gold ring which I had brought Osada-san in appreciation for the laundry and other kindnesses she had done for me. Yoshie said again, "This too," and held up a figured satin purse woven all over in gold with figures of chrysanthemums. Next she displayed a fairly large oblong box of paulownia-wood; it contained a decorative metal band for an *obi* made up of ivy leaves worked in gold, copper, and silver. At last Yoshie, pointing out a comb and an ornamental bar for the hair, explained, "This is a *ranko* imitation, not real tortoise-shell. The real tortoise-shell was so expensive that she gave it up." I did not know the word *ranko*. Nor did Yoshie. But being a girl, she said, "This is the cheapest one, even cheaper than *shibobari*. Because it's glued together with egg white." When I asked, "What parts and how do you glue it with egg white?" she said affectedly, "Oh I don't know that sort of thing," and quickly dragged the cloth-pouch back into the adjoining room.

My mother showed me the garment Osada-san would be wearing on her wedding day. It was of sky-blue silk crepe tinted with pale purple. It had ivy designs and the skirt was patterned with bamboo.

"Isn't this a bit too quiet for her age?" I asked my mother.

"But otherwise it would be too expensive," was her reply. Then she added, "Even this, you know, cost twenty-five *yen*," which was enough to shock an ignoramus like me. About three rolls of the undyed material had been acquired from a Kyoto weaver who brought it on his back the previous spring, and I was told it had been kept until recently in a dresser.

For some time Osada-san refused to show up in company. She probably felt awkward, I thought, and wishing to witness her embarrassment personally I asked my mother, "Where is Osada-san?" At that moment my brother said, "O, I'm forgetting. I meant to say something to Osada-san."

Everyone looked puzzled; and across my sister-in-law's thin lips flashed an intensely derisive smile. Altogether regardless of the others, my brother said to Okada, "Will you excuse me a moment," and went upstairs. Soon after his footsteps died away, Osada-san came to the door of our room and made a polite bow to Okada.

As Okada invited her in, she said, "Right now I must go up to the study; I'll be back a little later," and rose. Noticing her flushed face we, perhaps out of pity, did not even try to detain her.

Although my brother's footsteps going upstairs had not been heavy, we had heard the slapping sound of his slippers quite distinctly. Because Osada-san's feet were bare, and also perhaps in keeping with her feminine modesty, she was completely silent as she ascended, and I could not hear even the creak of the door up there when it was opened and closed.

During the half hour that the talk lasted upstairs, my sister-in-law, displaying none of her usual indifference, talked and laughed more cheerfully than the others. Nevertheless, I could well see that behind all this there was a strained attempt to conceal her displeasure. Okada remained nonchalant.

As Osada-san was passing by our room after her talk with my brother, I noticed her footsteps and quickly went out in the hallway as if on an errand. When we met, her face was still red and she looked quite abashed. With eyes lowered, she slipped by me and I thought I caught the glint of tears in her eyes. But what kind of talk she had alone with my brother in his study I still do not know. I rather imagine, in fact, that no one except the two involved yet knows the details about it.

35

My parents asked me to attend Osada-san's wedding ceremony as one of her relatives. It happened to be a drizzly day, the dreary weather hardly suitable for a wedding. I rose earlier than usual, and when I arrived at Bancho, the bride's trousseau was scattered all over the eight-mat room.

Walking back from the toilet, I happened to peep through the half-open sash-door of the dressing room and caught a glimpse of Osada-san preparing herself. Just as I looked in I heard her say, "O, please don't touch that," and I guessed that Yoshie was, half in jest, engaged in some sort of mischief. Much as I was tempted to join Yoshie in this fun making, considering the occasion I refrained from it and returned to the living room.

When a little later I went back to the eight-mat room they were all busily helping her into her wedding dress. "Look," Yoshie was shouting around, "Osada-san has painted her hands, too." As a matter of fact her hands and feet were an even darker red than her face.

"So you've painted yourself all white. It's not fair to cheat the groom," my father kidded her.

"I'll bet he will be surprised tomorrow morning," my mother laughed. Osada-san, too, grinned with her face averted. She had had her first *shimada* coiffure, which somehow struck me as un-expectedly fresh.

"It must be uncomfortable for her to wear such heavy orna-ments on top of her head," I commented. "Well, no matter how heavy, at least once in a lifetime . . ." said my mother as she fussed nervously with the fit of her own black-crested coat and white collar. As for Osada-san's *obi*, my sister-in-law went be-hind her and tightened it up.

My brother paced up and down the wide veranda smoking one of his reeking cigars. Every now and then he looked into the room where we were with such an equivocal attitude that one might think that either he took no interest whatever in the wed-ding or he was inwardly exercising his habitual criticism. He merely paused at the door for a second, never attempting to step inside, and never betraying any impatience. He was wearing his frock coat and silk hat.

Finally it was time for us to leave and my father, choosing the cleanest ricksha, helped Osada-san in. The ceremony was scheduled for eleven o'clock, and we were already a little late. Okada was waiting for us, at the steps leading to the Grand Shrine at Hibiya. As we all crowded into the lounge we found the bridegroom all alone seated on a chair and looking like an ornamental piece held in pledge. As he rose and greeted us individually I looked around the lounge, at its tables, its carpets, its unstained wooden ceiling, etc. At the farther end of the room hung a bamboo blind screening something which I couldn't clearly discern since it was hidden in the darkness of the inner section. In front of the blind stood a pair of gold-leafed folding screens covered with the traditionally propitious painting of cranes and waves.

A man fully dressed in *haori* and *hakama* came out and explained the order of the processional: first the bride with the go-between's wife, then the bridegroom with the go-between, and after them the relatives. But as Okane-san had not accompanied Okada, the very person to serve as the go-between, he consulted my father. "I'm sorry to trouble you," Okada stated, "but would Ichiro-san and Onao-san mind taking the parts on this occasion?" My father replied simply, "I guess that will be all right." My sister-in-law said as always, "Whatever you will," and was echoed by my brother, who then added, "But it would be somewhat unfair to the bride and groom to have an odd couple like us serving as their go-betweens."

"Unfair? You'll do more honor to them than I. Isn't that right, Jiro-san?" said Okada in his usual bantering manner. Obviously my brother wanted to elaborate, but on second thought said presently, "Then, I'll assume this big burden for the first time in my life, though I confess I know nothing about the job." "You'll have no trouble, since they tell you exactly what to do. In fact, everything is so arranged that you really don't have to do anything," my father explained.

36

While crossing the arched bridge we momentarily stopped as someone ahead of us was blocked by something. Seizing on the chance I pulled the tail of Okada's coat.

"You are really easy-going," I said.

"What do you mean?"

He seemed totally unaware of his own carelessness in having failed, as go-between, to bring his wife. When I told him this, he replied, scratching his head, "As a matter of fact I meant to bring her with me, but well, I thought I could muddle through . . ."

Crossing the bridge we came to the entrance of the interior part. There sitting before the completely mirrored wall the bride was washing her hands in the black-lacquered basin. When I stood on tiptoe and saw her figure from behind, I realized what had kept us waiting, and I nearly burst into laughter. A dipperful of holy water was now ruthlessly restoring her hands, which had been painted over with such care, to their natural dark red.

On either side of the inner shrine was a room. My brother accompanied by Sano entered the one on the right, and my sister-in-law with Osada-san entered the one on the left. Then emerging from both right and left, they took their seats. My brother and his wife were very serious, facing each other. Needless to say the bride and groom were very serious also as they sat solemnly face to face.

Facing the altar, the rest of us sat in rows at the back of the room and looked quietly at those two couples representing two very different phases, at the nicely painted drums, and at the bamboo blind which seemed mysteriously to conceal something.

My brother, whatever may have been on his mind, must have seemed to a casual observer in no way different from his normal self; his wife was of course as calm as usual, without any affected airs.

They were a couple who had already in the past several years come, in their own way, through a socially important experience called matrimony. And their own experience as part of human history was, to themselves, probably something precious that could not be repeated. Yet viewed from either side it seemed far from honey-sweet. Would this couple with such a bitter experience impose a share of their not very happy fate on these young people and create another unhappy couple?

My brother was a scholar, but also he was a man of sentiment. It seemed likely that behind his pale forehead such thoughts must have drifted, or perhaps he was thinking about even more profound things. Or even as he sat, probably cursing all marriages, he at the same time savored the comedy and tragedy of the role of go-between requiring the bride and groom to hold their hands together for their pledge.

Anyway, he sat solemnly as did his wife, Sano, and Osada-san. The ceremony started though we heard that one of the shrine maidens had had to retire halfway during the proceedings due to a stomachache, and her part was taken over by an assistant.

"It's quieter than at Big Brother's wedding, isn't it?" whispered Oshige, who was sitting beside me. And I recalled that that time there had been, besides reed-organs and drums, a procession of shrine maidens winding back and forth—radiant as fluttering butterflies.

"When you marry we'll make it as gay as at that time," I promised Oshige, who laughed.

Following the ceremony, when we returned to the lounge, Osada-san, while we were all standing, carefully placed her hands on the carpet and humbly thanked us for our past kindness, her eyes brimming with tears.

The bride and bridegroom, with Okada, left immediately for Osaka by the noon train. After we said good-bye on the rainy platform to Osada-san who was going to honeymoon for a couple of days in Hakone, I parted with my family and returned alone to my lodgings. Homeward bound I thought of my own marriage which must come inevitably—as if it might be one of the unhappy mysteries of life.

37

Even after Osada-san had disappeared as though carried off, the house had its usual atmosphere. As I now see it, Osada-san probably had been the most easy-going of all. After her ten-year-long stay with us, content with her dubious position as domestic, sweeping, washing and cleaning from morn till evening, perfectly calm and accepting, she had left Tokyo with Sano on a dismal rainy day. The working of her mind seemed as clear-cut and mechanical as her own repetitions and familiar daily chores had been. Even when our dinner table, the high tide of our happy family circle, had been temporarily oppressed by a greyish atmosphere it was Osada-san alone who, calm as ever, had waited on us with her tray poised. Shortly before her wedding day, she had been called into my brother's study and had come out with reddened face and teary eyes. I had no clue as to what her tears and blushes might signify regarding her future but, judging from her usual disposition, the impact was not likely to last long.

Just as Osada-san had gone, so had winter gone; it might be more proper to say that the exit of the season had happened without event. Spots staining the snow, winds shaking dry branches, ice covering the wash-basin—all passed unnoticed after having projected their annual image with such regularity. While nature moved through her cold cycle the house at Bancho remained inert. Somehow its inhabitants managed to maintain their old relationship.

Nor was there any change in my position. Only Oshige now and then visited me, partly for fun—and complained. Every time she came she asked, "I wonder how Osada-san is doing."

"You wonder how she is doing? Hasn't she written you?"

"Of course she has."

About Osada-san's married life she had far more information, I discovered, than I did.

Every time she came I made sure to inquire about my brother. "And how is he?"

"Are you asking how he is? You are to blame if you don't know; when you come to the house you always leave without seeing him."

"Oh, I'm not trying to avoid him. It's just that every time I go he is always out. Can I help that?"

"Don't try to tell me such stories, please. Last time you came you slipped away without going up to his study, didn't you?"

More honest than I was, Oshige turned red as she spoke. Actually ever since that incident I had wanted to re-establish familiar relations with my brother, but this was not possible, for he seemed somehow so unapproachable. Just as she pointed out, more often than not, I got away without seeing him even when I certainly had the opportunity.

Cornered by Oshige, I tried to laugh it all off as if surrendering without resistance, while stroking my short moustache deliberately or, at times, lighting a cigarette and puffing out tactical smoke.

At other times it was Oshige herself who said, "He is really odd. Now I can see very well it was perfectly natural for you to quarrel with him and leave the house." Although she surprised me with this point-blank assault, I felt inwardly happy at the thought I had won one more friend to my side. But I was not so childish as to echo her remarks openly; nor, on the other hand, did I pretend to rebuke her. After she was gone, however, whatever had been on my mind till then was turned upside down and I grew ever more concerned about the impact of my brother's mental agitation on those around him. I often felt more sorry than ever for the fact that he had apparently allowed himself to become immersed in books while alienating himself from living things.

38

My mother also came to see me once or twice. On her first visit she was quite cheerful and seemed interested in getting all sorts of information with which I myself wasn't very familiar—such as, where a law-school graduate in the next room was working and what he was doing. On that occasion she said nothing about how things were at home, but merely said, "Lately a flu has been prevalent in many places. So take good care of yourself. Your father has had a sore throat for two or three days, and is using wet dressings on it." Cautioning me, my mother left, and after she had gone I had no time to think of the problem of my brother and his wife. In fact, oblivious to their existence I had a good bath and ate a hearty dinner.

On her second visit, however, my mother's mood was a little different. Since our return from Osaka, and especially since I had moved away from home, she seemed to avoid criticizing my sister-in-law in my presence. For my part, perhaps due to some guilty feeling, I refrained from mentioning her name. Yet it was my mother, an extremely cautious person, who suddenly asked, "Jiro, just between you and me, is Onao good-natured or ill-natured?" Instantly I decided that something was going wrong at home as I had feared, and I felt a chill.

Since I had moved out of the house I had said nothing irresponsible or indiscreet about my brother or sister-in-law, and I'm afraid my mother left without getting any satisfaction from me. However, I must admit that I let her get away without finding out what had precipitated her abrupt and ominous question. I ventured, "Has anything serious happened?" But she merely answered, "No, nothing special in any way, though . . ." and stared back at me.

After she went away I began brooding about her question. But piecing together the general circumstances and recalling her attitude, I finally decided it was hardly conceivable that anything really new had developed at home.

Undoubtedly my mother had worried so much that for her it had become more and more difficult to figure out my sister-in-law.

Yet even as I came to this conclusion I felt as though caught up in a nightmare.

Although Oshige visited me in addition to my mother, my sister-in-law did not stop by even once to warm her hands over the brazier in my room, and I could well understand why she refrained from visiting me. When I had gone to Bancho, she had said, "I hear you're living in a high-class boarding house; and there are a fine alcove in the room and a nice-looking plum tree in the garden." But she didn't say, "Next time I might come over and see the place for myself." Nor was I bold enough to say, "Why, please come and see my place." And I must admit, incidentally, that the plum-tree she had mentioned was so shabby-looking indeed that one might think it had been pulled up wild out of some field and merely transplanted.

Perhaps for the same reason that my sister-in-law did not put in an appearance—or perhaps for some other reason—my brother never showed his face in my room.

Nor did my father.

Misawa came from time to time, and I finally had occasion to sound him out about his interest in marrying my sister.

"Say that's right, she is already of marriageable age and you'll soon have to think of marrying her off, won't you? You'd better find her a nice fellow and make her happy."

And faced with this obvious lack of interest in the matter I decided to abandon him as a prospect.

While things seemed to happen to me but nothing really did, the seemingly long but actually short winter—drizzling rains, thaws, dry winds—ran its own predestined course with monotonous regularity, and then it was gone.

Anguish

As the somber and severe winter was blown away by the new spring wind, I viewed the bright world like one emerging from a cold cellar. Somewhere within me lurked a feeling that this bright world would be as banal as the winter just gone by, yet I was not so old as to be insensitive to the thrill of the vernal fragrance that would flood my veins at every breath.

Every once in a while, when the weather was good, I slid open the doors of my room and gazed down at the street scene. Also I peeped at the blue sky spreading right up to the overhang. And I wished I could go somewhere far away. Had I still been in school, I would now have been getting ready for a spring vacation trip. However, no such freedom could be hoped for, now that I was tied down to a job. Even on those rare Sundays off I woke fretful and idled about my room all day, somehow unable to get started on a walk.

Thus partly I hailed spring and yet partly cursed it. When I returned to my room after work and had finished my supper, I sat by the brazier, smoking and vacantly trying to imagine my future. In the threads that wove my future flatteringly gorgeous colors always flickered from the flames of the newly supplied Sakura charcoal in the brazier; but at times they burned out, as bleak as the ashes themselves. Often, suddenly and by some chance I awoke to my own present self out of such a daydream, and wondered by what means fate would link my present and my future self.

Early one evening, while intently warming my hands over the brazier and wavering between reality and fantasy, I was suddenly aroused by the maid. Apparently I had been too absorbed in myself, for I really had not noticed the sound of her footsteps along the hallway. Then she had unexpectedly opened the sliding panels, and raising my eyes I was suddenly aware of her presence.

"Is the bath ready?" I asked instantly, for there seemed to be no other reason for her to come to my room at this hour.

"No sir," she said, standing quietly. I noticed a certain smile about her eyes, that flash of feminine pleasure at having fooled a man. "What is it, then? Standing there like that," I said sharply. The maid at once fell to her knees on the doorsill and said, a little more seriously, "Sir, you have a visitor."

"It must be Misawa," I said, for I was expecting a visit from him about some matter.

"No sir, it's a lady."

"A lady?"

Raising my brows doubtfully, I looked at her, but she remained calm.

"Shall I show her in?"

"Who is she anyway?"

"I do not know, sir."

"You say you don't know! Would you show a stranger into my room without even finding out who she is?"

"But she wouldn't tell me when I asked," the maid said, with the same teasing smile about her eyes. Withdrawing my hands from the brazier, I rose and almost thrusting aside the still crouching maid, I hurried to the entrance. There I saw my sister-in-law standing with her coat on in the corner of the cold dirt floor.

2

It had been cloudy all day, and the cold wind had blown steadily, driving away a long spell of fine weather. All the way back from the office I had walked with my overcoat collar turned up, fearing rain at any moment. A drizzle had begun, in fact, at about the time I had sat down to supper.

"Well, you have chosen a cold evening to come!"

"O yes," was her only reply. Turning over the cushion which I had been sitting on, and adjusting it in front of the three-foot wide alcove, I insisted, "Won't you come over here?" Slipping off one sleeve of her coat, she said, "I don't want to be treated like a guest." I looked at her face as I rang the bell to have the tea utensils washed. I was struck by the pallor of her cheeks, whiter than usual, and obviously chilled by the cold outside air. About her lone dimple wavered a new sense of solitariness, even as it disappeared.

"Anyway, please sit down there."

She sat on the cushion as I had insisted, and held her white hands over the brazier. In keeping with her fine figure, she possessed exceptionally beautiful fingers. In fact, of all her natural features, it was her delicately shaped hands and feet that had drawn my attention from the start.

"Jiro-san, you too. Hold out your hands and warm yourself."

For some reason or other I was reluctant to extend my hands. I noted the desolate sound of the rain outside the window. As the northwesterly wind which had risen during the day had dropped with the beginning of the rain, all was exceptionally quiet. At regular intervals there was only the sound of the water dripping into the eaves trough. Calm as usual, she looked around the room, saying, "A very nice room, as they said. And so quiet, too."

"It looks nice only at night. If you could see it in the daytime you'd realize it's really shabby."

I chatted with her for a little while. But as I must now confess, my mind was not as calm as my tone of voice might have suggested. Until that moment I couldn't have imagined that she would call on me in my room, never even in my idlest fancy. I had been shocked upon seeing her standing on the dirt floor of the entrance. And it was a surprise that came from uneasiness rather than gladness.

What had brought her here? What had brought her all the way over here in such cold weather? And especially at this hour of the night? Suspicion caused the questions that flashed across my mind the moment I saw her. This suspicion had started gnawing at my mind from the very beginning, and I felt as if under constant pressure even as, in my usual manner, I chatted with her across the brazier. This gave an unpleasant hollowness to my comments, however, as well as to my expression of them. I was as clearly conscious of it as I was that she too sensed the hollowness. But there was nothing I could do about it. I said to her, "It has become really colder." I said, "What a rainy day you've chosen to come!" Also I asked, "What has brought you out at this hour?" Yet having carried our conversation to this point I did not feel any more relieved and, realizing this, I became stiffer. Indeed, I could only cower before her eery, Gioconda-like smile.

"You've become so formal all of a sudden since last time," she pointed out.

"By no means," I replied.

"Yes, you have," she shot back.

3

I rose suddenly and went around my sister-in-law. She was sitting with her back toward the alcove. The room was so cramped that her *obi* nearly touched the cedar alcove post. As I forced my foot in between, she bent herself forward uncomfortably, saying "What are you doing?" With one leg still suspended in midair, I pulled a black lacquered tier of boxes from the corner of the alcove and placed it down in front of her.

"Would you care for one?"

And I was about to remove the lid, when she smiled faintly. In the picnic box there were rows of rice cakes sprinkled with sugar; which reminded me for the first time that the previous day had been the spring equinox. Looking at her face, I asked in earnest, "Won't you try one?" In an instant she burst out laughing.

"You are really awful. These are the rice cakes we sent over just yesterday, don't you realize that?"

I could only grin, cramming one into my mouth. She poured tea into the cup for me.

But through some comment on the cakes, I at last found out that she had visited her family and their ancestral graves, and that she was stopping by on her way back to Bancho.

"I haven't been home for a long time; yet things are going along as usual there, I hope."

"Yes. Nothing unusual . . ."

That was all she said, with her characteristic taciturnity. "Now since you admit it, you certainly haven't shown up at Bancho for a long time," she added, looking at me sharply.

Indeed I had kept away from Bancho. At first I was quite anxious about it, so much so that I felt uneasy if I did not go once or twice a week, but in time it became my habit to keep out of the circle and observe it furtively from the periphery. And this feeling that there was no trouble so long as I was merely observing had led me to attribute the placidity to my own absence.

"Why don't you drop in now and then as you used to?"

"Because my work has kept me pretty busy."

"O really? But that isn't the reason, is it?"

I could hardly stand being cornered by her in that way. What's more, I was unable to fathom her intention. Until then I had been convinced that of all people she would not have the nerve to press me on this point. I was almost tempted to say once for all, "How daring you are!" But she had already looked down upon me as timid; I was indeed too much the coward.

"Yes, really busy. As a matter of fact for some time I've been getting ready to study, so I haven't lately felt like going out. Sick and tired of always frittering away my time, I have been thinking of reading books when I can, and going abroad one of these days."

"Going abroad, you mean to Europe?" she asked.

"Well, perhaps. Yes."

"Isn't that wonderful? Go quickly and ask your father to help you out. Shall I speak to him for you?"

I really had entertained such a dream, though I knew it was hopeless, and as I heard her speak these words I suddenly shook my head, "He won't, I'm sure." She kept silent for a moment, then said in a melancholy tone, "You menfolk are really carefree, I must say."

"Far from it."

"If you are not satisfied you can just go away where you please."

4

By then I was somehow already holding my hands out to warm them over the brazier. Tall and thick, the brazier was in size not much larger than any ordinary encased brazier, so that when sitting around it vis-à-vis, our faces were almost too close. My sister-in-law had been sitting somewhat bent from the waist, as if round-shouldered. And there was nothing to criticize about this completely feminine posture. But as a consequence I was obliged to sit with my head thrown back. Even so, never had I observed her Fuji-shaped forehead so closely and so intensely. I was dazzled by her pale cheeks which seemed like flickering flames.

Still in such an uncomfortable posture, I was suddenly informed that her relationship with my brother, even after I left the house, had grown worse. In the past it had been her policy to keep quiet about him unless I asked. And even if I did, she habitually had simply smiled and said, "Just as usual," or "O nothing to worry about." Now that she had herself reversed this policy altogether, and had started deluging me with the facts of the frustrating situation I, being essentially a coward, smarted as though acid had been dashed on me.

But once I found an opening I decided I would question her in detail. Averse to any bandying of words, however, she would not so easily let me have my own way. What she disclosed was, I was certain, no more than a flash of the unpleasantness that existed between them. And as to the immediate cause of that unpleasantness she never spoke a word. Pressed, she merely said, "I really do not know why." Indeed, she might not have known—or even if she did, she might be purposely holding it back.

"You see I was born dumb, so it can't be helped. No matter what happens, things turn out to be as they are. There's no other way, I suppose. If I think that way and become resigned to it, that's that."

Apparently she was from the start the kind of woman born with a religious faith that there was nothing for her to fear if such should be her fate. Likewise, by nature she didn't seem afraid of the fate of others.

"Menfolk, if they aren't contented, can fly off anywhere—just like you—but certainly we women cannot. I am no better than a potted plant; once planted by my parents' hands, I am never able to move an inch unless someone comes along and helps me to move. There can be no other way but to stand still —yes, no other way but to stand still until blighted."

I felt electrified by the unfathomable feminine strength behind such a seemingly pathetic appeal. And I was frightened as I came to imagine how this strength would affect my brother.

"He is just in an ill humor, isn't he? Is there any real change other than that?"

"Well, about that I can't say. After all, he is a human being; no one knows when and what kind of ailment he may suffer."

Then, pulling a small ladies' watch out of her *obi*, she glanced at it. The room was so quiet that the click of the lid as she snapped it shut sounded unexpectedly loud in my ears. I felt as though the surface of my tender skin had been prodded by a sharp needle-point.

"I must be going now. I am sorry I have told you such an unpleasant story. But I have never told it to anyone until now. You know, I even remained silent about it to my own people today."

I noted that the lantern of a ricksha man, waiting all that time at the entrance, bore her family crest.

5

Throughout the night a quiet rain continued to fall. Amid the sound of the raindrops dripping as though tapping my pillow, I somehow retained an image of my sister-in-law. No sooner had her dark brows and dark eyes appeared in my vision than her pale forehead and cheeks rapidly encircled them—automatically like iron filings attracted to a magnet. Each time her image collapsed another cycle immediately began repeating its ordered pattern. At last I even saw with uncanny vividness the color of her lips, and at both corners of her mouth muscles were quivering imperceptibly like the symbol of unvoiced words. And even her cheeks were constantly rippling in a minute, hardly visible, whirl, hesitating whether to form into a dimple or to flatten out completely.

With such intensity I envisioned her, her image quickened almost into life. And while the raindrops were dripping, wild and incoherent fantasies began to torture my burning brain.

So long as the relationship between her and my brother kept worsening my mind could never enjoy peace no matter where I might flee. Much as I sought more concrete detail from her regarding that relationship, unlike another woman, she refused to ground her complaint on petty facts, and ignored my request as if it was out of the question. Thus her visit had no result other than to heighten my suspense.

Everything she said was dark and shadowy. And yet it all pierced my heart with the flashing swiftness of lightning. Piecing together this shadow and lightning, I wondered if my brother had by now taken to beating his wife as a release for his pent-up petulance. The word beating, associated with chastisement and abuse, connotes something abominable and cruel. A modern woman, she might well view my brother's behavior altogether in this light. When I asked her about his health, she in fact declared coldly that he, being human, might succumb to any ailment at any moment. That I raised this question out of my concern over his mental function was apparently obvious to her too. Therefore her reply, colder than usual, might possibly be taken for the voice of revenge echoing through her husband's future the sound of his whip on her tender flesh . . . I was frightened.

I resolved that the first thing the next morning I would go to Bancho to get my mother's confidential report on their situation. Already, however, my sister-in-law had declared that no one knew the change in their marital state of affairs yet, that no one had been told of it. Thus it was solely on my heart that her shadowy yet lightning-like words engraved this news, even if vaguely.

Why did my sister-in-law, taciturn as she was, confide in me alone? She was usually calm; indeed she was calm tonight, too. It seemed inconceivable that she had come all the way to see me because there was no one else to whom she might appeal in her extremity. But certainly the word appeal didn't describe her manner at all, for her statement could only result, as I have said a moment ago, in a tantalizing suspense.

Looking at my face as I was warming myself over the brazier, she in fact asked, "Why are you so stiff?" When I replied, "But I'm not," she smiled, saying, "But you are drawing back your head." Her manner then was so familiar that she seemed almost about to reach across the brazier and poke at my cheek with a delicate finger. She also spoke my name and said, "Surprised, aren't you?" as though her surprising me by coming unexpectedly in a rainy, cold evening had been a very exciting kind of mischief.

My fancy and memory, accompanied by the dripping raindrops, kept on revolving aimlessly until far into the night.

6

In the following few days, incessantly haunted by my sister-in-law—even while drawing a plan on my office desk—I knew no means of exorcising this curse. Day by day and throughout each day I felt that impatience one gets at the realization that nothing is done without help from others. I also wondered how those around suspected nothing, even while in such a divided mood I somehow managed to keep up appearances. For some time I had ceased to be considered a jolly fellow around the office. Especially lately I seldom spoke. That perhaps explained, I thought, why my colleagues had failed to notice the change I had undergone in those last three or four days. Loneliness assailed me, the intense loneliness of one living in utter isolation.

Meanwhile I viewed my sister-in-law in various ways. Perhaps from the very day of her marriage she had been well beyond what even we males could hardly transcend. Or perhaps from the start there had been neither a fence nor a wall standing in her way. From the start indeed she was an unshackled and free woman. And every single act of hers had been but the manifestation of this inborn innocence which was free, bound by nothing.

At one moment she also appeared to me a person of strong character who would keep everything to herself, never laying bare her true self. And viewed in this light she passed far beyond the level of an ordinary person of strong personality. Her equanimity, her dignity, and her taciturnity were all evidence of just how extraordinary she was, perhaps even too much so. She was also certainly brazen-faced to an amazing degree.

At another moment, however, she seemed to stand before me as endurance itself. And latent in her endurance there was a kind of nobility which betrayed no trace of panic whatever. She smiled, instead of frowning; she sat straight, instead of throwing herself down in tears—as if waiting for her own legs to be devoured. In short, her endurance was more than the word endurance ordinarily signifies; it was almost part of her own nature.

My sister-in-law, extraordinarily at one with herself, yet appeared to me in these various guises. She appeared differently in different places—at my office desk, at my lunch table, on the homeward-bound streetcar, or hovering around in my lodgings. I contained my suffering and no one knew. It often occurred to me that the proper thing was to go straight to Bancho and size up the whole situation for myself, but I was too much the

coward to dare it. While well aware of the existence of something fearful right before my eyes, I closed them tightly in order
not to face it.

It was on the fifth day after her visit, a Saturday afternoon,
when my father unexpectedly phoned me at the office.

"Is this Jiro?"

"Yes."

"You don't mind my coming over to your place tomorrow
morning, do you?"

"Well—"

"Is it perhaps inconvenient for you?"

"No, not really . . ."

"Then wait for me, will you? You're sure it's all right with
you? See you tomorrow then."

And he hung up. I was more than a little embarrassed. There
had been no time even to ascertain what his business was, I
thought regretfully after leaving the telephone. I saw clearly that
if he had some business with me he could certainly have sent for
me. I became all the more uneasy as his unprecedented visit
seemed somehow related, I felt, to my sister-in-law's recent visit.

When I returned home, I found on the desk a picture postcard from Okada in Osaka. It was a souvenir of the half-day he
and his wife had enjoyed in the city's outskirts, together with
Sano and Osada-san. Sitting at the desk, I stared at the postcard
for a long time.

7

Although on Sundays it had
been my habit to allow myself to stay in bed as late as I could, I
rose rather early this Sunday morning. After breakfast I began to
look at the newspaper, but there seemed to be nothing news-
worthy, and soon I got tired of it, as anyone would who, while
awaiting a train, buys the paper and glances through it hurriedly. So I threw it away; but hardly five or six minutes had
passed when I took it up again. Smoking a cigarette, carefully
wiping off a smear from my eyeglasses, and going through all

sorts of other nervous rituals, I waited anxiously for my father's arrival.

He did not appear so soon, however. I knew very well that he was an early riser, and since my childhood I had been used to his impatience. Increasingly restless, I even thought of phoning him to ascertain his convenience.

While thoroughly familiar with my mother, I had, on the other hand, always been reserved toward my father, although the truth of the matter was that I was more afraid of my gentle mother than of my father. When my father scolded and lectured me, I of course felt small, but at the same time I often thought inwardly that he was just another man. But on this occasion I felt differently. I couldn't so easily treat him lightly. Much as I wanted to call him up, I did not dare to do so.

Finally at about ten o'clock my father appeared. He looked somewhat formal, dressed in his *haori* and *hakama*, but at the same time he seemed surprisingly gentle. Having grown up with him, I had developed considerable ability to judge from his look what was on his mind.

"I've been waiting for you quite a while, since I assumed you would come earlier."

"Waiting in bed, you mean. Of course, I might have come quite a bit earlier, that would have been no problem. But I have come late on purpose, in order not to disturb you."

My father, sipping a cup of tea which I had poured, scrutinized my room. In the room there were only a desk, a book case, and a brazier.

"Now this is a good room."

My father had a habit of saying nice things such as this even to us. He had somehow smuggled these trite expressions, used throughout his long public career, into even his supposedly informal family relations. Such a hackneyed compliment, therefore, sounded to me as empty as a "Good morning."

He peeped into the alcove and, gazing at a scroll hung there, declared, "Just the right match."

It was a half-size scroll I had borrowed from him expressly to decorate this alcove. Tossing it to me, he had said at the time, "Well, you may take this one." It was such an odd piece that it seemed like nothing to me, not to mention a right match. With a grin I looked at it.

On it there was a line drawn diagonally in thin India ink. And above the line there was a sentence praising the painting: "This stick doesn't move of itself; touched, however, it moves." In a word, it was a hybrid kind of thing which could not be taken as either a painting or a writing.

"You may laugh at it, but it's really tasteful, very. An excellent piece for a tea-room alcove."

"Who is the artist, may I ask?"

"That I do not know, but it may be from the Daitokuji collection or perhaps . . ."

"I see . . ."

But still my father would not terminate his lecture on the scroll, and insisted on telling me all sorts of wholly uninteresting things—of the Daitokuji Temple, the Obaku sect, and what not. And finally he badgered me with questions such as, "Now what do you suppose this stick means?"

8

That day my father took me to the Hyokeikan at Ueno. Since I had many times kept him company on visits to such places, it seemed very unlikely that he had taken the trouble to call at my lodgings expressly for this purpose. At every moment while we were on the way to Ueno after leaving the house, I expected him to bring up his business. For my part I didn't have the nerve to ask about it; in fact, in his presence the very names of my brother and sister-in-law, like forbidden words, stuck in my throat.

In the Hyokeikan my father stood in front of Rikyu's letters and bit by bit deciphered the almost illegible words, as if to reassure himself about his own reading: "I am hereby reporting to you, sir, of my having . . ." As he came to O-Gishi's writings in the Imperial collection, he was thoroughly impressed, exclaiming "Yes, indeed." Whereas I thought them so worthless that I couldn't refrain from commenting, "Certainly reassuring." "Why is that?" cross-questioned my father.

We both entered the upstairs hall. There hung in succession ten pieces or so by Okyo which formed one sequence; the one on the extreme right represented three cranes, and another on the extreme left, just one crane on spread wings, and the whole space between, about four or five yards in distance, was filled with waves.

"They were stripped off sliding panels and made into hanging scrolls, I gather."

My father pointed out to me, on each piece, the worn marks of handling, and white spots where the catches had been removed. Standing there in the middle of the hall, I learned from my father for the first time how to admire the Japanese artist of olden times who had created these magnificent paintings.

When we came down from the second floor, he lectured on jade works, on Korean pottery, and the like. I learned the name Kakiemon, and also decided that the most worthless of all were Nonko's teacups. Now tired, we left the museum at last. We strolled along the clean path, viewing on our right hand a pale-dark pine tree overtowering the front of the structure. Still my father said no word about his business, but instead offered, "Soon in blooming season."

"Yes."

We strolled on as far as the front of the Toshogu Shrine.

"Shall we lunch at the Seiyoken?"

My watch indicated it was already half past one. From my childhood it had been our custom to dine out whenever my father took me visiting, and even when grown I continued to expect to dine with him on such occasions. However, that day at least I was somehow impatient to part with him.

Although we had failed to notice it on our way, the entrance of the Seiyoken was decorated on all sides with strings of parti-colored flags, and welcoming groups of silk-hatted guests.

"Something must be going on there today. Apparently the place has been reserved."

"Yes, I see."

Pausing, he looked at the colors of flags here and there visible through the trees, and asked, as if he had just remembered, "Today is the twenty-third, isn't it?" Indeed, it was the twenty-third of the month; and it was the day for the wedding reception of my brother's friend K.

"It just slipped my mind. About a week ago an invitation came addressed to Ichiro and Onao."

"Hadn't Mr. K married yet?"

"No—I'm not sure though. Can't be his second marriage."

We walked down the hill and at length entered a western-style restaurant on the left.

"From here we can get a good view of the street. Ichiro may be passing by with his silk hat on."

"You mean with Sister-in-law?"

"Well, I am not sure."

We took our seats near a window on the second floor and looked down at the wide Mihashi Boulevard over a flat vase of flowers.

9

At the table my father chatted cheerfully, and until we had coffee he didn't mention anything at all business-like. As we came out he glanced in apparent surprise at a large white building opposite, saying:

"O I didn't know they'd converted the bazaar into a cinema. I wonder when."

The gilt-lettered signboard on the façade of the white building looked cheap indeed, bordered with innumerable flags. I confess I could feel only professional shame for this shabby building standing ostentatiously in the middle of Tokyo.

"It is really amazing to see how fast things are changing. Come to think of it, who can tell how soon I may be going to die?"

As it happened to be a fine Sunday and what's more, the busiest time of the day, the streets were jammed with holiday-makers. Therefore, what he said was bizarrely out of tune with our surroundings—the bright colors, the gay crowd and the light-hearted quick pace.

Where the street forked in two directions, towards Bancho and towards my lodgings, I was about to part from my father.

"Do you have something to do?"

"Well, uh—a sort of . . ."

"Come on along to the house."

I hesitated, still with my hand touching the brim of my hat.

"Now you just come along. After all it's your own home. You ought to drop in once in a while."

Conscious of the embarrassed look on my face, I followed my father, who soon looked back and said:

"Everyone at home is wondering lately what has kept you from coming around. 'What's the matter with Jiro?' they ask. Well, they say diffidence leads to silence, but your case is worse, since liberty leads to silence."

"That is not really the case . . ."

"Anyway, you'd better come along. First come home and explain yourself to your mother as best you can. All I have to do —my role—is to drag you home."

My father went quickly along and, grinning inwardly at my own attitude which was no wiser than a child's, I quietly kept pace with him. That day, unlike previous days, the southern sun was casting its warm beams upon us, truly worthy of the first day of spring. My father was wearing a heavy, otter-collared cloak and I a thick overcoat, and after our walk we felt overheated. It was a rare occasion indeed to spend a half day with him. Lately, I had had little chance to walk with him; nor was I sure at all how many more times I would be able to walk thus with my old father.

In this dull anxiety I felt a streak of gladness, followed by a certain sense of transience. And indulging myself in this sentimental mood which gripped me with such suddenness, I walked on.

"Your mother is shocked that you haven't answered or returned the picnic box even after having received the rice cakes on the equinox. It will do if you drop in for a moment. I don't see any special reason why you can't."

I made no answer.

"So today I thought of bringing you home and making everyone happy. You haven't seen Ichiro lately, have you?"

"Not since I said good-bye at the time I moved to my lodgings."

"Now you see. It so happens Ichiro is out today. Sorry I forgot that wedding reception at Ueno."

At last, accompanied by my father, I passed through the gate of the Bancho house.

10

When I entered the room my mother looked at me and merely said, "Now this is a rare visitor." Although almost forcibly brought home, I had all along felt grateful for my father's kindness. But the reunion scene with my mother which I had envisioned was thus shattered at her one word. Without consulting anyone in the family, and completely on his own initiative, my father had apparently lavished his favor on me, his thoughtless son. Oshige looked at me as though at a runaway house-dog and said, "Look. Our lost child has come back." "Welcome home," was my sister-in-law's only greeting, laconic as ever. She seemed to have altogether forgotten that she had recently dropped in alone to see me, and of course in the presence of others I thought it best not to say a word about that. My father was relatively gay as with somewhat exaggerated humor he proudly related to my mother and sister how he had lured me out. His "lure out" sounded to me ostentatious as well as comical.

"Now that spring is here everyone ought to cheer up. If you continue your gloomy silence as you have lately this place is going to be really depressing—like a ghost house. Why, they are even building a house in the paulownia place."

The paulownia place was the name of a corner lot near our

house. Until recently the lot had been vacant due to an old tradition that a curse would fall on whoever might choose to live on the lot. Recently, however, someone had purchased the lot and begun to build a big house. My father spoke animatedly to those around him, apparently hinting fearfully that his own house might become another paulownia place. Ordinarily he would stay in his familiar two-room inner suite, and call us in—my mother, brother or anybody else—as he saw fit. But that day, strangely, he did not go to his room but instead, having slipped off his *hakama* and *haori*, he sat down and chatted with us for a long while.

Thus once in a while coming back to the home I had long been used to, I somehow felt as if I'd been remembering things long forgotten. It had been still cold when I had left the house. Then, storm doors had covered most of the sash-doors of the parlour and the garden had been covered all over with the frost which cruelly tore the moss off the ground. Now, however, all those exterior partitions were stored away in their boxes; and the interior partitions were also thrown open, allowing the interior of the house and the outdoors to blend completely into each other. The trees, mosses, and stones struck me as nature itself. Everything put on an appearance different from what it had had when I had left the house. Everything here seemed in contrast with my own lodgings.

Sitting amid such relics of the past after so long a time I chatted with both my father and mother, with my sister and sister-in-law. Only my brother happened to be absent from this family gathering, and his name was not once mentioned by anybody. That day, I was told, he had been invited to Mr. K's wedding reception, but I couldn't tell whether he had accepted the invitation. As my sister-in-law then happened to be with me, it was clear that she had not attended the reception.

I was uneasy that my brother's name was not mentioned at all in our conversation; at the same time I was afraid it would be mentioned. When with this in mind I looked at everyone, there did not seem to be a single innocent face.

A little later I said to my sister, "Let me see your room that you have bragged of as being so pretty."

"Certainly, it merits my bragging. Please go and see it for yourself."

I rose to take a look into my old room, that familiar room I had used until I had moved to my lodgings. As I expected, Oshige followed me.

I I

Her room was not really as charming as her bragging might have led me to believe, but it was no longer neglected as when I had used it; and there was something attractive about it. On a gay-patterned cushion before the desk I settled down and looked around, saying "Yes, indeed."

On the desk there was a Japanese imitation of a majolica plate. An artificial rose was arranged in a single-stalk flower vase. A wall-piece embroidered with large white lilies hung horizontally.

"Quite stylish, I must say."

"Of course," she replied with an air of triumph and an affected look.

I teased her awhile but after five or six minutes I asked as casually as possible, "How is Brother doing lately?" "He is really odd," she said dropping her voice instantly. Her disposition, which was diametrically the opposite of my sister-in-law's, was very helpful in such cases. Once she started I had no need to draw her out any further. She spoke quite candidly of whatever was on her mind. In fact, finally her talk became almost annoying even as I quietly listened.

"In short, he doesn't speak much to anyone in the family, is that it?"

"That's right."

"Then he isn't any better than when I left the house, is he?"

"I am afraid not."

I was disappointed. Still pensive, I unthinkingly flicked some cigarette ash into the majolica plate, and Oshige made a face at this.

"That's a pen-tray, not an ash-tray."

Now realizing I could get nothing out of Oshige, who was not nearly so intelligent as my sister-in-law, I was about to go back to rejoin my parents in the other room, when unexpectedly she related a strange story.

As she explained it, my brother seemed lately to be seriously studying mental telepathy or something of that sort. Having her stand outside his study, he pinched his own arm and then asked, "Oshige, just now I pinched this spot; didn't you feel a pain at the same spot?" Or drinking a cup of tea alone in his room, he then asked, "Oshige, didn't you feel a gurgling sensation in your throat as if you were drinking something?"

"I was really astounded; I thought his mind was slipping until I was told what it was all about. He told me afterwards it was an experiment done by a certain Frenchman. And he said it didn't work on me because I was so dull. I was so happy."

"Why is that?"

"Because to me it's more frightening than cholera."

"Really?"

"Of course. It's so weird to do that sort of thing even for study."

Much amused as I was, I also felt somewhat uneasy. Returning to the room, I discovered that my sister-in-law was no longer there. In a lowered voice my father was talking with my mother, and he did not look at all like the person who had just now kept all of us gay and merry. As I entered, a voice said, "We never meant to raise him that way."

"It's really very embarrassing," another voice replied.

12

It was on that occasion that I heard, from both my father and mother, the latest account of my brother's recent condition. Their facts added nothing especially new and merely confirmed what I had already heard from

Oshige. But their looks and words made it painfully clear how seriously concerned they were about his difficulty. My mother in particular complained that on account of him the family atmosphere had become very depressing. Their concern was made all the more pitiful by their conviction that they had cared for him more than parents ordinarily would. Implicitly they seemed to insist that they in no way deserved to be made miserable by their own child. As I sat before them, they talked only about my brother, and laid the blame on no one else. This time even my mother, who was usually dissatisfied with the way my sister-in-law treated my brother, uttered no word of complaint against her.

Their complaint also reflected what was really their sincere sympathy; they were not a little worried about his physical health. Moreover they were not unmindful of his mental condition which was, to some extent, dependent on his physical condition. In short, my brother's future to them seemed an ominously unknown factor.

"What is to be done?" was the question repeatedly raised as they talked it over. Indeed, it was the question constantly resounding in their minds even when they separately brooded about the matter.

"Yes, quite often in the past this sort of thing has happened to him, being such an oddity, but for that very reason he has gotten over it quickly too. But this time it's really puzzling."

Despite the fact they had learned thoroughly how to humor him since his childhood, my brother's recent condition was puzzling indeed. His depression had remained unrelieved from about the time when I moved to my lodgings. And it had been proceeding steadily from bad to worse.

"It makes things really difficult for me even," my mother declared appealingly, looking at me. "And although he makes me mad of course, I can't help feeling sorry for him."

After I talked it over with my parents, it was decided that my brother was to be urged to take a trip. As they said they were hopelessly unsuited to the task, I proposed to work on him indirectly through Mr. H, his most intimate friend, and they readily gave their consent. As for the task of approaching Mr. H, I had to take it on myself. There was still a week before the spring vacation was to begin, but his school lectures were about over. Clearly, if I was going to approach Mr. H at all, I had to move quickly; otherwise, it would be very difficult.

"Then, within two or three days, I'll go either to Misawa and have him talk to Mr. H or, depending on the situation, go myself and speak to him personally."

Since I was not very well acquainted with Mr. H, it was plainly preferable to go through Misawa. Mr. H had been Misawa's sponsor while he was in school, and even after graduation Misawa had frequented his house almost like a member of the family.

As I was taking my leave I looked into my sister-in-law's room just to say good-bye. With Yoshie before her, she was dressing a naked doll in a pretty kimono.

"Yoshie, you've really grown up."

I put my hand on her head as I rose. Fondled so suddenly by her uncle whom she had not lately seen around, Yoshie looked a little abashed and smiled shyly with twisted lips. It was nearly five o'clock when I came out of the gate, but my brother was not yet back from Ueno. Although my father suggested that to make up for a long absence I ought to dine with them and wait to see my brother, I didn't feel I could spend that much time.

13

The next day I called on Misawa on my way home from the office. He had just gone out to have his hair cut, so unhesitatingly I decided to go in and wait for him to return.

"It's become awfully warm in the last two or three days. Soon flowers will also be blooming," said his mother, entering the room where I was awaiting the master of the house, and speaking to me in her usual mannered language.

His room was covered all over with paintings and sketches,

leaving little space. Some of them without frames were pinned directly to the walls.

"I have no idea what they are," she explained apologetically, "but he is so fond of them that he must put them all over." On the bookshelf at one side an oil painting next to a round jar caught my eye.

The painting showed the head of a woman with large dark eyes. The gently dimmed blur of these dark eyes gave a certain pervasive dreaminess to the entire canvas. Noticing my intent gaze, his mother nodded with a grin.

"That one, too, he painted for fun the other day."

Misawa was good at painting. As part of my profession I too knew how to handle pigments but I was no equal to him in the matter of artistic talent. This painting somehow reminded me of the pathetic Ophelia.

"Yes, very interesting," I said.

"Drawing from a photograph, he complained he couldn't capture the true feeling. He said he should have had her pose for him while she was alive . . . Such an unfortunate person she was; she died two or three years ago. She was divorced after what we had done to help her marry."

The model for the painting was that young divorcee, Misawa's demented girl. And his mother, wholly unsolicited, had told me these various facts about her. But about the precise relationship between the woman and Misawa she did not say a word; nor did she mention the woman's mental disorder. I did not feel like asking her about that, either; in fact for my part I tried to change the subject.

So the conversation shifted from the woman to Misawa's marriage. His mother seemed happy.

"Yes, he has caused so much anxiety to everyone, but this time at last it has been settled . . ."

The previous day I had had a letter from Misawa indicating that he would soon come over to talk with me about his personal affairs; his mother's remark on his marriage finally gave me the clue. Even as I offered her routine congratulations I couldn't help wondering if the bride-to-be had as large, dark and liquid eyes as did the woman in this oil painting, and that was the first thing I would be curious to find out.

When Misawa did not return as soon as we expected, his mother said that perhaps on the way back he might have gone to the bath, and offered to send for him; I declined that, but to my dismay I could take little interest in the conversation with her.

Oshige, my own sister, about whom I had sounded Misawa's mind, hadn't yet married, and was idling away her time as I was also. My brother, although married and settled down, wasn't getting along so well with his wife.

On weighing and considering all of this, I could hardly be cheerful.

14

Finally Misawa came back home. Lately he seemed to be in good shape, and he looked exceptionally slick after a haircut and a bath. Indeed he radiated health and happiness as he sat cross-legged. In keeping with these his speech and manner were equally cheerful. In fact he was so lively that I hesitated to bring up my unpleasant business matter.

"What's the matter with you?" He asked when his mother had left the two of us alone face to face. With reluctance I had to inform him of my brother's recent condition, and then implored him to have Mr. H persuade my brother to take a trip.

"You see I can't be indifferent while my father and mother are so much worried," I concluded as he sat with arms folded staring seriously at his knee-caps.

"Why not come along with me, then? That would be better than my going alone, and together we can give him all the details."

If Misawa was willing to go out of his way that much, nothing could suit me better. He left the room to change but soon reappeared and said, "Say, this being a rare visit on your part, my mother wants you to have supper here, and she is now preparing it." I was in no relaxed mood to enjoy such hospitality. But if I declined I would still have to eat my meal somewhere anyway. Having given vague assent, I forced myself to settle down once more, though I was really impatient to leave at once. Every now and then my gaze fell on the woman's portrait on the bookshelf.

"Unfortunately I've asked you to stay when there is really nothing special, it will just be some left overs, so to speak," Misawa's mother said, appearing again in the room, followed by a maid carrying a tray, in the corner of which there were antique Kutani sake cups.

Yet it was still earlier than we had expected when Misawa and I together emerged from his house. After getting off the streetcar, we walked several blocks, and as we were shown into Mr. H's living room I noted that it was still around eight o'clock.

Mr. H, dressed in a silk kimono, belted with white crepe, sitting cross-legged on a chair, greeted Misawa, saying, "Well, you've brought with you a rare visitor, it seems." With his round face, and his close-cropped round head, he looked plumlike as a Chinese. He spoke slowly, as slowly as a Chinese would speak Japanese he isn't used to. And every time he opened his mouth his fleshy cheeks moved, which made him appear to be constantly beaming.

His disposition was as generous as his manner suggested. Perched with legs doubled under him on his rather shaky chair, he yet retained his usual calmness, despite a posture which might appear very uncomfortable to others. His look and temper, which were almost diametrically opposite those of my brother, rather did help in a way to bind him and my brother together. With him, who was unresisting, my brother probably would not feel like resisting. In fact, never once had I heard my brother speak ill of Mr. H.

"Is your brother studying hard as always? Too much work won't do him any good, I'm afraid," he said, characteristically relaxed and looking at the smoke he was puffing out.

15

In time Misawa broached the matter and, following his lead, I explained the main point. Mr. H inclined his head as if in doubt.

"That's a bit strange. Why, it can't be."

His doubt was apparently not pretended. It seemed that just the day before he had seen my brother at K's wedding reception at the Seiyoken. In fact they had left the place together. As they had not finished their talk they had rambled along together. At last my brother had said he was tired and Mr. H had taken him home.

"As a matter of fact he had supper with me here. There seemed to be nothing unusual about him."

A spoiled child, my brother had always been a difficult person at home, whereas he was very quiet once outside. But his present state certainly could not so simply be explained away on the basis of his wilfulness. So I attempted to find out as delicately as possible what sort of matters my brother had talked of with Mr. H.

"Well, he didn't say a word about his family."

He didn't invent it. Mr. H, who happened to have a good memory, remembered their talk clearly and related it to me as plainly as he could.

As Mr. H explained, my brother at the time had constantly alluded to the problem of death. Apparently his interest had been aroused in the studies of life after death which were currently popular in England and America, and he had done considerable reading on the subject. But none of his reading, my brother had declared, had satisfied him. He had read Maeterlinck's article too but deplored it as the same kind of rubbish as common-run spiritualism.

His information about my brother was altogether confined to the area of study or research; indeed he seemed to think all this was part of my brother's academic interest. All the while I was listening, however, in my mind I could not keep my brother as a scholar separate from my brother as a family man. To me it seemed that his role as the former was but the result of his role as the latter.

"Certainly, I can see he is restless," Mr. H admitted, "but whether that has anything to do with your family situation I do not know. In any case, one thing at least seems certain; intellectually he is disturbed and restless."

Moreover, Mr. H openly referred to the neurosis which my brother never tried to conceal. In fact, I was told that my brother had invariably complained of it whenever with Mr. H.

"Yes, it may really do him good to take a trip at a time like this, and if that's the case I'll try to prod him. But I wonder if he will say yes immediately. As you know, he can't be moved so easily; I'm afraid it may be difficult."

His words seeemed to lack confidence.

"But I think he will listen to you at least."

"I'm not so sure," he said, grinning.

It was nearly ten o'clock when we departed. Yet in this quiet residential section people could still be seen wandering about here and there, and leaving the peaceful echo of their footsteps. In the sky stars shone dully as though winking sleepy eyes. I felt wrapped in something opaque as I returned through the dim-lit streets with Misawa.

16

Anxiously I awaited Mr. H's word. No communication came from him, however, even a week after the newspapers of the capital were full of the first tidings of the blossoms. I was disappointed, yet I did not like to check with Bancho by telephone. I was in a mood to say "What does it all matter?" when Misawa arrived.

"I understand things haven't worked out well."

Matters had turned out exactly as I had thought. My brother had flatly rejected Mr. H's invitation. This left Mr. H no choice but to have Misawa convey the result to me.

"Have you come all the way for that?"

"Well, that's about it."

"Thanks for all your trouble."

I felt like saying nothing more.

"You know how Mr. H is. He seems to feel he himself is to blame. This time it came on such short notice he couldn't quite manage it, but this coming summer vacation he is going to get your brother away by all means, he told me."

I grinned, looking at Misawa who had brought me such consolations. An easy-going person like Mr. H might not see very much difference between the spring and the summer vacation; but to those of us laboring behind the scene, the summer vacation seemed very remote indeed. And between that remote future and the present there lurked enormous uncertainty.

"Well, I guess it can't be helped. We made a plan for our convenience and then tried to move my brother with it."

So at last I was resigned. Misawa made no comment but, with chin resting on his elbows on the corner of the desk, he merely stared me in the face. "That's why," he said a moment later, "You'd better do as I have suggested."

The other day, while on our way back from Mr. H's, after making the request regarding my brother, Misawa startled me by breaking his silence to state, right there in the street, "Wouldn't it be better for you to get married quickly than to try to cheer up your brother or to induce him to go on a trip? You'll be better off, I tell you," he said nudging my shoulder, although until that moment he hadn't spoken a word about my brother.

That evening was not the first time he had urged me to get married, however. I had always offered the excuse that there was no suitable girl available. He had once gone so far as to say he would find me one and indeed he almost kept his word.

That evening again I resorted to the same excuse although, as he recalled, it sounded somewhat cooler than usual.

"All right—whatever you say. But are you really going to find me one?"

"Sure. And a very good one too, if you'll only listen to me."

Indeed he spoke as though he really had someone in mind. Perhaps he had discovered a prospect through the girl he himself expected to marry soon.

No longer did he talk about the large, dark-eyed girl, the demented girl.

"Does your future wife resemble that girl?"

"Well, I'm not sure, but one of these days I'll introduce you to her and you'll be able to see for yourself."

"When is your wedding?"

"It may be postponed for her convenience until this fall."

Apparently he was happy as he projected the poetry of his own past into his future life.

17

April passed all too soon. The cherry blossoms bloomed and then fell in one place after another, at Ueno, at Mukojima, and then at Arakawa. I idled away this blossom time, the most welcome season of the year. And as a new month came and the world began to be adorned with green foliage, I looked back at the bygone spring—with profound dissatisfaction. Yet I was grateful for the very fact that I had at least been able to idle my time away.

Not once did I visit my old home. Nor did anyone from home come to see me. Once or twice my mother and sister did phone me, but only about a new kimono for me. I did not see Misawa at all. From Okada in Osaka came another picture postcard when the cherry-blossoms were in full bloom. As before, it was also signed by Osada-san and Okane-san.

I was living the mechanical life of an animal going daily to work at the office. Then toward the end of May, Misawa surprised me with a large invitation card. Rashly taking it for his wedding announcement, I broke the seal. To my astonishment, however, it was an invitation from the Conservatory of Court Music in Fujimicho. It read: "We request the pleasure of your company at the music recital which is to be held at one p.m., the second of June." I didn't have the slightest idea why Misawa had sent me such an invitation, since I was quite certain he had no special interest in court music. Half a day later I received a letter from him in which he urged me to attend without fail. Since he suggested that I come without fail, there seemed no doubt that he himself would come. In view of his special insistence I thought I might as well go. But as for the music itself, I must admit I had no great expectation. Rather, it was his casual post-script that inspired a change in my mood:

"Mr. H is no liar. He finally persuaded your brother. As I understand it, they have agreed to take a trip together somewhere this June as soon as they wind up their school lectures."

I was happy for my parents as well as for my brother. If he was in a mood to promise to join Mr. H on a trip, that alone seemed to indicate a great change in his condition. Never one to hedge, he no doubt meant to carry out his promise.

I did not verify this news with either my father or my mother, though. Nor did I even take measures to confirm it with Mr. H himself, since I wished first simply to hear a few more details from Misawa. That could be taken care of when next I saw him, I thought, and thus I was looking forward to the second of June and the date he urged me to keep without fail.

On June 2, as it happened, the weather was wet. Around eleven o'clock the rain did let up somewhat, but it did not turn as clear as was normal at that time of the year. Passers-by kept raising and lowering their umbrellas as the weather changed. The willows outside Mitsuke were drooping their long branches like smoke. As I passed under them, their pale pollen or mouldy substance stuck fast to my clothes instead of settling to the ground.

Inside the gate of the Conservatory many rickshas were drawn up. There were a couple of carriages but no automobiles. At the entrance I handed my hat to a page wearing a brass-buttoned uniform. Another page ushered me to a seat.

"Kindly be seated over there," he said and returned to his post at the entrance. The seats were only sparsely occupied. I took a seat at the rear, trying to avoid notice.

18

Fully expecting to find Misawa I looked around, but he was nowhere. The gallery itself surrounded the stage on three sides. I was taken to a center seat after turning to the left from the entrance, then to the right at the end of the aisle, and passing by the golden folding screen. In front of me were seated two or three women in crested coats. Behind me were two khaki uniformed army officers. A half dozen other people were scattered here and there.

A couple of seats away from me two persons were commenting on the curtain hanging on the stage in front of us. I noted that on the curtain in many vertical rows a quaint-looking crest was repeated which had no apparent connection with court music.

"You see that is Oda Nobunaga's crest. It all started when Nobunaga, lamenting the decline of the Imperial Court, presented that curtain. Ever since, I understand, it has become traditional to hang the curtain with the ringed melon crest dyed on it."

Examining the curtain I saw that the top and bottom were hemmed in by a kind of purple frill with a golden arabesque design.

Before the curtain a drum was placed at mid-stage. The drum was prettily painted green, gold, and red, and was set in a thin, round frame. In addition, arranged before the curtain were a pair of *koto*, and another pair of Japanese lutes.

In front of the instruments was spread a blue carpet for dancing. The structure, like the Noh stage, was altogether separated from the gallery on three sides by four or five feet of open space to let in the sunlight and air.

While I was curiously observing the staging, guests constantly came in one after another. Among them was Marquis N, whom I remembered just having seen at a certain concert. "Can't come today because of the meeting of the Educational Association . . ." Apparently he was remarking about his absent wife, to a

small, portly man with a shaven head. This portly little man was
Prince K, as I later learned from Misawa.

As for Misawa, he came in a frock coat only a few minutes
before the music started. At the folding screen at the entrance he
stood hesitant, glancing around the gallery, but as soon as he
caught sight of me he came over directly and sat down beside
me.

Almost following on his heels a tall young man also came to
the center gallery, accompanied by two young women. He was
also in a frock coat and the women, of course, were in crested
coats. From the resemblance between the man and one of his
female companions I could easily see that they were brother and
sister. They exchanged greetings with Misawa across several
rows of people. The man smiled broadly, and the woman
blushed slightly. Misawa courteously rose. As most of the front
seats were occupied by women they did not come near us.

"She is my future wife," Misawa said to me in a low voice. I
made mental comparison between that demented girl with the
large, dark eyes, on the one hand, and this blooming young lady
who had just now taken her seat four or five yards in front of
me. She sat, only her black hair and white nape revealed; I could
barely see that clearly, for my view was obstructed by the
crowd.

"And the other one—" Misawa began to speak again in a low
voice. But then suddenly he put his hand in his pocket and, pulling out a slip of white paper and a fountain-pen, he began writing down something. On the stage in front of us the musicians
had already appeared.

19

Their headgear was so peculiar
as to be distinguishably neither cap nor hood. But from what I
knew of the Noh song, *Fuji Drum*, I guessed that it was probably the dancers' so-called bird helmet. The rest of their costume, like their headgear, was out of date; they were wearing
brocade ceremonial dress which, unboned, fitted skintight about

their shoulders, forming a gentle curve. To the white end of each sleeve was attached a red piece of silk about three inches wide. They all wore white padded *hakama*, and all sat alike with their legs crossed.

Misawa suddenly crumpled up the slip of white paper on which he had just begun writing something on his lap. I glanced askance at the crushed paper ball, but without a word of explanation he stared straight ahead. On the blue carpet appeared dancers, carrying halberds, from behind the curtain on the left hand. They also, like the instrument players, had sleeveless brocade tops.

I waited and waited, but Misawa did not complete his comment. Everyone in the gallery was quiet; everyone hesitated to speak even to his neighbors. I had to keep myself from pressing him any further. For his part, Misawa was calm, pretending not to notice, and being as much a stranger here as I was he seemed somewhat stiff.

Before a solemn audience the dancers, in accordance with the fixed order of program, proceeded patiently with the monotonous but elegant postures. Their costume changed with every new piece, and they paraded before us a spectrum of the graceful colors of ancient eras. Some stuck cherry blossoms in their crowns; showed bright flame-colored decorative crests under their large sleeves of silk gauze; or girded on gold-mounted swords. Others looked like hunters swathed in rich brocade, the sleeveless Chinese brocade tunic reaching to the knee, over vermilion gowns gathered at the wrist. Still others wore loose blue gowns which resembled straw rain capes, and also blue sedge hats hanging at their sides. All looked somehow dreamy; all radiated the scent of the age-old relics of our ancestors. And although everyone watched them with apparent admiration Misawa and I sat somewhat bewildered.

When the intermission halted the dancing and music someone announced that refreshments were to be served, and those around us rose from their seats and began moving toward another room. Just then the man, brother of Misawa's fiancée, came over and talked familiarly with Misawa. Apparently well acquainted with this circle he had recognized those invited that day. Misawa and I learned from him the names of various nobles, high-ranking officials, and celebrities.

In the other room they were serving coffee, sponge-cake, chocolate, and sandwiches. Unlike ordinary parties, there was no ill-mannered behavior, but as the place was somewhat jammed, some of the women decided not to stir from their seats. Misawa and his friend carried trays of sweets and coffee to the ladies. I stood at the door, peeling the silver foil from a chocolate, and stole a distant glance at them.

Misawa's fiancée bowed her thanks and took only a cup of coffee, not touching the cake. But her companion did not care to take even a cup of coffee. Therefore, still holding a tray, Misawa stood there, undecided what to do. Her face showed more of child-like innocence than I had noted a while earlier, a somewhat painful expression.

20

For some time I had been carefully studying the other woman. No doubt this was due largely to Misawa's look and attitude; but apart from that, she was indeed pretty enough to command my attention. At intervals during the performance I had constantly observed her and Misawa's fiancée from behind. They were seated so conveniently that from my seat I could see them without so much as turning my eyes purposely in that direction.

I had thus far looked at only the napes of their necks, but now I found myself in a freer position and was able to observe their features from a sharper angle. As I decided that they might happen to turn their faces in my direction, even while I was cramming my mouth with chocolate, I was yet furtively alert to seize the moment should it come. However, neither she nor Misawa's fiancée turned around. I had to be content with only this distant side view of only two-thirds of their faces.

Meanwhile Misawa returned to me, still carrying a tray and

passing by me he smiled, saying, "Well, what do you say?" I said merely, "Much obliged." Following him, his fiancée's tall brother came over.

"Well, won't you come over there for a smoke—in the smoking room at the far end?"

This again spoiled the possibility for a talk which seemed about to start between Misawa and me. The three of us went together to the rather small smoking room which was quite animated with smoke and men.

In one corner I noticed only one familiar face. He was a large-eyed man from a family of musicians. As an important member of a certain dramatic society he made skilful use of his large eyes on the stage. He had been talking with someone, in his deep-sounding stage voice, but left the smoking room at almost the same time we entered.

"He has finally turned to an acting career, I hear."

"Is it paying?"

"It must be."

"The other day I read in the newspaper that he is going to play some part or other—is he?"

"Yes, so they say."

After he left the three men in the middle of the room were talking about this sort of thing. Misawa's friend told us their names. Two of them princes and the third a count, they all three were peers descended from court nobles. From their conversation it seemed that none of them had any real knowledge of or interest in drama.

We again returned to our seats and heard two or three selections of western music, and at about five o'clock we finally came out of the Conservatory. When we were alone, Misawa started talking about the other woman. It turned out to be just as I had guessed from the start.

"What do you say? Didn't you like her?"

"She has a pretty face."

"You mean just a face?"

"For the rest I have no idea. But isn't she a bit old-fashioned?

She seems to think it proper to be so reserved about everything."

"It's her family, I guess. But you can at least be sure about her type."

We walked along the embankment where the pine trees, wet with rain, stood pale and dark against the sky.

2 1

Misawa and I never quite tired of chatting about the women. It seems that the one he was going to marry was a daughter of an official connected with the Imperial Household Department. On my behalf he had arranged with her to invite her companion, a good friend of hers. I obtained as much information as I could from him about her family, her social status, her education, etc.

But I put the cart before the horse, so to speak. Until I met Misawa at the Conservatory I had decided to focus our discussion on the trip Mr. H and my brother were going to take together the coming summer. Yet when we left the Conservatory it turned out to be a matter of secondary importance. Only at the last moment of our parting did I pause for the first time at the corner of the street.

"Today I had really hoped to hear more from you about my brother's summer plan. So things have at last worked out the way Mr. H said?"

"There is no mistake about it, since Mr. H sent for me to tell me just that. You can depend on him."

"I wonder where they are going."

"Well, that I don't know—but where they're going won't matter so long as they go, right?"

To Misawa, who was after all a distant observer, my brother's fate was clearly a matter of little consequence.

"Rather, let's pursue the other matter more vigorously. What do you say?"

As I continued on alone toward my lodgings I nevertheless kept thinking of my brother and sister-in-law. Yet more than of them, I probably thought of the woman whom I had just seen that day, despite the fact I had not exchanged so much as a word with her, nor had I even heard her voice. That the occasion might not seem any more unnatural than necessary, Misawa had contrived to have it appear that nature had happened to bring the two of us together in one room to barely glance at each other. He had not even bothered to introduce us. Or so he explained it all to me. His way was so simple and natural as not to cause trouble or inconvenience either to her or to me. Yet that's exactly why it had been all the more disappointing. I wished that he had done a little more than that. "But I didn't know your intentions," Misawa explained. And indeed he was quite right, for I did not plan to pursue her any further.

During the following two or three days I often envisioned her face. But in no way did it incite in me any eagerness or anxiety to see her again. While the excitement of the impression that day faded away, matters at Bancho remained as urgent as before. In reaction perhaps to my incomplete and half-hearted sniff at a woman, I became rather slovenly. On the way to and from the office I often touched my rough cheeks, and to my chagrin, felt just like a streetcar-riding badger.

A week later I had a telephone call from my mother, who reported that on the previous day Mr. H had called at the house. As my sister-in-law had had a slight cold, my mother had entertained the guest, and in taking my sister-in-law's place she had happened to hear Mr. H and my brother talk about their anticipated trip. Completely delighted, my mother thanked me, and through her my father also sent his regards. "O I'm very glad things have worked out all right," I replied.

That night I thought about many things. Being convinced that travel would do my brother good, I had gone so far as to tax Mr. H with the job, but quite frankly it was my brother's opinion about me that troubled me the most. Just what was his feeling toward me? To what extent was he resentful or suspicious of me? That was what I wanted to find out most. My concern was, therefore, not only with what my brother might become in the future, but also with what he really was at that moment. Long cut off from any opportunity to talk with him, I had almost no first-hand knowledge about his recent self.

2 2

I felt it necessary to see Mr. H prior to their trip. Also I was duty-bound to thank him for expediting my request so smoothly.

On the way home from the office I again called at his house and sent in my card. As soon as I was announced the plump figure of Mr. H appeared.

"To be frank with you, right now I'm struggling with tomorrow's lecture. If it isn't a pressing matter, would you excuse me today?"

Ignorant as I was of a scholar's life, these words of Mr. H's nevertheless suddenly reminded me of my own brother's daily routine. If they locked themselves up in their dens, it was not necessarily the result of their rebellion against family or society. I found out which day would be convenient for him, and agreed to come back.

"Excuse me, but would you mind doing that, please. You see I'm trying to wind up my lectures as soon as I can so that I can go on the trip with your brother."

I could only bow politely to Mr. H.

A few days later, one clear evening just after the rain I called on him once again. Being a fat man, he complained of the warm weather and sat with his chest stripped of his *yukata* almost to the top of his stomach.

"Let me see. Where are we going? We haven't decided yet whether it will be the sea or the mountains."

Quite characteristically, he didn't seem concerned a bit about their destination, and I myself was indifferent. But . . .

"There is one favor I'd like to ask you."

As for the family situation in general, I had already informed Mr. H of it on the previous occasion when I had come with

Misawa, but I did not say a word to him about the somewhat peculiar relationship between my brother and myself. It was the sort of thing I could not possibly disclose to him. Even what Misawa knew about it, intimate as we were, was little more than his own conjecture. Mr. H might have that from Misawa second-hand, but how valid it might be, and how well he knew it, I could not ascertain without broaching the issue openly myself.

Yet I was very anxious to know how my brother now looked at me and what he thought of me. It seemed, therefore, that if I was to enlist Mr. H's help at all, I would of necessity have to lay bare the whole matter before him. When I had decided to call on him alone, leaving Misawa in the dark about the problem—and perhaps making it appear consequently that I was deceiving him—it was precisely because I wanted to keep the truth from others as best I could. But clearly, if I could not bring myself to divulge matters to Misawa, I certainly could not mention them to Mr. H.

Consequently I felt obliged to present the specific problem in more general terms.

"I am afraid this may give you a great deal of trouble, but I wonder if you could inform us as fully as possible about what-ever you may notice as to my brother's behavior and speech, his thoughts and feelings while traveling with him. Whatever we can learn thereby will prove very helpful, I'm sure, to my folks as they try to cope with him at home."

"Well, that may not be altogether impossible though it will be a little difficult, I'm afraid. In the first place, there will be no time for it, as you can see. And even if there is enough time, there will probably be no such need. Wouldn't it be preferable for you to come for a long talk with me when we return from the trip?"

23

Mr. H was right, to be sure. For a moment I was silent with my eyes downcast, and at last lied.

"To tell the truth, my parents are so worried they would, if possible, like to be kept informed of whatever may happen during your trip, at every stage of it . . ."

I pretended to be at my wits' end, but he began laughing.

"There is no need for you to worry so much. It's going to be all right, I can assure you."

"But you see they are so old . . ."

"That's too bad. That's why I don't care for old people. But you go home and tell them everything is going to be all right."

"Couldn't you find some way? Some way that won't give you too much trouble and yet also keep them happy."

Again he grinned.

"You really don't expect me to handle it that easily, do you? But since you insist on it, how about this? I'll write to you if anything worth mentioning should happen while we're traveling. If you don't hear from me, you may be sure everything is going along as usual. I should think that will do."

I could not possibly expect anything more from him.

"That will be fine. But please don't limit your report to what might be called an unlooked-for event; that is, I hope you will write of anything at all you think unusual about my brother's feelings and thoughts?"

"Now this thing is becoming awfully complicated, isn't it? But that's all right with me. Yes, I may well do that."

"Also my brother may talk about me, my mother, and his family, etc., and I hope you won't mind letting us know whatever he says quite frankly."

"Well, I'll do what I think proper."

"Even if it is something you don't think proper, I hope you will feel free to reveal it. Otherwise, it might inconvenience us at home."

Mr. H started smoking in silence. I then realized that for someone new at this sort of thing I had gone somewhat too far. I became painfully aware of my own awkwardness. He was gazing at the garden, in the corner of which were five or six butterburs that the landlord was said to have transplanted all the way from Akita. An early summer sky cleared just after the rain was

still showering its bright light over the ground, and in the twi-
light the thick stalks of those burs stood out in all their blue
freshness.

"You know, over there huge toads are coming out," said Mr.
H.

We chatted for a while until it was time for me to take my
leave before dark.

"By the way, what about this talk of your marriage? Misawa
came the other day and, all elated, said he had found you a nice
girl."

"O yes, he loves to look after others."

"On the contrary; he doesn't seem to be doing that just to be
meddlesome. Isn't it time for you, too, to get married? I hear she
is not bad-looking at all, eh? Or aren't you satisfied?"

"It is not that—I am not satisfied."

"Ah, then, you liked her all right," said Mr. H laughing. And
leaving his house I thought that even out of my sense of obligation to Misawa I would have to do something about that matter
soon. But as long as my brother's problem remained unsettled
one way or another I could hardly afford to divert my attention to that other matter. Rather I wished she would just fall in
love with me once and for all.

24

I called on Misawa once again.
As I did so without having made up my mind I had no desire to
take a forward step. I was completely indecisive, and talked of
the woman in a merely casual way.

"Now what are you going to do?"

Approached in this manner, I was just unable to reply pointedly, and he continued:

"I may be floating around like a fellow out of employment;
but as a family man I, such as I am, think I am steadfastly solidi-
fying my position according to a certain fixed policy. However,
you are exactly the opposite. When you come to the matter of
becoming independent or getting married you deliberately sus-

pend your will power, and yet jobwise you promptly decided and settled down."

In fact, I had just received a letter from Okada in Osaka urging me to come there for a suitable position which happened to be open, and thus I was thinking about the possibility of quitting my job.

"But until recently you were so excited about going abroad."

Misawa persisted in his exposure of my own self-contradiction. At that very moment in need of a change I saw little difference between Europe and Osaka.

"It's hopeless if you are so capricious about everything. I alone am taking your marriage problem seriously—that's ridiculous. Let's call off the whole thing."

Apparently Misawa was pretty annoyed; so was I—at myself.

"What does she say? You are blaming me alone, but how do I know her mind?"

"How can you? I haven't told her anything yet."

Misawa seemed a bit excited and, I suppose, with reason. Yet he had not said a word about me either to her or to her family. That is, he had merely placed her and me within sight of each other, so that nothing might affect their good name no matter which way the die was cast. It was his great pride that there was nothing obtrusive about his handling, and that all he had done was to make use of nature.

"There is nothing I can do so long as you can't make up your mind."

"Then, let me think a little about this."

Misawa seemed impatient. I was disgusted with myself.

It was hardly a week after I had gone to see him that Mr. H and my brother left Tokyo together by train. I was not aware of the time and date of their departure. Since I had had no notice from either Misawa or Mr. H, I learned of it for the first time via a telephone call from home. Surprisingly, it was my sister-in-law who was on the line.

"Your brother has left this morning. I'm calling you because your father has told me to inform you of this," she said in slightly formal language.

"He's with Mr. H, isn't he?"

"Yes."

"Do you know where they are going?"

"As I understand it, they are going to travel around the coast of Izu."

"Do you mean by boat?"

"No. From Shimbashi Station as usual . . ."

25

That day I went to Bancho directly from the office, instead of returning to my lodgings. No doubt I was being quite obvious in going there immediately after assuring myself of my brother's departure. I had no desire to conceal it, however. There seemed to be no one in the family from whom I needed to conceal it.

In the living room my sister-in-law was looking at the frontispiece of a magazine.

"Thanks for your call this morning."

"Oh, it's you, Jiro-san. What a surprise! Are you just returning from Kyobashi?"

"Yes. It's become quite warm, hasn't it?"

I pulled out my handkerchief and wiped my face. Then I took off my coat-jacket and flung it onto the mat. She handed me a fan.

"And how is Father?"

"He is not home. He's off to some social engagement at Tsukiji today."

"You mean the Seiyoken?"

"No, I don't think so. It may have been another tea-house."

"And Mother?"

"She is in the bath right now."

"And Oshige?"

"Oshige-san also . . ."

My sister-in-law finally started chuckling.

"Also in the bath?"

"No. She is out."

The maid appeared and asked whether strawberry or lemon was to be added to the ice.

"Have you already started using ice?"

"O yes. We've been using the icebox for the last two or three days."

I fancied that she had gotten a little thinner since I had last seen her. Her cheeks had lost some fullness, it seemed, as my eye caught her shifting face—in the late sunlight. She was sitting with her left cheek turned toward the veranda.

"Well, Brother apparently made up his mind and went on the trip, didn't he? I thought he might put it off."

"No, he didn't put it off."

She cast down her eyes as she said this. And then she continued in a voice far more calm and melancholy than usual.

"Well, he has such a strong sense of obligation that once he made a promise to Mr. H, he must have meant to carry it out . . ."

"Not exactly for that reason. Not for that reason really—yet anyway he wouldn't put it off."

I stared vacantly at her face.

"Then, for what reason wouldn't he put it off?"

"For what reason? O you know. It's obvious."

I really did not know.

"No. I don't think I do know."

"He is disgusted with me."

"Do you mean to say he's gone on the trip to be rid of you?"

"No, not that. I mean he was disgusted with me and that's why he has gone on the trip. In a word he doesn't think of me as his wife."

"So . . ."

"So he doesn't care a bit about me. That is why he has gone on the trip."

With this she lapsed into silence. Nor did I speak; just at that moment my mother came out of the bath.

"O, when did you come?"

My mother frowned as she saw the two of us sitting there.

26

"Now it's time to wake up Yoshie; otherwise she may stay awake at night again."

My sister-in-law rose in silence.

"And give her a bath as soon as she wakes up."

"Yes."

My sister-in-law's retreating figure disappeared down the hallway.

"Is Yoshie taking a nap? No wonder it's so quiet."

"A little while ago she became touchy about something and was crying; and then she fell asleep. Anyhow we ought to wake her up; it's already five o'clock . . ."

My mother appeared displeased.

That day, unusually enough, I sat down at the table and had dinner with them. My father, who I heard had been invited to a restaurant or a tea-house in Tsukiji, naturally hadn't returned yet, but Oshige came back in time.

"Hey, come in here quickly and sit down. Everyone has been waiting for you to come out of the bath."

She flopped down on the veranda, and was fanning fresh air into the front of her *yukata*.

"Don't you rush me like that, please. Remember you are, after all, our very occasional guest."

She put on a prim air and turned purposely towards the Japanese fatsia right next to her. My mother looked at me, smiling as much as to say, "Up to your old game again." I felt encouraged to continue making fun of Oshige.

"If you're going to treat me as a guest, please don't make such a display of your big bottom, and come over here quick and sit down, will you?"

"Don't bother me, please."

"Where were you hanging out in such hot weather?"

"Wherever I was, it's none of your business. Hanging out— what kind of vulgar language is that anyway? O never mind.

Today I've been to Sakata-san's, and found out Brother's entire secret."

Oshige used to call my brother Big Brother and me simply Brother. At first she had called me Little Brother, but because this Little Brother gave me a peculiarly unpleasant feeling every time I heard it, I at last had her drop that Little.

"You don't mind my telling it to everyone, do you?"

Oshige turned her still bath-steamed face fully toward me. I winked at her twice in succession.

"But haven't you just now made it plain that it is my secret."

"That's right, your secret."

"Of course, it's no good telling it if it's a secret."

"On the contrary, that's why it is all the more fun."

I was inwardly uncomfortable since I had no idea what this rash Oshige might be about to say.

"Oshige, you don't have any idea of what in logic they call contradiction in terms, do you?"

"I don't care about all that kind of snobbish English you're displaying. Just because you think I don't know it."

"Enough of your nonsense. You are no longer fifteen or six-teen years old."

My mother joined in at last, reproving us equally. Seizing the opportunity, I dropped the verbal fencing. Oshige also threw her fan out onto the veranda and meekly sat down at the table.

Once the matter had been dropped there was little chance during the meal for her to disclose any serious secret. Neither my mother nor my sister-in-law showed any sign of taking it seriously. A fellow named Heikichi appeared from the rear of the house, and began watering the garden until stopped by my mother who ordered, "That's enough. It isn't so dry yet."

27

It was early in the evening, shortly after the lights had come on, when I left Bancho. For an hour and a half or so following supper I had remained and chatted with my family.

During that time I had found myself in a nice fix when at last Oshige insisted on exposing what she had called my secret. Fortunately, it turned out to be only that marriage question which to me was anything but a secret.

"Mother, I have heard that Brother had a secret interview with his prospective bride the other day."

"Not at all secret, I tell you."

I interrupted Oshige before my mother said anything.

"I got it from a reliable source. It's no use pretending you didn't."

When she used a phrase like a reliable source, I grinned, in spite of myself.

"You really are a fool."

"Who cares?"

And with such glibness she started telling my mother and sister-in-law all about what had happened on June 2. I was a little amazed at the precision of detail in her account, and became so curious about the source of her information I felt compelled to cross-question her. However, Oshige wouldn't divulge her source, and said only with a rather mean smile, "You are keeping it from us because there is—no doubt—some peculiar reason you don't want to tell us about it. Isn't that so?"

Not only did she refuse to gratify my curiosity but instead set out to tease me. "O well, say what you please," I said. When my mother asked me quite seriously about the details I merely told of the event as it had happened.

"That's all there is to it. Besides, I want you to know that the other party knows nothing about this. I don't care if, like Oshige, you go round chattering so loosely, but it may be embarrassing to them."

As though she apparently could see no reason why it might be embarrassing to them, my mother ventured several detailed questions as to the extent of their property; whether they had poor relations; whether any hereditary disease ran in the family; and so on. I simply did not know how to answer such questions. Not only that, I finally became weary of even listening to such stuff. Beating a hasty retreat, I left Bancho.

That evening, all the while my mother had been pestering me with her pointed questions, my sister-in-law hardly spoke at all regarding this topic. Nor did my mother even once attempt to elicit a comment from her. Their respective attitudes clearly indicated their differences of temperament. But it did not seem the kind of contrast that could be due merely to their differences of temperament. Perhaps in order to maintain her position wholly as an outsider, my sister-in-law had all along busied herself with looking after Yoshie. That evening Yoshie, who usually was sent to bed at dark, had not yet slid beneath the mosquito-net when I left—as a result of her too-long nap.

On returning to my lodgings I felt acutely the stuffiness of my room. I turned off the light and sat quietly in the dark. Where was my brother staying at that moment? What kind of talk was Mr. H having with him at that moment? The image of Mr. H's magnanimous face returned to my mind and I also imagined that rare smile about my brother's sunken cheeks.

28

From the next day on I anxiously awaited a letter from Mr. H. One, two, three, I counted on my fingers the days that had passed. No letter had come from him, however—not even a picture postcard—and I was disappointed. There was no levity in him, such as might make him forgetful of his responsibility; there was evidence, on the other hand, of the kind of liberality that might make him neglect to discharge his duty as punctiliously as expected. That's how I, a member of the impatient tribe of humanity, looked at him from a distance.

Then, on the evening of exactly the eleventh day after their departure, I at last received a ponderous missive. Mr. H's penned words entirely covered the finely lined stationery. From the number of the pages I could tell it was not the sort of thing which could have been done in a couple of hours. Sitting immobile as a mannequin chained to the desk, I began reading it. My eyes shone with a burning determination not to miss a single

278

word, written in tiny black characters. My mind was riveted to the pages, yet it glided over them as smoothly as a sleigh over the snow. In a word, I had not the slightest notion how long it took me from the very first line of the first page of Mr. H's letter to the final word of the last page.

The letter read as follows:

As I invited Mr. Nagano to travel with me, I also promised to comply with your request. But in doing this I had misgivings that once I faced the situation, I might find it very difficult to carry out your wishes; even if possible, it might not be necessary; and whether necessary or not, it might not be proper. And on the first and second days of our journey these three attitudes worked together in varying combinations, so that I became increasingly convinced that I might have to break my word. On the third and fourth days some reconsideration seemed demanded on my part; and then on the fifth and sixth days and so on, as the days went on, I gradually came to the conclusion that it might be necessary after all not merely to think it over but also to write to you as I had promised. Though the word necessary may mean something quite different to you than it does to me, I shall not explain it here, for you will find that out for yourself by the time you come to the end of this letter. As for my initial feeling that ethically it is not quite proper to accede to your request, I do not think I can get rid of it no matter how much time may elapse. On the other hand, the degree of necessity is plainly becoming great, so great as to override that ethical feeling. Probably there will be no time for me to write a letter. (This being the only trouble that dogged me wherever I went.) We both sleep in the same room; we eat meals together in the same room. And together we go out for a walk, and take a bath too, as long as the structure of the bathroom can accommodate us both. All these things considered, the only time when we move separately is when we go to the toilet.

I do not mean to say that we two are rattling on from morn 'til night. There are times when we each read our own books and also lie down to rest quietly. However, ignoring someone's very presence, to write about him and confide it to a third person is a very difficult thing for me to do. Thus while I do realize the necessity of reporting, I still find it very trying. Such an opportunity does not come so readily, however I may wish it. But chance has proved kind enough to take me in hand and finally let me do what I deem necessary. Trying not to be much concerned with your brother's presence, I have begun to write this letter. And I hope to finish it under similar circumstances.

29

Two or three days ago we came into the valley of Benigayatsu and dropped exhausted into this glen. We are now staying in a small summer house owned by one of my relatives. The owner, who can't leave Tokyo before August, had offered to put the place at our disposal any time before that, and we have chanced to avail ourselves of his kind offer during our travel.

Although the word summer house may sound very respectable, the truth is that it is a shabby and cramped place. As for its appearance, it is no better than the places of those petty government officials, with monthly pay of forty or fifty *yen*, which you can find on the outskirts of Tokyo. But as it is in the country, there is at least some land, some space around it. A yard or a vegetable garden, difficult to say which, slopes down under the eaves and extends as far as the fence, which is overladen with the berries of sweet viburnums. Over the foliage is seen only a quarter or so of the straw-thatched roof of the neighboring house.

From under the same eaves we have a clear view of the opposite hill across the glen. As the entire hill is some count's country seat, at times we catch glimpses through the trees of colored *yukata* and hear women's voices coming over a cliff. On the top of the cliff a tall pine soars into the sky. We regard it as our lofty task to look up at this tree, from under our low eaves, morning and evening.

Of all the areas we have so far passed through, this place seems to please your brother the most. For this there may be various reasons, but the main one, as I see it, is that the feeling that the two of us alone have become masters of an independent residence brings to your unsociable brother a certain tranquillity. Although he hadn't been able to sleep well any place else, since the night we came here he has been sleeping well. In fact now, while I am driving my fountain-pen forward, he is sound asleep.

Chance has also favored me in seeing to it that we need not loll about in one room, sitting knee to knee with each other, as is usual in the ordinary inn. But the house, as I have just said, is cramped indeed. On the hilltop to the right of our gate there is a western-style house built by a millionaire, in comparison with which ours is no better than a matchbox. Even so, it is a solitary independent house enclosed by fences, and altogether insulated from the surroundings. Cramped as it is, the house has five rooms. Here, however, we need not arise at the same time, as at an inn. One of us may rise, while the other can sleep as long as he wants. I can leave your brother undisturbed, and sit at the lacquered papier-mâché desk provided in the next room. The same is true in the daytime: when we get tired of being face to face, either of us may keep out of sight and do whatever suits him for as long as he wishes. And then at a suitable time he may return.

By taking advantage of such a chance, I am writing this letter. It is fortunate for you, I think, that I can unexpectedly take advantage of this chance. At the same time it is unfortunate for me to have thus come to recognize the necessity of taking advantage of it.

What I am saying does not have the orderliness of a diary; nor may it have any scientific precision. However, I can only remind you that it is the consequence of two negative factors—one inherent in travel itself, the trains, rickshas, inns, etc., bound to obstruct all regular chores; and the other in the very nature of this task of mine which cannot be tackled with ease. It is surprising to me that I am now able to report to you even as much as what follows, fragmentary as it may be. This, I owe altogether to chance.

30

Neither of us has any great taste for traveling. Consequently the plan we set up was as commonplace as our own experience itself. We decided our purpose would be just as well served if we toured several nearby and conveniently located spots as do many other tourists. With this vaguely in mind, we first thought of trying Sagami and Izu or thereabouts.

I was still better off than your brother, for I had some rough idea about main points and transportation to get there; whereas your brother almost transcended geography and directions. He could not tell whether Kozu is this side of or beyond Odawara, although perhaps he merely doesn't care rather than cannot tell. What really amazes me is that your brother, while thus indifferent to such an extreme, is incapable of taking a detached attitude toward anything relative to human affairs. But that is an aside. As it is difficult to return to the subject from such a digression, I shall henceforth keep as close to the main stream as I can.

Originally we agreed to start from Zushi as a jumping-off point. But that morning, while rushing to Shimbashi Station by ricksha, I had a different idea. Ordinary as our trip was going to be, to go straight to Zushi seemed just too ordinary to interest me. At the station I talked it over with your brother once more, and suggested that by reversing our itinerary, we might go first from Numazu to Shuzenji and then cross the mountains and go down to Ito. There was of course no objection on the part of your brother, who could not even tell whether Odawara is beyond or this side of Kozu; we at once bought tickets for Numazu and boarded a Tokaido train.

On the train nothing happened worth reporting. Following our arrival at our destination—while we bathed, ate, and sipped tea, there was nothing that could command my special attention. Not until that night did I come to realize that I might have something to convey to your folks about your brother.

It was too early for us to turn in. Already we were tired of chatting. I was overcome with the kind of ennui every traveler experiences. Then happening to notice a heavy-looking *go* board standing beside the alcove, I instantly carried it out to the middle of the room. Of course, I meant to play against your brother. And I am not sure whether you know this, but anyway while in school, though you may not think it of me, I had frequently played *go* with your brother. Although later on we stopped playing suddenly as if by preconcerted notion, the *go* board at this time seemed an ideal way to pass the hours that already somehow seemed to hang heavy on us.

Your brother stared at the board for a moment, and then said, "Well, I'd better not play." "Now don't say that. Come. Let's play," I countered quite determinedly. "No. No, I'd rather not," he said, however. And as I looked at his face there was a peculiar expression around his eyes, an expression which, oddly enough, betrayed no sign of either dislike of the game or indifference to it. Reluctant to force him, I nevertheless picked up the *go* stones and began arranging the white and black stones on the board for a match. Your brother watched for a little while. As I continued playing by myself, however, he abruptly rose from his seat and went out in the hallway. I thought he had probably gone to the toilet, and paid no more attention to him.

31

As I expected, your brother came back almost at once. And hardly had he said, "Let's have a game," than he snatched the stones from my hand. Noticing nothing, I said "All right," and began the game immediately. We were such wretched *go*-players that we could make our moves rapidly and finish quickly. We could easily play two games in an hour, a rate that could bore neither lookers-on nor players. But your brother said it was very trying to wait out the finish of even that rapidly changing *go* board, and at last gave up playing halfway through a game. I wondered if he might be feeling ill, but he merely smiled.

Not until we were about to turn in did your brother mention

anything about his mental state at the moment. It seems that he felt it repugnant to do anything, even to play a game of *go,* and that at the same time he could not stand doing nothing. This conflict was already painful to him, and he had foreseen that once the game started he would surely be oppressed with the feeling that he could not afford to play a game like *go.* Yet he could not help playing it. So he had had no choice but to face the *go* board. And no sooner had he faced it than he lost all his patience. At last the white and black stones scattered over the board began to look like monsters which were purposely gathering and parting, separating and joining only to torture his brain. In a few seconds' time he felt he might have played havoc with the board to drive away these monsters, your brother told me. Although I had all that time noticed nothing, I was now somewhat startled and felt sorry that I had been so inconsiderate.

"No, this is not just with *go,*" your brother said and apparently forgave my blunder. Then he launched into an account of his day-to-day life. His attitude was calm enough even when he stopped playing halfway through a game. It may be that you people do not understand his feeling, which shows no abnormality whatsoever on the surface. To me at least this was a discovery.

Whether reading, reasoning, eating, walking, whatever he is doing and around the clock, he says he cannot find any peace of mind. No matter what he does, he is bedeviled by the feeling that he just can't afford to do that sort of thing.

"Nothing is as frustrating as when what I am doing is not related to the end I have always in mind," he told me.

"Isn't it good enough if what you are doing becomes a means?" I inquired.

"Yes, that would be fine. But only when you have your end can you determine your means."

Your brother is frustrated, for he thinks whatever he does, no matter how, becomes neither his end nor his means. He is completely insecure; as a result he cannot stay still. He gets up because he cannot sleep in peace, so he contends. Once he gets up, he cannot stand being merely awake, so he walks. Once he walks he cannot just keep walking, so he runs. And once he starts running he cannot stop no matter where he may run. Not only must he not stop anywhere, but he cannot help accelerating his speed every moment. And he says it frightens him to imagine what it will ultimately lead to; he says it is so frightening that he breaks into a cold sweat. Yes, he says it is unbearably frightening.

32

Your brother's explanation came to me as a surprise. Though having never once in my life experienced this sort of insecurity, I could understand it all right, even if I couldn't really feel it at all. I listened to him with the feeling of one who has no experience of a headache, and yet has to put up with someone's complaint about a splitting headache. I mused awhile; and while I was musing, I came to envision, though vaguely, the fate of man. I thought I had found fitting solace for your brother.

"Now what you call insecurity is the insecurity of the entire human race, and it isn't peculiar to you alone—if you realize this, that's that. Constant motion and flow is our very fate."

What I said here was not only vague but really disgustingly feeble. It was bound to wither beneath your brother's sharp, disdainful glance. But he replied:

"Man's insecurity stems from the advance of science. Never once has science, which never ceases to move forward, allowed us to pause. From walking to ricksha, from ricksha to carriage, from carriage to train, from train to automobile, from there on to the dirigible, further on to the airplane, and further on and on—no matter how far we may go, it won't let us take a breath. How far it will sweep us along, nobody knows for sure. It is really frightening."

"Yes, it is frightening, indeed," I agreed.

Your brother laughed.

285

"When you say it is frightening, it is simply because you feel it convenient to use the word frightening. That is no genuine fright. In other words, it is nothing but the fright of the head. Mine is different. Mine is the fright of the heart. It is a living fright which beats like my pulse."

In your brother's words there was no particle of falsehood, I assure you. And yet it is hardly possible to experience personally his fright.

"But if that is everyone's fate, it is hardly necessary that you alone be frightened," I offered.

"It is a matter of fact, if not of necessity," he returned, and then continued:

"It is frightening because the fate which the whole of humanity will reach in several centuries, I must go through—in my own lifetime—and at that all alone. And an average lifetime would be advantageous; but whether it be ten years, one year, or further shortened into one month, even one week, I must go through the same fate just the same. That's what frightens me. You may think I am telling a lie; but let me tell you this: cut my life at any point and in any fragment; and whether the length of that fragment be an hour or thirty minutes, you will find it goes through precisely the same fate. That's why it is frightening. In short, I gather within myself the insecurity of the whole human race, and distill that insecurity down into every moment, that is the fright I am experiencing."

"It won't do you any good. You ought to take it a little easier."

"It won't do me any good, that much at least I know."

In front of your brother I was quietly smoking. I wished I might help him escape this anguish somehow. I forgot everything else. Just then your brother, who had been staring me in the face, said suddenly, "You are a better man than I am." As I happened to be quite convinced of his intellectual superiority, this praise was neither gratifying nor flattering. Still I quietly puffed my cigar, and after a while he calmed down. Then we both got beneath the mosquito-net and went to sleep.

33

The next day we stayed in the same place. In the morning, as soon as we were out of bed, we strolled around the beach; it was then that your brother gazed at the deep somnolent sea and said joyously, "I like the sea as quiet as this." Lately he seems to long for anything that is at rest. For that reason, apparently he preferred mountains to water. This preference of his, though, differs from an ordinary person's enjoyment of nature, I think. This is evident in the following words by your brother:

"From the way I grow a mustache, wear a suit, hold a cigar in my mouth, I may look outwardly like a respectable gentleman, but in reality my mind is like a shelterless beggar wandering around from morning to night. All the time I am pursued by insecurity. Hopelessly restless. And at length I think that in the world there is no poor devil as crude as I. Then as often happens, in the streetcar or elsewhere, I raise my eyes, look across and catch sight of a face which seems completely carefree. The moment my eyes are fixed on such an undepraved, blank face, a deep thrill of joy runs throughout my frame. My mind revives just as the stalks of rice withering in dry weather welcome rain. At the same time that face, the one which is devoid of any thought, and completely relaxed, takes on nobility for me. Yes, it seems full of nobility, be his eyes slanted, his nose flat, his features plain. Before that face I feel like kneeling down and expressing my gratitude with a pious feeling very close to religious sentiment. My attitude toward nature is exactly the same. Long ago I used to enjoy things simply because they were beautiful, but that feeling is something I cannot afford now."

He now assigned mine to the category of such holy faces as he happened to come across in the streetcar. I declined such an unsought-for honor. Then, your brother said in earnest:

"Once or twice a day, I'm sure, it occurs to you too that your face automatically mirrors the natural state of your mind, which neither craves loss or gain, nor bothers about good or evil. I use the word holy for you at those particular moments—only at those moments."

Probably in an attempt to offer concrete evidence to me since I was still uncertain about all this, your brother, as illustration, referred to what I had been like at the time we turned in the night before. As he admitted, your brother had been overly agitated then, as a consequence of our talk. But as he had looked at my face his agitated state had calmed by degrees. Whether I would affirm this or not, it was none of his concern. One thing was certain, he declared, that under my favorable influence at the moment he had been able, even if temporarily, to escape from his agonizing insecurity.

I've already related what my attitude was like at that particular moment. I was quietly smoking. Nothing else. I was then oblivious to everything other than the desire to help him out of this insecurity. But I did not expect my wishes to communicate themselves. Nevertheless, in it there might have been genuine sincerity. Did he then perceive that sincerity in my face?

Your brother and I wandered along the sands, and while wandering I pondered: isn't he the type of person who cannot find peace until he goes into religion? More emphatically stated, isn't your brother now suffering in order to become a man of faith?

34

"Have you not lately thought about God?"

At last I asked such a question. When I said specifically lately, I was prompted by an old memory of our student days. In those days we both were still naive and full of random ideas; even so, your meditative brother and I had often discussed the existence of God. Incidentally, even then his brain worked somewhat differently from others'. As often happened, while idly walking he became suddenly conscious of the fact that he had just been walking, and this now became an insoluble problem which he had to wrestle with: it is undoubtedly I who walk if I will myself to, but whence do both my will to walk and my strength to walk spring? This was a big question for him.

Hence we had frequently used terms such as God and prime mover. As I now think about it, we used them without any real understanding. Even God, thus verbally abused, soon became trite. Then we would become silent as if by tacit agreement. How many years has it been, I wonder. Then one quiet summer morning I stood in front of that vast vessel holding the deep color called sea and, facing your brother, I uttered the word God once more.

But your brother had forgotten the word altogether. He showed no sign even of recalling it. In reply to my question only a faintly ironic grin flashed across the corners of his lips.

Yet I was not so timid as to be daunted by such an attitude. Nor were we on such delicate terms that we had to retreat warily before speaking out fully what was on our minds. I ventured one step farther.

"Now you say a nobody's face often makes you feel so glad; then you would be many hundreds of times happier if you might always be able to be with God and to worship his perfect image, wouldn't you?"

"What is the use of toying with such empty, sheerly verbal logic? Perhaps you'd better bring me God."

Your brother's tone as well as his wrinkled brows were quivering with impatience. He suddenly picked up a pebble at his feet, and dashing four or five yards toward the water's edge he threw it far out into the distant water. The sea received the pebble calmly. He repeated the act two or three times, as one would who is angered by his own futile efforts. Your brother stamped around in the seaweeds which had been washed ashore and whose names I didn't know—perhaps *kobu* or *wakame*. And then he came back to where I was standing.

"I prefer the living man to a dead God."

So your brother said, gasping for breath. And together we slowly walked back toward the inn.

"Whether it be a ricksha man's, a lazy bum's, or a thief's, whatever face—at the very moment it gladdens me—is God, after all, isn't it? Mountains, rivers, seas—nature at the instant when I feel it sublime is nothing but God, is it not? What other kinds of God are there?"

"Well, yes—" was the only answer I made. And for the moment your brother looked anything but satisfied. But afterwards, by look or manner, he betrayed that he had been impressed by my remark nevertheless. To tell the truth, although he snubbed me I was somehow more impressed.

35

We stayed in Numazu for a couple of days. When I suggested that we take advantage of the opportunity to go as far as Okitsu he said no. I had not the faintest idea why on that particular occasion your brother, who had so far let me have my way about our itinerary, ventured to reject my proposal. Later, when I asked why, he explained that he didn't care for the place renowned for Miho's Pine Grove and the Angel's Feather-Robe. Certainly his brain works in an odd way, I must say.

At last we returned as far as Mishima. There we transferred to an Ohito-bound train and finally arrived in Shuzenji. From the start your brother apparently was very much pleased with the idea of this watering-place. And yet as soon as we got to our destination he groaned with disappointment. That is, what he really liked was the name of Shuzenji, not the place itself. This may seem a trivial matter, but still to a degree it's characteristic of your brother, so I am taking this occasion to add it.

As you know, this watering-place is located in a town sunk deep into the bottom of a ravine and embraced by mountains. Once in, you face the verdant cliffs closing in on you on all sides, and you have no choice but to look upward. So cramped is it that if you walk with downcast eyes you can hardly notice the color of the earth. Your brother, who had so far preferred mountains to the sea, felt hemmed in the moment he came to Shuzenji, surrounded by mountains, and at once I took him out.

Where there would be a main street in an ordinary town we found a river-bed through which flowed a stream of blue water dashing against the rocks. As a consequence there was scarcely any room to walk around freely. I lured your brother to the hot spring gushing from some cracks in the rock in the middle of the stream, for there men and women, interestingly enough, were all bathing together. Its uncleanliness was also something to talk about. Neither he nor I had the nerve to throw off our *yukata* and hop in. Instead, we stood on the rock for a long time, looking curiously at the black mass of bathers. Your brother seemed delighted. As we returned by way of a precarious plank bridge between the rock and the bank, he mumbled the phrase pious people. Evidently he did not mean it ironically; that seemed the way he really felt.

The following morning we were steeping in the indoor bath, brushing our teeth, when he said, "I couldn't sleep last night either." As I happened to be convinced that insomnia was most harmful to him particularly at that time, I considered that problem.

"When you can't sleep you are trying very hard to get to sleep, are you not?" I asked.

"Exactly. That makes it all the more difficult for me to sleep," he said.

"Now, tell me whether you feel guilty about someone if you don't sleep?" I asked again.

Your brother looked puzzled. Sitting on the edge of the piled-stone tub as he was, he was staring at his own hands and stomach. He is not very fleshy, as you know.

"There are times I can't get to sleep too. But insomnia is also fun," I said.

"How is that?" This time it was your brother who asked. I then cited an ancient poet's phrase which I happened to remember, "Wakeful in the light of a lamp, and mindful of exquisite fragrance." You brother instantly smiled at me.

"A fellow like you can understand such sentiment!" he remarked with an incredulous look.

36

Later that day I dragged him out again, and this time we climbed the mountain. If you look upwards, there are mountains to climb; if you look downwards, there are springs to dip yourself in—there is nothing else to do. This is that sort of place.

Your brother, his lean legs flashing, walks briskly up a narrow path. And for that reason he seems to get tired faster than others. As I followed him up, hulkingly in my obesity, there he sits at the root of a tree, gasping for breath. He is not waiting for others; out of breath, he can only collapse.

Every now and then he stopped and looked at the lilies blooming amid the bushes. Once, for instance, he pointed expressly to the white petals and declared, "Those are mine." I could not catch his meaning; nor did I have a mind to ask, and finally we reached the summit. As we rested at the tea booth there, pointing to the woods and ravines unfolding under our feet, he said once more, "They are all mine too." Hearing these words repeated, I at last had become curious. Yet I was not to have my doubts dispelled on the spot, for in reply to my question he merely smiled a lonely smile.

On the stools at the tea booth we drowsed for a little while as though dead. What your brother was thinking about during the time, I do not know. For my part I only looked at the white clouds drifting along in the clear sky. The sun glared in my eyes. I became concerned about the heat we would have to brave on our way home. I hurried him along, and we started down the mountain. And it was just then that he suddenly grabbed at my shoulder from behind and asked, "How far do your mind and mine meet together and from where do they part?" Halting, I was shaken by the left shoulder two or three times. Just as my body was jarred, so was my mind. I always regarded your brother as a thinker. Since we had undertaken this journey together I had also concluded that he was one who was trying to go into religion and yet was having difficulty finding the entrance. In fact then my mental shock was due to my wondering if this question was possibly prompted by that sort of viewpoint. By nature I am indifferent to things—and also so dull-witted that I am not easily perturbed. But on account of your various requests prior to our departure, I tended to be particularly sensitive toward your brother at least. I felt then that I was almost on the point of slipping off my usual unperturbed way.

"*Keine Brücke führt von Mensch zu Mensch.*" (There is no bridge leading from one man to another.)

In reply I cited this German proverb which I happened to remember—though it was no doubt partly contrived strategically to keep the problem from getting complicated.

"Probably so," said he, "at this moment you cannot answer in any other way."

"Why is that?" I at once asked.

"One who is not truthful with himself can never be truthful with others."

I could not think to which aspect of myself I should apply his remark.

"You are traveling along as my nurse, are you not? I am grateful for your goodwill. But your behavior thus motivated is no more than hypocrisy, I think. I as your friend am moving away from you, that is all."

Such was your brother's declaration. And leaving me behind, he rushed down the mountain path alone. As he did I heard him exclaim, "*Einsamkeit, du meine Heimat Einsamkeit!*" (Loneliness, loneliness, thou mine home.)

37

With much anxiety I returned to the inn where I found your brother pale and lying in the middle of the room. When he saw me he neither spoke nor moved. I adopted a policy of leaving him as he was—one who valued naturalness. Sitting beside him, I had a smoke in quiet. Then I picked up a towel and went to the bath to wash off the unpleasant sweat. As I was standing by the tub, washing myself, he came to join me. Then for the first time we spoke to each other. "Tired, aren't you?" I asked. "Yes, I am," he replied.

From about lunch time by degrees he recovered his humor. At last I mentioned the melodramatic scene that had taken place between us a little earlier on the mountain path. At first he smiled but finally drew himself up, became serious, and declared that he was wretchedly lonely. For the first time he made the painful confession that he was invariably lonely not only in society but also at home. And he seemed more suspicious of his own family than he was of me, his intimate friend. In his eyes, both your parents epitomized hypocrisy itself. And especially was this true of his wife. He mentioned striking his wife on the head.

"At a first blow she is calm. At a second she is still calm. And at a third, although I expect resistance, there is none. The more blows the more lady-like she becomes. This helps all the more to make a ruffian out of me. It's just like venting my wrath on a lamb, only to prove the degradation of my character. Isn't she cruel to use her husband's wrath in this way to display her superiority? Now look. Women are far more cruel than men who resort to force. I wonder why the devil she didn't stand up to me when I hit her. No, she didn't need to resist, but why didn't she say so much as a single word back to me?"

As he said this, his face was filled with pain. Strangely though, while describing so graphically his own disagreeable behavior toward his wife, your brother would say almost nothing concrete about what really had motivated him. He merely insisted that on all sides he is besieged with hypocrisy, and yet he would not illustrate that hypocrisy to me. I wondered why in the world he was so excited about the empty-sounding word hypocrisy. In fact, your brother reminded me that my stupid doubts were due to the fact that I knew the word hypocrisy only in a dictionary sense, and rebuked me for being ignorant of its actual meaning. In his opinion I am far separated from actuality. I did not force out of him what he meant by hypocrisy. Consequently I have not the faintest idea about what sort of trouble besets his family. I left it that way, for in the first place it is a point I am not happy to pry into; also, whether I do or not, it is something I need not report to you, who are a member of the family. Yet, let me say a word just for your information: while saying something, though abstract, about his parents and his wife, he never mentioned your name. Nor did he say anything about your sister, Oshige-san.

38

It was on the night we arrived in Odawara from Shuzenji that I told your brother about Mallarmé. Mallarmé is the name of a famous French poet. I hope you won't mind my telling you, since it's out of your line. Although I say this, I confess I know nothing but the name. What I said about him is therefore no criticism of his works. The fact is that before leaving Tokyo I had come across an anecdote about this poet while glancing through a foreign magazine to which I regularly subscribe. It was such an interesting piece that I happened to remember it, and I used it as something for your brother to think about.

This Mallarmé, it so happens, had many young admirers. And these admirers were in the habit of gathering at his house and listening to his talk far into the night. No matter how many came his place was always before the fireplace and his seat was always the rocking chair. This had gradually become the kind of time-honored custom that no one dared violate. One evening, however, there was a new visitor. This visitor, who I understand was an Englishman named Symons, unaware of the long-established custom, and probably thinking that all places and chairs were the same, seated himself in that special chair which Mallarmé always took. This disturbed Mallarmé; so much so that he could not concentrate on his talk. Naturally this spoiled the gathering.

"Now that is really rigidity," I concluded after having related the Mallarmé anecdote. And then turning to your brother, I said, "But your rigidity is even greater than Mallarmé's."

Your brother is a sensitive person. Aesthetically, ethically, and intellectually he is in fact hypersensitive. As a result, it would seem that he was born only to torture himself. He has none of

that saving dullness of intelligence which sees little difference between A and B. To him it must be either A or B. And if it is to
be A, its shape, degree, and shade of color must precisely match
his own conception of it; otherwise he will not accept it. Your
brother, being sensitive, is all his life walking on a line he has
chosen—a line as precarious as a tight rope. At the same time he
impatiently demands that others also tread an equally precarious
rope, without missing their footing. It would be a mistake,
though, to think that this stems from his selfishness. Imagine a
world which could react exactly the way your brother expects;
that world would undoubtedly be far more advanced than the
world as it is now. Consequently, he detests the world which is
—aesthetically, intellectually, and ethically—not as advanced as
he is himself. That's why it is different from mere selfishness, I
think. Indeed, it has nothing to do with the rigidity of Mallarmé
who was so disturbed by the loss of his seat.

But probably greater still is his suffering. I sincerely wish to
help him find relief from this suffering somehow. For his part,
scarcely able to bear it, he is struggling as desperately as a
drowning man. I can very well see the struggle that is going on
in his mind. But I wonder whether it would be worthwhile,
merely for the sake of the peace he might find, to blur that
vision which is so sharp by virtue of his inborn capacity and
long cultivation. Supposing that it is worthwhile, is it a humanly
possible task?

I knew very well. I knew very well that his brain, over-
wrought with thinking, was echoing with the word religion
which is written in blood and tears.

39

"To die, to go mad, or to enter
religion—these are the only three courses left open for me," your
brother declared at length. At that moment he looked rather like
a man riding into the abyss of despair.

"And yet I do not think I can possibly enter religion; nor can
I take my life, being too much attached to it. That leaves me

only one way out—madness. Aside from my future, do I seem to you even now to be in my right mind? Hasn't something already gone wrong with me? That is what really frightens me."

He rose and went out to the veranda. There he leaned over the railing awhile, gazing at the sea. Then he paced back and forth in front of the room two or three times before returning to his seat.

"Blessed is Mallarmé, whose peace of mind was disturbed by such a thing as the loss of his chair. I for one have lost almost all. Even this body—even these limbs—the little that is left in my possession, betrays me mercilessly."

These words were not a mere hollow expression. Long superior in his capacity for introspection, your brother is now suffering from its coercion as a result of his excessive thinking. No matter in what frame of mind he may be, no longer is he able to go forward unless he first subjects his action to scrutiny. That's why the flow of his life is being interrupted every moment. It must be as trying as being called to the phone every other minute during mealtime. But it is his mind which interrupts, as well as his mind which is interrupted; in the last analysis he is controlled by these two minds which accuse each other from morning till night just as a wife and her mother-in-law might. As a consequence he cannot have even momentary peace.

From what your brother had told me, I could now understand what he meant when he asserted his discernment of nobility in the face of one who thinks about nothing. This conclusion had been altogether a product of his thinking. Yet because of this very thinking he is unable to enter that desired state. He has pursued a study of happiness in hopes of becoming happy. Yet no matter how much he might study, happiness always eludes him.

At last I once more mentioned the word God to your brother. And quite unexpectedly he struck me on the head. But that was the last scene which took place at Odawara. There was yet another scene before this blow came; so let me tell you about that first. As I have said earlier, however, since our fields are altogether different, what I am writing may at times appear to you mere pedantry and uncalled-for elaboration. Consequently when

I insert foreign words which may mean little to you I become all the more hesitant. Since I am trying to leave out such outlandish words unless I deem them absolutely necessary, I hope you will understand this and read on without prejudice. Should you entertain misgivings about my sincerity what I have written so far can serve no purpose whatsoever.

While still in school I came across the following legend about Mohammed. Mohammed is said to have declared that he would summon before him a big mountain which happened to stand in the distance, and he invited interested witnesses to be present on a certain date.

40

The day came around and, as a multitude of people gathered around him, true to his word Mohammed called aloud upon the mountain to come to him. Not an inch would the mountain move, however. Still composed, Mohammed repeated the command. The mountain stood as still as before, and Mohammed was compelled to repeat the command a third time. But seeing, even after three repetitions, that the mountain showed no sign of motion, he said to the crowd: "In keeping with my promise I summoned the mountain. But the mountain seems reluctant to come. And since the mountain does not come I have no choice but to go to it." Saying this, he walked quickly toward the mountain.

I was too young when I read this story. I thought merely that it was an excellent vehicle for witticism, and told it around to various people. Among them there was one who was my senior and, while everyone else had a laugh, this man commented, "Ah, that is a great story. The true substance of religion is in it. It contains everything." I listened attentively to his comment, though it was beyond my comprehension. Many years had passed when I repeated the same story to your brother at Odawara. Yes, the same story just as it was, and I didn't mean it to be a joke.

"Why not walk toward the mountain?"

When I suggested this, he remained silent. For fear that I might have failed to make myself understood I added:

"You are the kind of fellow who summons the mountain, and who becomes irate when it doesn't come, the kind of fellow who stamps the ground with chagrin, and only thinks of criticizing the mountain. Why not walk up to the mountain?"

"What if it has a duty to come to me?" said your brother.

"Whether it has the duty or not, you just go if you need to," I said.

"Why should I when I have no duty?"

"Then go for the sake of happiness, if you don't like to go out of necessity," I replied.

At this your brother became silent again. He understands very well what I am driving at. But he cannot live without erecting in the center of his life his own lofty standard, the standard which he has laboriously built up thus far, of distinctions between right and wrong, between good and evil, and between beauty and ugliness. He does not care to throw it all away even to seek happiness. Rather, clinging to it all, he yet becomes desperate for happiness. And he himself recognizes full well the very contradiction that enmeshes him.

"If you stop regarding your own self as the axis of life and fling it overboard altogether, you will feel more comfortable, believe me, I again suggested.

"Then, what would be the axis to live by?" he asked.

"God," I replied.

"What is God?" he asked again.

Here I must confess something. As you go through the dialogue between your brother and me, I might sound as though I were a man of religion—as though laboring to lead him somehow to the way of faith. But I am no more than a common mortal who has nothing to do with either Christ or Mohammed. I am a wild creature of nature who has grown up aimlessly, without feeling the slightest necessity for religion. If our talk somehow gravitates toward it, it is entirely because I am dealing with such an intensely troubled person as your brother.

41

And precisely therein lay the reason he had dealt me a blow. Although I knew nothing about God, I dared to use the word God. When your brother questioned me about this in return, I should have said vaguely that it has the same meaning as Heaven or Fate. But circumstances did not allow for such an explanation. Our dialogue at the time, as I recall, proceeded in the following manner:

"Since there are things in the world that just don't turn out as you wish, you must acknowledge the fact that there is at work a will other than yours, must you not?"

"Yes."

"Furthermore, that will is far greater than yours, isn't it?"

"Perhaps greater, for I am being beaten. But most of them are not as good, not as beautiful, not as true as mine. There is no reason why I should be beaten, and yet I am. That's maddening."

"You are talking about the feeble struggle between man and man. That is not what I am talking about. I mean something larger than that."

"Where is something as vague as that?"

"If you deny it, then there is no way of saving you. That's all."

"Then let us suppose for a moment that . . ."

"Leave everything to it, and let it do as it pleases. Now look. When you ride a ricksha, can't you trust that the puller won't drop you and therefore sleep peacefully while in it?"

"I do not know of any supreme being as trustworthy as a ricksha man. You don't either. What you are saying is a sermon made up just on my behalf; it is not the religion you yourself are practicing, is it?"

"By all means, it is."

"Then have you renounced your ego altogether?"

"Well yes, in a way."

"That is, death or life, you are at peace, trusting that God will take care of you as he pleases?"

"Well, yes."

The more he pressed me the less certain I felt myself growing. But as I was completely at the mercy of circumstances there was nothing I could possibly do. Just then suddenly your brother raised his hand and slapped me in the face.

By nature I am insensitive as you well can see, thanks to which I have thus far managed somehow to survive, without either getting into serious brawls with others or incurring their wrath. Probably because I was dull-witted, even as a child I was not spanked by my parents, so far as I can remember. Still less as I grew up. Thus, when for the first time in my life I was slapped in the face, I immediately took offense in spite of myself.

"What do you think you are doing?"

"Now you know."

I did not understand what he meant by this, "Now you know."

"This is outrageous."

"Now you know. You do not trust God at all. You get mad just the same. You lose your balance over trifles. Your peace is upset."

I made no answer. Nor could I make any. Meanwhile your brother abruptly left his seat. And all that I heard were his footsteps rushing down the stairs.

42

I called a maid and inquired about my companion.

"He has just gone out. Probably to the beach, sir."

As the maid's answer coincided with my own guess I abandoned any further worry and threw myself down. At that instant I took notice of your brother's summer hat hung on the end of a clothes rack. That is, he had rushed out somewhere, hatless in the heat of the day. To someone like you, so much

concerned with every move he makes, the way I stretched myself out on my back might seem too carefree. This is no doubt
because I am a dullard. Yet this, I think, involves something
noteworthy—something more than my slowness can explain
away; so let me dwell on it for a moment.

I had confidence in your brother's intelligence. I thought
highly of his power of comprehension. Time and time again he
will unexpectedly speak out things incomprehensible to the
average person. To those who do not know him or have little
education, these might sound as strange as a cracked bell, but to
those who understand him well these are rather more welcome
than any conventional remarks. In them I used to find his origi-
nality. That is why I did not hesitate to declare positively to you
that there was nothing to worry about. Then we set out for our
journey. And exactly how he has been getting on since we
started out I have so far described, but because of what I have
learned about him during our trip it has become necessary for
me to revise my initial opinion by degrees.

That your brother's brain is in better order than mine I still
believe there is no doubt whatsoever. As a human being, however, right now he is somewhat confused, as compared with his
former self. And that confusion, I think, stems from the precise
and orderly functioning of his brain. For my part I would prefer
to admire his ordered brain while reserving some doubts about
his disordered mind. As far as he is concerned, however, his
ordered brain is his disordered mind. This is what puzzles me:
his brain is all right, but something may be wrong with his mind
—dependable and yet not to be depended upon. If I say this, can
it be accepted by you as a satisfactory report? Since I know no
other way of describing it, I myself am already completely at
sea.

I let your brother rush down the stairs, and then threw myself
down to rest. To that extent I was at ease. As he'd gone out
without wearing his hat I had no doubt that he would soon be
back. On the contrary, however, he did not return as readily as I
had expected. No longer could I remain stretched at full length
and at ease. With frank misgivings, I rose at last.

Out on the beach I noticed that the sun was already behind the clouds. Both the leaden, overcast sky, and the shore and the sea below, tinted grey, looked melancholy, and a peculiarly tepid wind blew, carrying a briny odor. A white dot on that grey expanse, as I gradually became aware, was the figure of your brother crouching on the beach. When I approached him quietly and spoke to him from behind, he rose instantly saying, "I'm sorry for what I did a while ago."

After having rambled about aimlessly and endlessly, he at last had become exhausted, and had crouched down to rest on the spot where I had found him, he told me.

"Let's go to the mountains. I am sick of this place. Let's go to the mountains." He seemed eager to be off.

43

That night we finally decided to go to the mountains. The only mountain we could reach easily from Odawara was Hakone, and to this worldly spa I took your brother, the least worldly of men. From the start he said that the place would surely be noisy. Yet he insisted that he would be able to stand two or three days of it simply because it was a mountain.

"What a waste it is to go to a resort merely to put up with it!"

That was another remark your brother then made in a self-mocking tone. As might be expected, from the very night we arrived there he was subjected to the mercies of a boisterous guest in the next room. Although we couldn't decide whether he was from Tokyo or Yokohama, this guest was apparently a merchant, a contractor, or a broker—anyway something of that sort, judging from his manner of speech. Every now and then he raised his braying voice completely regardless of other guests. It was quite hard even on me, though I am ordinarily unmindful of such things. On account of this fellow, however, your brother and I retired that night without any complicated discussion. In other words, the fellow next door made such a hell of a noise he destroyed our meditation, so to speak.

On the following morning when I asked your brother, "Could you sleep last night?" he shook his head, saying, "Not a wink. How I envy you!" While he had had difficulty getting to sleep it seemed that I had snored loudly all night long.

From dawn that day it drizzled, and at about ten o'clock the drizzle turned into a regular rainfall. Shortly after noon it showed some signs of an approaching storm. Suddenly your brother rose, and tucking up his *yukata*, asserted that he was going out to roam around the mountain. He insisted that he was going to get some exercise no matter what, braving the downfall, scaling hill and dale. "What a chore!" I thought, but since it would be less troublesome for me to go along with him than try to dissuade him I presently said "All right," and also tucked up my *yukata*.

In no time he was rushing into the teeth of the choking wind. Like a bouncing ball he was leaping in the midst of those indescribable reverberations—the splashes of water or the booming from the sky. And he was shrieking with violence enough to rupture his blood vessels. He was many times more violent than the guest next door had been the previous night. His voice sounded even more like a wild beast's than that fellow's. His savage cries, once out of his mouth, were borne away by the gusts, to be smashed into pieces by the pursuing rain.

Then, soon afterwards, he lapsed into silence, although he still roamed about. He kept walking around until he was well out of breath.

I think it was an hour or two after we left that we returned to the inn dripping wet. I was chilled to the bone and your brother's lips had changed color. As we warmed ourselves in the bath, he kept saying, "Splendid!" To him it was perhaps splendid indeed, to be conquered by nature which harbors no hostility. "But what a chore!" I said simply, glad to stretch out my legs comfortably in the bathtub.

That night the next room was as silent as a grave, contrary to our expectations. From the maid we learned that the guest who had given so much trouble the previous night was already gone. It was that evening when, to my surprise, I heard your brother's views on religion. Indeed, I was somewhat shocked.

44

As a modern day youth you may also have little sympathy for the time-worn word religion. I wish I could possibly manage without referring to such knotty matters. But understanding your brother necessitates our touching on it. To you it may be uninteresting if surprising, but so long as you shun it the only result is that your brother himself will remain an enigma. Therefore I want you to have patience and read on without skipping this portion. If only you have patience, I am sure you can understand it. Please read it and understand him well, and then try to explain the matter to your parents, to their satisfaction. I feel really sorry for your old parents who are overly concerned with your brother. But as it is, you are the only means by which I can describe to his family what he really is. I hope you will pay serious attention to my report which may sound odd. I am certainly not trying to discuss such a complicated problem for fun. I cannot help it, for this complicated problem is itself part of your brother. Separate one from the other, and we will no longer have your brother in flesh and blood.

Your brother dislikes to erect any other authority than himself, whether it be God, the Buddha, or what not. (I use the word erect here following your brother.) Yet it has nothing to do with the Nietzschean assertion of ego.

"God is myself," says your brother. Should strangers happen to overhear the way he draws such a forthright conclusion, they might think him a bit out of his mind. Indeed, he speaks in such a violent way that perhaps they may not be able to think otherwise.

"Well, isn't that tantamount to asserting that you are absolute?" I criticize, but not an inch will he yield as he answers.

"I am absolute."

The more we repeated such dialogues the more peculiar your brother's tone grew. Not just his tone, but also what he said by degrees slipped more and more out of the ordinary. Had he been arguing with someone unlike myself he would most certainly have been dismissed as a case of sheer madness. However, I never took him so lightly as to give him up in that easy way. At last I pushed him to the brink.

Your brother's so-called absolute turned out to be no mere abstraction which a philosopher had spun out of his head. It was something plainly psychological, the kind of state which one could enter and experience in person.

He argues that one who has attained a pure peace of mind should naturally be able to enter this state without seeking it, and that once he enters the state the universe and all creatures—every possible object—would vanish, and there would be only self; and that self at the moment would be something existing and yet non-existing, it would be impossible to say which. It is something great and yet minute. It is something beyond description. In short, it is absolute. And should some partaker of this absolute hear all at once the sound of a fire-bell, then the sound of that fire-bell would be his self. In other words, the absolute becomes the relative itself. Consequently, no longer is it necessary to trouble oneself to project things and objectify others besides himself; nor need one fear even the possibility.

"The fundamental principle should remain the same, whether in death or life. Otherwise, there could be no peace of mind. A clever fellow might exhort, 'Rise above the times, by all means'; I, for one, believe that one must rise above life and death as well."

So asserted your brother, almost clenching his teeth.

45

In this instance also I must admit that your brother was over my head. Never had it occurred to me that it is humanly possible to attain the state he was referring to. On hearing his argument out to the conclusion which arrived with such logical precision, I thought that such a conclusion might be the case. Yet I also thought that such might not necessarily be the case at all. At any rate, I only proved to be unqualified to question it. Confronted by his impassioned words I sat perfectly silent. Then your brother's attitude changed. Until then my silence had frequently taken the edge off his argument, though all that had happened by sheer chance. Being such an intelligent person your brother would surely have seen through me had I merely played silent to some purpose. Perhaps, that is, my slowness somehow proved to be my advantage.

"Now look. Please do not despise me as a mere talker," your brother continued and suddenly placed his hands on the floor. I was stuck for an answer.

"To a staid fellow like you, I may indeed sound like a silly chatterer. Such as I am, though, I am anxious to practice what I am preaching. Day and night, never do I stop thinking that I should practice it. Yes, I am thinking continuously that I cannot live if I don't practice it."

Still I was at a loss what to say in reply.

"Now, tell me. Do you think my ideas wrong?" inquired your brother.

"No, I do not," I answered.

"Or do you think they are not quite thorough?"

"Fundamental enough, it seems to me," I answered again.

"But how can I change from a speculative to a practical man? Please tell me that," he beseeched me.

"Oh, but that's something beyond my power," I backed off, suddenly awe-struck at this turn.

"Yes, you can. You are a man born to be practical. That's why you are happy. That's why you can be so tranquil," your brother pursued.

It was evident that he was in earnest and, turning to him with a sigh, I declared:

"In intelligence you are far superior to me. It is certainly beyond my power to save you. I might touch those of duller intelligence than mine. But I could have no effect on you at all, for you are more intelligent than I am. In other words, you are born thin and tall, whereas I am fat and chunky. If you want to be fat like me, there can be no other way than for you to shorten yourself."

From his eyes fell teardrops.

"Plainly I recognize the absolute state. But the more distinct my *Weltanschauung* becomes, the further the absolute moves away from me. In short, I was born to explore topography only on a map; yet I have all along been anxious to have the same experience as a practical man in gaiters would have, ranging over hill and dale. I am stupid; I am inconsistent; I know my stupidity; I know my inconsistency; and yet I still struggle, nevertheless. I am a fool. As a man you are far more mature than I."

Once more he placed his hands before me, and as if to apologize he then dropped his head. Tears fell in streams from his eyes. I was overwhelmed.

46

As we left Hakone, your brother said, "I won't come to such a place again." Of all the places we had so far passed through there was none in fact that pleased him. I guess he is the kind of person who quickly becomes tired no matter where he may go and no matter with whom. Well, it must be so, for in the first place he is not pleased even with his own body or his own mind. He speaks of his own body and mind as though they were his knavish traitors. And that this was by no means a nonsensical half-jest I can well understand, after staying with him all these days. This, I am sure, you will also understand thoroughly from my own objective account.

You may wonder how your brother in this state, and I, can travel together. To me too this is something to marvel at. Once my head was filled with all that I have just stated about your brother, it might seem difficult for me even to deal with him, however thick-headed I might be. But the fact is that I do not find it so painful to live vis-à-vis with him. It is, I should think, at least much easier than outsiders might be led to imagine, although if asked why it is so, I am quite at a loss for an answer. Don't you have this same experience with your brother? If you do not, it would appear that I, a stranger, rather than you, his own brother, enjoy greater intimacy with him. By intimacy I do not mean mere friendship. I do mean that we both share somehow the unique nature which harmonizes us into unity, and thereby enables us to get along.

Ever since we set out on our journey I have constantly said and done what would hurt his feelings. And once I was even struck by him on the head. Yet with all this I think I can stand before your entire family and declare that I haven't yet fallen out of his good graces. At the same time I have not the slightest doubt that I still from the bottom of my heart love and respect your brother, despite his certain weakness.

Your brother is an upright man, upright enough to drop his head and shed tears before an ordinary fellow like me; he has the courage to dare it. He is a man of principle who discerns that it is proper to dare it. So clear-headed is he that he tends to go forward, leaving his own self behind. He is suffering, for the other implements of his mind fail to keep pace with his intellect. In terms of character this is a blemish; in terms of success it is an ominous danger. While I lament this conflict for your brother's sake, and trace all its causes to his overly active intellect, I cannot rid myself of genuine respect for that very same intellect. So long as we take him for a hard-to-please and selfish person, there may be no opportunity to approach him. In that case we will have to give up the chance for good, the chance to allay his suffering even if slightly.

We left Hakone, as I have already said, and we came directly to this summer house in Benigayatsu. Earlier and at my own discretion I had made a plan to stop over in Kozu, but I finally decided against bringing it up for his consideration. Since I was afraid he might again say angrily, "I won't come to such a place again." Besides, when he heard from me about this summer house, he was most eager to come here for a quiet rest.

47

As it is now, anything can easily excite your brother and yet he can hardly bear any excitement. For him, therefore, this hermitage-like summer house would seem to have been most suitable. When from the quiet room he looked up at a soaring pinetree on the cliff across the ravine, he said, "Good," and sat down.

"That pinetree is also yours."

Consolingly I tried to mimic his way of talking, for I remembered his words, "Those lilies are mine," and "That mountain and that ravine are also mine," whose meaning I had not quite been able to understand at Shuzenji.

The house had been kept by an old man who returned to his own place when we arrived. Still once every morning and evening he continues coming to sweep and clean the place and to draw water. As the possibility of cooking for ourselves was out of the question, we had him arrange with a nearby inn to deliver our three meals daily. Since this house is lighted by electricity we are spared the trouble of lighting lamps at night. Thus, all that we have to do from the time we leave bed till the time we retire at night is, at most, to make our beds and hang up the mosquito net.

"Well, it's certainly easier and more leisurely than doing our own cooking," your brother says. Indeed, this place is undoubtedly the most quiet of all those mountain and sea places we have passed through. As often happens, when we keep quiet by ourselves, we do not hear the rustle of the wind even. The only noise that there is is the creaking of the wheel-well in the shade of sweet viburnums, which your brother does not mind, oddly enough. Apparently he is gradually becoming collected. I should have brought him here earlier.

In the yard there is a patch of eggplant and some Indian corn. We talked about plucking off the eggplants to eat, but it would be too much trouble to pickle them, so we gave up the idea. As for the Indian corn, it is not ripe enough yet to be edible. By the well at the back door tomatoes are growing, which we eat in the morning while washing our faces. In the heat of the day your brother often goes down to this patch of land, hardly distinguishable as yard or garden, and crouches there fixedly. Every now and then he sniffs the cannas which, as you know, have no fragrance, or he examines the flower petals of the evening primroses. On the day of our arrival, for instance, he went over to the pampas-grass growing on the boundary between our place and that of our millionaire neighbor to our left, and stood stock-still there for a long time. From the room I watched him; he did not move for so long that at last I slipped on sandals and headed over to him. Dividing the neighbor's house and ours is a bank about two yards high, which is covered all over with pampas-grass in season. As I approached him, your brother glanced at me over his shoulder, pointing down at the roots of the grass.

At the roots of the grass a crab was crawling—a tiny one, no bigger than a thumbnail. It was not the only one, however; for, in time, while I was watching, there came another, a third, and so on, their numbers growing rapidly until at last they swarmed all over.

"Look. Some are crossing the blades of grass," he observed, still standing motionless. I left him where he was, and returned to my seat.

It makes me immeasurably happy to see your brother so absorbed in these trifles as to almost forget himself. And I even think it is worth all my trouble to have brought him out for our trip. And that night I told him what I meant by this.

48

"A while ago you were possessing those crabs, were you not?"

As I suddenly spoke, your brother, surprisingly enough, gave a merry chuckle. Ever since Shuzenji I had often used the word *possess* in such a peculiar way that your brother had taken it as merely a joke. To him, therefore, I might have sounded amusing. Well, to amuse is far more preferable than to anger. As a matter of fact, however, I was being quite serious.

"Yes, an absolute possession," I corrected myself at once. This time your brother did not laugh, either. Nor did he make any answer, and it was again my turn to speak out:

"The other day we had a difficult argument about what you called the absolute, but I fail to see why you need to go to so much trouble as to try to enter that absolute state. There would be no problem, I should think, so long as you could absorb yourself as you did in the crabs. To be first conscious of the absolute, then seize the moment when the absolute switches to the relative and thereby seek their unity—isn't this too difficult? In the first place, it's problematical whether it is humanly possible."

Your brother would not interrupt me yet. He seemed to be quite a bit steadier than usual, and I ventured a step further.

"Wouldn't it be handier to go the other way round?"

"The other way round?" he returned, his eyes sparkling earnestly.

"Yes—that is to say, to be so absorbed in the crabs, and thereby forget yourself. If you were thus perfectly one with your object, that would be the state you're talking about."

"Indeed," he responded uncertainly.

"Indeed? You are actually practicing it. Don't you realize that?"

"I see."

His response was still vague. Then suddenly it dawned on me that all along I had been saying something quite unnecessary. To tell the truth, I have not the faintest notion of the absolute. I had never given any thought to it; nor had I even tried to entertain such a thought as far as I could remember. Thanks to my education, I had only learned to mouth that sort of term. Nevertheless, as a man I was more stable than your brother, although I would, of course, be ashamed if you took this to mean that I am superior to him; let me put it this way: my mental state is closer to the general average than his. What, as a friend, I am working for with him is only to have him regain the position of the average person like me. To put it somewhat differently, it means the seemingly ridiculous act of converting the extraordinary to the ordinary. But for your brother's anguished suffering, it would make no sense for one like me to try to start such an argument with him. Your brother is honest. If he cannot quite understand, he yet keeps pressing me for an answer, and thus pressed for an answer I am at a loss how to respond. And worse yet, such a critical discourse, I fear, is likely to turn your brother, who is only just becoming practical, back to where he was, to his former injuring attitude. That was what I feared more than anything else. I do wish I could provide him with something that can captivate his mind completely, so completely as to leave no room for his inquiring attitude—something as engrossing, let us say, as all the works of art, as all the lofty mountains and mighty rivers, or as all the beautiful women in the world. And for a year or so I would like to keep him under their complete spell. After all, your brother's alleged desire to possess things would ultimately seem to mean being possessed by things, wouldn't it? Consequently, to be absolutely possessed by things, I think, is to possess things absolutely. Only then and there will your brother, who does not believe in God, find his peace of mind in this world.

49

The night before we had gone out to the beach for a walk. From our place to the beach it is about a fifth of a mile. We follow a narrow path to the road and then must cross it to have a view of the color of the sea. There was still some time before the moon was to rise. The waves were darkly in motion, and the division between the water and the beach was hardly distinguishable until our eyes became adjusted. In this darkness your brother continued boldly on his way. From time to time lukewarm water came running over my feet. The waves, after breaking on the shore, rolled in, unexpectedly spreading far out like a flattened rice cake.

"Don't your clogs get wet?" I asked him from behind.

"Tuck up the bottom of your *yukata*," he urged. Apparently he had already tucked his up behind, and was ready to get his feet dirty. It was so dark that I had not noticed although we were only a few yards apart. Probably because it is the best season in this resort place we ran into many people, and invariably they were couples—silently groping their way in the dark. Consequently we could not discern them at all until they suddenly confronted us. Then as they passed close to us I raised my eyes to scrutinize them only to find that they were indeed all young couples, just the sort I had come across many a time.

It was then that I heard from your brother about a certain Osada-san. It seems that she had lately gotten married and had gone to Osaka. Those young couples we saw must somehow have reminded your brother of her in bridal costume.

Osada-san, according to him, was a good-natured person, the least selfish in the family. Her kind was born happy, he declared enviously, and admitted he wished he could be that way too. Unacquainted with Osada-san, I had no comment but merely mumbled, "I see."

"She is something like you made into a woman," your brother said and paused there on the sands. I did likewise.

A dim light came into sight on the height beyond us. By day in that direction we could see a red building through the trees, and this light probably belonged to the owner of the red western-style house. Solitary in the thick shades of night, it glittered like a star. But while my face was directed toward this light, your brother stood facing the rolling sea.

Just then suddenly the notes of a piano rang out above us. The house stood on the stone wall piled regularly two yards high above the sands. From the end of this stone wall notched steps slanted up to the garden, so as directly to connect the garden and the beach. I ascended the steps.

Over the garden fell a streak of light from the house. Bathed in its faint glow, the ground was covered all over with grass. Flowers which I could not see distinctly since the garden was so dark and spacious seemed to be in bloom here and there. The notes of the piano were coming from a brightly lighted room of the western-style building in front.

"It looks like a foreigner's summer house."

"Probably it is."

Your brother and I sat together on the top of the steps. The notes of the piano, scarcely audible, reached our ears from time to time. Both of us remained silent. Every now and then the tip of his cigarette glowed red.

50

Certain that your brother would tell me more about Osada-san I waited somewhat anxiously in the dark for him to speak. But as though absorbed in his smoking he merely made the tip of his cigarette glow from time to time, and would not say a word. When he threw the butt down at the foot of the steps and turned toward me, I expected that our topic might drift away from Osada-san. I was a little puzzled, in fact, for his thought now had nothing to do with her; nor did it have any connection with the notes of the piano, the spacious lawn, the beautiful summer house, resort, travel or anything else related to our surroundings and the present moment. Instead, it was about an ancient Buddhist bonze.

The name of this bonze, I recall, was Kyogen. He was said to be both so intelligent and sagacious that a word was clue enough to express a whole thought. Yet this very alert intelligence, as your brother explained, had hindered his spiritual enlightenment for a long period of time. What this means is clear even to me, although I know nothing about spiritual enlightenment. Still more so, painfully clear, must it be to him who is wrestling with the burden of his own intelligence. "The source of his trouble was in fact his erudition itself," your brother declared emphatically.

For several years the bonze had studied and practiced Zen under the guidance of his master, Abbot Hyakujo, but the master passed away before he could obtain results. Then he had

gone to Isan. Isan denounced him, saying that there would be no
hope as long as he took pride in flaunting his learning. Isan is said
to have told him to come back in the form of existence prior to
the time of his own parents. Kyogen, the bonze, returned to his
living quarters. After reviewing what he had till then acquired
from volumes of books, so it has been said, he sighed that no
such painted cake could appease hunger. So he burned all the
books he had collected.

"I'll give it all up. From now on I'll live on gruel."

Henceforth he ceased to think of even the word Zen. He
flung off good and evil, the form of existence prior to the time
of his parents, and in fact any and every thing. Then it occurred
to him to choose a quiet place and there build a little hermitage.
He cut the grass on the lot; he dug out the stumps; he cleared
away the stones to level the ground. Then it was that one of the
stones he hurled aside struck the nearby bamboo thicket with a
thud. And with this sound the spiritual truth burst upon him.

"One single blow has done away with all my learning," he exclaimed joyously.

"I wish I could somehow be like Kyogen," said your brother.
What he means is clear to you too, I think. He wishes to be relieved of every possible burden, and he has no God to entrust
that burden to. Therefore, he wishes to dump it all into a dust-
bin or some such place. In high intelligence your brother much
resembles Kyogen. For that reason he envies Kyogen all the
more.

Thus, your brother's story had nothing to do with the foreigner's summer house or the fashionable musical instrument.
Why at the summit of the dark stone steps, in the midst of the
pervading smell of brine, he chose to tell this particular story, I
do not know. But by the time he had finished his story, the notes
of the piano could no longer be heard. Either because of the
proximity of the tide or of the night dew, our *yukata* had become damp. Upon my urging, we retraced our steps. As we
came out in the street I stopped by my favorite candy store and
bought some bean-jam buns. Nibbling them, we returned to our
place quietly through the dark. The old man's boy whom we

had asked to look after the house while we were away, was fast asleep, in spite of the buzzing mosquitoes. Giving him the remaining buns, I sent him home at once.

5 I

Yesterday morning, while we were having our breakfast, I took your brother's bowl and filled it with his first serving of boiled rice. At that time he once again mentioned Osada-san's name. As I understand it, before marriage she used to wait on him just as I was doing then. Just the previous night I had been compared to her in point of personality, and I was now compared to her in the way I waited on him.

This prompted me to ask him, "Do you think you could be happy if you lived like this with that Osada-san?"

Your brother thoughtfully raised his chopsticks to his mouth. But from his attitude I inferred that he was perhaps reluctant to reply, and I did not press him further.

Then suddenly, after swallowing two or three mouthfuls, he blurted out, "I did say Osada-san was born to be happy. But I am not saying she could make me happy."

His retort sounds logically very consistent and straightforward. In its dark depths, however, it already harbors inconsistency. For once he had told me plainly that he rejoices almost gratefully at a natural face which shows no concern with anything. Is this not the same as saying that one born to be happy can also make others happy? I smiled at him. In a case like this he just cannot let you off scot-free; he snaps back at you directly.

"Yes, I mean exactly what I say. I do not want you to doubt that. You can be sure that what I said is said, and that what I didn't say hasn't been said."

I did not want to contradict him, but it seemed to me slightly amusing that, clear-headed as he was, he showed no reluctance to toy with that verbal logic he always despised. I therefore exposed freely what seemed to me the self-contradiction he had lapsed into.

Still saying nothing, he crammed rice into his mouth a couple of times. Then his bowl was empty, and since the server was still beside me, out of his reach, I held out my hand before him to receive his bowl for another serving. This time, however, he would not accept my offer, but insisted instead that the server be handed over to him.

So I pushed it over to him and, picking up the large scoop, he heaped his bowl with rice. Then placing the bowl on the table he asked without even attempting to pick up his chopsticks: "Do you think that a woman remains the same after marriage?"

On this occasion I could not answer offhand. Perhaps this was because I usually gave no thought to things like that, and I in turn busied myself cramming rice into my mouth, while awaiting his explanation.

"Osada-san before marriage was altogether different from the married Osada-san. Osada-san as she is now, I tell you, has already been spoiled by her husband."

"What sort of fellow did she marry, anyway?" I interposed.

"Once married, a woman becomes perverse on account of her husband, no matter who he may be. As I say this I don't know how much I have already corrupted my own wife. Wouldn't it be really shameless to expect happiness from the very wife one has debased? Happiness is something you just can't demand from a woman whose innocence has been destroyed by marriage."

No sooner had your brother said this than he took up and emptied the over-loaded rice bowl.

52

Now I think I have described as fully as I can how your brother has behaved since we set out on our journey. It seems as if it were only yesterday that we left Tokyo, but in reality it has been by count already more than ten days. To you and your aged parents who have been looking forward to my letter these ten days may have been perhaps too long, I am afraid. That I understand too. But under the circumstances, as I explained at the beginning of this letter, I had little time to take up the pen until we finally came here for a restful stay. Hence my inevitable delay. In reporting on your brother, however, I haven't skipped any of the last ten days. In this letter I have taken special care to note down how he has been each day. That is my excuse; that is my satisfaction, as well; for I am closing this letter with the confidence that I have done my duty better than I had initially expected.

I cannot figure out the time I have spent on this, it being the kind of labor whose extent is not to be measured by the clock. All the same, it is no doubt a very painstaking task. This is the first time in my life I have written a letter of such length. It just couldn't have been written at one sitting; nor could it have been written in a day. Snatching every spare moment, I sit at the desk and begin where I left off last time. But it is nothing. If I could make your brother come to life in this letter, just as I have observed and understood him, I would not mind taking the trouble and would tax my strength many times more than I have done so far.

I am writing this letter in behalf of your brother whom I care for; also I am writing this letter in behalf of you who equally care. And last, I am writing this letter in behalf of your loving parents, the father and mother of both you and your brother. Your brother as I have found him may perhaps be different from your brother as you people have found him. Your brother as I understand him also may not be the same brother as you people understand him. If my letter is worth this effort its value, I want you to bear in mind, rests in precisely that. That is, its value lies in the different reflection I received as I looked at the same person from a different angle. This, I want you to note and use for your benefit.

It may be your wish to obtain some especially clear knowledge about his future, but I, being no prophet, have no right to meddle with the future. When the sky is covered with clouds it may rain or it may not rain at all. One thing at least is certain, that while it is cloudy we cannot enjoy sunshine. All of you people seem to lay a certain amount of blame on your poor brother for making those around him miserable, but I don't think that one who is not happy himself has the strength to make others happy. If we demand warm sunshine from the cloud-covered sun, we are simply demanding something impossible. While I am here with your brother I am trying to dispel this cloud for him. Before expecting warm sunshine from him it would be well for you to banish first the cloud that surrounds his head. Should you fail to do this, something unfortunate may befall your family. For your brother himself too there will be sadness, and I as I state this will be saddened too, in that event.

I have described your brother as he has been during the last ten days, and the question now is what he will be in the next ten days. That question, no one can answer. But suppose I could answer for him in the next ten days, who then could answer for the following one month, and for the following half year? All I have presented is a faithful account of only the last ten days. This account, which I, being thickheaded, have merely written down without rereading it, may certainly have inconsistencies. For that matter, even your brother's speech and behavior may also have inconsistencies which I have failed to notice. Nonetheless, I do declare this: your brother is in earnest; he is not trying to fool me. I am honest too and I have not the slightest intention of misleading you.

When I started writing this letter your brother was snoring loudly. So is he now as I am finishing it off. It seems strange that I happened to begin writing while he was sleeping, and am now finishing while he is again sleeping. Somehow or other I feel how happy he would be should he never awaken from this sleep. Yet at the same time I feel that he would be very sad indeed should he not awaken.

GLOSSARY OF JAPANESE WORDS

(Words whose meanings are apparent in the context are not included.)

gidayū	a kind of ballad drama.
go	a popular indoor game; a kind of chess.
hakama	a pleated over-skirt; full pleated trousers for men; ankle-length culottes.
haori	a loose coat worn over the kimono: "in *haori* and *hakama*," that is, "in full dress."
jōruri	a kind of ballad opera. Osaka has been known as a center of its culture.
kobu	Laminaria japonica; also known as *kombu*; edible seaweed.
koto	a Japanese lyre.
musumesan	*musume* signifies a daughter or a girl.
obi	a broad sash worn by women; also a sash worn by men.
okusan	usually used for addressing married women; more politely *okusama*.
rankō	an imitation tortoise-shell for which egg white is used.
samisen	a three-stringed Japanese guitar.

sen	a small Japanese monetary unit.
shihōbari	glued handiwork.
shimada	coiffure worn for formal occasions.
shosei	a student dependent.
tabi	Japanese socks made like mittens.
takuan	pickled radish.
utai	chant of a Noh drama, a kind of highly stylized classical drama.
wakame	Undaria pinnatifida, edible seaweed.
yen	a Japanese monetary unit, equal to 100 *sen*.
yukata	a bath kimono; a summer dishabille.

NOTES

miserably constituted now that I can't love a woman if I do not feel her soul, and that there is force therein to wrestle with the facts of life (called the Angel of the Lord). But I envy those who are attracted by what is given to the eye; —yes, even those who have a special taste for woman flesh, and this or that particular little tit-bit—I envy them! It lasts not beyond an hour with me."

155   Feast of Lanterns: the great Buddhist festival of *Bon* (July 13–16), when the spirits of the dead are supposed to revisit the scenes of their life on earth.

179   Tanyu: Kano Tanyu (1602–1674), Japanese painter responsible for the prosperity of the Kano school during the Edo period.

180   *Kagekiyo:* a Noh drama about Hitomaru's visit to her blind father, Kagekiyo, former Heike warrior who is now exiled in Hyuga. For its English rendition, see Arthur Waley's *The Nō Plays of Japan.*

that vital "shomon" passage: This passage recited by Kagekiyo is technically a most demanding one, which reads: "Behind this gate, /This pine-wood barricade shut in alone/ I waste the hours and days; /By me not numbered, since my eyes no longer/ See the clear light of heaven, but in darkness,/ Unending darkness, profitlessly sleep/ In this low room./ For garment given but one coat to cover/ From winter winds or summer's fire/ This ruin, this anatomy!" (Waley's translation)

209   Sankatsu and Hanshichi: The lovers' double suicide (Sankatsu being a courtesan) was much popularized by novelists and dramatists during the Edo period.

243   Hyokeikan: erected at Ueno Park in celebration of the Crown Prince's (later Emperor Taisho) wedding in 1909.

Rikyu: Sen-no-Soeki (1521–1591), Japanese tea ceremony master who founded the Senke school.

O-Gishi: Wang Hsi-chih (321–379), Chinese calligraphist.

Okyo: Maruyama Okyo (1733–1795), Japanese painter who founded the Maruyama school.

244   Kakiemon: Sakaida Kakiemon (1596–1662), Japanese ceramist who evolved the famous overglaze technique.

Nonko: a popular name for Donyu, Japanese ceramist.

256 Maeterlinck's article: probably his article, "Ueber das Leben nach dem Tode," which appeared in *Die neue Rundschau* for February 1913.

261 Oda Nobunaga: Japanese military ruler (1534–1582).

280 sweet viburnums: Viburnum odoratissimum; popularly known in Japan as *sangoju*.

290 Miho's Pine Grove and the Angel's Feather-Robe: Miho's Pine Grove is much celebrated in Japanese poetry and art alike. It is also the scene for *Hagoromo* (or The Robe of Feathers), one of the most fanciful Noh dramas. For its English rendition, see Waley's book.

291 "Wakeful in the light of a lamp, and mindful of exquisite fragrance": from a poem by Tu Fu, Chinese poet (712–770).

295 the Mallarmé episode: from A. Hass' article, "Pariser Bohemezeitschriften," which appeared in *Die neue Rundschau* for August 1913.

306 "Rise above the times, by all means": made by Takayama Chogyu (1871–1902), an influential critic of the Meiji period.

315 Kyogen: Hsiang-yen (n.d.), Chinese Buddhist.

Hyakujo: Pai-chang (720–814), Chinese Buddhist.

Isan: Wei-shan (771–853), Chinese Buddhist.

Beongcheon Yu was born in Korea, attended the First Higher School in Tokyo, Japan, and received his A.B. from Seoul National University, Korea. His A.M. degree was obtained at the University of Kansas City, and his Ph.D. from Brown University. He is an associate professor of English at Wayne State University.

The manuscript was prepared for publication by Ralph Busick. The book was designed by Edgar Frank. The type face for the text is Linotype Janson based on a design originally cut by Nicholas Kis about 1890. The display face is Mistral designed by Roger Excoffon in 1953.

The book is printed on Warren's Olde Style Antique and bound in Interlaken's cloth over boards. Manufactured in the United States of America.

326